The dangers of love . . .

"Come here," Colton said softly, pulling gently on Kate's hand. "Closer," he whispered.

He reached up and began to ease the pins from her hair. He pulled them out one by one, then placed the handful of hairpins on the heavy oak table behind them. "I never grow tired of touching your hair," he murmured, bringing his hand back to her, running his fingers through the thick locks.

Kate held her breath. The quick thunder of his heart beneath her palm matched the staccato of her own.

Colton buried his fingers in the hair at the nape of her neck and gently drew her down toward his lips. Don't even touch her, his conscience warned. *Just a little kiss or two*. You're playing with fire. *I can't resist her . . .*

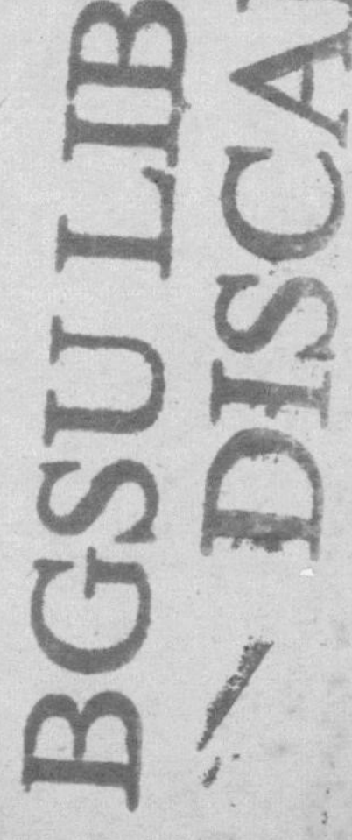

CHARTER/DIAMOND BOOKS, NEW YORK

HEATHER MOON

A Charter/Diamond Book / published by arrangement with the author

PRINTING HISTORY
Charter/Diamond edition / December 1990

ISBN: 1-55773-423-2

Charter/Diamond Books are published by The Berkley Publishing Group, 200 Madison Avenue, New York, New York 10016. The name "CHARTER/DIAMOND" and its logo are trademarks belonging to Charter Communications, Inc.

PRINTED IN THE UNITED STATES OF AMERICA

10 9 8 7 6 5 4 3 2 1

To Hugh and Carol,
the best in-laws a gal could have.
Thanks for loving me
like a daughter.

Chapter 1

January 1814

Colton Lydell, the Duke of Ryland, hurried up the steps of his mother's London home. Stopping at the doorway to knock the snow from his boots, he nodded his greeting to the footman holding open the door.

"Good day, Your Grace. Looks like we're in for quite a storm this time."

"Yes, the streets are already slick. They'll be impassable after nightfall." He handed his greatcoat, hat, cane, and gloves to the footman. The lad shot an uneasy glance toward the wide mahogany staircase, then looked back at the duke.

"Is there something amiss, Harlan?"

"Wot?" The young man flushed, briefly losing control over his carefully cultivated speech and countenance. "Your pardon, Your Grace. You were frowning. I was wondering if you brought bad news about the war."

The duke's expression settled into its normal sober lines. "No. The last dispatch indicates we are holding our own against Napoleon. I have a friend who is traveling in this weather, and I was thinking of his safety. Nothing more. Is my mother upstairs?"

"Yes, Your Grace. She's in her sitting room."

Pausing in front of a gilt mirror in the hall, the duke

smoothed back a lock of medium-brown hair from his forehead. A movement on the second-floor landing was reflected in the mirror and caught his eye. He adjusted his cravat while surreptitiously watching a pretty, well-endowed maid come down the stairs.

Ah, the real reason behind Harlan's nervousness, he thought. She must be new, and the servants have placed wagers as to whether I'll notice her or not. He almost smiled but carefully schooled his features into the cold, sober expression that was his trademark. Servants had been placing such wagers since his salad days.

The woman moved slowly, as if she suspected he might be looking at her. The duke silently checked her assets. He appreciated a pretty face and a shapely body as well as any man, although he knew the servants believed otherwise. His father had taught him never to let a servant know that he found her attractive, whether she worked for him or for someone else.

From his earliest years Colton had been trained for his position in life, one of great wealth and power. Along with that power came responsibilities—for his country, for those in his care, and especially for his own actions.

He lowered his gaze before the maid confirmed that he was watching her. No, he decided easily, she'll not win her wager. Pretty enough but far too brazen. His mother would be all of a heap if she saw the woman parading around with such a low-cut gown. No doubt she had removed the tucker from her bodice only moments before.

Colton brushed a loose thread from his dark blue superfine coat and turned abruptly, dismissing the woman from his mind. He rushed up the stairs, not sparing her a glance as he passed by.

He had far more important things to be concerned with at the moment. The duke had spoken the truth to Harlan. He did have a friend who was traveling, but it wasn't just the weather that caused him concern. The man was one of many who worked for him in the Regent's service, slipping in and out of French-occupied territory with vital information. His men were in constant danger. The extreme cold and snow only served to increase their peril.

Angry whispers drifted up from the hall below, bringing him back to the present.

"I told you he was made o' granite." Harlan's hushed words did not hide his triumph. "And you said meltin' the cold ones was your speciality."

Colton shook his head at their foolishness and tried to think of something cheery to say to his mother. He smiled to himself. She really didn't need anything to cheer her up. Since her marriage three months past to Thomas Denley, the Earl of Blagden, she had been wearing a perpetual smile. The elderly earl was crotchety with everyone else but positively doted on his new countess.

"Come on, Rowan, be a good dog. Ye know ye canna be in here." The thick Scots brogue and lilting, musical voice slowed the duke's rapid pace. "Yer makin' a mess, ye big hairy beastie."

Colton hesitated, then moved slowly toward the music room and the beautiful voice. The scene that met his gaze brought a look of pure male appreciation to his face.

Apparently his mother had hired another new maid, and at the moment she was losing a tug-of-war with Lord Blagden's Irish wolfhound. The young woman bent over a little and pulled on the dog's collar, unknowingly giving the duke a very pleasing view of her backside. She was slender but with enough gentle curves to be very attractive. He shifted a little, trying to get a better view of her face, but the ruffle on her large mobcap thwarted him. From the little he saw, he expected a beauty.

The maid released the dog's collar and straightened. Rowan lay down, thumping his tail on the floor, and gazed up at her in contentment.

"Please, Rowan, I canna do my work with ye scatterin' all the sand about." She pointed to the side of the room. The dog's gaze followed her finger. "I had already swept that side. Ye dinna have to go trackin' all the dust and sand back over there." She chuckled softly and leaned down to stroke the dog's head.

Colton's heartbeat quickened slightly. He never thought he'd be jealous of a dog. He felt uneasy. He was always uncomfortable and awkward in the presence of a woman, whether she was one of the working class or one of his peers.

He could purchase the largest estate in England and never miss the money. He could persuade prime ministers and generals to implement his plans, but he had never learned to make small talk or flirt with the ladies or charm them out of stolen kisses. The ladies of the ton thought him cold and arrogant, but secretly the wealthy and powerful Duke of Ryland was shy.

Colton was not a recluse but still only attended a small number of parties each Season. Once he had held the hope of meeting a woman who would set him at ease, one who could break down his wall of reserve to reveal the warm, caring man underneath. Eight Seasons had come and gone, and so had his hope.

"Well, what am I goin' to do with ye?" The maid took a step backward just as the duke decided he must go to her aid.

A second later Rowan spied him and jumped to his feet. The dog made a beeline for the duke, crashing into the maid and hurling her backward with small stumbling steps. When she slammed into Colton, his arm went around her to steady her. He barely had time to gasp for air before Rowan jumped up, looped his paws over the duke's shoulders, and knocked them both to the floor.

Slightly stunned, it was a moment before Catriona Denley opened her eyes. Her white linen mobcap covered one eye. Her limited view was filled with a multitude of threatening teeth and a long curling tongue.

"Ach, I'm goin' to be eaten alive," she whispered, then squeezed her eyelids tightly shut to block out the fearful sight.

"He won't bite, but he might lick you to death."

Catriona's eyelids flew open. Not only had that warm, manly voice fluttered the lace beside her ear, but she had also felt it rumble beneath her back. To her mortification she realized she was sprawled on top of someone. A glance at the richly covered arm encircling her waist confirmed her fear; he wasn't one of the servants but a gentleman.

The dog stood over them, his gray forelegs straddling the man's shoulders. His hind legs were on either side of the gent's calves, near her ankles. Every so often Catriona caught a glimpse of Rowan's tail wagging back and forth in what seemed to be a happy rhythm. She relaxed a little.

She was about to apologize to the gentleman when she noticed the dog's mouth coming closer. With a small cry Catriona turned her head and buried the side of her face in the dark-blue wool coat beneath her. Pulling her hands up to protect the other side of her face, she squirmed, waiting for the onslaught from that big, sloppy tongue.

"What's wrong?" The duke's words were muffled as the wiggling bundle on top of him inadvertently stuffed part of her cap in his mouth. She gave a little squeak, then giggled. About the time Colton spat out the cap, the dog began to shower his face with kisses—not big, sloppy licks but tiny, gentle strokes with just the tip of his tongue.

"Rowan, stop!" The duke's command was accompanied by a strong push against the dog's chest. "Rowan, get off!" This time the duke's voice was more desperate than commanding, and his shove was fed by a surge of adrenaline.

The dog reluctantly stepped over them, moved a few paces away, and stretched out on the floor.

Catriona rolled off the gentleman and sat up, pushing her mobcap up out of her eye and wiping the dog slime off her face with her apron.

"Your Grace!" Catriona's face reflected her mixed emotions of chagrin and amusement. "Oh, dear."

The duke sat up, pulled his handkerchief from his coat pocket, and wiped his face. Then he looked down at one of the loveliest women he had ever seen. Her cap was still askew and the little ribbon tie at the throat of her linen chemisette had come undone, but her turquoise eyes sparkled with laughter as a soft blush kissed her cheeks. He wanted to kiss them too.

She smiled, and the duke questioned whether his legs would ever be strong enough to stand. He reached out and straightened her cap, noting the dark red curl that peeked out from under the lace in front of her ear. With great effort he kept his hand from seeking that curl and rolling it around his fingers.

With even greater effort he pushed himself up to stand and offered her a hand. She took it, lightly coming to her feet at his gentle tug. A smile twitched the corner of his lip. If he guessed correctly, she was barely suppressing a laugh.

Catriona studied the man standing in front of her. With his twinkling eyes and tiny smile he looked nothing like the somber, grave aristocrat in the painting in her ladyship's sitting room. In the portrait, he was the epitome of dignity, the ultimate peer of the realm.

She glanced at his mangled, twisted cravat. Her gaze went to his hair, where one thick, chestnut-brown lock stood straight up. In spite of her efforts, she chuckled. Without thinking, she reached out to smooth his hair, stopping herself just before she actually touched it. Embarrassed by her impudent action, she dropped her hand in front of her and looked down.

"I assume I did not come out of our skirmish unscathed." The duke laughed softly and ran his hand over his hair, smoothing down the wayward strand.

Catriona glanced back at his cravat and grinned. "No, Yer Grace." His deep, warm laugh sent gooseflesh racing down her arms.

"There's no help for this without a mirror." He jerked the cravat back around so that its drooping folds sagged down the middle of his chest. "In fact, there's probably no help for it without my valet." He hesitated, telling himself to let this frivolous exchange go no further. He ignored his own advice.

"You have the advantage over me, my dear. You know who I am, but I don't even know your name." He smiled down at her, a warm, tender smile usually reserved for playful puppies and innocent, laughing children. It was slightly lopsided, revealing a wonderful, unexpected dimple in his right cheek.

His smile went straight to Catriona's heart. As she lifted her gaze to his, the twinkle in his beautiful cinnamon eyes gave way to something deeper, something mysterious and compelling. He did not move, but she felt his caress just the same. She opened her mouth to speak—and almost told him her real name.

Catching herself before she gave away her true identity, Catriona looked down at the mangled cravat and shook her head. She would have to be careful where the duke was concerned. In his presence, she had forgotten about her masquerade. It would not do for him to discover she was the earl's granddaughter, a twenty-year-old grandchild the older gentleman probably did not even know existed. Someday soon she could tell them all, but not yet.

"I am Kate MacArthur, Yer Grace," she said, using a friend's last name. She gave him a deep curtsy and kept her eyes lowered. "I beg yer pardon for my poor manners."

The duke frowned. How had he frightened her? He sighed inwardly. For the first time in his life a servant had been more cognizant of her position than he had. Was she afraid she would be dismissed for her behavior?

"Kate, your manners are fine." He knew he should end this little encounter now, with both of them stepping back into their precisely defined roles. He could not. She made him smile—she made his heart smile. Colton couldn't remember the last time anyone had touched that hollow, lonely core.

He gently lifted her chin with his bent forefinger. "The circumstances were unusual, that is all." He glanced over at Rowan. As soon as he looked at him, the big dog began to thump his tail on the polished wooden floor. "Would you like me to take this big, hairy beastie with me?" he asked, lowering his hand.

Kate laughed softly. "Yes, please. I canna get my work done with him underfoot, knockin' the chairs about and scatterin' my cleanin' sand in every direction."

Colton smiled down at her. He saw her glance at his dimple before her own wide smile lit her face. He suddenly felt like whistling. He didn't, of course. The Duke of Ryland never whistled or acted foolish in front of others. But he felt like it just the same. With a jaunty grin, he called to Rowan and headed down the long hall toward his mother's sitting room.

Kate went back in the music room and leaned against the wall. She wasn't quite sure what made her heart pound so—was it the duke's warm smile and soul-searching eyes, or was it because she had almost given her secret away? She took a deep breath, deciding it was all of them.

She had come to work in her grandfather's house on a whim. She wanted to see the old man and get to know him for herself, even if just from a distance. Her father let her come because he wanted to know for certain that the earl's new wife loved him and made him happy. Addison Denley knew his daughter would be safe working as a maid in the earl's house, and he held a deep hope that she could find some way to reunite him and his father.

Remembering the warmth of the duke's finger beneath her chin, Kate muttered to herself. "He's supposed to be as cold as stone. I canna let him cause me trouble." She squared her shoulders resolutely, making up her mind to stay away from him. A little imp reminded her of the duke's heart-stopping smile, and some of her resolve faded. "Well, I'll try my best to avoid him."

She glanced down at the calluses on her hands, remembering the month she had worked as a part-time maid in her own house. The adjustment of her body to the rigors of manual labor had been painful, but now she was thankful she had done it. She never could have stood up to the present hard work otherwise.

She scooped up a handful of damp sand and scattered it across the floor. Picking up the broom, she began sweeping the room briskly. The sand picked up the dust and polished the floor, bringing out the beautiful grain of the wood. Kate barely noticed.

Colton was still smiling when he entered his mother's sitting room a few minutes later.

The countess looked up from the book she was reading. "Goodness! You're smiling!" Her tone sounded accusing. "What happened to you?"

"Your maid." Colton grinned and stopped in front of a mahogany-framed mirror, attempting to do something with his limp cravat.

"Oh, dear. Don't tell me Nell . . . Whatever am I going to do with that girl? First she practically undresses in front of Richard, then I hear her and Blake in one of the bedrooms doing . . . well, you know what they were doing." Embarrassed, the countess jumped up and fluttered about the room in agitation. "She's old Betty's niece. The old woman will be so disappointed if I let her go. I suppose she simply 'bumped into you,' like all the others."

"No." Colton gave the cravat one last tug, then turned toward his mother, devilment sparkling in his eyes. "Actually, I haven't met Nell. The maid I bumped into is Kate."

"Kate! Oh, dear. Oh, dear! Not Kate. She's such a sweet,

obedient little thing. Such a hard worker. I promised Lady Douglas I'd give her a job and let her stay as long as she wants. She'd worked for her for three years. Kate only came to town to see a bit of the world. Oh, dear. I never thought she would behave this way. And with my son of all people." She turned on him, her face full of irritation. "Your father trained you differently, Colton."

The smile faded from the duke's eyes. "Yes, I was trained well," he said with a slight trace of bitterness. He smoothed his hair absently and sat down gracefully on the green velvet settee.

"Come down out of the boughs, Mother. Kate did nothing wrong. Neither did I, for that matter. We shared a moment of laughter, little more. Rowan knocked her into me as I passed the music room; then he jumped up and knocked us both down." He glanced over at the dog as the animal stretched out before the fire. Colton grinned, unwilling to let his mother's disapproval spoil his lighthearted mood.

"I'm rumpled because he decided to wash my face." He sat quietly for a moment. He and Kate had shared much more in those brief moments, but he could not talk about those feelings to his mother or to anyone.

"I beg your pardon, son. I shouldn't have gotten so vexed. I'm a bit in the dumps today."

"Why?" Colton's expression became one of concern. "Are you and Thomas at odds?"

"He is at odds with everyone today. I've never seen him so blue-deviled." She sat down beside him, clasping her hands on her lap. "Bence told me Thomas disinherited his son twenty-two years ago today."

Colton draped an arm across the back of the settee. "I've never heard why Thomas disinherited him. Did Bence tell you what happened?"

"Yes. Addison married an Edinburgh shopkeeper's daughter. I know I shouldn't gossip with the butler, but Thomas forbids me to talk of his son. Bence was the only one who could tell me about it." She looked up at Colton for encouragement, and he smiled gently.

"Elizabeth, Thomas's first wife, flew into a rage when Addison brought his wife home to meet them. She could not bear the disgrace of her son marrying a Cit. The girl was a rare beauty and had as much grace and manners as the best of the ton, though she didn't have a drop of blue blood in her. Bence said it was obvious to all that they were deeply in love.

"But Elizabeth could only see the disgrace. She could only think of the scandal. I shouldn't speak ill of the dead, but when I think of the pain my Thomas has gone through all these years . . ." She took a deep breath and pulled a delicate handkerchief from her pocket and wiped her eyes.

"Elizabeth ranted and raved, nagging Thomas until he disinherited Addison. Thomas loved her deeply and was too blind to see what a horrible thing he was doing. He threw them out and renounced him before the ton." Fresh tears sprang to her eyes. "Addison was his only child, yet Thomas forbids anyone even to speak his name. I love my husband, Colton, but how can he live knowing nothing of his son? I doubt he even knows if he's alive. He has lost twenty-two precious years."

Lady Millicent began to cry harder, and Colton slipped his arm around her shoulders. For once, he was at a loss for words. He had only seen her weep twice in his life, five years past when his father died, and long ago when his younger brother drowned in a small lake on one of the family's estates. He pondered for a moment. It had been twenty years since Erwin died.

Colton cradled his mother's head against his shoulder, guessing that only part of her grief was for her husband's pain. She wept for the son she had lost and the stepson she might never have, the one person who might help fill the void left by Erwin's death.

He knew his parents had not been particularly close. His father had been wrapped up in politics and his mother had been busy with parties and various charities. She had always been a loving mother, but he had never realized how much love she had to give until now.

The countess sniffed loudly and sat up. Wiping her eyes and blowing her nose, she gave her son a weak smile. "Oh, dear, I do beg your pardon. I don't know what came over me." She blew her nose once again, took a deep breath, and relaxed back against the cushions. "I do feel much better."

"Good." Colton removed his arm from her shoulders, considering his words carefully. "Mother, I'm acquainted with Addison Denley."

"You are?" Her face lit up. "How do you know him?"

He's one of my intelligence contacts. The words ran through his mind but he didn't speak them. "A chance meeting in Scotland two years ago."

"Well, why didn't you tell me?"

"I assumed you knew as much about him as I do. He is still happily married to his Cit. I didn't meet her, but he spoke highly of her. He is a prominent businessman in Edinburgh. Has done quite well for himself. I think he mentioned having a child. A girl, I believe."

"Oh, Colton. How wonderful! Do you know how old she is?"

Colton searched his memory. Addison was on the fringes of his network, providing information only occasionally. At times he would hear of supply shipments being smuggled from Scotland to France or of suspicious activities by Frenchmen living in Scotland. Many Scots were loyal to England. Some were not. There were those who hated the English enough to join forces with France, mistakenly believing Napoleon would give them home rule.

"Unfortunately, I don't recall."

"Oh, Colton, just think. If Thomas and his son could mend their differences, I'd have a grandchild." She frowned up at him. "I've given up on *you*."

He laughed. "I'm not in my dotage yet, Mother. I've plenty of time to father children. I just haven't met the right woman." A pair of sparkling turquoise eyes flashed across his mind, but he quickly squelched the thought.

"You won't meet her if you don't attend more functions this Season. She's not going to fall right out of the blue into your lap."

The faint aroma of jasmine teased his memory. The duke frowned, trying to remember where he had smelled that elusive scent. *Her hair*. When Kate's mobcap had been scrunched up in his face, it smelled of jasmine. He gave himself a silent rebuke for acting like a foolish young buck, then turned his attention toward making small talk with his mother.

An hour after the duke left her, Kate finished cleaning the music room. She had pushed the furniture back against the walls in order to clean the floor. When she started to move the chairs back to where they belonged, she stopped, allowing herself a moment to daydream. The duke had been in her thoughts most of the past hour.

What would it be like to waltz around the room in his arms? she thought. Wonderful but not likely. The waltz was not done among the ton, although it had been a popular dance on the Continent for fifty years. Her father had learned it years ago on a trip to Austria. She and her mother often took turns playing the pianoforte and dancing with Addison, so she knew the music and dance well. She began to hum a Viennese waltz and whirled across the floor.

Colton walked down the hall, wondering if Kate was still working in the music room. Common sense told him not to stop, but at the moment he was not feeling very sensible. As he paused outside the door, a softly hummed tune reached his ears. He stepped forward and looked into the room, watching in silent amazement as Kate executed the waltz steps perfectly.

Kate swirled around the room, pretending, just for a moment, that she was in the duke's arms. Suddenly, she came to a halt. He was standing there in front of her.

He closed one warm hand over hers and slid the other one around her waist, heating the small of her back through the black gown. For a long moment, they simply stood there, gazing into each others' eyes, silently asking questions to which there were not yet answers.

The duke smiled gently and began to hum the same song, sweeping her in wondrous circles around the room. Kate rested her hand on his wide shoulder. She couldn't wipe the brilliant smile off her face, nor did she even want to. She felt as if she were floating on air. Waltzing with her father, as good a dancer as he was, was nothing compared to dancing in the duke's arms.

Much too soon, the song ended. Reluctantly he stopped. When she removed her hand from his shoulder, he released her, dropping his hands down at his side.

"You dance wonderfully, Your Grace." Kate smiled up at

him, suddenly a little shy. "I dinna know the English knew how to waltz."

"Most don't. I learned how on a trip to the Continent last year. Surprisingly it is one of the few dances I do well." He smiled down at her, his eyes twinkling. "You also dance wonderfully, little maid. I didn't think the Scots knew how to waltz, either."

Kate jumped guiltily, and her face flushed deeply. She quickly lowered her gaze to hide her confusion. *What am I thinking of?* she thought desperately. Of course, Scottish maids dunna know how to waltz.

"I do believe I've embarrassed you. Don't tell me a suitor taught you how to dance." *Please don't tell me that.* "A French dancing teacher, perhaps."

"Yes, yes, you're right. A French dancing teacher. He instructed my former employers' daughters on how to dance. He came to call a few times and taught me a few dances. He was no suitor; we were nothing more than friends."

The duke breathed a quiet sigh of relief, even as a tiny alarm sounded in his head. One of the reasons he was so good at espionage was because he caught little things in people's behavior that might go overlooked by others. His eyes narrowed slightly as he watched her, wondering why the thickness of her brogue had suddenly lessened. Her speech was not that of an uneducated maid but an odd mix of cultured English and Scots. It suggested a genteel Scots lady who might have had an English governess. Also, Lady Douglas had no daughters, only sons.

Kate wanted to cry. Until she embarked on this wild scheme to learn about her grandfather she had never told a lie in her life. Even here she had tried very hard to keep to the truth as much as possible, but she had purposefully lied to this man. She felt dirty and disappointed in herself.

What would he think of her when he discovered the truth? What would her grandfather think? Or the countess? Suddenly Kate felt very foolish, trapped by her own duplicity. The plan had seemed so simple when she thought of it. Now all she could think of was the line from Sir Walter Scott's poem, *Marmion*—"Oh, what a tangled web we weave when first we practice to deceive."

Colton watched the different emotions rush over her face. Something else was amiss. Was it something to do with the dancing teacher? Perhaps the man had been more than a friend. Perhaps a lover. A surge of jealousy shot through him.

She looked up at him uncertainly, and he wanted to wipe away any thoughts of an old lover. He ached to kiss her, but it was the wrong place, the wrong time.

A lock of dark red hair had come loose from her cap while they were dancing. It was clean and shiny and curled across her collarbone. He picked it up, letting the end wrap around his finger. Bending slightly, he brought it up to his nostrils. The scent was subtle, as if she had washed her hair the night before. He breathed deeply, filling his senses with jasmine. Colton let the silky hair slip from his fingers before capturing her gaze with his.

"You're a bonnie lass, Kate MacArthur."

"You're no piece of granite, Your Grace." Her bemused smile told him she didn't quite know what to think of him.

He chuckled. "To everyone else, Kate, but never to you." He turned abruptly, leaving her staring after him as he walked out of the music room.

As the duke came down the stairs, Harlan stared, too. Colton grinned. The boy acted like he had never heard a man whistle a Viennese waltz before. He pulled on his coat, hat, and gloves. With a twirl of his cane he stepped out into the storm, resuming his tune.

Chapter 2

At the sound of a familiar voice below, Kate cautiously peered between the elegantly carved Adam balusters. Richard Denley, her father's cousin, came up the stairs from the ground floor, accompanied by a younger man.

Kate swallowed a lump in her throat. Richard was her father's friend and occasionally had visited their home, the last time being the past summer. Addison had been under the impression that Richard usually spent the winter at his home in Kent.

She drew back slightly as they came closer, straining to understand their words.

"When are you leaving?" asked the younger man.

"Tomorrow, if the weather holds. Are you certain you won't come down for a visit, Blake?"

"No, there are too many diversions in town. I'd only plague you with my boredom."

"Ah, a new piece of muslin, eh?"

Kate moved backward a few steps before turning and going down the hall to dust one of the guest bedrooms. "Drat!" she muttered once she was safe. "First the duke, now Richard. I'll have to stay out of his way, or with a certainty he'll recognize me."

She had never met the other man, but she guessed from some of her father's past conversations that he was Blake

Denley, Richard's youngest brother. Since the countess had caught him and Nell in the bedroom next door, his reputation as a ladies' man had preceded him. He was handsome enough, Kate decided, but she was not impressed by his slight build.

Her father had mentioned another brother, Howard, but she did not think he would be popping in at her grandfather's house. Howard was very ill and lived in Brighton, where he gained some comfort from the sea air.

She brushed the cloth duster carefully over a porcelain figurine of a hunting dog. If she had not been so preoccupied, she would have noted its beauty, but her thoughts were on beauty of another kind.

She had been unable to get the duke out of her mind. The other servants had said he was cold and arrogant. Priscilla, one of the older maids, had gotten quite a laugh out of the way he had ignored Nell. A small smile curved her lips. *They dunna know the duke I met,* she thought. *But I have to stay away from him, too,* she reminded herself sternly. *Later, when things are resolved between Papa and Grandfather, we can meet as equals.*

On the floor below, the earl and his nephews discussed a few news items pertaining to the war. When talk turned to some of Richard's and Lord Blagden's joint business ventures, Blake excused himself. He quietly climbed the stairs, looking for Nell.

He did not find the blond maid, but he did find Kate. Quietly pushing open the bedroom door, he took his time looking her over. When she moved to dust the pictures on the wall adjacent to him, he was finally given a good view of her face. He let out a long, low whistle and stepped into the room.

Kate glanced up in alarm, then quickly dropped her gaze and curtsied.

"Aren't you the pretty one." Blake walked across the thick carpet, stopping in front of her. She stood quietly, her gaze lowered with pretended respect.

"I must say my new aunt isn't opposed to hiring pretty servants. First Nell, now you." He tipped her chin up with his knuckle, but Kate kept her eyes lowered.

"Nell is over in the other wing, sir."

"Why should I go look for her when I have you?" He traced

the line of her jaw with his fingertip. "What's your name, little Scot?"

"Kate, sir."

He ran his hands lightly down her arms, taking hold of one hand. "There's a nice bed here. Shall we try it out?"

Anger shot through her. "No, sir," she said sternly. "Let me pass."

"Ah, the little Scot has spirit. I like a woman with spirit. I don't even mind a woman who fights me." He moved one hand to her upper arm, gripping it firmly while the fingers of his other hand slipped under her cap just beneath her ear. "Are you going to fight, Kate?" he asked softly.

"Aye, I'll fight ye," she spat. Fear and rage threatened to overshadow rational thought. "I'll kick and claw and scream if ye dunna let me go. I willna be dismissed because of the likes of ye." She looked up at him, her angry gaze meeting his directly.

His eyes narrowed, as if he saw something familiar in her face. Kate looked down quickly, even though the fear of being ravished overwhelmed her fear of discovery. There was a hardness in his face, a cruelness in his eyes unlike any she had ever seen before. He would take great pleasure in subduing her. She began to tremble and felt his grip ease. He pulled his other hand from beneath her cap.

"Please, sir, Lady Millicent will dismiss me if she finds me with ye. She was very angry with Nell."

"Uncle always was against us having a bit of sport with the servants, but Nell was willing, very willing."

"I am no'. Let me pass." She forced her voice to remain strong, although his grip tightened once more.

Blake wanted her, but not badly enough to upset his uncle again. There was too much at stake.

"I would have made it enjoyable for you, little Scot." He released her arm, drawing his hand back with a little flourish.

Kate's face flamed, and she kept her gaze averted as she rushed from the room. She wanted to go to her room and hide until she could calm down, but she guessed she would be much safer with others around. Hurrying down the back stairs, she raced breathlessly into the kitchen.

Mrs. Jackson, the housekeeper, paused in removing the

silverware from its box. She took in Kate's flushed face and shaking hands. "Priscilla told me Mr. Blake was here. Looks like he might have found you. Did he harm you, girl?"

"No, ma'am." Kate slumped down in a chair. "But he gave me a fright."

The housekeeper thrust a soft cloth into Kate's hands. "Here, dearie, you can polish for a while. A little bit of good rubbing will take your mind off that rake. He won't venture in here." The housekeeper watched Kate work for a moment. Satisfied that the girl knew what she was doing, the older woman left the kitchen.

Blake waited in the guest room for a few minutes, then ventured back downstairs to his uncle's office. As he slipped into the room, it was apparent that his brother and uncle were having a heated discussion.

"I want you to live at Heartlands this spring, Richard. You need to become familiar with the tenants and the lands. I don't want you taking over as a stranger when I'm gone."

"Don't talk nonsense, Uncle Thomas." Richard shifted uncomfortably in his chair. "You're going to be around for years yet."

"Most likely, but I want you to spend some time there every year. You'll be the next earl. I want my people to know you and feel comfortable with you."

Blake watched intently, covering his tension like a consummate actor as his brother drummed his fingers on the arm of the chair. If Richard persuaded the old man to reconcile with Addison, all would be lost.

"You know I do not want the title or Heartlands, Uncle. It belongs to your son."

"I have no son!"

"Yes, you do. He is alive, well, and worthy of his heritage. It should be his," Richard said gently.

"No! Do not speak to me of that ungrateful whelp." Sweat broke out on the earl's forehead and his face grew red. "He dishonored this family and sent his mother to an early grave. And now he's a traitor, a spy for Napoleon."

Blake's eyes sparkled and his tension eased. His rumor had finally reached the proper ears. He was hard-pressed to retain his smile.

"Surely you do not believe such a thing!" Richard jumped to his feet. "Addison would no more betray England than you or I would."

"He betrayed his mother by bringing that strumpet home as his wife. Why wouldn't he betray his country as well? He thinks only of himself. He's a Scot now, and it's no secret some of them think Boney would be a better ruler than the Prince Regent."

"Myrna is no strumpet. She's as fine a lady as you'd meet in any Mayfair drawing room." Richard tried to control his temper. "Addison Denley would never betray England. Never."

"I'll speak no more of him! Now get out. I don't want you here!" shouted the earl.

"Very well, my lord," said Richard stiffly. "I shall send my card around next time I'm in town. If you want to see me then, you'll have to tell me." With a sharp jerk of his head in Blake's direction, Richard stormed from the room. His patience strained beyond endurance, he flung the door back against the wall, sending a picture crashing to the floor. Blake strolled nonchalantly after him.

Lord Blagden jumped to his feet and followed him, shouting. "Never speak of him again, I tell you. Never!"

Lady Millicent came rushing down the stairs as Richard and Blake hurried out the front door. The earl was standing in the hallway, shaking his fist after them. His heavy jowls quivered in rage. "He is dead to me! Do you hear? Dead, like his mother!"

At the sound of her grandfather's shouting, Kate slipped from the kitchen and tiptoed quickly down the hall. She hid behind a partially opened door and peered around it as Lady Millicent reached the earl. His face was blood red, and even from where Kate stood, she could see his pulse throbbing in his temple.

"Thomas, calm yourself," the countess cried softly. "You'll give yourself a stroke." She cradled his face in her hands, calling his name softly until he looked down at her. "I didn't marry you, so I could play nursemaid. Please calm down."

He forced himself to relax, taking several deep breaths. The color slowly began to drain from his face.

"What were you arguing about, my love?"

"Addison." His face contorted with deep pain. Lady Millicent put her arms around his wide waist.

Tears filled Kate's eyes.

"My son, my traitorous son." The venom in his voice was like a knife thrusting into Kate's heart. "His mother expected so much from him. He could have had his pick of the ton, but he turned his back on us. He married a nobody and killed his mother." His voice cracked with grief.

"She just withered away after that. A year later she was gone. The doctor said it was some kind of disease, but it wasn't. She died of despair and dishonor. He brought dishonor to this family, and she couldn't live with it." Thomas clutched Millicent tightly as a tear slid down his anguished face.

Kate drew back and tiptoed away. She had no right to intrude on their privacy, but as she turned the corner, their words still reached her.

"I love you, Millie. You're as dear as life, but I loved her, too."

"I know, Thomas, and I love you. I'm not jealous of Elizabeth, but can't you see you're destroying yourself? You'll never have peace until you set aside your grief and forgive your son."

"I cannot, Millie—" His voice broke. "I cannot."

Kate polished the silver for the next hour. With a heavy heart she considered the futility of her quest. She thought of her friends and family back in Scotland, guessing that most would tell her to abandon her mad scheme. But her father wouldn't.

Kate smiled softly, thinking how much Addison loved the earl. It had broken his heart when his father sent him away, but he had understood his reasons. He had known his mother would not forgive him, for she had always been more concerned about what her peers thought than of his happiness. He had felt, in time, his father would have a change of heart, but Elizabeth's death put an end to that hope. Richard had gone to Scotland to tell him of her death. He told him, too, that Thomas had forbidden his son to come home for the funeral.

No, her father would not want her to leave yet. He was almost as stubborn as she was. Both her parents had a tendency to be mulish, but they often said she had inherited the trait from both of them. She could not leave. She had to find a way to tell her grandfather who she was and how much his son loved him. She had too much unfinished business to attend to.

The duke's face flashed across her mind. No, she could not leave yet.

Several days later, Colton arrived late in the evening amid swirling snow and plunging temperatures. The weather was too foul for any parties, and the earl and his lady had been about to retire for the evening.

"What brings you out on a night like this?" asked Lord Blagden, eyeing the duke's valet, Gregory, and the bag he was holding.

"One of our chimneys clogged and filled the house with smoke before anyone could figure out which one it was." Colton wearily looked over at his mother. "I was in council most of last night and since six this morning. I had just crawled into bed when smoke came rolling under the door. Could you spare a couple of beds for a few days?"

"Of course, dear. You look tired unto death." She wrinkled her nose. "You'll need a bath, Colton."

He nodded. "I'm so exhausted, I think I could fall asleep in spite of smelling like smoke, but it would only stink up the bedroom. I apologize for being such a bother so late."

"Glad to oblige you, son," said the earl affectionately. "Now go on upstairs. We'll have the water brought up straightaway." The earl instructed Bence to have the footmen, as well as the maids, carry up the water, so the tub was filled in record time.

Kate was given the added task of putting fresh linen on the duke's bed. When she entered the room, carrying the sheets and pillowcases, she heard the slosh of water as he bathed in an adjacent antechamber. It was an intimate sound, sending a little shiver of awareness down her spine. The image her mind conjured up brought a blush to her face.

She dumped the sheets on a chair and quickly pulled the heavy bedspread from the bed, folding it carefully and setting it on another chair in front of the fireplace. Kate hurried to put the sheets on the bed and, in her haste, got the top one crooked. Grumbling at her foolishness, she jerked it off the bed and started over. At the sound of a soft, deep chuckle behind her, she whirled around—and gasped.

The duke grinned as she stared openmouthed. He was clothed, in a manner of speaking. He was apparently wearing one of the earl's old dressing gowns, from the days before Kate's grandfather had reached his present large girth.

When Colton absently began drying his hair with a small towel, the robe stretched taut across his wide shoulders. Kate thought if he moved his arm forward any farther, it would split down the back. The hem of the garment had been made to hit the wearer at the ankles. It struck the duke at mid-calf.

He shifted the towel to the other side of his head, and the upper part of the dressing gown gaped open, revealing a strong, muscular chest liberally sprinkled with reddish-brown hair.

Kate's mouth went dry. She had the oddest longing to rest her cheek against his chest, to smell his freshly bathed skin and let the coarse hair curl around her fingers. She had never had such thoughts before about any man, and they shocked her. Her eyes moved slowly upward, past the solid column of his neck and his square jaw to stop briefly on his lips. He was no longer smiling.

Colton stood perfectly still, watching her gaze roam over him. The innocent desire reflected on her face sent a jolt through him, filling him with a craving unlike any he had ever known. He wanted to bury his fingers in her hair and cradle that beautiful heart-shaped face in his hands. He wanted to taste her lips and feel her tremble beneath his touch.

When Kate raised her gaze to his, she stifled a tiny cry and took a step backward. Her expression of desire gave way to one of confusion tinged with fear. The duke silently cursed himself for not hiding the hunger in his eyes and forced himself to look away toward the fire.

He heard her move and caught a glimpse of blankets being jerked from an oak chest at the foot of the bed. The lid dropped shut with a soft thunk as Kate tossed one of the covers over the bed. Glancing at her surreptitiously, he found her hurrying around the bed to tuck in the cover. Her face flamed, and he tried to think of something to say to put her at ease.

"Aren't you finished with the bed yet?" Gregory's irritated

voice grated across the duke's nerves. Kate jumped guiltily and threw another blanket up in the air, and it floated gently down over the mattress. "Such sluggardly be—"

"Gregory!"

The valet looked at his lord in astonishment. In ten years of service, the duke had never spoken to him in such a sharp, angry tone.

Colton wearily rubbed his hand over his face. "It is late. I'm certain Kate is as tired as the rest of us. Let her be."

"Yes, Your Grace." Gregory slanted a glance at the young maid, curious as to how the duke knew her name. "I'll take your things downstairs to clean and air. You should have a fresh suit of clothes by morning."

"Thank you. Don't stay up all night worrying about it."

Gregory left the room as Kate smoothed a wrinkle out of the third blanket. She grabbed the bedspread from the chair, laying it across the top of the blanket chest. Keeping her eyes downcast, Kate backed away from the bed and stood near the door.

"Will there be anythin' more, Yer Grace?" She was half afraid to ask the question, but as a servant she was obligated to do so.

Yes, much more. He smiled slightly, pleased with himself for keeping his mouth shut. She was as skittish as a new colt, ready to bolt out the door. When he didn't answer, she peeked up at him and his smile grew gentle. "No. Thank you for making the bed. Now go and see to your own rest."

Kate bobbed a quick curtsy and dashed through the door. She raced up the back stairs to her room without thinking of taking a candle. She groaned softly as she sank down on her small bed.

"He must think I'm a strumpet!" she muttered quietly. Tightly squeezing her eyes shut, she pounded her fist on the feather mattress. "I canna believe I stared at him like he was some confection from Gunter's. My mouth was practically watering," she said, moaning.

The room was like ice, and though at first she was warm from her embarrassment, it did not take long for the chill to permeate her clothes. She did not know why, but the servants were not given any coal to heat their rooms. It seemed totally out of character for either the earl or the countess to treat them so poorly, but she felt she had not been there long enough to ask the countess about it.

Groping around in the dark, Kate pulled out two linen nightdresses from her small trunk. She was shaking all over by the time she had removed her day wear and dressed in the gowns. Both garments had five buttons that she struggled to fasten with trembling fingers. She put on two pairs of woolen stockings, then pulled her long, loose braid from beneath her cap. Letting the braid drape across her neck and over one shoulder, Kate added another mobcap over the one she had worn all day.

Scurrying under the covers, she curled up in a tight little ball, trying to get warm. She doubted if she would ever go to sleep, even if her shivering subsided. Every time she closed her eyes she pictured the duke standing there drying his hair.

Kate had been courted by several young men and had even been infatuated with a couple of them. She had felt an attraction for one gentleman in particular the year before and had allowed him a couple of chaste kisses.

But nothing in her experience had prepared her for the flood of desire she had felt while watching the duke. She was not completely naïve; the smoldering hunger in his eyes told her he had felt the same. A shiver of a different sort rippled through her. Gradually her thoughts of the duke became a beautiful dream as her weary body conquered her racing mind. She fell into a deep sleep.

The Duke of Ryland enjoyed sleeping in a cool room but not a cold one. When he awakened at about a quarter to three, he was definitely cold. Colton rubbed the sleep from his eyes and glared at the low coals in the fireplace. Knowing he would never get back to sleep unless he stoked up the fire, he finally jerked back the covers and dragged himself from the four-poster bed.

He threw more coal onto the fire and pumped the bellows a few times for good measure. As the fire slowly began to grow hotter, he stood and turned his bare back to it to warm that side also.

Feeling toasty, he hurried back to bed. He had just settled in nicely when he heard the sound of his door opening and closing. Cautiously Colton raised up a bit, looking over the sleek mahogany footboard of the bed. He blinked his eyes and looked again.

"Kate?" he asked softly, squinting in the flickering light of the fire.

She didn't answer but walked across the room and picked up the heavy brocade bedspread from the top of the oak chest. Lifting the spread to the bed and laying it across his feet, she methodically unfolded it.

Colton watched her, amazed because she was in his room and puzzled by her actions. Now that she was closer, he could see her clearly in the light from the fire. She did not look at him but moved up the other side of the bed, drawing the curtain up to the head of the bed. She calmly returned to the foot of the bed and pulled the spread up with her. He dropped his head back down on the pillow, smiling sensually.

"There's no need for more cover, Kate. I'll make sure you're warm." Suddenly the bedspread was flipped up over his face. "What the devil!" His cry was muffled by the thick, somewhat dusty, spread. He shoved it off his face and chest and leaned up on one elbow to scowl at her.

She very calmly placed a pillow on top of the spread to his right and folded the coverlet over it, tucking it around the top and bottom edges of the pillow. A little frown creased her brow when she tried to straighten the bedspread on the side of the pillow nearest him.

The duke's frown deepened. He hung on to the cover tightly.

Kate tugged, but he held firm. She released an exasperated little sigh and turned, walking around the end of the bed and up the side where he was lying.

By now the fire burned brightly. Colton was getting too warm. He threw the spread back down toward the foot of the bed, remaining in a sitting position when she stopped beside him. He took a closer look at her and almost laughed out loud.

She was between him and the fire, so he expected to see her silhouette through the nightdress. He did not. Instead he studied two ruffles from two distinct heavy linen gowns, one trimmed with white lace, the other with dark green. The top one was primly buttoned from her throat down past her bosom.

He suspected the undergarment was fastened in the same manner.

"Kate, what are you doing?"

She tilted her head slightly to one side. "Making the bed."

Colton studied her expression. She was strangely subdued. There was no laughter in her eyes, no excitement, no guilt, no nervousness. Her thoughts seemed to be a thousand miles away. His eyes narrowed. He had seen that look before, on a classmate when he was at Oxford. The young man had been a sleepwalker.

"Kate," he said gently, "I've misplaced my timepiece. Do you know what time of day it is?"

"No' precisely, Your Grace, but 'tis near noon. Time to straighten the bedrooms. I have to make the bed."

"But I'm in it." He hurried on before she could say anything. "Why are you wearing two caps?"

"Cold." She stood very still.

He reached out to take her hand. Even in the warm room it was like ice. He felt her cheek. It was just as cold. She sighed quietly and closed her eyes, rubbing her cheek against his palm.

"Come, Kitten," he said softly. "You woke up much too early. It's not time for chores now. Crawl in bed and get warm."

He had heard it was unwise to try to wake a sleepwalker suddenly; the shock might be too great and cause a heart attack. He did not really know if it was true, but he was not about to take any chances. At the moment he was more concerned about her taking a chill than he was about waking her.

He scooted over in the bed, gasping when his bare skin touched the cold sheets. Drawing back the covers a bit, he tugged gently at her hand.

"Come, let's warm you up, Kate." His voice was soft and soothing. She smiled slightly and crawled in beside him. Colton pulled the covers up over her as she slid in next to him. He choked back a groan. This was going to be even more difficult than he thought.

His arm was beneath her neck, and her head rested on his shoulder. As she turned on her side and snuggled up against him, he ran his hand up and down her arm. "Better?" His voice was low and husky.

"Mmm." She wiggled a little more, tickling his chin with her cap. Her hand slid slowly across his chest, stopping at his collarbone.

Colton shuddered. He glanced down at her out of the corner of his eye. Was she really asleep or just pretending? He lay very still. So did she. In a few minutes the sound of her slow, even breathing convinced him that she was asleep.

He tried to think about the war or the ailing king or the Prince Regent's latest farce, about anything except the woman sleeping in his arms. It was impossible. Her hand and face had grown warm—he was burning up.

Colton shifted away from her a little and shrugged the covers off his shoulder. Moving slowly and carefully, he eased the mobcaps off her head and tossed them on a bedside table. He pulled the green silk ribbon from the end of her braid and gently worked his fingers through the silken strands. When he turned his head, resting his chin against the top of her head, she gave a soft little sigh.

"I think I'd better wake you up," he murmured. He smiled against her hair and breathed deeply of her special scent. "If I do it right, maybe you'll decide to stay."

He eased his arm out from beneath her, bending it so he could rest on his forearm when he raised up. Colton gazed down at her in the soft glowing light of the fire. She was beautiful! Why wasn't she some man's wife or even a mistress?

An odd thought struck him. The few times she had spoken tonight, her brogue had been light. In fact, there had been hardly a trace of Scottish dialect. He frowned, remembering the first day he met her. When they were discussing the dancing teacher, her brogue had softened also. And there was that little lie about Lady Douglas's nonexistent daughters.

He looked down at her peaceful face. She was not a simple maid. She was far too lovely, too direct with her words and her gaze, too refined when she let her disguise slip. Why was she hiding? What had forced her into working as a servant?

Colton might have considered these things longer, except she chose that particular moment to turn over on her back, murmuring something softly about "my braw man." He wondered if she dreamed of him. He brushed a wispy curl from her cheek, then lowered his head to kiss her gently.

Her response was sweet, innocent, and lingering. He trailed tiny kisses up her jaw, then back down again to her lips. Colton kept a tight rein on his desire; still, he could not refrain from increasing the pressure of his lips against hers. Her eager, passionate response was almost his undoing.

He slowly broke off the kiss, nibbling tenderly at the corner of her lip. She gave a tiny whimper, and the duke smiled. She learned quickly. He sensed she was beginning to wake up and shifted slightly away from her.

A tiny smile danced across her face. With a little chuckle she turned on her side, away from him and facing the fire. He leaned over her just far enough to see another soft smile curve her lips as she whispered, "What a wicked, wonderful dream."

He leaned over a little farther, being careful not to touch her. "It was wonderful and perhaps wicked, but sweet, sweet Kate, it wasn't a dream."

Chapter 3

"Your Grace! What are you doing in my bed?" Kate stared up at him, her eyes wide.

"I'm not in your bed," he said softly. "You're in mine." He moved back so he did not loom over her.

Kate shot upright, looking around the room in alarm. *Of course he isna in your bed, you dolt,* she thought. *Your bed is barely big enough for you, let alone for him, too.*

"But how?" she asked weakly, finally glancing back at him.

He was half-reclined, leaning on his forearm. He shifted his weight slightly, unconsciously drawing her gaze to his naked chest with the movement.

"Mercy of heav'n!" Kate scrambled from the bed, running for the door.

"Do not leave this room." The authority in his voice stopped her cold. That tone would stop Napoleon, she thought in irritation. Kate took a quick peek back over her shoulder. He started to rise, exposing one long, muscular leg as he stretched it from the bed to the floor. His fingers were poised to flick back the blankets as he pushed up off the bed. Kate quickly looked away.

"S-stay where you are," she cried softly. Her face flamed.

"No. Keep your head turned if you don't want to be embarrassed."

Kate kept her eyes glued to a painting in front of her. After a moment she realized it showed a fox cornered by a hound. Appropriate, she thought. The sound of rustling cloth eased her apprehension only slightly. Her imagination taunted her by picturing him as he slipped into the robe.

"As to how you got here . . . ." The duke paused when she shivered. "For pity's sake, Kate, go stand by the fire." When she obeyed, he continued. "Did you know you walk in your sleep?" He moved across the thick rug, stopping closely behind her.

"I havena in a long time. I used to, most often when I was upset."

He put his hands on her shoulders, kneading gently. Lowering his lips to her temple, he brushed a tender kiss across it before resting his cheek against her hair. Colton smiled when he felt another shiver race through her.

"Do I upset you, Kitten?"

"Yes." She wondered vaguely what she had done to earn the nickname but decided she didn't really want to know. She didn't want to know how her hair had come loose from the braid, either.

"Because I want you?" He touched his lips again to her temple and then to her cheekbone.

She knew she should protest. She should pull away, but it felt so wonderful, it seemed she couldn't move. He nudged the hair back from her face with his cheek, kissing her below the ear. Kate gasped. She had never imagined the sensitivity of that particular spot or how his touch there could drive the strength from her legs. She felt his hot breath on her ear.

"Or is it because you want me?" he whispered.

"Of all the conceited, arrogant . . . ." Kate's quick flare of temper settled into a slow simmer. He knew exactly what he was doing to her. "You ill use me, Your Grace."

"Nay, Kate." As he turned her around to face him, he took a half step backward and slid his hands down to her upper arms. "Your virtue is intact." His gaze skimmed the still fastened buttons of her nightdress. "I only took a few kisses."

"Aye, took," she said hotly. "I had no say in the matter."

A smile touched his lips. "You didn't seem to mind."

She glared at him, tipping her head to one side and resting

her fists on her hips. "What more would you have taken, Your Grace, if I had not awakened?"

"Nothing." For an instant he was angry with her for even asking such a thing, but he reminded himself she did not know him. "What I want from you must be freely given." He brushed her hair back from her face, allowing himself a moment to rub the silken strands between his fingers before lowering his hand to his side. "It must be shared to be of any value." He smiled ruefully. "I was only trying to wake you. Although I must admit that I was hoping to make you want to stay."

Kate stared up at him. How could she remain angry with him when he looked down at her so tenderly with those beautiful cinnamon eyes? She had come into his room in the middle of the night. She hated to think what he considered her to be. Kate turned her head away, embarrassed.

"Did I simply walk in and crawl into your bed?" Even to her own ears her voice sounded tired and dejected.

"No, I had to coax you." She frowned up at him. He removed his hand from her arm and shrugged. "You were freezing, Kate. I had to get you warm and wake you up slowly. Everyone knows you can't awaken a sleepwalker suddenly."

She made a disparaging sound in her throat and glanced away. "A nice gentle shake usually works well."

"But 'tis not nearly so enjoyable." He grinned at her scowl, then relented, deciding to put her mind at ease. "You thought it was morning and you were doing your chores. You came in to make the bed."

"Were you in it?"

"Yes, but it didn't matter. You simply covered me up." He laughed softly.

"I dinna!" She ventured a peek up at him, knowing she would find a warm, tender smile. She was not disappointed. She smiled in return.

"Yes you did. You really should shake out that bedspread. It's a bit dusty."

"Oh, my. I do beg your pardon, Your Grace."

"You have it. And I suppose I should apologize for taking advantage of the situation."

Kate nodded her acceptance of his apology, using the

movement as an excuse to break eye contact. His warm regard was playing havoc with her heartbeat again. They both knew she should leave, but neither one really wanted to end the encounter.

"Why are you wearing two gowns?"

Kate's face flamed once again. It had not occurred to her that she was still in her nightclothes.

"Don't be embarrassed. You're decently covered. I wasn't even given the pleasure of seeing your silhouette against the fire." He glanced over at the mobcaps lying on the table. "Is your room so cold that you must bundle up in two of everything?"

"Yes, Your Grace." Kate squirmed uncomfortably. She felt as if she were telling tales on her grandfather.

"Then you should ask for more coal."

"We are given no heat for our rooms, Your Grace," she answered in a small voice.

"What?" His voice boomed.

"Shh." Without thinking, Kate put her fingers to his lips. He kissed them. She jerked her hand away, as if she'd touched a live ember. "Please keep your voice down, Your Grace, or you'll wake the whole house," she said primly.

The duke chuckled but his smile faded quickly. "I do not understand why you are not given any coal. Our servants never lacked for heat. I cannot imagine the earl doing such a thing."

"Nor can I." Colton's mention of servants reminded Kate of who she was pretending to be. She had completely forgotten about speaking in dialect. "With yer permission, Yer Grace, I be leavin' now." She had intended to increase the brogue only slightly, but in her nervousness that he would notice, it came out thicker than ever.

He glanced at her sharply, his eyes narrowing. He started to tell her there was no need to pretend with him, but the fear in her eyes stopped him. Colton decided she would tell him the truth after he gained her trust. He only hoped she was not wanted for a crime.

She held her breath, waiting for him to confront her. Instead he took a small stick from a stack of kindling and held it against the hot coals. When the wood caught fire, he walked across the room and lit a small candle. Picking up the candle holder, he returned to her side, tossing the stick in the fire.

"Pull one of the blankets off the bed and wrap it around you. I'll see you to your room."

"There's no need to go with me, Yer Grace. I can find my way without a candle." Seeing his stony countenance, she added lamely, "I found my way down here in my sleep."

A smile flickered across his face before he said soberly, "Get the blanket, Kate. I want to see for myself just how cold your room is."

With a huff of irritation Kate jerked the top blanket from the bed and wrapped it around her shoulders. She grabbed the mobcaps from the table and yanked them down over her hair. Her quick movements jostled the blanket from her shoulders, and it fell to the floor. With a low growl of frustration Kate snatched it up off the rug and threw it around her shoulders again. She stomped across the room in her stocking feet, halting beside the duke.

A grin twitched at the corners of his mouth, but he fought valiantly to keep it under control.

"Dunna you say a word," she said crossly. "I'll no' have the whole household learn of my foolishness."

He laughed in spite of his efforts but quickly smothered it when she glared at him. Definitely not a servant, he thought, still grinning. He took her arm and silently escorted her upstairs to her room.

Once inside the room his countenance became as cold as the air itself. The layer of ice on the inside of the window was not uncommon during this cold spell, but when he spotted the solid chunk of ice in the water pitcher, he grimaced and muttered something unintelligible.

"This is despicable. You cannot stay here," he whispered. "Come back downstairs."

"No!" She noticed he was shaking from the cold. "Please go back downstairs, Your Grace. I'll use this extra blanket and will be fine. It's almost time to rise for the day, anyway. Now please go before someone sees you."

He opened the door and peeked out. No one in sight, he stepped through the doorway. To Kate's surprise he turned back to her, cradled her jaw in his hand, and whispered,

"You'll have heat before the day is out, Kitten, even if I have to buy the coal myself."

As he walked away, Kate watched him for a moment before she stepped back into the room and shut the door silently.

In the darkened corridor neither of them noticed as Nell quietly closed the door of her room, located across the hall.

At breakfast the next morning the duke confronted his mother and Lord Blagden about the servants' comfort. "It has come to my attention that your servants on the upper floor have no heat." Cool and confident, he relaxed against the back of his chair.

"But of course they have heat, dear." Lady Millicent gave her husband a questioning look. "Don't they, Thomas?"

"Well, I certainly thought they did." The earl frowned, puzzled over the situation. "No one has ever mentioned the lack of heat." He turned to the butler. "Bence, what about it?"

The elderly butler blushed and actually stumbled over his words. "W-well, no, my lord, er, that is, the maids and footmen have never been given any coal. Lady Elizabeth, God rest her soul, said they didn't need any. She said they didn't feel the cold as much as their betters and that enough heat filtered up from below. I—I thought it was on your orders, my lord."

Colton sat his coffee cup down with a clatter. "I've never heard such rubbish."

"Well, dear, now I know it sounds a bit eccentric, but I've heard some prominent people say the same thing." Lady Millicent watched her husband carefully. She was appalled by what the butler had revealed, but she would not cross her husband in front of anyone.

"It is so cold, the water in the pitcher is frozen solid. In my opinion such treatment is inexcusable."

The earl stared at his cup. He had forgotten about Elizabeth's peculiar views regarding servants and the lower classes. Those poor people had practically frozen each winter because of an order Elizabeth had given so long ago. It must have been bad enough in past winters, but intolerable this year. The past few weeks had been the harshest in twenty years. He slammed his fist on the table, startling the others.

"Yes, Colton, it is inexcusable. I was unaware that such an order was ever given; still, I should have learned of it long ago. Millie, I suspect I was wrong when I told you my household ran along smoothly. Would you look into it? Talk to the servants and make certain they are not being mistreated in any other way. You have my permission to change, discontinue, or add any rules as you see fit." He looked at his wife, his expression thoughtful.

"That includes any rules Elizabeth laid down. You are mistress here now. This home will be run as you want it to be. I regret I did not see the need sooner." Turning to the butler, he said briskly, "Everyone is to have sufficient coal for their rooms. While it is cold, I want fires burning constantly. They may be low during the day when the room is not in use, but I want everyone to be comfortable. See to it immediately. Take Harlan with you."

"Yes, my lord." The short, balding servant rushed from the room, followed by the footman.

After the servants' departure Thomas turned his penetrating gaze on the duke. "Now, son, tell me how you know the water is frozen in the pitchers. I did not realize you were so well acquainted with my staff."

Colton controlled the urge to squirm in his chair. The earl was not one to mince words. The duke knew that if he did not take the initiative, the old man would soon ask which of his maids had been playing the whore.

"Did you know your maid, Kate, walks in her sleep?"

"Yes, I believe Millie mentioned something about it last week, didn't you, love?"

"Yes. Last week Priscilla found her sweeping the music room in the middle of the night. Thank goodness she only had the broom instead of using sand, too. She had already cleaned it once that day." His mother frowned at him. "In fact, Colton, it was the day you came to call. I believe you met her that day, did you not?"

"Yes." Colton smiled, revealing his dimple. He had disturbed her even then. For a moment he was lost in the memories of that afternoon. He blinked and brought his thoughts back to the present. "Last night Kate came to my room."

"Oh, dear!" Lady Millicent began to toy with her napkin.

"Don't fret, Mother. Her intentions were honorable. She was walking in her sleep and evidently thought it was morning. She came in and started making the bed." He grinned again and his dimple was even more prominent. Colton slipped his hand in his jacket pocket and absently toyed with a strand of green silk ribbon.

His mother wiggled in her chair, now fidgeting with the tablecloth. He's smiling again, she thought. No, he's actually grinning. Oh, dear! She began to worry in earnest.

"She practically smothered me."

The earl chuckled, but his expression sobered as he watched his stepson's face. Colton's eyes sparkled with merriment and, unknown to him, with something more.

"I finally convinced her to quit trying to tuck me under the covers and was able to awaken her gently. Poor Kate, she was appalled to discover herself in my room, but even more so to realize that she was clad in her nightdress, or actually, nightdresses. She said her room was so cold that she wore two of everything, gowns, socks, even caps."

"So you decided to inspect it yourself?"

Colton caught the skeptical note in the earl's voice. "Yes, I did. However, you should know that she was reluctant to say anything against you, Thomas. If I had given her a choice, I'm sure she would have said nothing. She had come downstairs without a candle, so I took it upon myself to escort her back to her room." He smiled faintly, remembering her irritation. "She was not impressed with my gallantry."

Lady Millicent and her husband exchanged a speaking look. The countess smiled brightly. "Well, my dears, I must run. So many things to do, you know." The earl rose and pulled out her chair, giving her a peck on the cheek as she stood. Colton rose politely, too.

"Are you off to meetings again today, Colton?"

"Yes, Mother, I fear I'll be gone until dinner. I'll have Gregory check on my house today. If things are set to rights, we'll move back home tomorrow."

"Of course you may stay as long as you like." She lifted her cheek for his kiss, then left the room.

The duke remained standing and took one last sip of coffee.

"I'd like a word with you, son, before you go."

Colton met the earl's gaze, suspecting something of what the older man had to say.

Thomas cleared his throat. "I'll be blunt, my boy. It's my way." Colton nodded. "Did Kate warm your bed last night?"

No, it warmed her. "No, my lord, she did not." To his surprise he found himself opening up to his stepfather. He shrugged and colored slightly. "I'll admit my methods of waking her were a bit devious, but once she was awake, she wanted nothing to do with me." He smiled wryly. "I am not exactly known as a rake."

"Still, she's a maid and you're a duke." The earl watched him keenly. "She's a pretty little thing, although I've never seen her eyes. She's almost too conscious of her place, always keeps her head lowered when I'm around. I'd wager she looks *you* straight in the eye, though, doesn't she?" He nodded his head decisively. "You want her and you mean to have her."

"Only if she is willing." The duke's voice was deceptively soft. He was growing more uneasy by the moment. He'd expected Thomas to come right out and tell him to leave Kate alone. It was well known that the earl did not tolerate misconduct on the part of his maids or his guests. Now he was not sure what the man intended to do.

"She makes you burn, boy. You'll find a way to convince her." The duke's back stiffened, but Thomas ignored him. "Just don't do anything under my roof. Take her someplace else for a day or two. If she pleases you, set her up in a nice little house somewhere. If she doesn't please you, tell her she can come back here with no questions asked. As long as she does her work well and keeps away from other men, she'll have a position. I'll allow her to go once with you but with no one else."

Amazed, Colton could only stare at the earl. "But why? I thought you were adamant about the moral character of your servants. Why would you do this for me? Or for her?"

Thomas turned away and walked over to the window. He lifted the drapery aside with one hand and silently watched the snow fall for several minutes before he spoke. He kept his back to Colton, and the duke sensed that the older man was not watching the snow at all but reliving memories from long ago.

"You know as well as I that for a man to have a mistress is perfectly acceptable in our society. It is accepted, even expected in some cases. But let me give you a bit of free advice, son. Take your mistress before you're married. Once you're leg-shackled, it can only bring you pain. It will hurt your wife deeply, and because you're an honorable man, the guilt will drive you beyond all limits to make amends."

The drape slipped from the earl's fingers, but he did not notice. Leonore's face loomed in his mind's eye, eternally young and beautiful. He'd been married for almost twenty-three years when he'd met her. Her father was a hatter, and she helped out in his shop on Tuesdays and Thursdays. A brief smile flickered across his face. After all these years, he still remembered which days she worked.

He had loved his wife but had grown discontent about how seldom Elizabeth allowed him in her bed. From the first time he had laid eyes on Leonore she had made him burn. He knew it was not love that had drawn him to her, although he wanted to think so. He had not been her first lover, nor was he the last, but for the month they were together, she had made him feel like he was the most passionate, most wonderful man in the world.

He turned around to look at Colton. "I wasn't always an old man. I understand what you're going through, and I know you'll treat the girl fairly."

"And what of Kate?" Colton asked softly, trying to understand the earl's inexplicable behavior.

The earl pondered the question a moment, realizing that oddly, intangibly, Kate reminded him of Elizabeth. He shook his head, thinking how, in some perverse sort of way, he was still trying to make amends. "She reminds me of someone," he said quietly.

The duke nodded and left the room, understanding that Thomas wanted to be alone with his thoughts. Shortly thereafter he was en route to Cumberland House to visit the War Office, where he stayed in council meetings for the day.

All day Kate expected to be summoned either by the earl or by the countess for a reprimand. No call ever came. Once, when she met the earl in the hallway, he stopped and looked at her with a strange sadness but never said a word. She wanted desperately to throw her arms around his neck and tell him who she was, to convince him of her innocence. But she couldn't. Now more than ever, she could say nothing.

She slept fitfully that night, afraid she would sleepwalk again. Her room was warm and comfortable, as were the other servants' quarters. Somehow the others heard about her sleepwalking, and Bence told them about the duke bringing the lack of coal to the earl's attention. She expected the other servants to tease her about the duke, but no one did. Instead they were all only grateful for the heat, regardless of how it had come about.

She dragged about her duties the following day, weary from lack of sleep and from trying to avoid the duke. She finally breathed a sigh of relief when Gregory left in the afternoon, taking all the duke's things with him.

He was still in her thoughts the next week as she trudged along the ice-covered streets in what she hoped was the correct route to the River Thames. According to rumor, it was frozen solid. Since it was her day off, Kate had borrowed a pair of skates from Priscilla and gone off in search of the river. She knew a lady would never venture out on the streets of London without a chaperon but assumed that in her disguise as a maid no one would pay any attention to her.

"The way my luck's been going, I'm walking in the wrong direction," she muttered, and pulled her scarf tighter around her face, shifting the skates to her other hand. For the first time in a week she could see more blue sky than clouds. Ice and snow sparkled from tree branches; icicles several feet long hung from the eaves of the houses.

She paid little attention to the sights and sounds around the houses of Mayfair, for she had come on this walk as much to be alone and to think as to get some fresh air. Kate was confused, homesick, and falling in love.

She was no expert on love but she was no fool, either. She knew her feelings for the duke went far beyond the realm of infatuation. One look could send her blood racing; one touch made her forget everything else. She was sliding into love faster than a sled on a slippery hill.

He invaded her thoughts when she was awake and even

more when she was asleep. He interrupted every time she tried to figure out some way of telling her grandfather who she was. What would the duke think of her when he discovered she was supposed to be a lady instead of a maid?

"He'd laugh in my face," she muttered thickly through her wool scarf. She kicked a clump of snow and reluctantly accepted the conclusion she had reached earlier in the day. "I'll go home," she said to herself. "As soon as the mail coaches are running again, I'll go home." *'Tis the coward's way out,* she thought, *but I canna see any other way. I must get away before he has the power to hurt me too deeply.*

Kate glanced around her. She had reached the male domain of St. James Street. No lady ever set foot on this street in the afternoon, and only in the morning accompanied by a maid or a footman. *Well, since it is mid-morning,* she thought, *and a maid probably wouldna have a footman walking with her, I suppose it willna hurt.*

Her other option was to go farther down and take Haymarket, but since it was a well-known resort for prostitutes, it seemed more hazardous than St. James. A quick look up and down the street reassured her. Apparently few gentlemen had ventured out yet.

She strolled past Berry Brothers wine merchants and ducked her head as a gentleman left Lock's, the hatters. To her relief the man was busy admiring his new hat in the reflection of the store window and did not notice her. She hurried past the coffee and chocolate houses, telling herself that she could not be tempted by the wonderful smells drifting out into the street.

Pausing in front of a jewelry store, Kate had a few minutes to admire the display before the proprietor waved her away. She stopped again near Boodle's, the club to which her grandfather belonged. He was not a gambling man, but the club had a reputation for good food. Its members were mostly country gentlemen, a position in life to which the earl proudly professed.

A few more gentlemen appeared on the street. Kate picked up her pace, hurrying past wine shops, picture dealers, and a chemist shop. She slowed down a bit as she approached White's, sneaking a peek up at the club's famous bow window to see, if by chance, Beau Brummell or some of his cronies happened to be sitting there. The window was empty.

At the corner of King Street and St. James, Kate stopped for a moment and studied the facade of Almack's Assembly Rooms. She did not particularly yearn for a voucher from society's matrons, which would enable her to be accepted into Almack's hallowed halls. *Still, just once, I'd like to go there on the duke's arm,* she thought. *There I go again. Why canna I keep that man out of my mind?*

When the street came to an end, intersecting with Pall Mall, she crossed over to the south side. A few minutes later she was walking in front of Cumberland House, home of the War Office, and where, she had learned, the duke spent a great deal of time. She slowed down, looking up at the windows of the building in the hopes of getting a glimpse of him.

Suddenly it occurred to her that if he did see her, he would probably order her to go home. She lowered her head, not looking up until she was farther down Pall Mall, beside Carlton House.

Kate took her time strolling beside Carlton House, the Prince Regent's London palace. She could see little other than the outside, but with its great Ionic colonnade, even the outside was majestic.

Just past the palace she halted, trying to get her bearings. Up ahead, the quality of the street drastically changed and was inhabited by bad, abandoned characters.

Suddenly a burly young man stepped in front of her, blocking her path. "Look wot we got here, lads. Where ya goin', lovey?"

"Let me pass."

"Did ye hear that, lads? We got us a little Scottish chickie." Kate moved to the side, trying to step around him, but another man barred her way. The first man flicked the laces on her skates.

"Ye can't use those on the river, lovey. Ain't smooth enough. Now, we got us a nice little frozen pond just a few alleys down. Why don't ye come along and we'll show ye how to uh . . . skate." He smirked, looking around suggestively at his two companions. They guffawed as he grabbed her arm.

Kate tried to twist away, but he pulled the scarf down from

her face as one of the other men jerked off her hat. Dark red hair tumbled around her shoulders and down to the middle of her back. The sunlight glinted off the soft curls, framing her face in a fiery halo.

"'Adzooks! Ain't ye a beauty," he breathed. For a moment the three men simply stared at her.

A cold shaft of fear rushed down her spine. All of the men were short and stocky, but any one of them could easily overpower her. Even if she could break free, the ground was too icy. She would not be able to run. She glanced frantically around for help, but no one was paying them any mind.

"Come here, lovey."

"No!" Kate struck at him with her reticule as he tightened his grip on her other arm. "Let go of me." She tried to shift the skates to her other hand to use as a better weapon, but he ripped them from her grip and threw them on the ground.

"Let me be!" She twisted and hit and screamed at him in Gaelic, until he grabbed a fistful of hair and brought his foul mouth down over hers. Kate gagged as tears of pain and humiliation stung her eyes.

"Release her." The cold, hard voice was accompanied by the sharp rap of a cane across the back of the hooligan's neck.

"Wot the—" The man released her, giving her a little shove, then whirled, catching the cane square in the nose. He yelled and covered his broken nose with his hands as blood began to flow. He lost all interest in Kate.

"If any of you so much as touches her again . . ."

Kate shook her head to clear it, thinking she was having some peculiar daydream. But when she raised her face, her gaze fell upon the one man she most longed to see. "Your Grace!"

The hooligans fell back as if some giant hand had pushed them aside. The duke lifted one arm, and Kate scurried to his side, resting her cheek and hand against his chest as his arm closed about her.

"Have you been harmed?" he asked gruffly, not taking his eyes off the other men.

She shook her head, not trusting herself to speak. Such fear, followed so quickly by intense relief, made a shambles of her emotions. She clung to him, wondering how in the world she would ever be able to leave him.

"We didn't mean no harm, Guv. We was just havin' a bit o' sport," said the thug who had pulled off Kate's hat. The men backed away another foot or two, intimidated by the man who stood a head taller than any of them.

"At the expense of an innocent young woman." The duke's harsh voice made them wince and Kate jump. "I ought to beat you to a pulp."

"Well, we didn't know she was cozy with no duke," the hooligan said sullenly.

Swiftly Colton raised his cane. The muscles in his jaw tightened as he clenched his teeth in an effort to contain his anger. It was a moment before he spoke, his voice quiet, controlled, deadly. "Get out of my sight or you'll rue the day you were born."

The men scrambled away, slipping and falling on the ice, only to struggle to their feet again after glimpsing the duke's dark look.

Colton folded his arms around her, drawing her snugly against him. He buried his face in her hair, lost in a garden of jasmine. He smiled, rubbing his cheek gently across her silken strands. She'd stirred up such a commotion, he'd heard her from the other end of Carlton House. He'd died a thousand deaths when he'd spotted that flowing mane of hair, afraid he couldn't get to her before they hurt her.

The duke never doubted his ability to protect her; he'd fight twenty men to protect his Kate. *His Kate*. His arms tightened, squeezing until he heard her muffled protest. Realizing he was standing in a very public place with a woman in his arms, Colton slowly released her. When she looked up at him, he groaned softly.

"Kate, if you keep looking at me like I'm Sir Lancelot, I'm going to kiss you right here in front of everyone."

She smiled, even as her face turned red. She stooped to pick up her hat, scarf, and skates. "You play the part so well." Her expression grew sober. "Thank you, Your Grace. I fear I really walked into a hornet's nest this time."

He took the skates from her hand, raising one eyebrow

dubiously. With the other hand at her elbow he carefully escorted her over the icy walk to his sleigh.

She eyed the vehicle and the sturdy, surefooted horse with appreciation. Another driver gingerly made his way down the street, both carriage and horses sliding back and forth on the ice.

"I should have known you'd be better prepared than anyone else." She grinned when he lifted her into the sleigh.

He pulled a large beaver lap rug from behind the seat and spread it over her. When he leaned over to smooth it around her, his face was inches from hers.

Kate held her breath. He was so close, she could smell the spicy scent of his Hungary Water. His cheek looked firm and smooth, and she felt an almost overpowering urge to touch her lips there. He turned, looking deeply into her eyes. She could have sworn her heartbeat stopped before it skipped to double time.

"Are you warm enough, my pretty Kate?" His voice was low and intimate.

"Yes." The word came out in a whisper. Much too warm, she thought, as a wave of heat stormed over her.

"How do you always smell so nice?" he murmured, reaching out to smooth her hair. "You have such beautiful hair. I've never seen the like. I realized you were the woman in trouble when I saw the sunlight glinting in your hair."

"But you would have intervened even if it hadna been me," she said quietly.

His eyes narrowed as he considered her statement. "Yes, I suppose I would have, but I wouldn't have been nearly as frightened." He met her gaze.

"You, afraid? I dunna believe it."

"I wasn't frightened for myself. I knew I could handle them." He brushed her cheek with the side of his gloved finger. "My fear was for you, that they might hurt you before I could get to you."

Kate's eyes grew misty as remorse filled her heart. "Forgive me, Your Grace. It was foolish of me to come out alone. I thought no one would pay attention to me."

"Kate, it is dangerous for any woman to go about the streets alone, whether she is a lady of quality or a scullery maid. With your beauty you are only inviting trouble."

"Yes, Your Grace. I willna do it again." Kate swallowed hard, fighting the tears, which threatened to overflow. She felt foolish and frightened as the reality of what might have happened sank in.

"Hush, now. Don't cry. Your tears will freeze and you'll have icicles on your cheeks. I'll have to chip them off." Colton knew if he did not put a little more distance between them, he would start to kiss her tears away. She smiled weakly as he straightened.

The duke drew in his breath sharply. She had been pretty in her plain, dark gray pelisse, but in the brown fur she was vibrant. "The sable," he murmured.

"What, Your Grace?" she asked quietly. Her expression was slightly puzzled.

"You should be dressed in furs, Kate. Only such richness begins to do your beauty justice."

"What flummery!" Kate laughed, swiping her cheeks with her gloved hand. Colton could tell she was greatly pleased by his compliment. As he walked around to the other side, she shook the snow off her hat and scarf and put them on, tucking her hair up as best she could.

He climbed up and picked up the reins, carefully guiding the horse back into the street. "I assume you were planning on skating somewhere."

"Yes. Everyone is talking about the Thames being frozen. I thought it would be a good place."

The duke shook his head. "No, it's too rough. It doesn't freeze smoothly like a lake but in deep ridges."

"Harlan said there was some kind of fair out on the ice."

"Aye, but it is definitely not a place a woman should go alone." He almost smiled at the disappointment on her face. "Here, I'll show you, but you must stay in the sleigh."

He turned the horse and sleigh, traveling a short distance down Cockspur Street until it intersected with the Strand. The rich smells coming from the coffeehouses on the Strand made Kate's stomach growl as they passed by.

"But Harlan said there were food stalls and games and jugglers—"

"Juggling snowballs, no doubt. There are also prostitutes and pickpockets, thieves and gamesters. I trust you don't associate with that type of low life, do you?"

"Well, no, but—"

"But you're hungry."

"Starved. I should have brought something to eat, but I dinna realize it was so far, and I'd brought a bit of money to buy something anyway."

"Very well, I'll see if I can find someone to bring you something to eat, but we'll stay put. I don't want to have to fight off another bunch of thugs. By the way, did I tell you I have a fair understanding of Gaelic?" The duke glanced over at Kate and grinned at her gasp. "You were telling those men a thing or two, weren't you, my dear?"

Kate sputtered, trying to think of something to say in her defense. After a moment she closed her mouth. A smile twitched her lip. She had called the hooligans a few choice names in Gaelic, nothing profane but certainly not the kind of language used in polite society. She smiled slightly, remembering that at the moment she was not considered a member of polite society.

The duke watched her thoughts march across her expressive face and shook his head, his eyes twinkling. "Tsk, tsk. Such language for a lady."

At that moment the river came into view, and Kate was saved from making a response. When they drew near the Blackfriars Bridge, Colton pulled over to the side of the street.

Kate stared at the sight before her. Sure enough, the water was frozen solid, in mounds and ridges. In some places old wooden pilings stuck up through the ice. Skating was impossible.

A row of tents, set up by street vendors, ran down the center of the river with hawkers selling everything from food and drink to wagers on when the ice would thaw. From a distance all the merchants' cries melded with shouts of laughter, making an incoherent noise.

Kate was surprised at the number of people milling around. There were several well-dressed men and women, apparently members of the ton, strolling around between the booths, but the majority of the participants were from the lower classes.

There was a good number of young women near her age, but she had to admit that most of them either ambled around in groups or were escorted by men. She did notice some women walking about alone and started to point them out to the duke; however, she hesitated when two sailors stopped to talk to one of them.

She watched in amazement as the woman laughed and bumped the side of her hip against one of the sailors. Then, before Kate could even imagine what she intended, the prostitute unbuttoned her pelisse. She dipped one shoulder, sliding the top of her gown down to present a vulgar display of her wares. Kate gasped and looked away, a hot blush racing over her face.

"Welcome to the Frost Faire, Kitten."

Kate looked down at her lap, hoping the disgust she heard in his voice was caused by the scene they had witnessed and not her.

The duke drove the team a little closer to the river and stopped so Kate could watch a man juggling three flaming torches. He glanced at her to see if she had recovered from her embarrassment and smiled. She was completely engrossed in the juggler. "That's one way to stay warm on a cold day."

She nodded, never taking her eyes off the performer. "I wonder what he juggles in the summer."

"Probably something safe, like knives." The duke grinned as she smiled at him. "Are you still hungry?"

"Yes." She gazed across the ice longingly. It seemed like forever since she had been to a fair. It looked like so much fun. She glanced back up at the duke and found him watching her.

"No. You may not go."

"Please, Your Grace. There's so many things to see. I've never been to a fair in the winter, much less one held out on the ice."

"Neither have I," he admitted reluctantly.

She smiled prettily and, without thinking, laid her hand on his arm. "Do let us go. I'll stay right with you, I promise. And I'll even buy my own food. Please? I may never have the chance again."

He gazed down at her hopeful, upturned face, thinking no man could resist those lovely eyes and that smile. His gaze flickered to her hand, resting in supplication and trust on his arm. He didn't want to take her home and he didn't want to leave her, either.

Colton clenched his jaw and looked away. Suddenly he was very tired, tired of the war, of his responsibilities, of being alone. He'd seen so much pain and sorrow these last years. He rotated his tense shoulders. He needed to relax, to smile, to laugh. He'd smiled and laughed more since he met Kate than he had in the past two years.

"It has been five and twenty years since the last Frost Faire." For one of the rare times in his life he decided to act on impulse. "Very well, I'll take you." He laughed as she squealed and squeezed his arm in delight.

"I want you to be able to relax and have a good time. Since you seem to forget your heavy brogue half the time, why not dispense with it entirely?" He smiled gently at the fear in her eyes. "Be yourself with me, Kate."

She drew back her hand and dropped her gaze, feeling like the veriest fool. Earlier he'd so much as called her a lady, and obviously he'd realized her dialect was a sham. She'd let her disguise slip too many times when he was around. *Oh,* she thought furiously, *why does he do this to me? I never forget my role when I'm with anyone else.*

"Kate?" She jumped and looked up at him. He reached out, cradling her jaw in his hand. The leather was soft and warm against her skin. "I don't know who you are, only what you are not. I hope someday soon you'll trust me enough to confide in me."

"And if I can no'?"

He sensed her need to turn away and dropped his hand. She looked down at her lap, tying knots in the strings of her reticule.

"Are you in trouble? Have you committed some crime? How can I help you, protect you?"

"I've committed no crime." She wanted to pour out her heart but she could not. Instead she looked out across the river, her face filled with sadness. *But what I've done is very, very wrong. I've lied to Grandfather and to your mother. I spied on them.* She looked up at him, unaware that the pain she felt was reflected in her eyes and face. *I lied to you and I can never make it right. I have to go away and save us both from more pain.*

He searched her eyes, wanting to touch her soul. She was going to leave him; he could sense it in her pain. *No, I will not let you go.*

"Do you like the country, Kate?"

She watched him cautiously. "Yes."

"I have a cottage a little way out of London. It's not far; we could be there in about an hour. It's not large or fancy, but the caretakers are Scottish." He smiled. "You'll like Mrs. MacCrea; she's everybody's grandmother. There's a nice pond. We used to skate on it years ago. I'm sure it's frozen thick enough to use. After the fair, will you go out to Twin Rivers with me today?"

Everything in her upbringing shouted against it, but her heart begged her to go. She trusted him. He would never take more than she was willing to give. It was herself she was unsure of. Whenever he touched her, all conscious thought seemed to fly from her mind.

She looked back down at her lap. There was no room for any more knots on the string. *Surely,* she thought, *I can spend one day with him without doing anything immoral. Just this one day. It's all we will have.*

"Please, Kate?"

She looked back up at him. He was no longer smiling. Lines of weariness fanned out from his eyes. In that brief moment, he appeared almost haggard.

"Spend the day with me, Kitten. I need your laughter, your sweetness. I need to be with you."

Her heart rose to her throat as she made up her mind. "I'll go," she whispered.

He leaned over and kissed her. His touch was brief and tender, the simple brushing of his lips across hers, but it rocked her very soul. When he raised his head, a soft smile settled on his face, teasing her with the hint of his dimple.

Dazed, Kate took a slow, deep breath, wondering exactly what kind of agreement she had just made.

Chapter 4

Colton jumped down carefully from the sleigh, immensely pleased with himself. From the dazed look on Kate's face he knew he was not totally inept in the romance department. He pulled a striped blanket from the back of the sleigh and threw it across the horse's back. A bystander approached quickly, ready to watch over the duke's equipage for a bit of coin.

"Mind ye rig for ye, m'lord?" The young man waited courteously for the duke's reply.

Colton gave him a quick appraisal, particularly noting his honest, direct gaze. "Yes, thank you." He flipped a silver crown through the air to the lad, who aptly caught it. "There'll be more if I return and find everything in order."

"It will be, m'lord. I'll lead 'im about a bit to keep 'im warm."

"Very good." Colton walked around to the other side of the sleigh as the lad took hold of the horse's reins. The duke raised his hands, resting them gently on Kate's waist. "Shall we go to the fair?"

"Yes, Your Grace." Out of the corner of her eye Kate saw the young man straighten and his chest swell with pride. She doubted if he had ever worked for a duke before. He'd be even prouder if he knew this particular nobleman, she thought. There were few of his caliber to be found. She rested her hands lightly on Colton's shoulders as he lifted her down to the snow-covered ground.

When her footing was secure, Colton stepped back, meeting her gaze. The soft, warm glow in her eyes caused his chest to constrict. He held his breath as she studied him, wishing with all his heart that he knew what was going through her mind.

Kate reached up and gently touched the lines of weariness beside his mouth. The coarse woolen glove felt as soft and as precious as silk against his skin.

"This day is for you, Your Grace," she said softly. "You willna think about the war or Napolean or whatever worries you have." She moved her fingertip to where his dimple remained hidden. "You will smile and laugh and think of nothing but the joy of the moment."

He grinned. "Yes, ma'am."

She laughed and poked the dimple gently. "There, that's much better."

He caught her hand, leading her carefully around the sleigh. He glanced at the lad and found him watching them curiously. For a moment he hesitated, knowing they would receive many such speculative looks on their outing.

"Your Grace, is something amiss?"

Colton looked down at her expectant face. Although her expression was one of concern, she could not quite hide her excitement. "No, nothing. Come, let us enjoy ourselves."

"Yer Grace . . ." The lad waited until the duke looked at him before he continued. "I saw Fast-fingered Willy workin' the fair a little earlier. 'E's about my 'eight and wearin' a brown-and-black-striped wool coat and a red 'at. 'E works with a couple of young'uns."

The duke nodded his thanks. "My money is secure, but I'll take extra care if a child runs into me."

The young man tipped his hat and bowed slightly. "Enjoy the fair, Yer Grace, Miss."

They made their way down a trail worn through the snow to the river. To Kate's surprise the ice did not come up to the riverbank. Instead a wide channel of icy water separated them from the fair.

"I thought rivers freeze from the bank outward. Why dinna this one?" She looked up at him with a small frown.

"It did, but the watermen need to make a living. With the river frozen they can't ferry people to the other side." He smiled slightly, motioning toward two approaching wherries. "They've always been an ingenious lot, so they cut a channel on each side of the river. The only way to get to the fair is for them to carry the people across."

Kate chuckled and shook her head at their cleverness.

"Oars, sculls, oars!" called one burly waterman, grinning lecherously at Kate.

"Be warned, my dear. These men are known for their ribald banter. At times it can be quite offensive."

She looked up in time to see his jaw tighten as he watched the waterman. The duke's look should have frozen the water beneath the boat. "I'll ignore them," she said quickly. After his actions earlier, she was afraid he might try to make the man apologize if he insulted her.

Colton relaxed slightly, a wry half smile warming his face. "Good. I would hate to have to defend your honor against one of them. They are as quick with their fists as with repartee."

"Oars, sculls, oars! I'll take ye from the shores. Yer bones me boat will bear to London's Great Frost Faire!" The second waterman gave a mighty push of his pole, shooting his shallow boat out ahead of the other one. He, too, grinned at Kate, but his look was only appreciative, not leering. He halted his wherry alongside them, wedging his long pole into the snow and mud by the bank to keep the craft steady.

"How much?"

"Threepence for ye, Guv, and two for the little lady. If I weren't so 'ard up, I'd let the pretty miss go for free." He gave her a cocky grin and a wink.

She glanced quickly up at the duke, worried about the waterman's daunting size and obvious strength. To her surprise there was an undisguised twinkle in His Grace's eye. He said nothing, but she could have sworn he handed the man a gold guinea instead of fivepence.

Colton stepped into the boat and turned back to Kate, taking her hand as she stepped into the wherry. He waited until she was seated, then eased down beside her, slipping his arm protectively about her waist.

When the mild rocking of the boat shifted her weight against him, he tightened his arm subtly, holding her there. Kate wished the waterman would lose his pole and let them drift down the river. Instead the man pushed the boat away from the river's edge with a sure hand.

"I'da given yer light-o'-love a free ride, Guv," called the other boatman as they passed by. His eyes undressed her as he uttered a vile oath. "I'd even pay to ride 'er."

Colton stiffened, his free hand coiling into a fist. He glanced down at Kate. Although her face flamed, she held her head high. He was struck by her poise and regal bearing.

"Shut yer yap, 'awkins," yelled their waterman. "Don't ye know a lady when ye see one?" He looked back at the duke and the beautiful woman beside him. She was quality, no matter how she was dressed. Any fool could see it. "I 'ear the war's goin' to end soon. What do ye think, Guv?"

"That's the rumor going round. It would appear Boney is running out of money and men."

"Aye. Should 'ave ended years ago. One impressment in the Navy was enough. I ain't lookin' forward to it again." He stopped the boat gently at the wide island of ice and snow in the middle of the river.

"You need not worry," murmured the duke as he stepped ashore. He turned back and lifted Kate from the boat, reluctantly dropping his hands once she was standing.

"Ye goin' to 'ave 'awkins fined by the Company for insulting the lady, or do ye want me to plant 'im a facer?"

"A broken jaw would do nicely." In spite of his irritation, Colton smiled at the waterman, whose name was John Pemberton. He had known the man for five years. Pemberton, too, kept his eyes and ears open for the duke and had gone along on several excursions when Colton needed someone of strength and intimidating size.

"I'll take care of 'im tonight, Yer Grace," he answered quietly.

Colton nodded curtly.

"Welcome to City Road, Miss. I 'ear the gingerbread is mighty good today." Pemberton tipped his hat to Kate and turned his attention to two young bucks ready to leave the fair.

The duke offered Kate his arm. When she had tucked her

hand securely around it, they started toward the row of makeshift stalls.

Curiosity got the better of her. "You knew him, dinna you?"

"I've ridden with him before. I often take the ferry instead of the bridge. I fear in years to come the watermen will be a thing of the past. Eventually more bridges will be built and the wherries will be obsolete."

Kate had the feeling the duke knew the waterman better than his casual answer implied. However, it was clear from his manner that he did not intend to elaborate, and she saw no need to pursue the matter.

As they drew near City Road, the din of street cries became discernible. "Hot pies! Hot!" "Twelve pence a peck, oysters!" "Beef! Beef! Ribs o' beef and beef fer yer ribs!"

"Oh, Your Grace, I've never seen anything like it!" Kate squeezed his arm as her radiant smile warmed his heart.

His gaze lingered on her face, memorizing her beauty, absorbing her happiness. "Neither have I," he said softly. Reluctantly he turned his attention back to the fair.

Kate sniffed the air mischievously. "Something smells wonderful."

"Beef. Over there." The duke pointed toward a crowd of people several spaces down. "Come, we'll buy some." They made their way through the crowd until they had a clear view of the spectacle. A whole ox was being roasted on the ice. Nearby were several pigs sizzling on individual spits.

"Mercy of heav'n!" For a moment Kate could only stare as the ox was slowly turned over the fire. Then her stomach rumbled and her hand automatically went to the front of her pelisse.

"Are you growling at me again?" Colton smiled down at her, his eyes sparkling.

"I'm afraid so," she said with a laugh. Her laughter stopped abruptly when she was jostled by the crowd, finding herself wedged against the duke. Somehow his arms went around her, protecting her from the rowdy, shifting throng yet pressing her body against the long length of his at the same time. As her fingers curled against his greatcoat, she regretted the cold and the necessity of wearing so many layers of clothing.

"We should buy a loaf before we get the meat." He made no

effort to push away from the crowd. He didn't move. Neither did she. He searched her eyes for a long moment before his gaze dropped to her lips.

The longing in his look made her legs grow weak. A sweet ache spiraled through her being, a yearning so intense that it made her tremble. He met her gaze.

"Are you cold, Kitten?"

"No."

Her voice was so soft, he did not actually hear the sound. He read the answer on her lips and in the soft, awakening desire in her eyes.

Kate felt a shudder run through him. Her eyes opened a fraction wider. "Are you?"

"No." His voice was low and husky. Colton took a deep breath and cleared his throat. "We'd better move or we'll freeze to the ice."

Kate looked down at the first button of his coat. When she nodded, her beaver hat brushed the tip of his chin, tickling it.

He chuckled and moved one arm, using his shoulder and upper arm to push their way from the crowd. He kept his other arm snugly around her shoulders. When they arrived at the bread stall, Kate reached to open her reticule.

"Don't be a widgeon." Colton stayed her movements with his hand. "You are my guest."

"But I said I would buy my own food."

"Kate . . ." His voice held a distant note of warning.

"Very well." She flashed him a warm smile, then glanced down ruefully at the many knots in the strings of her reticule. "The ice will probably melt before I can get into it, anyway."

Colton followed her gaze and grinned devilishly. Leaning over, he spoke softly into her ear. "Do I tie you in knots, Kitten?"

She moaned and rolled her eyes, then laughed despite her efforts not to.

The duke bought the loaves of bread and, leaving her under the watchful care of the baker and his wife, hurried back through the crowd for the meat. A few moments later he presented her with a loaf sliced down the middle and filled with a thick cut of roast beef.

Kate took a deep breath, savoring the fragrance of the

freshly baked bread, smoky meat, and pungent mustard for an instant before she took a big bite. "Mmm." She closed her eyes for a moment, relishing the hot food. When she opened them, the duke was smiling at her.

"Will this stave off starvation?"

"For a while." They enjoyed each other's laughter as they began walking. The crowd thinned as they moved away from the ox and pigs, for many of the people were gathered around the fires just to get warm. They strolled along the City Road, eating their luncheons.

"Coffee! It's so 'ot, it'll scald yer tongue. Coffee!" came the cry from one of the tents on their left.

"Gin, gin! Warm ye up and forget yer sin! Gin, gin!" cried a salesman on their right.

"Chocolate, 'ot chocolate, sweet! Buy some chocolate for yer sweetie, Guv?" This vendor did not even have a tent but had set up a small makeshift stove and tiny round table on which he prepared the chocolate. He held up a tin cup.

Colton looked at Kate, an imp dancing in his eyes. "Do you want some chocolate, sweetie?"

"No, thank you," she said with false politeness. "A drink of gin would be much better."

"What?" Colton's booming voice turned a few heads.

"Shh! I was only teasing. A cup of coffee, please."

He muttered something under his breath and shot her a sideways glance as he bought them each a cup of coffee. When he returned, he was still muttering, but his eyes were twinkling. He handed her a cup. "Careful. It's so 'ot, it'll scald yer tongue."

Kate laughed with joy. She could almost see him relaxing in front of her. His smile came easier and his laughter more often. She had never thought he would actually mimick a street seller's cry. She blew gently on the steaming liquid, then took a cautious sip, letting the hot drink rest inside her mouth for a second before swallowing. She felt its warmth all the way down to her stomach.

Colton popped the last bite of bread and meat into his mouth and curled both hands around his cup. After two more bites Kate did likewise. "Feels good, doesn't it?" His eyes smiled at her over the rim of the cup as he took another sip. She nodded murmuring about the coffee's good taste, but his thoughts had traveled beyond their food and drink.

The warmth of the coffee was only a tiny part of his feeling of well-being. In that moment, he was happy and content just to be with her. Somehow she brought out the carefree side of his nature, a part of his personality that had been stifled for so long that he had thought it lost. He had forgotten how good it felt simply to relax and indulge in a little frivolity.

"Lice, lice, penny a pair boot-lice!"

Kate stopped and gaped at the man walking by. He carried an open box on a harness slung about his shoulders. She could not quite make out what was inside the box.

"What did he say?"

"'Lice, lice, penny a pair boot-lice!'" The duke mimicked him perfectly.

Kate shook her head. "I know that's what he said, but what did he mean? Surely he isna selling lice."

"No, *buit* laces." His Scots accent was perfect.

"Oh, boot laces! Why dinna he just say that?"

"Because he's Cockney and they have a distinct form of speech. Many different people do, you understand, such as the Scots. Then, of course, there's you." He grabbed her arm when she stumbled.

"What about me?" She eyed him warily.

"Well, when you're not putting on that fake thick brogue, your speech is a combination of Scots and English." His eyes narrowed as her cheeks paled. "I suspect you've lived in Scotland, probably with Scottish parents, but you had an English governess."

He watched her face carefully as he spoke, but her expression changed so quickly that he was not sure if he had guessed the truth. One thing was clear; such talk frightened her. Still, he could not resist one final probe. "Or perhaps one parent is English and the other Scottish." Panic flickered across her eyes and then was gone, but Colton did not miss it.

"Oh, look!" she cried with just a little too much enthusiasm. "Punch and Judy!" She grabbed his arm and pulled him across the ice to watch the puppet show.

Not wanting to spoil her day, Colton dropped his interrogation. It had been years since he had watched a Punch and Judy show. These particular performers were adept at poking witty fun at the government. He found himself laughing even though some of their sarcasm hit close to home.

A printer had set up his printing press next to the puppet show and was busy printing out mementos of the fair. After paying the puppeteer for the privilege of watching his show, Colton and Kate moved over to the printer's.

The man had drawn a sketch of the fair as seen from the riverbank and printed it on small sheets of fine paper. Colton studied the drawing, which was surprisingly quite good. "Great Frost Faire of 1814" was printed in large type across the bottom.

"Print ye names, m'lord? It'll make the lady a nice keepsake."

"Would you like one?" Colton looked down at Kate, thinking he would have no need for a remembrance of their day. Somehow he knew he would never forget these moments with her.

"I willna need a reminder of this day, Your Grace," she said softly. Suddenly her eyes burned with unshed tears. "But I would like a memento." She took a deep breath and tried to control her swell of emotion. She forced a short laugh. "I'll keep it to show my wee grandchildren. What a tale it will make; the story of a maid and a duke going to a fair in the middle of the Thames." Her voice cracked slightly as she tried to force a note of laughter into her words. "They willna believe such a thing unless I have proof."

Kate had to look away. She did not think there would be any grandchildren to hear the tale, for she doubted if she could ever find a man to measure up to the Duke of Ryland. A sharp pain in her chest took her breath away. He already owned far too much of her heart to leave room for any other man. She pushed the hurt aside, drawing on her strong determination to make the day special, to store up memories she would treasure for a lifetime.

The duke looked down at her profile, watching her struggle with her emotions. He was fighting a battle with some unexpected and unusual feelings of his own. Grandchildren meant a husband, some phantom who would share not just a day but a lifetime with her. The strength of his jealousy and hatred for this unseen rival shocked him.

Another thought shook his inner composure: Could she already have a husband? He wanted to dismiss the idea out of hand. She had never been bedded; he was certain of it. However, she might be married. It was not unheard of for a wife to run away from her husband before the marriage was consummated. Colton took a long, deep breath. It would not do to cuckold another man.

His conscience prodded him. *You'll seduce an innocent,* he thought, *but not a man's wife?*

"Yer pardon, Yer Grace, but there be others waitin'." The printer looked from the duke to Kate and back to the duke. "If ye'd like to wait and come back later . . ." His voice trailed off.

"No, now will be fine," Colton said briskly. "Colton Lydell, Duke of Ryland and . . ." He met Kate's gaze, his eyes questioning, challenging.

Kate broke away from his beautiful, compelling eyes. *I canna tell you!* "Catriona," she said softly. She looked back up at him. "And beside it put Kate." She turned her attention to the printer's puzzled expression. "Kate is my nickname."

Catriona. So you are Scottish, he thought. Or at least half-Scottish, he amended. He curled his fingers around her upper arm, watching as the printer laid out the type. *Why won't you tell me who you are?*

He gave her arm a tight squeeze, and Kate looked up at him in surprise. "Your pardon," he murmured, and dropped his hand. "Make two of those," he directed the printer. The man ignored his curt tone and happily complied.

A few moments later the job was done. Colton paid the man and took the mementos, handing one to Kate. She carefully rolled it up like a scroll and tucked it into a tiny opening in her reticule. She was not sure if she would be able to remove it from the purse unless she cut the drawstrings. Kate glanced up at her companion. His jovial mood had disappeared.

The duke carefully placed his keepsake inside his jacket pocket, then offered her his arm. Kate could feel the tension in his rigid muscles. They strolled farther down the row of tents. When the crowd thinned, he looked down at her. "Did you run away from your husband?" he asked bluntly, watching her face carefully.

"Of course no'!" Her expression was one of surprise and puzzlement. There was no trace of fear or guilt in her eyes as she met his gaze.

Colton let out his breath slowly, only then realizing he had been holding it in anticipation of her answer. A tremendous feeling of relief washed over him.

"Why would you think I was married?"

"Your talk of grandchildren gave me pause. It occurred to me that you might have run away from an unwelcome marriage. It's not unheard of," he added dryly.

"I assure you, Your Grace, I am no' married." She laughed, relieved to see his face relaxed once again. She did not want to dwell on such things, for at the moment her future seemed bleak. Instead she spotted a skittle alley. Pulling on his arm, she hurried him over to it.

"I must warn you, Your Grace, I am very good at skittles." Her eyes sparkled as he paid the vendor and picked up the hardwood disk, known as a skittle ball.

He hefted the disk in his hand and peered down the alley at the nine wooden pins set up at the opposite end. He handed the skittle ball to Kate. "Here, you go first. Then I can see what kind of opposition I have."

She grinned and playfully wound up her arm before sending the disc sliding in a straight line down the alley. Eight of the nine pins tumbled over. The attendant handed her another disc. She promptly knocked the last pin down.

The duke let out a low whistle. He had not attended many fairs in his life. His father had considered them beneath his dignity. Still, he had once been quite good at the game, for he used to play it with his brother. However, he couldn't remember the last time he had played. It had been years. He took the disc from the attendant and tossed it down the alley. Seven pins fell.

Kate squealed in triumph, then clamped her hand over her mouth at his arrogant, very ducal glare. She giggled behind her hand. His lip twitched, but he maintained his haughty pose.

"I remind you, my dear, it is the number of throws that count, not how many pins fall each time."

"True. But you canna possibly get those two down at the same time." She looked at the pins. They were lined up at an angle on the right side of the alley. "You'd have to be left-handed."

He grinned wickedly and passed the skittle ball to his left hand. Stepping to the far left side of the alley, he gave the disc a hard throw, sailing it down the alley at an angle and dropping both pins. He let out a whoop and turned to look at Kate with a grin.

"You're no' left-handed! How did you do that?" She was mesmerized by his heart-stopping smile, thinking there should be a law against having a dimple on just one side. Her concentration was sorely affected.

"No, I'm not. But I've trained myself to use my left hand for some things. I can't write left-handed, of course, but being coordinated with both hands is useful sometimes." He could think of several pleasant ways to put that coordination to good use but forced his mind to think of something else.

"Obviously." She snatched the disc from the attendant and lined up on the alley, trying to gather her scattered concentration. Kate unconsciously wiggled her hips as she squirmed to get just the right angle for her throw.

It was Colton's turn to be distracted. At her happy cry he raised his gaze to find all nine pins down. She took the skittle ball from the vendor and handed it to the duke with a saucy smile. Deciding it was time to be on their way, he gave the disc a halfhearted toss down the alley, then stared openmouthed as eight pins crashed down. The ninth swayed precariously, then slowly tumbled over.

Kate frowned. "This is our last set of pins. We'll have to play again if we tie," she proclaimed with a decisive nod of her head.

"No we won't."

Something in his tone caught her attention, drawing her gaze to his face. The heat in his eyes touched off a shower of sparks throughout her body. Thoroughly rattled, Kate gave the skittle ball a feeble toss. It slid slowly down the alley and stopped a hair's breadth from the pins.

"You did that on purpose!" She turned on him, resting her hands on her hips.

"I didn't do anything." He ruined his look of innocence by chuckling.

Kate took two deep breaths, trying to calm down, and threw the ball with a vengeance. The pins flew in every direction.

"Whew! Remind me not to make you angry." Colton couldn't resist grinning at her. His throw was as powerful as hers and just as successful. He draped his arm around her shoulders and led her away from the game and the next players.

"You cheated." Her lips formed a slight pout. She was not really angry. It was impossible to be irritated with him when he had his arm around her.

"How?" The husky tone was back in his voice.

She looked up at him and stopped walking. He stopped, too, meeting her gaze. He was doing it again. The desire in his eyes set off a heat wave. She expected to drop right through the ice any second.

"Dunna look at me that way," she said quietly.

"Why? What does it do to you, Kitten?" His voice was like crushed velvet. His eyes told her what she was doing to him.

"It makes my insides melt."

He didn't say a word, but his arm tightened around her shoulders, and he swung her back toward the fair. He started walking as quickly as he dared on the ice. "We're leaving," he murmured.

A twinge of trepidation rippled through her, a little doubt that perhaps she had taken on more than she could handle. "Your Grace?"

Colton heard the hesitation in her voice and slowed his pace. He willed himself to put a damper on the fire she was unconsciously building inside him. "Your pardon, Kate." He gave her a rueful smile. "I know I keep telling you to be honest with me, but in this instance you probably should have shaded the truth a bit." At her blush he removed his arm from her shoulders. "Here, let's have some gingerbread before we leave."

He bought the sweet, spicy treat, giving her a piece so they could eat it while they waited for the return ferry ride. Colton looked back at the throng still frolicking around the fair. It occurred to him that he had seen no sign of Fast-fingered

Willy, the pickpocket about whom the lad had warned him. In fact, he thought wryly, he had not paid much attention to anyone other than his companion.

He was thankful they had not encountered any members of the ton with whom he was acquainted, for he knew they would have immediately assumed Kate was his light-skirt. The women would have snubbed her. The men would have ogled her.

Colton frowned, watching as she brushed the last crumbs of gingerbread from her gloves. She was a fever in his blood, but he was not sure he wanted to be the reason for her shame. He did not like to think of the treatment she would receive from others if he made her his paramour, so he tried not to think about it at all. Unfortunately, like a worrisome tooth, he could not quite put it out of his mind.

Chapter 5

Kate looked over her shoulder at the lad as the sleigh pulled away from Blackfriars Bridge. He tipped his hat for the second time and grinned from ear to ear. The young man had good reason to smile. The Duke of Ryland had just hired him as a stableboy.

She turned back, peering up at the duke out of the corner of her eye.

"Well?" He glanced down at her, knowing full well that she was itching to say something.

"Do you always hire people without references?" She smiled up at him to let him know she did not disapprove of what he had done. Still, she was amazed by his actions.

"No, but I'm usually a good judge of character, and I do need another stable hand. The lad has a natural feel for horses. He did a good job watching over Snowball."

"Snowball?" Kate looked at the stocky brown horse and giggled.

Colton grinned. "That's what I call him. His former owners called him Mercury, but that was ridiculous. Since I purchased him to pull the sleigh, something more pertinent seemed appropriate."

"That's no' quite as bad as Copper Halfpenny." She shook her head at the new stableboy's name. He had explained that he had been a foundling, left on the parish doorstep with a halfpenny in his hand. "Surely the officials could have thought of a better name."

He nodded with a grimace. "Unfortunately, there are many such children. I suppose they can only call so many John Monday or Mary Tuesday." His expression softened as he looked at her. "Not everyone can have a beautiful name like Catriona, but then not everyone is lovely enough to bear it."

She blushed slightly, thinking it was silly to be so flattered by his compliment. "Certainly no' everyone would be pleased to bear the name, Your Grace." Her lips twitched. "I can think of any number of men who wouldna be happy with it."

Colton laughed out loud, sweet music to Kate's ears. There was nothing cold and austere about the man sitting next to her. How could the other servants have been so mistaken? He was warm, caring, and generous. And he claimed a little more of her heart with each passing moment.

"Kate, I must stop at home before we go to Twin Rivers." His voice and expression were sober. If she were a lady of the ton, such a stop could prove scandalous.

Kate considered his words, realizing he was once again giving her an opening to tell him who she was. A lady of quality would never pay a gentleman a call at his London home. Nor, of course, would she even think of going alone with him to his country home. A country drive in an open carriage was acceptable, but to stop along the way was courting disaster.

What does it matter? she thought. *I'll be leaving soon. I'll never be a part of the ton. Even if I were, it wouldna matter to me what those self-righteous hypocrites thought of me.*

Old feelings of resentment welled up in her heart. Her father had been as popular when he was in England as he now was in Scotland. However, as soon as he had married someone from beyond their ranks, the ton had turned on him. Those he had believed to be his friends ignored him or, worse, openly disdained him.

"I hope you'll be quick," she said with a smile. "I'm anxious to skate."

He studied her thoughtfully as she fidgeted absentmindedly with her reticule. He had suspected she would not care, since she had already agreed to go to the cottage with him. Was she so naïve that she did not realize what would be thought of her? No, he decided, she knew. It showed in her slight nervousness.

When she had consciously cast aside her brogue, she had unconsciously put away all nuances of her disguise. Her grace, bearing, and manner of speech indicated she was a lady of quality despite the worn pelisse and equally used hat. However, either she truly did not care about her reputation or she was intentionally flouting society's rules of conduct.

"I won't tarry," he replied, deciding not to question her. "I only need to pick up my skates."

As they stopped in front of the duke's town house, a footman ran out to take the reins. "Take Snowball around to the mews and ask Lunan to give him a bag of feed. I'll want the animal and Lunan ready to leave in a quarter hour." Colton helped Kate down from the sleigh while the footman tried not to stare.

The duke's butler could not hide his shock when his master walked through the front door with a woman on his arm.

"Close your mouth, Jempson." The duke smiled slightly at the man, an action that caused the butler's eyes to bulge. It took a few seconds, but Jempson managed to put his eyes back in his head and clamp his mouth shut. Colton handed him his hat, gloves, and cane.

"I'll keep my coat since I'll be only a few minutes. Take Miss MacArthur to the front drawing room so she can warm herself by the fire."

Kate followed the butler toward the drawing room. A few steps before the door she glanced back over her shoulder to find the duke watching her. His gaze flickered to the butler's rigid frame, then back to her. Colton shot her an impish wink that almost sent her into a fit of giggles.

He turned away as Gregory hurried down the stairs. The valet recognized Kate as she disappeared into the drawing room, and his face mirrored his astonishment. Not only was it unheard of for the Duke of Ryland to bring a woman unchaperoned to his home, but the woman was a maid!

Colton ignored his manservant's amazed expression, acting as if the situation were perfectly normal. "Gregory, fetch my skates, please."

"Your skates, Your Grace?" Gregory's eyes bulged almost as much as the butler's had.

"Yes, I do need them if I'm going skating."

"But, Your Grace, it's been ten years since you skated."

"No, I don't believe it's been that long." Colton thought for a minute. "Only seven. I believe I was two and twenty the last time. You do know where they are, don't you?"

"Yes, Your Grace. In the attic. It will take but a few minutes to find them."

"Very well." Colton moved toward his study as the valet turned around and started up the stairs. "Oh, Gregory . . ."

The servant peered over the railing. "Yes, Your Grace?"

"Bring the sable also," Colton said quietly.

"The sable!" Gregory glanced uneasily down the hall, aware that he had spoken louder than he should have.

"Yes, the sable. It is bitterly cold out. I'm driving Kate out to meet Mrs. MacCrea, and I don't want her to catch her death."

"Yes, Your Grace." The valet started back up the stairs, shaking his head. He had known something was afoot. He had not missed the tender way the duke looked at the girl the night they were forced to stay at Lady Millicent's. Nor had he forgotten the way His Grace snapped at him when he scolded her.

He could not blame his master for being attracted to her. She was a beautiful girl. No, he thought, correcting himself, she was a beautiful woman, and she would be a real high flyer when His Grace decked her out in expensive, fashionable finery. But the sable! He shook his head once more, climbing the steep steps up to the attic.

The duke stopped in his study and wrote a brief note to his mother explaining that he was taking Kate out to meet Mrs. MacCrea. He simply said he had run across her on her way to the Thames. He did not actually lie to his mother but worded the message so she would believe he had been intending to go to Twin Rivers before he met Kate.

As an afterthought, he asked her not to tell the earl that Kate had gone with him. From their earlier discussion Colton knew the earl would believe he was taking her to Twin Rivers to seduce her. *Aren't you?* He drummed his fingers on the tooled green-leather top of his desk, still unsure of what he would do.

The longer he spent in her company, the more confused he

became. It was a very odd predicament for the Duke of Ryland. He was known for his decisiveness, for his ability to weigh the facts and make the right judgments, sometimes in a split second.

He sighed and picked up the note, leaving the room. He had finally met a woman he felt comfortable with, one whose company he enjoyed tremendously, and he didn't know what to do with her. He walked down the hall, thinking that if he were not in such a quandary, the situation would be amusing.

He paused at the door to the drawing room, studying Kate a moment before he entered the room. She had not removed her pelisse, scarf, or hat, although she held her bare hands out to the fire. Her gloves and reticule lay on a table beside the pale blue sofa. Jempson stood stoically on the far side of the room, looking as if he expected to catch her stealing something.

Colton glanced back at her gloves. The faded wool contrasted sharply with the shiny marble and gilt of the ornately carved eagle table. It was a stinging reminder of their different stations in life. For a moment his conscience pricked him. Then his gaze fell upon the knots in her reticule, reminding him of their banter and laughter at the fair.

Tenderness softened his face as he turned to look at her once again. No, he told his conscience, there was not as much difference in their stations as one might think. His eyes twinkled. Besides, he'd never liked those opulent eagles of his grandfather's, anyway.

"Are you getting warm?"

She turned to look at him, a happy smile lighting her face. "Yes, thank you. I hadna realized I was so chilled until I stepped up to the fire."

Colton flashed her a warm smile, showing his dimple. Out of the corner of his eye he saw Jempson's mouth drop open again. The duke almost laughed out loud, thinking that he had been far too stern these last few years. Jempson had served him for over a year, but evidently the man had never seen him smile.

"We will leave shortly." He signaled to Jempson, waiting a few seconds to look at him to give the man time to regain his somber facade. "Please have this letter delivered to my mother immediately."

He handed him the note and turned his attention to Kate. "I advised her that you are going out to meet Mrs. MacCrea. I did not want her to be concerned about your welfare." It did not occur to Colton that his mother would be just as concerned because Kate was with him as she would be if the girl were traipsing around London on her own.

"Jempson, I will be at Twin Rivers for the afternoon. We should be back before nightfall, but you can send a message to me if a crisis arises. I do not anticipate anything urgent, but it is always a possibility." There was a soft tap at the door. "Ah, Lunan."

As the groom walked into the room, he spotted Kate. For a second his face registered his surprise, then settled into its normal relaxed lines. "Where are we off to this time?"

Kate noticed that Lunan was much more at ease with the duke than Jempson. Evidently the groom had been with His Grace for many years.

"Twin Rivers. We should be back before night." Colton addressed both the groom and the butler. "I hired a new stableboy this morning, a lad named Copper Halfpenny. He should arrive sometime this afternoon." Colton had offered to give Copper a ride to his new home, but the young man had declined. He said he didn't think the lady would be comfortable driving through his part of town. His consideration for Kate had raised him a notch or two in the duke's esteem.

"Does he know anythin' about horses?" Lunan unbuttoned his heavy coat.

"He appeared to. I liked his manner, and he seems honest enough." Colton was intentionally vague with his answer, knowing the groom would understand and question him about the boy when they were alone. The duke had been given a horse of his own when he was ten, and Lunan had come with it. He had been with him ever since. He was more of a friend than a servant, and they both knew it.

Gregory entered the room, carrying the skates in one hand and a sable muff in the other. A beautiful, rich brown sable cloak was draped over his arms. Both Kate and the butler gasped.

Colton picked up the fur and turned to Kate. "You'll need to remove your hat. I don't think the hood will go over it."

Kate stared at him, her mouth opening and closing several times as she tried to think of what to say.

"My dear, you don't look at all like a fish, so don't try to imitate one." The duke's eyes twinkled with laughter. Even Lunan was somewhat taken aback by Colton's actions. While Kate continued to sputter, the duke waved his hand, dismissing the servants.

The men hurried from the room, waiting in the hallway for any further instructions. They practically held their breath, straining to hear what was being said in the drawing room, although none of them ever would have admitted it.

"Your Grace, I canna accept such a gift."

"I am not offering it to you as a gift." He paused. "At least not now." He draped the cloak around her shoulders. It stopped about two inches above the floor. From all appearances it could have been made for her. "It will keep you warm on the drive." He fastened the loop over the button at the throat and glanced up to where her hair was tucked beneath her hat. "Take off your hat, Kitten. Let your glorious hair frame your beautiful face. Let me see you dressed as you're meant to be."

It was a simple request—a harmless one, she reasoned. It was such a small gift to give him. Her deep affection for him and her own vanity would not let her refuse. She knew gray was not a good color for her; it was the reason she had chosen the pelisse as part of her disguise. Any shade of brown, however, made her coloring come alive. The dark fur would be especially flattering.

Slowly Kate reached up and removed her hat with trembling fingers, placing it on the table with her other things. She pulled the few remaining pins from her hair and shook her head, sending the thick locks cascading across her shoulders and down to the middle of her back.

Colton opened his mouth to speak, but no sound came out. He had always considered her beautiful, no matter what she wore. Earlier, with the beaver rug thrown over her, she had been vibrant. But now, with the rich sable and her dark red hair framing her face, she was breathtaking. Her satin-smooth skin was gently colored with the soft golden-peach glow of a healthy young woman, a woman comfortable with her beauty.

Her turquoise eyes were like sparkling jewels, made brighter by the red of her hair and her pleasure at his response. His gaze dropped to her lips. He almost groaned out loud. They were slightly parted and glistened with moisture. He swallowed hard. They reminded him of a slice of ripe peach, soft and sweet and gently tinted with pink. *Just one taste* . . . His head began to move toward hers.

"Your Grace," cried Kate softly.

He stopped, blinked, then shook his head. Straightening, he brushed her cheek with his fingertips. He was not surprised to find his hand unsteady. Borrowing one of her phrases, he smiled gently and said, "Mercy of heav'n, woman, what you do to a man."

Kate blushed and looked over at the fire. With any other man she would have made some flippant remark, but she found her wit had deserted her. She wanted him to be attracted to her as to no other woman.

"You're exquisite, Catriona." He ran his fingers through the long length of her hair, fascinated with the silky texture. As if compelled, he buried his fingers in the soft strands and lifted them to his nostrils, anticipating, then savoring, the subtle scent of jasmine he knew would be there. "I have never seen a woman to compare with you."

She had heard the phrase in one form or another before, but though the gentlemen had been sincere, it had meant little to her. But to hear him say it, for him to believe she was more beautiful than any other, brought forth a deep swell of pride and pleasure, a feeling so sweet that it was almost an ache.

Tears welled up in her eyes. She looked up at him, barely able to hide what was in her heart. "Thank you."

"Why do I make you cry?" He frowned and let her hair slide from his fingers, cupping her face in his hands.

She smiled, blinking back the tears. "It is foolishness, merely an overreaction to your compliments."

He slowly lowered his hands, but his gaze locked with hers. "My words were not just compliments," he said, allowing her a tiny peek into his heart. He held his breath. It would be a terrible blow to his pride if she were to make light of his attraction to her.

"I know you are sincere," she said softly. She knew she had to be honest with him about her feelings. She lifted her hand, resting it on his chest. She could feel the solid beat of his heart even through the thick material of his greatcoat. "I have received many compliments, some of them sincere." He stiffened and started to turn away. She jerked her hand back, shaking her head in frustration.

"Colton, wait!" Kate grabbed his hand in both of hers and drew it close to her heart. She had called him by name without thinking, but she was glad. It had taken him by surprise and given her another chance. He turned back toward her, relaxing slightly.

"I am having trouble saying what I want." She shook her head in dismay.

"I can wait." A tiny smile hovered around his mouth. He liked the musical way she said his name. He also liked the way she was clinging to his hand.

Kate took a deep breath, looking back up at him. She relaxed a little when she saw the mellow warmth in his eyes. "When others spoke of my appearance, their praise was appreciated, but it dinna signify. But to have you think I'm beautiful means a great deal to me." She glanced down, suddenly a little shy, and realized she was clutching his hand to her bosom. She released it, moving her hands away in nervous, fluttery motions. Though it took great willpower, he politely withdrew his hand without touching her further.

Embarrassed by her forwardness, she looked down at the floor. She wondered if he would take offense at her for using his given name. "Your words filled me with great joy and pride," she said softly, quickly adding, "Your Grace."

Colton breathed a sigh of relief. "Good. I would want nothing less." He took her hand and tucked it through the crook of his arm. "Now I suppose you must call me by my title when we are with others, but it would please me greatly to have you call me by my name when we are alone. I have never been fond of the name Colton, but I like the way you say it. You make it sound like notes of a sweet song."

It is a song. The song of my heart. She avoided looking up at him, knowing her feelings would show in her eyes. A part of her mind cried out for sanity. She must put a stop to this slide into love; only pain and heartache waited at the end. But she found it impossible to walk away. The memories of this day would have to last a lifetime.

She must not think of the heartache to come but rather concentrate on him, memorizing all the tiny facets that formed Colton Lydell. Her perception seemed to intensify, allowing her to notice and store away the tiniest details—the faint scent of Hungary Water on his skin, the hint of gingerbread on his breath, the play of muscles in the arm beneath her fingers, and the mild roughness of a callus on his palm as he put his hand over hers.

She looked down at his large hand, admiring the long, strong fingers, remembering the way he had cupped her face moments before. He was a powerful man, one with enough strength to break a man's nose with one blow of his cane, yet his touch had been as gentle as a drop of dew upon the grass. Her gaze wandered to his neatly trimmed fingernails and stopped short. One nail was black from the tip to the center.

"How did you smash your fingernail?" She looked up at him, concern reflected in her eyes.

"I was splitting wood a month or so back and dropped a piece on it."

She turned to the table and picked up her gloves, putting them on. "*You* were chopping wood?" she asked.

"I enjoy it." He took her hand and tucked it around his arm, flexing the muscles in his forearm as he did so. "Helps to keep me fit." He grinned at her doubtful expression as she reached over and picked up her hat and reticule. They moved slowly toward the door.

"But most Englishmen dunna burn wood; they use coal."

"True, but I have an abundant supply of trees at Twin Rivers, and we plant more each year. I've always thought a wood fire was nicer than coal, so I ride out to Twin Rivers every chance I have. Between the ride and swinging the ax, I get some exercise."

"I see." Kate swallowed hard. In her mind's eye she *did* see—the duke outside on a warm spring day, coats and shirt cast aside, the muscles of his broad chest and arms rippling as he swung the ax. *Oh, my,* she thought. *What a glorious sight that would be!*

"Kate?" Colton looked down at her, a puzzled little frown marring his perfect brow. "Is something wrong?"

"Uh, no, everything's fine. I was just thinking how much work it is to cut wood." Her face flamed.

"Oh, really?"

She chanced a peek at his face. From his smug grin she knew he knew that it was not precisely what she was thinking.

Why no'? she thought. *Why no' let him know how beautiful I think he is?* She stopped short, looking up at him. For a second her gaze wavered, then she forced herself to look him in the eye.

"No, it wasna what I was thinking, and you know it. I've seen you without a shirt, Your Grace—" She held up her hand as he took a breath to speak. "You'll be gentleman enough no' to mention the circumstances—and I can imagine what a glorious sight you would be swinging an ax. Now dunna go getting a swelled head because I think you're a braw man, Colton Lydell."

His head didn't swell, but his heart did. He took a deep breath, inordinately pleased. He knew he was fairly handsome and was conscious of his fine physique, but he could remember no woman ever telling him so. Certainly no one had ever called him glorious before. *My braw man* . . . Her words came back to tickle his imagination. He knew that to a Scot, braw meant handsome, fine, even splendid. Did she truly think he was splendid? Had she been dreaming of him the night she'd sleepwalked to his room?

Colton gazed down at her, smiling tenderly at her slightly defiant tone and the tiny, upward tilt to her chin. She looked as if she expected him to be amused by her thoughts. Her thoughts . . . Knowing she found him desirable triggered many feelings, but amusement was not one of them. Pride, pleasure, excitement, longing, need—these were the things her bold compliment produced.

Kate stared up at him, mesmerized by the range of emotions rushing across his face. Like never before, she was able to read his expressions, to understand what he was feeling. It struck her that he had permitted it, this openness, this window to his soul. He allowed her to see what her words did to him, that for all his supposed hardness he was as vulnerable as any man.

Oh, dear God, her heart cried. *How can I keep from hurting him?* She turned her head away so he would not see her guilt and pain.

He thought she was simply embarrassed by her plain speaking. He nudged her chin with his knuckle, guiding her face around toward him. She kept her eyes lowered.

"Thank you, Kate," he said gently. "A man likes to hear compliments, too, especially when he knows they are sincere." When she finally looked up at him, his smile was warm and tender. His eyes glowed with pleasure. "Thank you," he said again, brushing her jaw with the back of his fingers.

Kate tried to catch her breath, wondering how he could send her pulses racing with a soft word and a gentle touch.

Colton stepped back, offering her his arm. "Of course, we may have a problem going through the door."

"Oh?" She sounded a little distracted and hoped the duke would not guess she was concentrating on calming her thundering heart. She absently took hold of his arm.

"Yes, I believe my head has grown considerably fatter." Colton grinned when she looked up at him, her expression alert and her eyes twinkling. "Ah, good to see you've quit your woolgathering. Shall we go for a drive in the country, my dear?" He escorted her from the drawing room.

The three servants waited in the hallway, trying to appear totally disinterested in the duke and the young lady. All three men failed miserably. They could not take their eyes off her.

"Perhaps the sable was a mistake," muttered the duke. He watched the men stare at Kate as she pulled the hood up over her head, carefully tucking her hair beneath it.

Colton held out his hand for his hat. Without looking away from Kate, Gregory handed him the skates instead.

The valet held out the muff so Kate could slip her free hand inside. She waited a minute for him to release it. He didn't. "Thank you, Gregory."

"What?" Startled, the valet dropped his hands and stepped back with a blush. "Oh, you're welcome, Miss." He glanced at the duke, wishing he could fade into the wallpaper when he saw his employer's piqued expression. "Oh, lud!" He grabbed the skates from the duke's hand and thrust them at Lunan. The groom reached for the straps but missed. One skate bounced off his knee on its path to the floor.

"Ow! You little dandy! Why don't you watch what you're doin'!" Lunan bent over to rub his knee, nudging Jempson with his shoulder.

Jempson came out of his trance and tried to help. He reached over to a small table for the duke's hat. Both he and Gregory seized it at the same time, tugging in different directions. Lunan let out a groan when the butler bumped him in the head with his elbow.

"Enough!" At Colton's bellow everyone froze. All except Kate. She was doubled over with laughter and could not have stopped if her life had depended upon it.

The duke again held out his hand for his hat. With a disparaging look at Jempson, Gregory jerked it away from the butler and gave it to His Grace. Lunan picked up the skates, wrapping the long straps around his hand, and slowly straightened, carefully avoiding any contact with the butler or anyone else.

"My gloves, Jempson." Colton's lip began to twitch. Kate straightened, taking huge gulps of air in a valiant attempt to control her laughter. "And my cane." He was proud of himself for remaining cool and calm. It wouldn't do to completely destroy his servants' image of him. He was careful not to meet Lunan's gaze when he nodded for him to go on ahead.

Kate took several more deep breaths and swallowed her laughter. When the duke offered her his arm, she wiped the tears from her cheeks with the back of one gloved hand and shrugged. Both hands were full, one with her hat and reticule, the other with the muff. Colton congratulated himself for not losing control and took hold of her elbow. They started out the door behind Lunan.

When the groom sensed that His Grace was following him, he began to walk with an exaggerated limp, leaning over every few steps to rub his knee. Colton glanced down at Kate. The second he looked into her twinkling eyes, they both burst out in whoops of laughter.

He drew her back inside, waiting until their peals of merriment had subsided before going out to the sleigh. The duke wiped a tear from his eye and lifted Kate up to her seat.

Taking the hat from her hand, he passed it back to Lunan for safekeeping. He glanced at the town house as the footman shut the door. Jempson and Gregory were still standing in the hallway, completely dumbfounded.

The trip to Twin Rivers was pleasant and uneventful. Kate sat beside the duke as he drove, with Lunan riding in the seat behind them. The sun played hide-and-seek with the clouds, but with the exception of her cheeks and nose, Kate stayed nice and warm. Although she owned a pretty, fur-lined, velvet cloak, which she had left in Scotland, she decided it could not compare with the sable.

She did not want to speculate on the duke's intentions in having her wear the cloak. Unfortunately the luxurious fur only served to remind her of what he said when he put it around her shoulders. She expected to be offered *carte blanche* before the day was out. She made up her mind not to be offended by the offer when it came, since her actions could only lead him to believe she would be open to such an arrangement.

She turned the muff this way and that, admiring the varying shades of color brought out by the sunlight. She was about to burst with curiosity. Had he purchased the fur recently and for whom, or had it been in his possession for some time? She did not think it had been bought specifically for her, since he had seemed to think of it only after he wrapped her up in the beaver rug.

"It's beautiful, isn't it?" Colton watched the sunlight ripple across the muff. It almost looked as if the fur itself were moving.

"Yes, it is. I've never seen one so lovely." Kate hesitated a minute, then plunged ahead. "Did you buy it in London?"

"No, it was a gift."

"A gift? But it's a lady's cloak."

"I'm glad you noticed." Colton chuckled at her miffed expression. He knew she was dying to know who gave it to him and why. "Very well, I shall tell you the tale of how I came to be the proud owner of such a fine *lady's* cloak. Several years ago Gregory and I were traveling outside of Moscow when we happened upon a coach robbery. We were able to thwart the villains without any injury to the occupants of the coach." He grinned. "Contrary to my valet's actions today, he is quick of mind and an accurate shot with a pistol." He glanced over his shoulder at Lunan, his eyes twinkling. "Poor Lunan was abed with a cold and had not made the short journey with us. He missed out on all the entertainment."

The groom waved his hand carelessly. "I like my sport a little less excitin'."

"As I said, Gregory is an excellent shot. When we came over a rise and saw the robbery in progress, he took careful aim while I drove the team at breakneck speed toward the highwaymen." A bubble of laughter welled up in his chest as he heard Lunan snicker behind him. He had never told the tale with quite so much embellishment.

"I swung the team and the carriage to the left so Gregory would have a better angle. As he pulled off his shot, I slowed the team with one hand and pulled out my pistol with the other." Lunan coughed, sounding as if he might choke to death, but Colton ignored him. "Gregory's shot was true, and of course mine hit its mark also. One of us—we never did determine which one—shot the gang leader, so the others rode off in a flash."

Kate sent a skeptical glance back at Lunan, who only winked and nodded, then burst into laughter.

"Pay no attention to my friend in the backseat," said the duke with exaggerated priggishness. "He is only jealous because he was not there."

Kate giggled. "And, who, pray tell, was inside the coach? The Tsar?"

"No, alas, it was only a beautiful young woman." His lips twitched as he detected a spark of jealousy in her eye. "And her baby. She was the very young and much loved wife of an elderly fur merchant, and her son was the man's only child. We escorted them to their destination some twenty miles away. The gentleman could not thank us enough for saving the joy of his life. He rewarded Gregory handsomely with coin. Of course," he said matter-of-factly, "I could not accept any reward."

"Of course no'." Kate suspected that many men, if not most, would have happily taken the man's money.

"When we returned to England, the sable, along with a

matching one for me, were waiting. His letter said they were gifts, tokens of his appreciation, not a reward. I knew he would be greatly offended if I returned them."

"Why dinna you wear it today?" She glanced at his dark-blue greatcoat. The collar, cuffs, and lapels were sedately, yet elegantly, trimmed in silver fox. The sable wouldna be his style, she thought. Still, it would bring out the red highlights in his hair, and he would be so handsome.

"It didn't occur to me." *I was only thinking of you.* "I should wear the cloak more often, I suppose, but it is a trifle excessive for my tastes." Colton shifted his weight in the seat and turned his concentration back to the road. They were passing through a shaded area, and the going was more treacherous.

He was glad to have the diversion, since it would be awkward to tell her the real reason the merchant had sent something for a woman. "The sable is the finest fur I have in my possession," the man's letter had stated. "By saving my beloved, you gave me my life. Someday, when you are in love, the cloak will be a fitting gift for the light of your life."

He shifted again, wondering for the second time in less than an hour if having her wear the sable had been a mistake. The first time he had been joking. This time, however, his thoughts were serious. He turned down the lane leading to his estate and dismissed his concern from his mind. There would be time to analyze his motives later, when and if he understood them.

When the duke stopped the sleigh in front of Twin Rivers, Kate looked first at the house, then at him, and shook her head. "You said this was a cottage."

"Isn't it?"

" 'Tis no'. 'Tis more like a small mansion. There must be at least ten rooms."

"Actually, I think there are eleven."

"Eleven rooms do no' a cottage make, Your Grace."

He looked sheepish. "I suppose not, but my family always called it the cottage. It is the smallest of my houses." He frowned because it sounded as if he were bragging. "I normally use only part of it, so it seems cozy. I apologize for misleading you, my dear." He wondered why it was so important to him for her to like it but did not dwell on the problem long enough to reach any conclusions.

"It doesna matter, Your Grace." She let her gaze roam over the red brick mansion, admiring its simple lines. Turning a dazzling smile on Colton, she said, "It is beautiful, even if no' what I expected."

The duke's description of Mrs. MacCrea, however, was accurate. She and her husband were surprised when they arrived, but she bustled them inside with loving affection. She treated the duke more like a grandchild than a high-ranking member of the ton, fussing over how tired he looked and pampering him with hot tea and a freshly baked cake. He loved every minute of it.

Kate knew the caretakers were curious about her relationship with the duke, but they were polite and acted as if it were an everyday occurrence for His Grace to bring a maid out to call on them.

"Did you grow up in Edinburgh, ma'am?" asked Kate.

"No, lass. Both Angus and I were raised near Aberdeen. We're country folk. We wouldna be happy in a city, even as fine a one as Edinburgh. We like things peaceful and quiet. I be happiest when my neighbor lives down the road aways."

"Aye, I know what you mean." Kate smiled. "I always enjoyed it more when we were in the country than at the house in town." She caught a glimpse of Colton's interested face and almost bit her tongue. "There's more to do in the country," she finished lamely.

"Ach, that be the truth! Sometimes there's more than a body can keep up with."

Colton frowned slightly. "Do you two need more help around here?"

"Nae, except when Anne takes it in her noodle to do her spring scrubbing."

"Ye could use help chopping the wood, Angus MacCrea, and ye know it. Ever since ye took that killiecoup, yer shoulder's been a-paining ye."

Angus grumbled that there was no need to tell everyone about his clumsiness. He stuck his pipe in his mouth, drawing in several deep breaths as he lit it. He blew the smoke out in a puff, his bushy gray eyebrows angled in a frown. Lunan stopped working on the horse he was whittling and joined the others in looking at his old friend.

"You took a fall?" Kate asked, concerned.

"Aye. Slipped on the ice the vera first day of the cold spell."

"Tumbled head over heels, he did," cut in Mrs. MacCrea. "Aboot scared the life oot o' me."

Colton frowned at both of them. He loved these two elderly people like family. They had taken care of Twin Rivers since before he was born. "Angus, I want you to hire one of the neighbors to chop wood for you." He held up his hand when the man started to protest. "At least until your shoulder mends. Then you can decide whether you want him to continue or not.

"And you, madam, will hire all the help you need when you do your spring cleaning." He grinned at her. "I remember how you turn this place upside down and inside out when you get a bee in your bonnet." His grin softened into an affectionate smile. "There's no need for either of you to work so hard."

Colton pushed his chair back from the table. "Now, Angus, let's go see how high your woodpile is." He turned to Kate, his eyes sparkling with mischief. "I'll swing the ax a few times, then we'll go out to the pond. Too bad it isn't summer," he murmured.

Although her cheek turned a soft pink, she refused to rise to the bait. "If it were, we couldna go skating." Her eyes sparkled with warmth and laughter.

Lunan put his piece of wood and knife back in his pocket and rose from his place before the fire. The three men put on their coats. As they went out the door Kate stood and began picking up the dirty dishes to carry them into the kitchen.

"Nae, Miss. There's no need for ye to do anything," Mrs. MacCrea scolded. "Ye are the duke's guest." She took the plates from her hand.

Kate smiled and trailed along behind Mrs. MacCrea. She had been pretending to be a maid for so long that the role came naturally. She had not thought twice about clearing off the table. She shook her head ruefully. Living the life of a rich young woman again was going to take some adjustment. She glanced down at her red, work-worn hands and was suddenly anxious for her charade to end.

"May I sit in your kitchen for a while? I'd like to hear about Aberdeen. I've been there a few times, but the visits were brief."

"Of course, lass." Mrs. MacCrea shot her a sideways glance. She didn't know what to think of Kate. Everything about her, except for her clothes and red hands, suggested a lady of quality. Still, she had never known a lady to help with the dishes. If she were the duke's light-skirt, she would have been wearing a new gown instead of one that was a few years old. She had never heard of one of *that* kind helping with the dishes, either.

Then again, she thought, putting the plates down on the floor for the cat to lick, the lass had been wearing the beautiful cloak when they'd arrived. The duke did not treat her like a Cyprian, but she was more than a friend. She felt like throwing up her hands in bewilderment.

Mrs. MacCrea shoved her musings aside to tell Kate about Aberdeen. They chatted for half an hour, talking about places with which they both were familiar, as well as sights Kate had not seen.

She enjoyed her visit with the housekeeper but found herself growing more homesick. Some of her ways and little sayings reminded Kate of her mother.

The duke and the other two men came through the back door, stomping the snow from their boots. Colton grinned at Kate. "Are you ready to skate? I've warmed up, so I shouldn't break anything if I fall."

"I canna believe you would fall." Her smile held a hint of coquetry. "I dinna think there was anything you canna do."

"How kind you are, my dear." The duke made a great show of straightening to his full height. "But I must admit it has been a few years since I put on a pair of skates. I hope you don't have to pick me up too many times."

Kate cocked her head a little to one side and looked him up and down, appraising his size. She met his gaze, a teasing glint in her eye. "I'm afraid I'd have to come get Lunan to help."

The duke laughed and waited while she put on her pelisse, scarf, hat, and gloves. He picked up both pairs of skates and held the door open for her.

"What if I fall on you?" he asked, a teasing gleam dancing in his own eye.

"We'd freeze and be buried under the snow." She glanced

up at the large flakes that were slowly drifting down, wondering when the sky had clouded over.

Appearing very thoughtful and overly concerned, the duke turned to Lunan and winked, reminding the groom of a much younger Colton Lydell. "If we don't return within the hour, send out the Saint Bernards."

Kate's trill of laughter drifted back to the kitchen as he shut the door behind them.

Mr. and Mrs. MacCrea turned expectantly to Lunan. "Don't ask me what he's about. I never saw the woman until today." The groom took his piece of wood and knife out of his pocket and pulled a chair close to the fire. Angus lit his pipe and propped his booted feet up on the hearth. Mrs. MacCrea started to move away but stopped when Lunan spoke again.

"No, I never saw her until today, but I've sure heard a lot about her." He looked at his friends, knowing they loved Colton as much as he did. His face reflected his hope and his concern. "And if a man was ever besotted, it's our duke."

Chapter 6

The duke placed the wooden footpad of the skate beneath the sole of Kate's boot and frowned. "They're a little big."

"I dunna think it will matter. I used my mother's skates for years and they were always a little too large."

Colton nodded and adjusted the footpad once more to make sure the steel blade was straight. Bringing the leather thongs around the top of Kate's foot, he tied them securely. A few minutes later the second skate was also in place.

"There you are." He stood and took her hand, helping her out onto the ice. He stood in the snow at the edge of the pond and smiled. "You go ahead if you want. I'll put mine on and join you in a minute."

He sat down on the rock she had just vacated and tied his skates in place. He stayed there for a few minutes, watching as she glided smoothly around the pond. When he tried to stand, his legs were far too wobbly. He regretted not having worn boots that fit more tightly at the ankle. He sat back down with something less than his usual grace.

"Are you no' coming?" Kate stopped in front of him.

"I'm not certain this was a good idea." He grinned sheepishly. "I'm not sure I can stay on my feet."

"Of course you can." She held out her hand. "Here, I'll help you."

He hesitated a minute, then gritted his teeth and took her

hand, pushing himself to his feet. He swayed this way and that; his arms, as well as hers, flailing around wildly to keep him upright. After a long, scary minute he was able to steady himself.

"Kate, I don't know about this. I'm not even on the ice yet." He looked down at his skates, which were buried in the hard snow.

"You'll do fine. Just hang on to me." She smiled at him mischievously.

"How can I refuse such an offer?" He grinned and took a deep breath, bravely stepping out onto the ice. They slipped and slid precariously for a minute until he achieved a shaky balance. He settled his right hand on her waist as they skated at a slow pace around the pond.

With one hand at her waist and the other holding her hand securely, Colton began to relax. In a few moments they were skating with reasonable smoothness.

"There, now dinna I say you could do it?" She looked up at him, pleased, happy, and excited to be by his side.

"Yes, you did." He grimaced. "But it won't be for long, Kitten. My ankles are killing me already. I should have worn tighter boots. Unfortunately mine don't lace up like yours do."

"True. One more time around, then you have to take a turn by yourself."

"Are you giving me orders, young lady?"

"Yes." She smiled impishly. "I'll no' have you thinking you must hang on to a woman's skirts every time you want to go out on the ice. You need to know you can do it on your own. It'll build your confidence." She nodded sagely.

He slipped a little and his grip tightened. "I'm not hanging on to your skirts, I'm hanging on to you. There's a very nice difference, you know."

"Yes, I know," she said softly. They were quiet the next time around the pond, enjoying their closeness, the beauty of the sparkling white meadow around them and the gentle brush of the snowflakes on their faces.

Kate slowed, releasing his hand. "Now, Colton, do it on your own."

"Kate, I don't want to." His voice held an odd note of apprehension and a great deal of stubbornness.

"But you must. Someday you'll want to teach your children, and you canna be afraid to try."

Colton saw the sense in her statement, but his ankles were beginning to throb and his legs felt weak. *Why did she want to skate?* he asked himself silently. *Why couldn't she have wanted to do something I'm used to?* Walking, riding, fencing—obviously none of his varied forms of exercise used the same muscles as ice skating.

"Very well," he said with a resigned sigh. *If I don't cooperate now, she'll keep me out here until I do,* he thought. At that particular moment it did not occur to him that in the past no woman, not even his mother, had ever forced or persuaded the Duke of Ryland to do anything he did not want to do.

He carefully eased his hand away from her waist, and she turned off to the right, moving away from him.

"Very good, Your Grace."

"Colton," he called softly, concentrating on making it around the pond. He almost lost his balance as he made the wide turn at the end but regained it amid waving arms and stifled cries.

When he had gone completely around the oblong pond, he slowed to a stop along the bank and promptly fell on his backside in the snow. His long legs were still stretched out on the ice. He plopped back on the snow, catching his breath.

"Are you hurt?" Kate rushed over.

"Only my dignity." He sat up and began removing one of his skates. "I've had enough. Do you want to stay a little longer?"

"No, I've had enough too. You did very well."

"Thank you." He sat still as she walked past, grinning as she slipped a little and had to grab for his shoulder for balance. "I'm not sure I'll be able to walk tomorrow." When Kate was safely past, he bent over and took off the other skate. He cautiously pushed himself to his feet and walked over to help her.

"I canna get this knot undone." She had untied one thong, but the other one was proving difficult.

"Here, let me give it a try." Colton worked at it for a few minutes until he was able to loosen it enough to slip the skate from her boot. "We'll have to try again when it dries out." He quickly untied the thongs on the second one, then picked up both pairs of skates and stood.

"You look in pain."

"I am in pain. Please, don't ever ask me to ice-skate again. I'm getting too ancient for this kind of thing."

"You're no' old." Kate walked lightly along the path in front of him.

"I feel like an antique at the moment."

With a laugh she started down the snow-covered path back toward the house. The duke walked along behind, limping somewhat. Kate hurried on ahead and scooped up a handful of snow, packing it into a nice snowball.

"Kate, put that down."

"Yes, Your Grace." She threw it at him, hitting him square on the front of his expensive beaver hat. It sailed off his head, was caught by the wind, and rolled across the snow.

"Kate!"

"Oops!" She covered her mouth with her hand, but a giggle still slipped out.

Colton threw down the skates and chased his hat, grumbling and groaning the whole way. Finally catching it, he took great pains to make sure she knew how much snow was on the inside. He tried to glare at her, but found it hard to laugh and glare at the same time.

"I beg your pardon. My throw was a wee bit off. I truly dinna intend to knock it off your head. Oh, no. Oh, no!" She turned with a squeal and ran down the trail as Colton stopped and scooped up a large handful of snow.

He took a minute to pack it tightly into a huge ball before picking up the skates and following her. Although his ankles hurt, he covered the ground quickly, having too much fun to be bothered by the pain.

"Now, Kate, you know it's not nice to throw snowballs at your elders." He had her cornered against a fence. He dropped the skates and crept up on her slowly, prolonging the agony.

"I told you, you're no' old." She watched him warily, her eyes glistening with excitement and enjoyment as she tried to judge which way to jump. As he grew closer, she turned, putting her back to him, and watched him over her shoulder.

"My dear, I've been old ever since I got out of the nursery." There was a subtle note of sadness in his voice, a weariness that told her he had missed many of the joys of childhood. She quickly decided sympathy might be the wrong response.

"Well, you dunna look old. Why, I'd wager you're no' above five and thirty." Shock lit his face, and she laughed, knowing he did not look a day over his nine and twenty years.

"You minx! Five and thirty indeed!" He threw the snowball at her, aiming for her back. She dodged to the side, but her foot slipped on an icy spot and she fell backward, twisting slightly. She grabbed hold of the fence, keeping herself reasonably upright, but the snowball caught her in the face.

"Aiiiiii!" Spit, splutter, spit. Kate made a great show of getting a clump of snow out of her mouth.

"Kate! Did I hurt you?" Colton was at her side in an instant, brushing the snow off the side of her face and chin.

"A wee bit." Her cheek stung like the very devil.

He faced her, draping his arms across her shoulders. "I was aiming for your back. I didn't throw it hard."

"Thank goodness. You're a worse shot than I am."

"My aim was true. You should have cringed and shrieked in terror like a normal woman." He frowned, looking down at the red welt forming on her cheek. "I did hurt you. I'm truly sorry, Kitten."

" 'Tis no' bad. I asked for it by being so childish. I started it."

"You weren't being childish, but you certainly know how to enjoy life. You make me feel young," he said softly. His arms closed around her.

She thought he was going to kiss her but he didn't, at least not on the mouth. Slowly and with painstaking care he moved his lips over her cheek and chin, kissing away the last remainder of the snow, bringing soothing warmth to her cold red skin.

"Is it painful?" His lips hovered above hers.

"No." She barely felt it. Kate wondered what he would do if she stretched up and kissed him. "Your hat is covered with snow." She thought she'd die if he didn't kiss her. "So is your coat." *When did you become such a blockhead?*

Colton leaned back to inspect her hat. "You're covered with

snow too." He almost smiled as her face flooded with disappointment. He knew she wanted him to kiss her, but he was enjoying teasing her a little. It was a new experience for him. He had never felt comfortable enough with any other woman to try it.

She unconsciously licked her lips.

All thought of teasing her flew out of his mind. He lowered his head toward hers, his voice a low groan. "Kate, I know I have no right . . ." His voice trailed off as her eyelids drifted closed and she stretched up on tiptoe to meet him.

Kate had never experienced anything so wonderful in her whole life. His lips caressed hers gently, as if she were the most delicate creature on earth. Love spiraled through her body, shouting to every molecule that this man had been made for her. She breathed a little sigh and leaned against him.

He nibbled on the corner of her mouth, then traced the outline of her full bottom lip with the tip of his tongue and nibbled on the other corner. "So sweet. Ah, Kitten, you're like a violet in the snow or the first sunbeam after a rain." His arms tightened as her hands slipped up around his neck. "You fill my dark, empty soul with sunshine," he whispered huskily. "I'm lonely, Kate, so very lonely."

With a tiny cry she closed the narrow distance between their lips, kissing him with all the pent-up love in her heart. He crushed her to him, deepening the kiss as her lips parted for him. Gone was his gentleness, her delicacy. To her surprise she discovered the same power within herself that she felt in him, even though her head swam and her legs grew weak. It was a power bred of longing and loneliness, the need to fulfill and be fulfilled.

A strong gust of wind buffeted a branch above, sending a barrage of snow down on them. Colton jerked back with a start, then cradled her head against his shoulder, breathing deeply. After a long moment he released her reluctantly.

Kate looked up at him, wanting to say what was in her heart, knowing the words must go unspoken. He searched her face so intently, she wondered what he saw there.

Abruptly he leaned down and gave her a hard, possessive kiss. "We'd better go back to the house," he said roughly. Kate caught her breath and nodded, waiting as he picked up the skates and tossed them beyond the fence. Then he lifted her over and climbed over himself. In a few minutes they were brushing the snow from their coats and shaking off their hats at the back door.

Kate went upstairs to the guest room Mrs. MacCrea had shown her earlier and tidied up her hair. She was shaken from those passionate moments in the meadow and wondered what she would do if he touched her again. Sinking to her knees on the soft rug beside the bed, she leaned her forehead on the embroidered counterpane. "Please, dear God, give me the strength to resist temptation. Oh, Lord, I love him so much! How can I untangle this mess I've made?"

She struggled with tears for a moment but quickly wiped her cheeks and dried her eyes on her petticoat when she heard the duke pass by her door on his way downstairs. "I must no' keep him waiting for supper," she muttered, checking her reflection in the mirror.

With pins borrowed from Mrs. MacCrea she pinned her hair up in a thick chignon at the nape of her neck. It was the only style she could successfully maintain due to the weight and length of her hair. She smoothed the back one last time and fluffed the shorter, soft curls around her face. Her skin was pale, causing the reddened area from the snowball to stand out predominantly. Kate pinched her other cheek in an effort to even out the color but was only mildly pleased with the results. With a resigned sigh she made her way downstairs.

Contrary to most of the ton, the Duke of Ryland did not mind a simple meal. He had traveled enough and eaten so many different kinds of food that he appreciated a tasty dinner whether it consisted of many courses or one of Mrs. MacCrea's thick, juicy shepherd's pies.

Nor did he mind keeping country hours and having early suppers. To Kate's surprise they all ate together in the dining room. She was glad for the company of the others. Colton had seemed tense and distracted ever since their last kiss. He barely talked during the meal. The minute he finished his cake, he excused himself and pushed away from the table.

Kate found him in the drawing room half an hour later. She had purposely waited until everyone else had left the dining room, thinking that perhaps he needed to be alone with his thoughts.

"Your Grace, may I join you?" Kate asked, waiting by the door.

"Only if you quit calling me Your Grace. I thought we agreed for you to use my name." He smiled as she moved into the room.

"We did. I just thought it might be better to address you properly with others about."

"They're at the far end of the house. And even if they weren't, I would not mind. They are not fools. They know there is something between us." He ran his fingers through his chestnut hair, mussing it slightly, then rested his hand on his hip. "Kate, we cannot go back to London today."

"Why no'?" She watched as he walked over to the window and pulled back the drapery. The light was fading, but it was easy to see the thick snow flying almost horizontally.

"But when did the storm hit? I dinna notice anything before."

"Nor did I, until the wind knocked that volley of snow down on us and we started back from the pond. I had not been attending before, at least not to the weather." He gave her a rueful smile and moved back across the room to her side. He took her arm, guiding her over to a brown-and-gold-striped sofa in front of the blazing fire. "I was too preoccupied with the storm you had stirred in me to pay attention to anything so trivial as a blizzard."

Kate flushed a becoming pink and sat down. For one of the few times in her life she wished she had her needlework. She did not seem to know what to do with her hands. He eased down beside her.

"When we returned to the house, I realized we might be in for trouble. I considered leaving then but was afraid we would be stranded along the way. It would appear my fears were well founded. We would not have had time to get to London before the bulk of the storm hit."

"Then you made a wise decision, Colton."

"Yes, I suppose there was no other choice."

They both sat quietly staring at the fire, each lost in their own thoughts. Kate had mixed emotions about staying the night or possibly more at Twin Rivers. She wanted to be with him, to make their time together last as long as possible. But she was afraid of the power he had over her. A few more kisses like those this afternoon and she would be clay in his hands. If he was determined to attack the fortress, she was not sure she had it in her to make him keep his distance.

If her grandfather learned of her absence and found out she had spent the night at Twin Rivers with the duke, it would be impossible to tell him her true identity, ever. She knew how he loathed misconduct on the part of his servants. She shuddered to imagine what he would think of his granddaughter doing such a thing. A picture of his red, angry face flashed through her mind. Such a scandal might kill him.

Sadly Kate admitted she had let her heart rule over her head, and now she must pay the consequences. She feared the door had been closed forever. There could be no reunion between her grandfather and her father. She had failed Addison, after all.

Tears stung her eyes. For a moment she considered curling up against Colton's chest and giving herself freely. She stopped when she remembered what he would think of her if she did such a thing and reminded herself that she must not willingly sin. The world might paint her a harlot because of her trip to Twin Rivers with him, but if she returned to London with her innocence intact, at least Colton, and God, would know the truth.

The duke did not know what to do. He should be thankful for the storm, for the additional time it provided to entice the beautiful woman sitting beside him. He was distinctly uncomfortable with such dishonorable intentions. He took her hand in his, threading his fingers between hers. She glanced up at him uncertainly, but when he said nothing, she turned back to the fire.

He believed she was willing to follow along and see where their liaison would lead, or that she trusted him implicitly not to harm her. He shifted a bit so he could look at her. She was wearing a blue calico gown, but it was the wrong color blue for her eyes and skin. It went well enough with her hair, but he suspected she had intentionally chosen her wardrobe in the wrong colors in an effort to detract from her beauty. He imagined how wonderful she would be wearing gold brocade or green silk or a soft peach muslin—or much, much less.

He released her hand and jumped up from the sofa to fiddle with the fire. He warned himself to keep a tight rein on his desire, to wait and see how the evening unfolded. He wanted her in a way he had wanted no other woman. That in itself told him she was special, that what he felt for her was out of the ordinary. He threw another log on the fire and knelt on one knee to shift the wood around with the poker. *Am I falling in love? Or is it simply against my principles to corrupt an innocent young woman?*

He stood, resting his hand on the mantle, watching her quietly. She glanced over at the pianoforte in the corner.

"Do you play?"

Kate hesitated, then decided to tell the truth since he had already guessed she was not a maid. "Yes. I'm told it's one of my best talents."

He stepped over in front of her and held out his hand. "Will you serenade me? I don't believe I've ever had a woman play for me alone."

"Yes, Your Grace . . . I mean, Colton. It has been a while, so I may make some mistakes."

"I will not mind. I already know you don't sing off-key." He grinned, remembering the day in his mother's music room. "If only the room weren't so cluttered, we could hum a duet and waltz."

"We shall dance in our minds." *And in our hearts*. Whether he wanted her for a mistress or for his love, she knew his heart was involved, as well as her own. She could see it in the intimate, tender way he had of looking at her at times, as if she were precious to him. She took his hand, rising gracefully, and crossed the room at his side. "Do you play, Colton?"

"Only a trifle. I love music, but singing has proven to be the better choice for me. My fingers and my mind do not communicate well with each other when I'm trying to read the notes."

"I know about that," she said with a laugh. Kate sat down and lovingly ran her fingers over the keys. It was a fine instrument and perfectly in tune. "There are some songs I canna get right no matter how much I practice them."

Colton stood beside her for a few minutes while she played, then he walked back over to the sofa. "Do you mind if I stretch out here? I suppose it isn't very gentlemanly of me, but my feet are sore."

"Go ahead." Kate smiled indulgently. The whole day had been out of the ordinary, so why should the evening be any different? "You try to rest and I'll play for you."

Colton stretched out on the sofa, leaning back against the thickly padded arm at a forty-five-degree angle. He had changed to slippers after dinner, and he thought about taking them off but decided it would be a little crude. Since they were house slippers, he reasoned they could not be too dirty and would not damage the furniture.

Kate played for over an hour, the tunes ranging from Bach and Mozart to a simple children's lullaby. She sang several Scottish ballads, switching to English ones when she experienced a wave of homesickness.

Colton closed his eyes, relaxing and enjoying the music. A tiny smile played across his face as she missed a difficult passage. She grumbled in frustration and started again. He opened one eye to see her expression. Even her little frown of irritation warmed his heart. This time she played the stanza perfectly and her face relaxed. *How nice it would be to spend every evening like this,* he thought.

He continued to listen to the music and allowed himself to dream a little. In his fantasy, the war was over and he was no longer occupied with so many affairs of state. He and Kate were together every day, spending much of their time at Twin Rivers. It was not until he pictured a small, red-haired babe playing on the rug in front of the fire did he realize where his thoughts were leading.

When Kate finally stopped, she believed Colton was asleep. She quietly closed the cover on the pianoforte and tiptoed by him on her way to the door. He reached out and grabbed her hand.

"Thank you. It was beautiful, and I agree with your admirers. You are very talented." He scooted over a few inches toward the back of the sofa and drew her down to sit beside him.

"I'm happy you enjoyed it. I thought I had put you to

sleep." He wound his fingers through hers, gently caressing her palm. Her heartbeat quickened as she sensed his tension. She met his gaze uncertainly.

"I am too aware of your presence to sleep." Seeing the wariness in her eyes, he made up his mind to be strong and not take her innocence. Still, he could not resist kissing her.

"Come here, Kitten," he said softly, pulling gently on her hand. He released it as she leaned forward, resting her hands against his chest. "Closer," he whispered.

He reached up and began to ease the pins from her hair. He pulled them out one by one, then stretched his arm over the back of the sofa and placed the handful of hairpins on the heavy oak table behind them. "I never grow tired of touching your hair," he murmured, bringing his hand back to her, running his fingers through the thick locks.

Kate held her breath. The quick thunder of his heart beneath her palm matched the staccato of her own.

"You're still too far away." He buried his fingers in the hair at the nape of her neck and gently drew her down toward his lips. Don't even touch her, his conscience warned. *Just a little kiss or two.* You're playing with fire. *I can't resist her.*

Kate came willingly. She did not think she had it in her to deny him, or herself. You're courting trouble, a little voice warned. *Just a kiss or two.* You know what he does to you. *I canna help it.*

Colton touched her lips gently, just for a second. With a groan he moved one arm down to her back, pressing her tightly against his chest. The fingers of his other hand gripped the back of her head as her lips opened for him. His mouth moved urgently over hers, caressing, demanding, claiming.

Kate gave him all he asked for and more. She gave him her heart. Willfully. Joyfully. Totally. He broke away from her lips to pepper little kisses along her throat. When he stopped to nibble on her earlobe, she leaned her head forward, covering his face with the curtain of her hair. He dipped the tip of his tongue into her ear and Kate cried out.

Weakness swept over her. The desire flowing between them was enchanting, a sweet intoxication that made her head spin. She eased her head down to rest on his upper arm and shoulder. With exquisite tenderness he cupped her face in his hand, lifting her slightly with his other arm. He touched his lips to her eyelids, to one delicate brow, then the other.

He dropped little kisses across her cheek and down her jaw as his hand moved up her side, evoking a gasp of pleasure from Kate when his fingers brushed the gentle curve of her breast.

"Oh, Colton," she whispered with a sigh. She could not think. She was lost in a world of feeling, wonder, and love. She sought his lips, wanting the beauty of his touch to go on forever, seeking a way to ease the overpowering yearning of her soul.

When she lifted her lips to his, Colton's restraint almost shattered. He needed her, oh, how he needed her, but a part of him, the part that believed in honor and morality and rules of conduct, wanted her to have the integrity to stop him. He hungered for her passion and fire, but, ironically, he wanted her to have morals, too.

Why doesn't she stop me? Don't be a hypocrite, his conscience chided. You shouldn't have put her in this position.

His frustration manifested itself in an almost unbearable need to feel her skin beneath his fingers, a powerful and alarming urge to rip her gown out of the way.

Kate felt his fingers grasp the material on her back as he gathered her gown in each hand. The muscles in his arms were hard and tense as angry strength radiated from him. It penetrated her passionate haze, frightening her. She raised her head to look at him.

"Colton?" She held her breath, watching his face as he fought his frustration. He closed his eyes, his jaw tightening. Finally, his fingers relaxed against her back.

"Your pardon, Kate. I misjudged my limits." His breathing, like hers, was rapid. He moved his arms from around her as she pushed on his chest to sit up.

She had known it would come to this. *Did he plan to seduce me all along?* she wondered. She knew she should not be angry with him, but to her surprise, she discovered it hurt to have him think she would be so loose with her favors. She hesitated to say anything, but she needed to know if he cared for her or if she had just been someone to entice into his bed.

"Are you trying to seduce me?" she asked in a tiny voice.

Driven by his frustrated desire, Colton resisted his conscience and hedged. "Am I succeeding?"

Kate flushed from her throat to her forehead. She was too embarrassed to reply, since he obviously knew he had been succeeding very well.

"Were you planning to offer me *carte blanche*?" she asked.

"Do you want me to?"

Confused and irritated by his reply, Kate scowled at him. Jumping up from the sofa, she paced around the room, biting a fingernail. *Why does he have to be so typical? I thought he was different from the other men of the ton. Do all women fall into two categories, either ladies of quality or whores?* Kate stopped beside the pianoforte and rubbed her forehead, questioning why she should be angry with him. Her actions had not exactly been those of a noble, moral lady. Still, her pride argued, he should have known I am a woman of integrity. He should have believed in me.

He stepped up behind her, gripping her upper arms gently. "You know I would treat you kindly and protect you. You would lack for nothing. Is it what you want, Kate?" His voice was low and urgent.

"No!" She twisted away from him, fighting his magnetism, fighting her treacherous heart that longed for any crumb he would toss her.

"What do you want?" he asked softly. The softness held a thread of menace. His expression had grown hard, and he watched her through narrowed eyes.

"To be happy." Tears sprang to her eyes and burned her nose. She sniffed and blinked hard to keep them back. "And to make you happy. But it canna be. It was wrong of me to come here. I knew it this morning, but I wanted to be with you so badly." She stopped and turned away as tears choked her throat. In a few minutes, she continued. "I'm going back to Scotland as soon as the roads are clear enough. I decided this morning I would give notice when I returned to Lord Blagden's. Then, when you rescued me from those thugs, I couldna bear the thought of going away without some memories of you to treasure in my heart."

"You're not a little girl who dreams of knights in shining

armor," he said harshly. "This is no storybook to open and close at will. Didn't you realize what I would assume when you came out here with me?"

"Yes," she said weakly. "But I thought I could spend the day with you without . . . without . . ." Her face flamed. She lowered her gaze to the floor in shame. She had not wanted to believe how improper and shameful her behavior had been. To lead him on, to act the tease must make her despicable in his eyes.

"Without being ravished?"

She looked up quickly, her eyes wide. "You wouldna have done such a thing." His jaw was clenched, his face immobile, but his eyes burned with anger.

He seethed at the position she had put him in, the position he had put himself in. "I'm only a man, Kate." He turned away, trying to calm down, striving to understand his unreasonable rage. *Don't take your frustration out on her; she's young and naïve. She doesn't realize what she does to you. She doesn't know how close you came to acting like an animal.*

It dawned on him that part of his anger, a large part, was because he had let his baser instincts dictate his actions. He had not lost command of his emotions since he was eighteen years old.

"Colton, you wouldna hurt me. You're a good and honorable man." She stepped up beside him, putting her hand on his arm without thinking. When his gaze shot to her hand, she jerked it away in embarrassment. *He canna even bear for me to touch him!* Pain flooded her heart.

"This good and honorable man came within a heartbeat of tearing the clothes right off your back." His voice was grim and filled with derision. At her gasp he turned to face her. He took a slow, deep breath, running his fingers through his hair in consternation.

Her heart ached to see him appear so weary and disillusioned.

"Kate, you don't know the effect you have on men. You're so beautiful, you make a man ache just to look at you." At her soft blush, he decided she wasn't as naïve as he first thought. His voice grew gentle as his anger ebbed. "Kissing you is like holding a torch to straw." He lifted her chin with his forefinger until she met his gaze. "You're fire, Kitten. Pure and simple. If you kiss other men the way you kissed me, you're going to be hurt. Badly hurt."

"I dunna make it a habit to go around kissing men, Colton Lydell." She raised her chin a notch, lifting it away from his finger. "I've only kissed one other man in my life, and *he* certainly dinna make me act like a wanton." As a tiny, smug smile lifted the corner of his mouth, she rolled her eyes and turned away with a huff of exasperation. She had only been trying to mend her shredded honor, not blurt out that he was the only man to ignite her passion.

She walked over to the fireplace, feeling cold, empty, and very tired. Shivering, she held her hands out to the warmth. Colton immediately followed her and tossed another log on the fire. He stood up, moving behind her. He didn't touch her but only shielded her body from the chill of the room.

"Kate, you don't have to go back to Scotland." He caught one of her hands in his. "I will not trouble you any further. There is no need to run away. You were running from me, weren't you?"

"Yes, partly. And from myself. But you are no' the only reason I must leave." She leaned back against him, unable to stop herself. As she rested her temple against his jaw, he slid his arm around her waist. There was nothing passionate in either of their actions. She sought comfort and security; he gave it.

He held out her hand in front of them, examining the rough, red skin. "I could help you find another position, something more suitable for you. You weren't meant to be a maid, although I'm told you do an excellent job."

"I do?" She was momentarily distracted from her present sorrow, wondering if the compliment came from her grandfather.

"Yes, both Mother and the earl have spoken highly of you and your work. But if they were looking, they would see you are of gentle breeding." He moved his hands to her shoulders and guided her around to face him. "Tell me who you are, Catriona, and what kind of trouble you are in. If I can't help you resolve the problem, then I'll do my best to find you a better position, perhaps as a companion to one of my mother's friends."

Her face reflected her dismay. Such an action would only broaden the scope of her deception, making it more likely her grandfather would be subjected to the ton's ridicule. "No, please, I could no'."

"Why are you so afraid? Who is trying to harm you?"

"No one."

His hands tightened on her shoulders. "Who are you? Why did you say the dancing teacher taught Lady Douglas's daughters when she has only sons? Do you really know her? Did she write that letter to my mother?" He fired the questions so fast, it made her head spin.

Kate's eyes widened in fear. "Yes, I know her. You caught me off guard when you mentioned the dancing teacher. I jumped at the excuse and made up the lie. I couldna tell you my father taught me how to dance because a maid's father wouldna know how to waltz."

"True. Why did Lady Douglas write the recommendation to my mother?"

Kate took a deep breath, trying to think of a way to sidestep the question without him realizing she was being evasive. "I have known her for a long time. She knew I needed to come to London without being recognized, and she knew I would be safe working for Lady Millicent and Lord Blagden."

"Why did you come to London?"

"I canna tell you."

"Why must you go back to Scotland?"

"I canna tell you! Please, Colton, there is no need to worry. I have family in Scotland who will welcome me back." Her voice cracked and she found she could no longer look at him. "They will forgive me for the jumble I've made of things."

"Kate, I care about you. I'm concerned about your welfare." *And I don't think I could bear it if you leave.* "Please, tell me who you are. Whatever has happened, I'll stand by you. I want to help you." He could feel her drawing away, not physically, but emotionally. In desperation, he dug his fingers into her shoulders, trying to keep her close.

"Colton, please, let me go." His grip instantly slackened.

She knew he had not meant to hurt her, yet she was reassured by the gentle caress of his fingers as he tried to erase the pain. "It is better if you never find out who I am."

"We could work together to solve whatever is wrong. Then, perhaps we could begin again, on different terms."

Her heart leaped, but she quickly quelled any thought of meeting him again as his equal. It could never be. She shook her head, tears of sadness welling up in her eyes. "I am the only one who can solve my predicament, and the only solution is to go home." She reached up and lifted his hand from her shoulder, holding it tightly to her heart. "There is no tomorrow for us, my shining knight. There canna be anything more between us, only this day and the joys we have had."

The tears began to slide down her cheeks as she raised his hand to her lips, kissing it lingeringly. She squeezed her eyes tightly shut for a moment. "Ask no more of me, I beg you." She looked up at him, his face wavering through her tears. "Dunna hate me, Colton. I shouldna come here today, but I willna forget these hours with you. In the years to come, remember me once in a while, no' with hatred, but with fondness."

He broke free of her grasp, asking one last time. "Trust me, Kate. Let me help you."

"I can no'."

Colton turned away, struggling to deal with the emotions running rampant through his heart and mind. He had finally found her, this woman who could bring glorious light to the dark, hollow shadows of his soul, but she did not want him. She could not trust him with her troubles. She did not consider him man enough to help her.

It had been many years since rejection of any kind had affected him. He had not been rebuffed by a woman since his salad days; he had never given another the chance until now. *I'd forgotten how much it hurt,* he thought. *No, nothing ever hurt like this.*

Colton straightened and squared his shoulders, gathering his frustration, hurt, and anger, burying them deep inside, beneath the mantle of his pride. His face became cold and hard, his carriage proud and tinged with arrogance as he turned to leave the room.

Kate wept silently as he walked out the door without a glance in her direction. She sank to her knees in despair, burying her face in her hands. Before her eyes the Duke of Ryland had turned into a piece of granite.

Chapter 7

The storm stopped the next afternoon, allowing them to return to London shortly before nightfall. The journey was made in practical silence with only an occasional conversation between the duke and Lunan. Kate sat beside the duke, her misery increasing with every wordless mile. She alternated between grieving over the mistakes she had made and being irritated with Colton because he was so angry with her.

When they were two streets away from Lord Blagden's, Kate handed the muff over the back of the seat to Lunan. Then she unbuttoned the cloak and shrugged out of it. The sleigh hit a bump as she raised up off the seat to pull the fur out from beneath her, and she almost fell off.

"Sit still," commanded the duke, his voice overly harsh.

"I know everyone at Lord Blagden's thinks I'm a strumpet, but I willna arrive looking like your fancy piece." She raised up again and jerked the fur out from under her, throwing it over her shoulder to land in Lunan's face. Out of the corner of her eye, she saw him gather it up and fold it carefully, tucking it down behind the front seat.

Colton's rigid stance grew even stiffer, and a muscle jumped in his jaw as he resisted snapping back at her. He stopped the carriage in front of Lord Blagden's as a footman came rushing out the door. The duke stared straight ahead, determined not to say a word to Kate, expecting the footman to help her down from the sleigh.

However, she scrambled down before the lad could reach her. She rushed into the house, past the curious footman, and without a backward glance at the duke. Once inside, she raced up the stairs, almost knocking Bence on his backside in the process. He called out to her, but she ignored him, desperate to reach her room before she gave in to her tears.

She slammed the bedroom door, dropped her reticule on the floor, and collapsed on the bed, burying her head in the pillow to muffle her sobs. She thought she had cried out her sorrow the night before, but found it had been only a temporary reprieve. To have Colton treat her so coldly, as if she were too despicable to even merit a word or a glance, pushed her pain into a new realm.

How he must hate me! she thought. *I hurt his feelings and his pride, but how could I ask him to help me? None of them must find out who I am. I will have shamed him in front of his mother and grandfather. To compromise a mere maid is one thing, but to bring dishonor upon his stepfather's granddaughter would be another.*

She wiped her eyes and sat up on the side of the bed, noticing that a small fire still lingered on the hearth. Kate pondered her problems for a moment, deciding that as an act of love, she must take all the blame for the scandalous episode upon herself. Perhaps, by doing so, she could keep him from being humiliated. *Indeed*, she thought, *I was the one who enticed him into taking me to the fair and who let him know I wanted to be with him. I could have refused to go to the country, but I dinna*. She shivered and held back the tears that burned her eyes, finally admitting that everyone, especially her parents, would consider her actions brazen.

When Kate removed her pelisse, she realized she had left her hat in the sleigh. "It doesna matter," she murmured wearily. "He'll probably take great delight in smashing it." She smiled sadly, thinking she could not blame him. She had just enough time to smooth her hair before a sharp knock sounded on the door.

"Lady Millicent demands your presence, Kate." Bence's clipped words grew from soft to loud as she opened the door in the middle of his sentence. She had expected a snide comment or demeaning look, but his expression was more of concern as he scanned her white face and red, swollen eyes. He said nothing, motioning with his hand for her to precede him.

Half a mile away, Lunan glared at the back of the duke's head as they made their way toward his town house. "Ain't right to leave the girl to beard the lion alone," grumbled the groom.

"Kate can take care of herself. She made it quite clear she does not need my assistance."

"It still ain't right. Never knew you to be a cad, Your Grace."

"You'd be wise to keep a civil tongue in your head, Lunan." Colton flicked the reins twice, encouraging Snowball to go faster than safety allowed.

"Ain't never known you to put your animals in danger, neither," muttered the groom. "Don't go breakin' a horse's leg just because you had a battle-royal with your light-o'-love."

"She's not my light-o'-love," growled Colton, but he pulled back on the reins, slowing the horse to a reasonable pace.

Although she was trembling inwardly, Kate entered Lady Millicent's sitting room with the grace and dignity of her upbringing. Kate was unaware of it, but the countess immediately noticed the distinct sign of a lady of quality.

Kate was so relieved to find Lady Millicent alone that she easily fell into her role of a maid. Dipping into a deep curtsy, she lowered her eyes in a manner befitting a servant. She straightened, looking down at the lady's hands as they fluttered nervously around in her lap, and waited for the countess to ring a peal over her head.

"Was going to Twin Rivers with my son his idea or yours?"

"His, milady, but I fear I made him think I would be willin' to go with him." She was careful to speak in the thick brogue.

"How? Look at me, child. I want to see if you tell me the truth."

Kate looked up at Lady Millicent, meeting her gaze directly. "I was on my way to the Thames to do a bit of skatin' when some hooligans grabbed me. The duke was drivin' by and saw me fightin' with them." Her face softened, her eyes glowing warmly. "Ye would have been so proud of him, milady. He sent those rounders packin' in a trice. He was goin' to bring me home, but I wanted to see the Frost Faire." Kate could see Lady Millicent was growing impatient.

"He drove by the fair so I could see it, but I wanted to go to it. I asked him to take me since he had ordered me no' to go alone. I wanted him just to escort me, no' pay my way. I had my own money. It took some beggin' but he finally agreed." She glanced uncomfortably down at the floor. The look on Lady Millicent's face was one of complete dismay.

"The Duke of Ryland went to a fair?" she asked, aghast. "The Frost Faire?"

"Aye, milady, and he enjoyed it too," Kate added impulsively.

"And how did you entice him to do such an outlandish thing, young woman? What favors did you promise him?"

Kate raised her chin, again unaware of the startling change it made in her demeanor. "Only to spend the afternoon in his company, nothin' more. He took me to Twin Rivers to skate and meet Mrs. MacCrea so I wouldna be so homesick. I shouldna gone with him, I know, but I had made up my mind to go back to Scotland and knew I wouldna see him again."

Her voice softened, and though she looked at Lady Millicent, the lady knew she was seeing Colton in her mind's eye. "The duke is a very charmin' man, milady. I couldna resist spendin' the afternoon with him."

"My son? Charming?" Lady Millicent's face was filled with astonishment as she rose from her chair.

"Aye, milady. He has a way of makin' me laugh when I least expect it. And he's gentle and kind. He's a good, fine man. We had a nice visit with Mr. and Mrs. MacCrea." She relaxed a little. Lady Millicent was so obviously astounded by this unseen side of her son that Kate hoped she would forget about chastising him or punishing her.

"When he found out Mr. MacCrea had trouble cuttin' wood because he fell on the ice, His Grace went outside and split enough to last them for several days." Lady Millicent sank back down in her chair, her mouth hanging open. "Afterward, he took me skatin' on the pond."

"Skatin'—I mean, skating?" asked the countess weakly. "My son went ice skating with a maid?"

"Aye, milady. He did pretty well too. He only fell once, but he was tired then anyway. He dinna even have enough energy left for a decent snowball fight."

"Snowballs? Oh, dear. Oh, dear! What have you done to him?" Lady Millicent fanned her face with her handkerchief.

Her question reminded Kate of the more painful part of her time with Colton, sobering her. She poured the countess a cup of tea from the silver tray nearby and set it on the table beside her. Kneeling in front of the countess, she drew the lady's gaze once again.

Kate smiled sadly. "For a little while, I gave him laughter and the joy of bein' alive." Her eyes misted with tears. "But I hurt him, too, milady. I did him a great disservice. I dinna mean to, but I let him believe I was . . . was willin' to give him more than I could. Please, dunna lay any blame on him for what has happened. I take full responsibility for my actions."

Lady Millicent straightened, studying Kate's face carefully. The countess was often a little flighty, but she was very intelligent and usually a good judge of character. When Kate entered the room she had realized that the young woman had been pretending these past several months. *This gel is no more a servant than I am,* she thought. It eased her mind to know Colton had not been captivated by a common maid.

"Look at me, child." When Kate looked up, the light caught the impact of her turquoise eyes, giving Lady Millicent a sudden revelation. She had seen those very eyes before, staring at her from Elizabeth Denley's picture on the earl's study wall. Several different trains of thought rushed through the countess's mind. Her son was not the only one capable of split-second decisions when the need arose. She decided to deal with the current problem and see how the others worked themselves out.

Of one thing she was almost certain. Kate MacArthur, or whatever she really was called, was the earl's granddaughter. She'd wager a Season's new wardrobe on it. The countess resolved to say nothing to the chit at the moment, but she was not about to let her leave for Scotland without finding out the truth. She wanted to know precisely why she had come to work in Lord Blagden's house. She felt the young woman was not after money. If she were, she would not be so quick to take the blame for going to Twin Rivers, nor would she be planning on returning to Scotland.

She had another suspicion. This one she decided to pursue. "So you do not think I should place any of the blame for such scandalous conduct on my son's head?"

"No, milady," said Kate, frowning a little in her earnestness. She blushed as she remembered some of the things that had transpired between them. "He only acted as any man would have under the circumstances. Please, the fault is mine and mine alone."

Just as I thought; the girl is in love with him! A vision of half a dozen little red-headed grandchildren popped into Lady Millicent's mind, and she almost laughed out loud in delight. If Colton was so taken with the girl as to risk a possible scandal, no doubt children would start coming as fast as they could make them. Lady Millicent surprised Kate by reaching out and taking her hand.

"You sound to me like a young woman in love," she said kindly.

Kate gasped and looked down at her knees. "It would be pure foolishness for a maid to fall in love with a duke, milady."

"Yes, that is true. It is equally ludicrous to think my son might become enamored with a mere maid, no matter how lovely the chit might be." She released Kate's hand and leaned back in the chair, talking sadly, as if to herself. Kate looked up at her, listening in fascination.

"Colton is such an uncaring, unreachable man," said the countess. "If he ever does marry, it will be to some plain little mouse who doesn't make him tongue-tied. She'll probably be a bluestocking, and they'll spend their time discussing Greek mythology or something else equally useless. She'll be content to stay in the country and come to town once in a blue moon."

She sighed heavily. "I'll be fortunate if I ever get any grandchildren. Two cold fish don't make much of a spark." Lady Millicent shook her head sadly, blinking her eyes quickly as if she were about to cry. "I doubt if there's a drop of passionate blood in him. Sometimes, I'm so disappointed in him."

Completely taken in by Lady Millicent's playacting, Kate

was quick to defend the man she loved. "Oh, milady, but you're wrong! He's warm and caring, and can be very passionate." She dropped her gaze, blushing profusely when she realized what she had said.

Lady Millicent sat up alertly. She wondered if the girl realized the thick brogue had disappeared completely with her impassioned cry. "Oh?" Her eyes narrowed and her voice became very serious. "Are you telling me I might have a grandchild after all?"

"Oh, no, milady!" Kate scrambled to her feet. "We did nothing to . . . that is, nothing like that happened."

"Are you certain, my dear?" Lady Millicent stood, watching Kate's beet-red face carefully. "If you find you are breeding, I will want to know immediately. I will give the child a grandmother's love and make certain my son provides well for you and the baby."

"There will be no baby, milady. Things . . . things dinna go that far."

"Very well. When do you plan to leave for Scotland? I would like a few weeks to find a replacement."

"I had meant to give two weeks' notice, if you would let me stay that long. I may have to stay longer if the weather doesna clear." Kate bit her lip, then asked hesitantly, "Does his lordship know I went to Twin Rivers with the duke? I know he has rules against such things. Is he very angry with me?"

"The earl does not know." Relief flooded Kate's face, reenforcing Lady Millicent's earlier suspicion that she was Thomas's granddaughter. "Colton asked me not to tell him and I followed his wishes, although I thought about doing otherwise when you did not return last evening. I realized, however, that more than likely you had been caught by the storm." *Either Colton wasn't paying attention to the weather or he hadn't planned to come back until today,* she thought. She frowned. *It wasn't like Colton to lie to her.*

"His Grace intended to come back as he said, but we were having such a nice visit with Mr. and Mrs. MacCrea that we dinna notice the storm. I'm sorry if we caused you to worry, milady."

"I wasn't worried about your safety, my dear. Colton would never jeopardize others by taking them out in a storm. I knew even if you ran into bad weather after you started, he would either go back to Twin Rivers or stop at an inn along the way. Now, you go along to your room. I'll have Nell bring you up a tray. You look as if you've been awake for days.

"There will be no punishment for you, Kate, at least none that I will administer. I suspect your own troubled heart will be punishment enough. I gave Nell another chance after her debacle with Blake. You deserve one, too, especially since my own son was involved. You know not to do such a thing again?"

"Yes, milady."

The countess dismissed the young woman with a wave of her hand. As Kate neared the door, she spoke softly, but just loudly enough for Kate to hear. "It is unfortunate you are not a lady of quality, my dear. It is a rare woman who can see the finer side of my son's nature, and still an even rarer one who can bring out his passion."

Kate paused at the door, wondering whether to turn around or not. Out of the corner of her eye, she could see Lady Millicent cross over to the corner of the room and lift the lid on a pot of potpourri.

"You have such beautiful eyes, my dear," murmured the countess. "I've seldom seen such a unique turquoise color." Lady Millicent picked a book from her new revolving bookcase and sat down near the fire, apparently finished with the discussion.

Kate left the room and slowly walked up the stairs, her heart fluttering and her mind racing a mile a minute. *Does she know? Or is my imagination running away from me?* Exhausted, she dropped down on her bed and pulled the blanket up over her. She was so tired she did not even take off her boots.

Kate had only been gone a minute when Lady Millicent rang for Bence. He appeared at the doorway quickly. "Yes, milady?"

"Send a message to my son. I require his presence here immediately," she said, closing the book with a snap and setting it on the rosewood cabinet nearby.

"There is no need to send a message, milady. His Grace is waiting below. He arrived a few minutes ago, but I did not think you would want me to show him up until you had finished your interview with Kate."

"Quite so. Summon him now. We are not to be disturbed, unless the house is on fire or some other dire emergency arises."

"Yes, milady." The butler bowed and left the room.

When Colton came through the door five minutes later, carrying a woman's worn hat in his hands, Lady Millicent decided she had never seen him more aloof and unreadable. *Either he doesn't care a fig for the gel*, she thought, *or he is extremely ashamed of himself*. What a position for the proud Duke of Ryland! For a moment, she felt sorry for him, then decided a little dose of embarrassment and shame might put a dent in that overbearing Ryland pride.

She met his ice with spirit, raking her gaze over his country attire. She doubted if he had even gone all the way home before his conscience convicted him. It pleased her to see that he was not capable of leaving Kate to bear the burden of reprimand alone.

"I see you still have some honor left," she shot at him. "Or did you think that by leaving Kate here to face me alone, you would be exonerated?"

"I did not," said Colton stiffly, tossing Kate's hat on the yellow marble top of the rosewood cabinet. He stopped briefly in front of the fire. His mother's attack was unexpected. Somewhere in the back of his mind, it occurred to him that she must feel more secure since she had remarried. The possibility that she had been afraid to speak her mind before troubled him.

"I am very angry with her," he added. "I let my anger cloud my judgment." He forced himself to sit down instead of pacing around the room as he would have preferred.

"How unlike you, Colton."

"This whole affair is unlike me, is it not?" Colton's jaw twitched as a surge of self-directed disgust and anger raced through him. He had opened his heart to Kate, given her a peek at his soul but she had thrown it all in his face. "Did you dismiss her?"

"No, I did not." She caught the brief flicker of surprise in his eyes. "She has given notice. She plans to return to Scotland. That is sufficient."

Colton drew in a slow, painful breath. *So, she truly is going to leave,* he thought. He was unprepared for how much the confirmation hurt. "When is she leaving?" He tried to sound disinterested, but knew he was not completely successful.

"She will stay for two weeks, longer if the roads are not clear by then. I could not turn her out in this weather with no place to go and no references." Lady Millicent rose from her chair and walked across the room, replacing her book on the shelf. She spun around, watching her son through narrowed eyes. "Do you know she took all the blame upon herself, claiming you to be as pure as the fresh fallen snow?"

Surprise registered on his face for a second before he effectively wiped away the expression. *Why would she do that?* Colton broke away from his mother's gaze and stared at the fire, considering her words. He came to the conclusion that Kate had taken the blame upon herself because she had decided it would sit better with Lady Millicent if she did not malign the lady's son. He would not believe it was because of any feelings Kate held for him. He could not, for if he did, it would open the door to hope.

"No, I did not know what she would do." He looked back at his mother as she returned to her lavender wing chair and sat down. "She had made it clear, however, that she did not want my help on other matters. In my anger, I decided she would not welcome my help in this one." He shifted slightly, crossing his legs so that the calf of one rested on the knee of the other. "Needless to say, the fault is not hers alone. I am also to blame, probably more so."

"Yes, you are," snapped his mother. *If you've soiled my Thomas's only grandchild, you'll do right by her.* "She is young and inexperienced in the ways of the world. If you deflowered that girl, Colton Lydell, you'll marry her!"

The duke stared at his mother in total astonishment. "Doing it a little too brown, aren't you, Mother?"

"Do you know who she is?"

"No. Do you?" Colton tensed. He would be unreasonably angry if Kate had confessed her identity to his mother when she refused to do so to him.

"No, but I know she's quality. I don't know why she's hiding all that breeding under the charade of a maid, but she let her disguise slip enough that I know she certainly isn't who she says she is." Lady Millicent leaned back in her chair, suddenly weary of the whole thing. "I'll ask you once, Colton, and I want the truth. Did you have your way with that girl?"

"No, Mother, I did not." Colton remained calm, although his mother's unaccustomed direct approach made him uneasy. *Thomas's ways are rubbing off on her,* he thought. His eyes narrowed. "Did she tell you I did?" he asked with deadly softness.

"No, she did not. She assured me things did not go that far. She was much quicker to defend you than herself, Colton. She strikes me as a young woman of rare integrity."

Colton made no comment about Kate's character. He was still puzzling over why his mother was so adamant about marriage if the girl had been dishonored. If she were a member of the ton, then marriage would be the most noble way of handling the situation, but not necessarily the only one.

"I offered Kate my assistance. She made it perfectly clear she did not want it."

Lady Millicent snorted. "What did you offer her? The high honor of being your mistress?"

"I offered to help her in whatever way I could," Colton answered stiffly, guessing what Kate must have told his mother. He flushed slightly in embarrassment. "She is in some kind of peril; otherwise, she would not have run away from Scotland. However, she obviously does not believe I am the man to conquer her foe. She was quite adamant that there can be nothing between us, Mother."

For a brief instant, Lady Millicent glimpsed the pain in her son's eyes, and her heart went out to him. It was also apparent that his pride had been sorely wounded by Kate's rejection. The countess shook her head. Hurt feelings would mend and could eventually be set aside, but to a Ryland, a blow to the pride was an unforgivable offense.

"Go home, son," she said wearily. "I am tired from thinking about this mess you've made. Thomas had dinner at his club and will be returning anytime now. I would just as soon you not be here when he arrives."

"Am I so out of favor, Mother?" Colton's voice and expression were totally devoid of warmth.

"I have very mixed feelings about you at this moment, Colton. I am sorely disappointed in your behavior, but then such actions are more tolerated by your peers than your mama. I cannot fault you for being attracted to the girl, and I can only hope that when we find out who she truly is, you are not shamed beyond measure.

"I suspect you knew, or had good reason to believe, she was a lady of quality before you took her to Twin Rivers. If that is the case, then your actions are beyond the pale. If she is a daughter of the ton, no matter how remote, you will have brought dishonor to your name as well as hers.

"Now, go, son, before Thomas gets home. I'll not have him asking nosy questions about why you're still in your country clothes."

"Does he know Kate went to the country with me?" Colton rose from his chair. He did not want Thomas to know about the trip to Twin Rivers, even though he knew the man would not find fault with him for going. It surprised him to discover that he still felt protective of Kate, even though he was angry with her.

"No, I did as you asked. I did not tell him. I don't believe he even noticed the girl was away from the house. That is why I want you to leave. I will not tell him an out-and-out lie. If he starts asking questions, I will be obligated to answer."

"I understand. Unless you need me, Mother, I will not be visiting for the next few weeks. It would be better for both Kate and I if we did not chance to see each other. Of course, if the weather drags on, I will not stay away too long. That is, if I will be welcomed."

"You are always welcome, son." Lady Millicent smiled up at him. "Even when I'm irritated with you, I'm happy to see you. I can always arrange to have Kate working in the other wing when you call." *I can arrange it*, she thought, *but I won't. It might do you both good to see each other again once you've cooled off.*

Colton dropped a brief kiss on his mother's cheek and left the room. It did not occur to him until he reached the sleigh that he had been listening intently for the sound of Kate's voice all the way down the hall.

* * *

That same evening in Edinburgh, Addison Denley, Kate's father, buttoned up his heavy greatcoat and bade his companions a good evening. Addison stepped out into the icy night, pleased with the financial negotiations that had transpired over the evening meal at his club. Usually, he held such dealings at home, with the gentlemen discussing the business matters over port after the meal. However, Myrna was recovering from a cold, and he did not think she was up to entertaining.

He glanced at the clear sky, admiring the stars that peeked past the occasional street lamp. Since the weather was clear, he had chosen to walk the short distance from the club to his home.

As he turned the corner, a tall, rough-looking character stepped out in front of him, effectively blocking his path. He heard the crunch of snow behind him and glanced over his shoulder. Two large men sprang from the shadows of a wall and grabbed his arms. Addison struggled, but he was no match for their strength. He called for help, but the first man took a quick step and struck him in the face with his fist.

"We got a present for ye, Denley."

Agony shot through him, and he cried out as the man buried a knife in his side. Addison gasped for breath, bracing himself for what was to come. He looked up at his attacker's face and felt the knife twist. From the nasty grin on the man's face, he knew he planned to slit him open like some dead animal. The assailant began to move the knife, and Addison moaned in pain and lost consciousness.

"What's going on there!"

The attacker quickly looked up at the three gentlemen running down the street and halted the movement of his knife.

"Release that man!" One of the men whipped off the outer casing from his cane, revealing a sword.

The attacker jerked the knife from Addison's body as the two accomplices released his arms, letting him crumple to the ground. Before the gentlemen could reach them, the others had faded into the darkness.

Colin MacAllister knelt in the bloodstained snow beside his unconscious friend. His fingers trembling, he felt for Addison's pulse. "He's alive!" Jerking off his scarf, he quickly folded it into a pad and pressed it against Addison's side. "For the love of heaven," he moaned as the flowing blood soaked through to his hand.

His companions tore their scarfs off, too, using one for a pad and one to wrap tightly around Addison's waist to hold the compress in place. "Peter, run ahead and tell Myrna we're coming. It's the sixth house down. Then go for the doctor."

MacAllister and the other man lifted Addison to a sitting position, then put his arms across their shoulders, hoisting him up as they stood. His feet dragged in the snow, but it was the quickest way they could get him to his house.

Peter met them a short distance from the Denley home, followed by four footmen. They quickly took over the job of carrying him, lifting him by his shoulders and legs. Peter ran down the street to the doctor's house.

Addison's wife, Myrna, waited by the front door. "Oh, dear God!" She took one look at Addison's white face, then rushed after the footmen as they carried him upstairs to his bedroom. One of the maids scurried in with an armload of bandages; another followed with a bucket of hot water.

Myrna worked quickly, removing the scarfs and applying fresh bandages. She had the footmen carefully lift him, removing his coat, then his boots. By the time the doctor had arrived, she had changed the dressings several times, cut away his shirt and pants and had him covered with several layers of blankets.

The doctor hurried up the stairs, complimented Myrna on the way she had slowed the blood loss, then promptly banned her from the room. "Your husband is unconscious, madam, so he willna feel it when I stitch up the wound. You go and rest a few minutes. You're going to have a long night ahead of you."

Reluctantly, Myrna went downstairs to the drawing room where the three gentlemen waited. MacAllister came to her side as she stepped through the door. He had been a friend of the Denley's for over twenty years. Like Addison, he was fiercely loyal to both Scotland and England. He also worked for the Duke of Ryland, although he had been more involved than his friend, occasionally making trips to the Continent at the duke's request.

"How is he?" asked MacAllister, taking her hand.

"I dunna know. We slowed the bleeding before the doctor arrived, but he lost so much blood anyway. He's still unconscious." Her eyes filled with tears. "It is such a deep and nasty wound. Colin, why would anyone try to kill Addison? It doesna make any sense."

"I canna think of any reason either, except mayhap robbery. Most every other night of late has been stormy. The footpads may be gettin' desperate."

They sat downstairs, making small talk, waiting for the doctor to come down. It took him almost an hour, an hour that seemed like an eternity to Myrna and her friends.

"It is a bad wound, Mrs. Denley," said the doctor, taking a glass of brandy from Colin. "But I was able to stitch everything up clean. We can be thankful it is winter. His heavy coat kept the blade from going so deep that I couldna repair the damage. There was no harm done to any of the organs." He nodded his agreement as Myrna breathed a prayer of thanks.

"There will be some bleeding yet, but it shouldna be much and should stop soon. The main worry now is infection. I'll come back on the morrow and check it. Keep him warm. I've left some laudanum. If he wakes, you can give him a dose. He'll need it for several days."

"Will he recover, Doctor?"

"Canna tell at this point. It could go either way. But I've known Addison Denley for fifteen years. He's a strong man and he's got a lot to live for. He'll fight, Mrs. Denley, and sometimes that makes all the difference."

The doctor left, along with MacAllister's companions. He stayed a few more minutes, after peeking in on Addison. When he arrived at his home, he roused two of his hardiest men. They had worked with him on assignments from the duke and could be trusted.

"You've got to take a trip to London town, lads." He quickly explained what happened, instructing his men to take a message to the Duke of Ryland. He wrote a letter to Colton, but also told the men the basics of the message in case the letter was lost along the way.

"His Grace needs to know what happened. He may decide to come, I dunna know. If he does, there's no need for you to return with him. You'll be at the end of your ropes, so stay a few weeks in the city before you start back." He handed them the letter and a supply of money. "Get through as fast as you can, lads. I dunna know how long Denley will last."

The men left immediately, thankful for the bright moon overhead, but wishing the roads were not still covered with ice and snow. MacAllister had them take a coach, so they could trade off driving and sleeping. It would be a hard journey and a long time before they slept in a warm bed.

Myrna sat up all night with her husband, making sure he was warm, comforting him in the moments when he briefly regained consciousness. The doctor came the next morning and proclaimed his patient to be holding his own. After he left, Myrna rang for the butler.

"Send Rory and John for Catriona." She gave the butler the address and a letter she had composed during the night for Kate. She had tried to ease the blow but found there was no gentle way to say that Addison might be dying. Finally she simply explained what had happened, told her what the doctor said, and begged her to return immediately.

"If you can, dearest daughter, make peace with your grandfather before you leave. Tell him about Addison and beg him to come with you. Assure him we dunna care about the money or the title, but that his son needs his forgiveness before he stands before God." Tears stained the paper. "I canna bear the thought of his dying with bitterness still lying like an open sore between father and son. Bring your grandfather with you, Catriona, and come quickly."

Chapter 8

Colton walked slowly up the staircase to see his mother. Bence had confirmed that the earl was home, but Colton wanted his mother with him when he told Lord Blagden of Addison's injuries. Colin MacAllister's letter weighed heavily in his pocket and on his heart. It had taken the Scotsmen ten days to travel from Edinburgh to London to bring him the news of the attack on Addison. Anything could have happened to him in those ten days.

The duke had not decided whether to go to Edinburgh or await further news. Foreign Secretary Castlereagh was in Switzerland, setting up a congress with the Allies. There was hope Napoleon would send an emissary and that a settlement to the war could be negotiated. Colton needed to stay in London to make judgments on any information that came in from his men and to forward anything vital on to Castlereagh.

As he neared his mother's sitting room, he decided his loyalty to his mother and Thomas must come first. There were other men working with him who could make good judgments about the war. He was not vain enough to believe himself completely indispensable. If Lord Blagden decided to go to Edinburgh, Colton would not let them go alone.

A soft, musical laugh drifted out of the sitting room, stopping him in his tracks. He eased forward until he had a clear view through the open door. If the young woman had been dressed fashionably, the scene might have appeared to be one played out many times in Mayfair drawing rooms—a young lady of the ton paying a late-afternoon call upon the countess, entertaining her with a witty story. However, this particular young woman wore a maid's uniform and a frilly white mobcap on her head.

Kate sat at an angle to the door as she chatted with Lady Millicent. Since her return from Twin Rivers, this was the third time the countess had asked her to join her in the sitting room, simply to talk. Lady Millicent did not have her normal number of callers due to the icy weather, and Kate assumed the lady was simply lonely.

"Lady Douglas should have boxed her son's ears, but she only laughed." Kate's voice softened. "She's a fine lady." *And a dear friend.*

"Yes, she is, and a dear friend. I've known her for over forty years. We had our come out together." Lady Millicent's gaze grew distant as she reminisced for a moment.

Colton watched Kate's every move, soaking up the sight of her. He frowned. She was pale, with dark half circles beneath her eyes. Her merriment seemed forced, her laughter quick but somehow hollow. For a brief moment, he wondered if she had been as miserable as he had since their day at Twin Rivers. The thought only served to remind him of his pain and the reason behind it.

He told himself that if she was unhappy, she deserved it. It was her own doing. She was the one who had rejected his offer of help—and him. For the past week and a half, Colton had buried himself in his work, driving himself to the point of exhaustion in an effort to keep her out of his mind. Still, she haunted his dreams.

Lady Millicent's wistful smile faded when she noticed the duke hovering outside the door. "Colton, dear. Do come in."

Kate jumped to her feet, almost dropping her teacup. She practically threw it on the table, hoping no one noticed how much it rattled when she set it down. "I'll be about my duties, milady," she murmured. Lady Millicent nodded, dismissing her.

Kate hurried toward the door, keeping her gaze lowered. *I willna look at him. I willna look at him.* As his boots came into her line of vision, her pace slowed and she lifted her gaze to his face. She instantly regretted it.

He met her look directly, but his eyes were cold and cynical. "You're keeping rather exalted company, aren't you, little maid?" His voice was low and quiet so his mother would not hear. "Be careful with your games." The subtle menace in his tone caused her to hold her breath. "Remember, you'll answer to me."

Kate straightened, lifting her chin defiantly. The pain of seeing him again was shoved aside by resentment and anger at his overbearing manner. Sparks snapped in her eyes. "Dunna threaten me, you arrogant poppinjay," she said under her breath. "If your mother enjoys my company, then she'll have it." She rushed from the room, not giving the duke a chance to rebuke her. She scurried down the hall and hid in the music room until she could regain her composure.

Colton looked across the room, meeting his mother's amused gaze. "I like that gel," said Lady Millicent with a chuckle. "She has spirit. Too bad she's not a member of society. She'd run you a merry race."

"Only if I chased her," snarled the duke. "And I have absolutely no inclination of doing so."

"Of course, my dear," said the countess, her voice placating. She patted the cushion beside her, smiling sweetly as Colton sat down next to her on the settee. "Now, what brings you out tonight?"

"Bad news, Mother." Colton's anger faded. His expression turned grim. "Addison has been gravely wounded."

"What happened?"

Colton quickly told his mother what he knew. "I understand Thomas is downstairs in his office. Will you go down with me to tell him?"

"Of course, dear." Lady Millicent rose, her mind filled with worry for Addison and about the earl's reaction to the news. "I'm not sure how he will take it. He seems to hate his son so very much."

"Still, we must tell him." Colton rose and offered his mother his arm.

"Yes, of course. How did you find out?"

"Addison has sent the Cabinet information over the years,

little things that sometimes turned out to be very important. On occasion, the information passed through me. We have a mutual acquaintance who sent me the message of the attack. He is a good friend of Addison's and knows you and Thomas were recently married. He thought I might best serve as the one to break the news."

"How kind." Lady Millicent hesitated. "Colton, you know I've never pried into your work for the government. I've always felt it better not to know exactly what you do for the War Office. However, it would seem to me that if Addison helped the English government, the rumor about him being a French spy is ludicrous."

"Completely. You'll not find any man more loyal to England. He has served his country well."

"Well, I never believed for a minute he was a traitor, but the rumor was troubling because it upset Thomas so. It does set my mind at ease to hear you reaffirm his innocence. Thomas may not be as easy to convince, however."

"I will do my best to reason with him," he said as they walked out into the hallway.

Kate opened the door of the music room, her initial anger and hurt finally calmed. She peeked out the doorway and saw Colton and Lady Millicent walking toward her. She ducked back inside, leaving the door open a crack so she would know when they passed.

"I hope we can persuade Thomas to go to Edinburgh," said the countess as they hurried by. "He desperately needs to make peace with his son. I'm afraid it will destroy him if Addison were to die before we can get there."

Kate gasped, hugging her back to the wall of the music room. She pressed her fist against her lips to keep from crying out. *Papa dying? No, dear God, it canna be!* Fear thundered in her heart and set her body to trembling. Cautiously, she pulled open the door and discreetly followed Colton and the countess down the stairs. When they entered the earl's office, closing the door behind them, Kate raced across the hall and put her ear to the door.

"Colton, my boy. Good to see you." Lord Blagden's booming voice was accompanied by a wide smile. "It's been far too long since you dropped by. Keeping you busy at the

War Office, eh? Heard anything more about the peace talks?"

"Castlereagh is having some success in setting up a meeting. If all goes as planned, the allies will open the Congress of Châtillon in early February." Colton's expression grew somber. He took a deep breath and glanced at his mother. "Thomas, I fear I am the bearer of bad news."

"What? Has something happened to Richard? I was too rough on that nephew of mine last time he was here. Regretted it ever since."

Colton noticed a glimmer of fear in the old man's eyes and caught the nervous fidgeting of his fingers. *He knows. He knows it's Addison, and he cares.* "No, as far as I am aware, Richard is well. It's Addison." Colton's voice grew even softer, even kinder. "Your son has been gravely wounded."

Terror shot across the old man's face, just a flicker, but Colton caught it. "I have no son! My son has long been dead to me!" blustered the earl. He raised a trembling hand to his throat and tugged unconsciously at his already loosened cravat.

"Thomas, don't," pleaded the countess gently. "He may die. Please don't turn your back on him now. We should go to Scotland right away."

"Did that strumpet of his send you to me?" He glared at Colton. "If she did, it's all a lie. They just want to get back in my good graces, that's all. That's all it is. Just a story. Just a ruse to get me to forgive him."

"No, Thomas. Addison's wife did not send me the message. It came from a mutual friend. A man I trust completely. He would have no reason to lie. Addison was attacked and stabbed one evening after dining at his club. He had decided to walk home and was accosted only a short distance from the club. It happened ten days ago. When the messenger left, the doctor did not know whether Addison would live or die."

The earl turned away from the others in an attempt to hide his feelings. Pain, anguish, and guilt poured over him like suffocating ash from a funeral pyre. Addison had been on his mind a great deal for the past two weeks—since his discussion with Colton had brought back memories of Leonore. For the first time, he had forced himself to consider his part in Elizabeth's despair. If she had not found out about his Cit mistress, perhaps she would not have been so outraged when Addison brought home a Cit wife.

He did not like the conclusions he had drawn. It was much harder to accept his own guilt than to blame someone else, even his son. Now, it was probably too late. Heartbreak and self-condemnation overwhelmed him. *I should have made peace with him years ago. Now, it's too late. Too late!* For a moment, the earl thought he would collapse under the weight of his sin and pain.

He struggled with the burden, feeling too old and too tired to bear it. In desperation, he took refuge in the habit of twenty years. It was easier to fall back into bitterness against his son, easier to blame him for all that had happened, easier to hate him than to face up to his own wretchedness.

"I won't go to Scotland," said the earl, turning back to look at his wife.

"Thomas, please, you must," she pleaded as tears welled up in her light brown eyes.

A leaf on the wooden panel left its imprint on Kate's cheek as she pressed her ear to the office door. She cursed her thundering heart for blocking out all but the loudest sounds. She had learned nothing more of her father's condition or what had happened to him.

"I will not go to Scotland," the earl boomed. "I was right to send him away. He broke his mother's heart and sent her to an early grave. Now, he's a spy, a traitor. I want nothing to do with him."

"Thomas!" Lady Millicent clamped her hand over her mouth in shock and shame.

"I assure you, my lord, your son is not a spy for France. Nor is he a traitor to England. Far from it."

Distraught, the earl didn't seem to hear him. "He's no good, I tell you. He's a traitor and he deserves to die!" he shouted.

Unable to bear such talk about her father, Kate threw open the door and burst into the room. "No! He would never betray England! Never! He has always worked for England's victory. He's no' a traitor, I tell you!"

Three stunned faces turned to stare at her, but Kate did not notice their surprise. Hot tears poured down her cheeks. She trembled so badly she had to grab the edge of the desk to stand.

Looking at Colton, she begged in a tiny, broken voice, "Tell me what happened to my father, please."

The duke glanced from those sorrowful turquoise eyes to the matching ones in Elizabeth's picture and everything fell into place. He quickly stepped around the desk and put his hand to her back to steady her.

"He was attacked ten days ago near his club. He was stabbed, Kate, and is badly injured. MacAllister and some of his friends chased the attackers away and took him home. MacAllister sent me a message, but it took his men ten days to reach us. I have no further word."

"W-What did the doctor say?"

"He said it could go either way. He was encouraged by your father's strong constitution and his will to live."

She looked up at him, his face blurred through her tears. "Where was he stabbed?" she whispered.

"Here." Colton held his hand to his left side, moving it several inches toward the center of his belly.

"Oh, my God!" Kate covered her face with her hands.

"Thankfully, his heavy coat prevented damage to the organs. The doctor was able to stitch everything up and said his main concern was infection." Colton reacted to the circumstances. He gave no thought to what had happened between them. At the moment, she was only someone for whom he cared deeply, and she was hurting. He put his arm around her and drew her head against his shoulder.

It took a moment for the earl to come out of his shock, but when he did, it was at a full roar. "Look at me, girl."

Kate dropped her hands, swallowed hard, and raised her head to meet her grandfather's gaze squarely. His thick gray eyebrows drew together in the center of his forehead in a horrible frown. His brows naturally slanted upward on the outer edge and, at that moment, he seemed like some wrathful, mythical god.

Thomas looked directly at his granddaughter's face for the first time. All he could see were her eyes—Elizabeth's eyes, Addison's eyes. Years of anger, frustration, and pain swelled to the surface; anger at Addison for disappointing his mother, anger at Elizabeth for driving the earl to disinherit his son.

Kate braced herself as the old man took a deep breath. An explosion was imminent.

"What are you doing spying on me? Did you think you would find some deep, dark secret to use against Millie and me? Something you could use to force us to take Addison back as my heir?"

"No, Grandfath—"

"What's wrong? Is my son tired of being a commoner? Did he decide, after all these years, that he wanted to be an earl when I'm gone? Or is it that scheming, conniving mother of yours? Does she want to be a countess?"

"No, Grandfather, please. You dunna understand." The earl put both hands on his desk and leaned toward her. Kate winced and felt Colton's arm tighten.

"Or did you spy on us out of your own selfish motives, gel?" roared the earl. "Did you think you could persuade me to present you to society so you could snare a rich, titled husband? You, with your pretty face and saucy ways. And, if that didn't work, were you prepared to go to any length to capture a husband—such as pretending to sleepwalk and wind up in the duke's room? Did you enjoy making a fool out of my stepson, missy? Well, speak up, what do you have to say for yourself?"

Kate squared her shoulders, gently shrugging off Colton's hand. "Grandfather, I dinna come to England for any of those reasons. I wanted to see you, to get to know what you were like. Papa wanted me to see if you were happily married. He only wanted to know if you were happy."

"Balderdash!"

"It's true! I did want to find a way to reconcile you and Papa, but no' because of any money or the title. Papa is a rich man in his own right. He wants there to be peace between you. He loves you. He only wanted your forgiveness."

"No! No, you lie. You spied on us. You deceived us. You wormed your way into my Millie's heart just to get to me, just to get the title back, or snare a duke for a husband. I can see what you're about. You're nothing but a conniving, deceptive little strumpet." The earl's face had grown almost purple in his rage. The countess moved to his side and put her hand on his arm.

"Thomas, please calm yourself. You mustn't get so angry."

"This is my house and I'll do what I want!" He glared at Kate. "Leave this house. I don't want to see your lying face again. Get out! Get out!"

Trembling, Kate turned away, crossing slowly toward the door. Her grandfather was enraged beyond all reason. She was afraid to try to talk to him again, fearful of what might happen to him if she persisted. She walked through the door with dignity, but once out of the others' sight, she flew up the stairs.

She made it halfway up the third-floor staircase before collapsing in a sobbing heap. A few minutes later, a gentle hand gripped her shoulder.

"Kate, don't punish yourself." Colton sat down next to her and gathered her in his arms. He cradled her head against his chest, letting her weep, and whispering soothing words in an effort to comfort her. "Let it out, Kate. Let go of the pain." He pulled the mobcap off her head and stroked her hair gently, hoping his touch would calm her.

"I failed Papa," she cried brokenly. "I failed them both. Now my grandfather will never forgive my father, and it's all because of my mad scheme." She cried harder, sobbing, "Oh, Colton, I canna bear it if Papa has died. Tell me he isna dead, please."

"I can't, Kitten. God knows how much I wish I could." His voice was filled with anguish as his arms tightened around her.

She cried awhile longer, until her heartache settled into a dull hurt and her panic subsided. She pushed a little on his chest and he released her. As she sat up, she dried her eyes on her apron. "Are the mail coaches running? I have to get home."

"I don't know if they are, but I sincerely doubt it. It took ten days for MacAllister's men to get to London. I don't think the Mail would even try such a trip yet." He made a quick, firm decision. "Kate, I'm going to go see about your father. If you want, I'll take you with me. I will be leaving in about an hour. Can you be ready?"

"Yes. But why are you going?"

Because you need me. "Let's just say I have an interest in your father's welfare that goes beyond family ties. He has worked for me on occasion."

Kate's eyes widened slightly. "You're 'the duke'?" she whispered. "The one my father sometimes sent information to?"

He nodded and touched his finger to her lips. "But no one else must know, understand? I'm going to tell Thomas the truth so he won't think Addison is a French spy, but for everyone's safety, it must be a family secret. If the war were not so close to an end, I wouldn't even speak of it now."

"I understand. I willna breathe a word. And I'll be ready. I dunna have a lot to pack."

"It will be a difficult journey."

"I know, but I must reach my father. Thank you, Colton." She reached down and self-consciously squeezed his hand. "I would be lost if you dinna help me."

"I suspect Mother would have found some way to get you home. She's been exercising a stronger side of her nature of late." He smiled ruefully. "I think your grandfather's directness is rubbing off on her."

Kate drew back her hand, wishing she felt at ease with him. Even though he had been nothing but kind and offered her help far beyond what she had hoped for, she felt an inexplicable reserve settling over him.

"I'll be back in an hour or so." He stood abruptly and trotted down the stairs, leaving Kate to stare after him in bewilderment.

Colton had briefly forgotten her rejection at Twin Rivers, but it had come crashing back unexpectedly into his mind while they talked. *No wonder she had not wanted him to know who she was,* he thought. Before he had been uncomfortable and more than a trifle embarrassed by the way he had treated her. He had known she was a woman of quality, yet he tried to seduce her and let her believe he wanted her for his mistress. That had been bad enough, but now, he was completely humiliated and thoroughly disgusted with himself.

The woman he had chased, lured, almost seduced, and seriously considered making his mistress was his stepfather's granddaughter. His actions, even his feelings and intentions, put him beyond the pale. Colton felt like an utter fool. He would be a laughingstock if anyone ever found out. He was not sure how he would face the earl, but knew he must. He had to convince Thomas that his son was not a traitor.

When Colton tapped softly on the earl's office door, his mother called quietly for him to enter. Lady Millicent had managed to calm her husband, but she had not been able to ease his hurt or dissolve his anger in such a short time. He sat slumped in his favorite chair, a glass of brandy in his hand.

The earl looked up at Colton as he entered the room. "Well, my boy, she made ninnyhammers out of all of us."

"Yes, my lord, I suppose she did." Colton appeared completely calm and indifferent to the circumstances. "Thomas, I want you to understand that Addison is not a French spy. You must not repeat what I tell you to anyone until the war is over, but I want you to know. Addison has served England well all these years. He has been our eyes and ears in Edinburgh. On several occasions, he has supplied us with information that was vital to our country's well-being. He is as much an English patriot as you or me."

The earl blinked at him in surprise, then cleared his throat, and took another drink of brandy. He turned his face toward the fire. "I'm glad he's not a traitor," he said gruffly. "But I still don't forgive him for what he did years ago. And I especially don't forgive him for sending that chit here to spy on us. I don't know what she's up to, but it was a contemptible way to go about it."

He looked back at Colton. "She made a royal dunderhead out of you, boy. Sent you wandering around here like some moonstruck buck. It's a good thing you never took her away for a few days like we talked about. Wouldn't that o' taken the cake if you tried to set her up as your piece of muslin!" The earl laughed disdainfully.

In spite of his efforts, Colton felt his face flood with color. He glanced at his mother, only to receive her most reproachful look. He felt like a complete idiot, embarrassed, humiliated, ridiculed.

"I shall return in an hour, Mother. Then I am going to Scotland to see about Addison's welfare." The earl and the countess both looked at him in surprise. "He is, after all, one of my men, and even more important, my stepbrother. I need to discover if this was a simple robbery attempt or if there is more behind it." He turned on his heel and walked to the door, where he stopped and looked back at them. "I will be taking Kate to her family. There is no place for her to go and no other way for her to return to Scotland."

A muscle twitched in his jaw as his mouth tightened. When he spoke, his voice was emotionless. "We will all fare better without her presence here."

Half an hour later, Kate came downstairs. She had changed into a forest green merino day dress. The soft, twilled wool glided over her curves gracefully from the high ruffled collar to the ankle-length skirt. The high waist was gathered beneath her bosom and accented with a pale green ribbon, as were the edges of the long sleeves. Although her long, flowing hair was unfashionable, she much preferred it loose than pulled up in a knot. Also, the heavy mass around her neck kept her warmer.

"My dear, how lovely you look." Lady Millicent stopped Kate in the hallway.

"Thank you, milady. I dinna bring many nice things with me." Kate shifted awkwardly. "Lady Millicent, please forgive me for deceiving you. I meant no harm, truly I dinna."

"I know, dear. And your grandfather will come to realize it as time goes by. I'm curious. Did you conclude that he was happily married?"

"Oh, yes. He dotes on you, milady. It's plain for all to see. I think you've made him very happy." Kate glanced down at the small coffer in her hands. The oak chest, about two feet long, with arched panels and delicately carved flowers, had been handed down from one generation of Denley's to the next since the reign of Queen Elizabeth.

It contained half a lifetime of letters, over two hundred and sixty of them, separated in twenty-two neatly tied bundles. She held them out to Lady Millicent. "Father wrote to the earl every month since he moved away. After the first several ones were returned unopened, he dinna mail them anymore, but he kept writing. He thought I might be able to give them to Grandfather."

"Yes, I think you should." The countess refrained from taking them. "He's still in his office. Why don't you go in and talk to him?"

"Oh, I couldna! I would only anger him again and I canna stand to do that. Will you give them to him?"

"No, my dear. This is something you must do. His wrath is spent. I don't believe he will break your eardrums this time. Stand your ground, but be gentle. He is dealing with many unwelcome feelings at this moment."

"Yes, milady." Kate took a shaky breath. "I dunna know if I have enough courage."

"Of course you do. You're a Denley, aren't you?"

Kate smiled. "Aye, for all my mistakes, I'm a Denley."

"I think everyone in the family has made their share of mistakes, Kate. This whole situation has been one big hodge-podge." Lady Millicent frowned. "I am upset by Thomas's reaction to your presence and your father's injuries, but I suppose I can understand why he feels the way he does. I wish I could have gagged him, however, the last time he talked with Colton."

"Why?" Kate frowned slightly. The countess seemed exceedingly irritated.

"He pointed out how addlepated Colton has been in regard to you. You know how direct your grandfather is. I'm sure he did it without thinking, but to ridicule Colton over his behavior is like a slap in the face. Of course, Thomas does not know you both went to Twin Rivers. I shudder to think what he would have said if he had been aware of it."

"Poor Colton. Was he terribly embarrassed?"

"Humiliated is more the word for it. I've never seen my son blush until this evening." Lady Millicent grimaced. "I fear his pride has been irretrievably wounded. You are in for a miserable trip, gel, and it won't just be from the cold weather. Colton can be daunting when he chooses. Indeed, until he met you, it was his normal demeanor. He has enough arrogance for ten men, thanks to his father. I curse that deuced Ryland pride!"

"Perhaps in time he will forgive me. I can only hope so, milady, for I do care for him greatly."

"I know you do, child, but he is as stubborn a man as you'll ever meet. Now, Kate, take those letters in to your grandfather. Colton will be here shortly, and it won't do to keep him waiting."

Kate nodded and carefully opened the office door. She stepped inside and closed the door behind her. Other than the blazing fire, only one brace of candles lit the room. The earl sat near the fireplace, his face shadowed by the wing-backed chair.

"Grandfather, may I speak with you?"

Silence.

Kate hesitated, then crossed the room quietly. She stopped a little in front and to the side of his chair. He stared straight ahead at the fire. She set the coffer on the floor and knelt near the earl's feet, looking up at him intently.

"Grandfather, I've come to beg your forgiveness, both for me and for my father. It was wrong for me to deceive you. I realized that soon after I arrived, but I dinna know how to get myself out of it. I dinna want to make you angry. I only wanted to see if you were happy. Like a silly child, I thought somehow I might find a way to get you and Papa talking again."

The earl did not speak, nor move so much as a finger. It was as if he were made of stone. Kate had the fleeting thought that if a rock is hit hard enough, it will shatter. *Lord, I dunna want to break him,* she thought in anguish, *but give me a little crack for love to pour in.*

"Grandfather, please dunna blame Papa for my ruse. It was all my idea. Papa is a loving father, but sometimes he gives in to my whims too much. He only wanted to know what Lady Millicent was like and if you were happy in your marriage. He has only spoken kindly of you all these years."

She opened the small chest and picked up a bundle of letters, holding them out toward the earl. "See, he has written you ever since he left England. There's a letter here for almost every month, twenty-two years' worth. He quit mailing them after the first ones were returned, but he kept on writing them. He always said someday you two would be reconciled, and you'd want to know what happened in his life. I dunna know what is in them, but I expect he wanted to share both his joys and his sorrows." Her eyes misted over. "He's had a good life with my mother, but there have been sad times, too."

When the earl still did not move, she drew back her hand and lovingly placed the letters with the others. Defeat and dejection filled her soul. Kate pushed herself to her feet, and picked up the coffer, placing it on the earl's desk. In one last effort, she raised the lid, leaving the letters in plain view.

"Please forgive us, Grandfather," she said softly. "Please go to Scotland and make peace with your son. He loves you so very much. He has missed you so badly all these years." Her voice cracked. "Please go to him. Dunna let him die without knowing you forgive him and love him."

With a heavy heart Kate crossed the room to the door. Just as her hand touched the door handle, the earl cleared his throat. She looked back at him. His fingers fluttered on the arm of the chair, but he did not look at her.

"Godspeed, child." His made a choking sound in his throat, cleared it, and took a deep breath. "Tell my son I will pray for his recovery. I wish him well."

Kate's heart leaped with joy. "Thank you," she whispered. She wanted to run to him but sensed he would be embarrassed by any display of affection at that delicate moment. Instead, she opened the door quietly and slipped out into the hall, closing the door once again after her.

When the earl heard the door click shut, he turned his head and let his gaze fall on the familiar old chest. Memories of the day he had passed it on came rushing back, poignant and bittersweet. The expression on Addison's face lingered still—pride, love, and a touch of humility, for the coffer had been given to each Denley heir on the day he reached his majority.

It had been a gift to the first earl by Queen Elizabeth as a token of her trust, and for over two hundred years it had represented the same token between father and son. The earl took a deep breath, releasing the air in a faltering sigh.

"Addison, my son!" His whisper was filled with anguish. In the dimly lit room, alone and brokenhearted, he reached for the letters with a quivering hand.

Chapter 9

Lady Millicent leaned over the back of her husband's chair and rested her chin on the top of his head. He reached up and took her hand, bringing it to his lips in a gentle kiss.

"Are you coming to bed, my love?" She brushed a thick, gray lock of hair from his forehead and planted a kiss there. "I know it's only half past ten, but it's been a draining evening."

"Yes it has, but no, I'm going to stay up a while longer. I need to think." His wrath had been spent, and it was as if some of his bitterness had dissipated, too. He felt tired but somehow mellowed, more at peace with himself than he had been in a long time. He tapped the ribbon-encircled bundle of letters on his lap. He found himself anxious to read them. "I need to take a look at these. Has Colton left?"

"Yes, about fifteen minutes ago." Lady Millicent straightened and moved around the side of the chair to sit in another one right beside it. She kept Thomas's hand firmly clasped in hers. "Kate is gone, too," she said softly.

The earl nodded curtly. "I don't suppose the chit meant any harm, but her spying on us don't sit well with me. Just plain rubs against the grain."

"I don't think it sat well with her, either." Lady Millicent's brow wrinkled delicately. "Thomas, I must confess I suspected who she was a week ago."

"What? Why didn't you mention it?"

"I wasn't sure and I didn't want to upset you needlessly. She let down her guard and let her upbringing show through. I first guessed she wasn't a typical maid, then it struck me how much she looked like Elizabeth. Their eyes are identical."

"Exactly. Addison has his mother's eyes, too. You should have said something to me, Millie." The earl's voice was stern.

"I suppose I should have, but I simply went with my instincts. She had just told me she was leaving and was quite upset. It didn't seem like the appropriate time to confront her. I had no intention of letting her leave for Scotland without getting to the bottom of it, though, I assure you."

The earl nodded grumpily; his thick brows furrowed in a frown. "Do you think she really would have just gone back to Scotland and never said anything about who she was?"

"Yes, I do. I've spent some time with her this week, chatting for a while in the evenings before I came down to join you in the library. She is a very intelligent girl, and I think by nature a very honest one. I believe she came here on impulse, positive as only the young can be that she could find some way to draw you and Addison together. Her charade proved very difficult for her. Oh, she was a good enough actress when she remembered the role, but at times of stress or in moments of deep feeling, the thick brogue would fly out the window. On several occasions, I saw her transform from a lowly maid into a lady of quality in the blink of an eye."

"Humph. She always played the part well enough when I was around." To his surprise, the earl was irritated that he had never noticed anything about her to lead him to believe she was other than a maid. "Suppose she knew I'd recognize her the minute I saw her eyes. By Jupiter, I've never received such a shock in my life as when I looked at her tonight. I suppose I was much too rough on her," he muttered.

"Yes, you were, but we all understood, even Kate. Bitterness doesn't just evaporate. It takes time to work these things out." Lady Millicent hesitated, wondering how much she could safely tell him about Kate and the duke. "Thomas, there's one other complication Kate had not bargained on."

"Colton?" he guessed. "How can there be anything between them when they've only seen each other a few times?" A look of horror crossed his face. "Good Lord, he didn't seduce her, did he?" He shook his head in bewilderment and added weakly, "He was so enamored with her, I told him to take her someplace and try to persuade her to become his light-o'-love."

Lady Millicent effectively hid her shock and decided a partial truth would be better than the whole one in this instance. "No, there was no seduction, but they did spend some time together. Kate got it into her head to go skating on the Thames. She borrowed some skates and headed off toward the river."

"By herself?" The earl was aghast.

"Yes." Lady Millicent shook her head. "Edinburgh must be a different city from London. The gel didn't think anyone would take notice of her since she was all bundled up in her old clothes. But she was accosted by three ruffians just past Carlton House. Thankfully, Colton was leaving the War Office and heard the commotion. He went to her rescue and saved her from a terrible tragedy."

"Thank God." The earl felt an inordinate sense of concern for her welfare. In the back of his mind, a little voice suggested that he already was beginning to think of her as his granddaughter.

"I suspect he was like a knight riding up on a white charger to the girl. We had already seen how enchanted Colton was with her. I've never known him to react to another woman with even a semblance of the interest he showed in her. At any rate, she persuaded him to take her to the Frost Faire on the Thames."

The earl's mouth dropped open. "Colton?"

"Colton. And, from what Kate says, he enjoyed himself immensely." Lady Millicent took a deep breath. "I believe the gel has fallen in love with him, Thomas."

The earl moved the letters to the desk and got up to throw more coal on the fire. When he had it blazing to his satisfaction, he sat back down and looked over at his wife.

"And what of Colton?"

"I don't know. As you said, he is or at least was greatly enamored with her. She didn't come right out and say it, but I believe he did offer her *carte blanche*. She refused, and he, no doubt, got his feelings hurt." She frowned, rubbing her front teeth over the tip of her fingernail. "I'm certain he has known for some time she was a lady of quality. I talked with him after their adventure on the ice. I got the impression that when she refused to be his mistress, he offered to help her in any other way he could.

"He was anxious to know if she had revealed to me who she was. Obviously, she had not told him, and it irked him beyond measure. You know Colton. He's so capable and so used to being in command of every situation. I fear that some people lead him to believe he is practically God."

"And of course Kate could not see her way to tell him who she was or how to help her. Oh, my." The earl leaned his head back on the chair, closing his eyes. After a minute he opened them and looked at Lady Millicent. "If he truly does care for her, it is deuced important to him for her to believe he can right any wrong or handle any problem."

The countess nodded mournfully. "I fear his pride has suffered quite a blow." Her expression cheered. "But he did go after her this evening when you sent her out of the room. He looked like a man intent on offering comfort."

"Aye, but when he returned, he wasn't happy. I didn't help matters any by mocking him," the earl said in disgust.

"Now, dear, you were still angry. You didn't mean any harm."

"I'm realizing that far too much harm can be done without meaning to, my dear." He picked up the letters and untied the ribbon. "Run along to bed, Millie. I want to see what my son has to say to me."

Lady Millicent kissed him tenderly and made him promise to keep warm. Tired, but with the hope of an optimist, she went to bed.

Lord Blagden sat up the rest of the night. Addison's first letters were filled not only with remorse for hurting his parents, but also with expressions of love for Myrna. His sadness at having the letters returned unopened showed up in the next ones. By the fifth he simply stated that he would no longer mail them but would keep them for his father in the hope that someday he would want them.

The earl read on, weeping at his son's grief over the death of

Elizabeth. The guilt over not allowing him home during her illness or to attend the funeral was like a knife slicing out his heart. Three months after his mother was buried, Addison joyfully proclaimed the birth of a daughter, Catriona, whom he had promptly nicknamed Kate. She was a healthy, happy baby. Six months later, he mentioned that she had the Denley eyes.

The earl read on, month after month, year after year. He read of business successes and a few failures, then mostly of successes again. When Kate was two, Addison shared his grief over the death of his infant son. The child was born prematurely and died ten hours after birth. Thomas wept again.

Throughout the night the earl read. As a rule, the letters were interesting, oftentimes witty. His son sprang to life, focusing Thomas's memory on his expressions and mannerisms. He remembered them all—the way he smiled, the tiny frown when he was thoughtful, the sparkle in his eyes when he was up to mischief, the sincerity there when he was serious about something.

But throughout the letters, through all the years, three things stood out. Addison loved his wife with a love few men ever attain. He doted on his daughter, often spending much of the letter telling of her escapades. But mainly it came to the earl over and over again how very much his son loved him.

Thomas Denley, eighth Earl of Blagden, leaned forward in his chair and buried his face in his hands, his elbows resting on his knees. In despair, he cried out to his loving God from the depths of his soul. "Please let him forgive me. Don't let me be too late!"

A short while later, just as dawn decorated the wispy clouds in the sky, the earl brushed a kiss across his wife's cheek. "Wake up, my love," he said quietly. "We're going to Scotland."

It took Colton and his party eight days to reach Edinburgh. To Kate's surprise and Lady Millicent's gratitude, he had brought along one of his maids to act as abigail and chaperon for Kate. The girl was in her early twenties, with a cheerful personality and strong constitution. Although the trip was grueling, she never made a complaint.

Kate was also surprised to learn that the duke had left

Gregory at home and brought John Pemberton instead. The duke's only comment about the waterman was that he could handle a team well and that on this venture, a strong back was more important than a perfectly tied cravat.

Lunan and the regular coachman, Jonesy, made up the rest of the group. Lunan, Jonesy, and Pemberton took the reins in two-hour shifts, with the duke filling in a few times a day. The coach was crowded, as only the one driving rode up top in the snowy weather, but the close quarters also served to keep them warmer. The duke had brought along plenty of furs and lap robes, but a few times Kate thought her nose would freeze anyway.

They traveled as much as possible each day, sometimes for twenty hours. The horses were changed approximately every five miles; otherwise they stopped only long enough for meals and a four- to six-hour rest each night. They encountered few actual snowstorms, but the roads were still heavily covered with snow and ice for most of the way.

At first Kate had hoped Colton was only distracted by the preparations for the journey, but it soon became clear that he was still very unhappy with her. He was formally polite, never unkind, never spoke a harsh or angry word to her; however, when she looked into those beautiful cinnamon eyes, there was nary a spark of interest or warmth. They were a brick wall, blocking her from his feelings, shutting her out of his life.

She ached to see him smile, to have him take her hand and offer a word of encouragement or comfort. But he did not. She did not try to break through his icy barrier. She told herself that if they had been alone, she might have tried to reach him, to apologize for all that had happened. Since there was not a chance for a private word during the whole trip, however, she made no effort.

Miserably, she believed she deserved the cold shoulder. At least he did not snap and snarl and regale her in front of the others. She had planned to leave London before the duke had the power to hurt her too deeply, but as the days wore on, she realized he had held that power from the first time he smiled at her. She wondered why a broken heart should hurt so badly and questioned whether she would ever recover.

Then, because she was a kindhearted soul by nature, she

wondered if his pain was as great. The thought that she might have crushed his growing love by her rejection at Twin Rivers filled her with profound sorrow.

Colton was not oblivious to the gulf between them; he felt it deeply. For one of the few times in his life, however, he was out of his element. He tried not to think of his hurt and humiliation, but since there was little else to do on the journey but think, it nagged at him day and night.

The earl's words came back to him, over and over, mocking him. *Royal dunderhead. Moonstruck buck.* He felt a fresh stab of anguish every time he thought about how he had run after Kate like some schoolboy to offer his comfort. That she accepted his solace and help this time only slightly mollified his wounded pride.

He reminded himself that she had said there could never be anything between them. On this point, they were agreed. Although his actions had been foolish, he did not take the blame upon himself for his hurt. She had deceived him not only with her disguise, but also by pretending to hold deep affection for him. Apparently she did not care for him as deeply as he cared for her, since she had out and out rejected him.

She had not trusted him enough to share her secret. Somehow, that hurt worst of all. He gathered his wounded pride and held it up like a shield, hiding his true feelings from himself as well as from the others. He silently justified his actions, telling himself he would not have treated her like a strumpet if she had not acted like one.

It was early evening when the carriage pulled up in front of Addison's Edinburgh home. Kate looked out the window, searching fearfully for signs of mourning. With a relieved smile, she closed her eyes and said a silent prayer of thanksgiving when she saw nothing.

Colton watched her out of the corner of his eye and was filled with such intense longing that he thought it must be visible to everyone else. He jerked his hat further down on his head. *You're better off without her, Lydell. She'd only cause you more grief.*

When he stepped out of the carriage and turned to help her

down, however, he could not refrain from giving her a tiny, encouraging smile.

"Oh, Colton, I'm still afraid." Exhaustion, fear, and the spark of hope generated by that little smile, set her to trembling.

The duke tucked her hand through the crook of his arm and covered it with his own. Squeezing gently, he said quietly, "Courage, Kate. At least, we know he still lives."

She nodded and took a deep, bracing breath as they started up the steps. The door was flung open, and two footmen hurried out.

"Welcome home, Miss Catriona!" The two young men stepped aside and bowed respectfully to Kate and the duke. As Kate entered the hallway, her mother scurried down the stairs.

"My bonnie lass, it is you!" Myrna swept Kate into her arms. For a few minutes, they stood there, sharing hugs, kisses, and tears.

"How's father?" Kate's worried eyes searched her mother's face.

"Good. He is weak and healing slowly, but the doctor says he will recover completely."

"Thank God!"

"I have." Her mother smiled tenderly. "Many, many times. Take off your hat and coat, and I'll let you go up and see him in a minute. He was asleep, but with all the racket, I'm sure he's awake now. Now, tell me, lass, who is this handsome gentleman you've brought with you?"

Kate blushed and turned to Colton. "Your pardon, Your Grace. Mother, may I present the Duke of Ryland. Your Grace, my mother, Mrs. Myrna Denley."

"It is a pleasure to meet you, madam. I am greatly relieved to hear that Addison is doing well. I assume MacAllister told you he was advising me of the attack."

"Yes, he did, but it never occurred to me that you would come all this way to check on him. I am overwhelmed by your generosity, Your Grace."

Colton shook his head. "Thank you, but generosity did not play a large part of it, I'm afraid. I am naturally concerned when one of my men is injured, but also in this instance, I felt

I should come as a representative of the family. And, of course, Kate needed a way to Edinburgh."

He glanced at Kate, feeling a little smug to see her startled look. It felt good to take *her* by surprise for a change.

"I am very grateful. Here, let's get you in by the fire." She turned briefly to the butler. "Oswald, have Cook prepare a quick meal. And make sure the duke's men are well fed and cared for." Myrna turned to the maid who had accompanied Kate. "If you'll follow Oswald into the kitchen, lass, we'll get you taken care of, too. You look like you're ready to drop."

"Yes, madam." The butler took their coats, then hurried away toward the kitchen with the maid following stiffly along behind him.

"Go up and see your father, dear, while I offer the duke something to drink." Myrna looked up at Colton. "You dunna mind waiting a bit to see him, do you?"

"Of course not. Kate should have some time alone with him first."

Kate shot him a grateful smile and hurried up the stairs as Myrna led the duke down the hall to a cozy back parlor. Outside her parents' bedroom door, Kate hesitated. She took a deep, bracing breath and opened the door quietly. A young maid hopped up from a chair near the bed, grinning from ear to ear. She left the room, closing the door softly behind her.

"Who is it, Bess?" Addison's voice was quiet but strong.

"It's me, Papa." Kate stepped up beside the bed, grasping the hand her father held up to her.

"Ah, lass, you're a sight for sore eyes."

"So are you," she said with a smile. Kate bent down and kissed his pale cheek. "How do you feel?"

"Like someone tried to cut out my liver." Addison grinned. "Thankfully, he was stopped before he could accomplish the feat."

"Do you hurt terribly?" Kate pulled the chair next to the bed and sat down, taking her father's hand once again.

"It's no picnic, but it's been worse. I even sat up in the chair a little while today. The doctor hasn't given his approval, but your mother and I decided it couldn't hurt. I thought I'd rot if I stayed another minute in this bed." He glanced at the closed door. "Did your grandfather bring you?"

"No." Kate shook her head, her expression regretful. "The Duke of Ryland brought me."

"The duke? I knew MacAllister sent word to him, but I never thought he would be the one to come."

"I think he felt someone should represent the family, and of course he was concerned since you work for him." Seeing her father's look of surprise, she continued, "He told me the night we found out about your injuries. It was his way of explaining why he was coming to Edinburgh."

"Did you make any headway with Father?"

"I think so." Kate broke away from her father's gaze and looked down at the coverlet. She picked at a loose embroidery thread. "I willna tell you the whole story now because it is long and would tire you. I hadna found a way to tell him who I was. Then I overheard Colton and Lady Millicent talking and learned you were badly hurt." She paused, her forehead wrinkling in a frown, then went on. "I listened at the library door when they went down to tell Grandfather, but I couldna hear anything. Finally, I couldna stand it anymore so I just barged into the room, begging the duke to tell me how you were."

She shook her head, grinning ruefully at her father. "It wasna the best way to break the news to Grandfather that I was your daughter."

He smiled back. "Did the windows rattle?"

"Aye." Her face grew serious. "He was very angry because he felt I had been spying on them. And, in truth, I suppose that's exactly what I was doing. But I went back down later and gave him the letters and tried to explain why I was there. I told him you loved him and only wanted his forgiveness. He dinna say a word until I started to leave. Then he bade me Godspeed and told me to tell you that he wishes you well and that he is praying for you. The duke and I left a few minutes later."

Addison closed his eyes and sighed softly, but his lips were curved in a smile. "He'll come around. He's really a kind man. He just keeps it buried beneath his bluster." He opened his eyes and looked up at her. "Did you have any problems in London? You came to no harm?"

The first thought that ran through Kate's mind was how

close she came to giving herself to Colton. In spite of her efforts, she blushed.

"Kate? What happened?" Her father frowned, studying the delicate pink of her cheeks. "Did some young buck try to force himself on you?"

"Well, Cousin Blake found me cleaning one day and made some lurid suggestions, but when I threatened to scream my head off, he let me go. He dinna harm me, Papa. And of course he dinna know who I was."

"I'll plant him a facer. I never have liked that scoundrel." Addison's free hand clenched into a fist.

"Now, Papa, you and who else? You're in no shape even to think such a thing. No harm was done, and he dinna have the slightest idea I was your daughter. I never saw him again afterward." She quickly decided the time was not right to tell him about Colton. "You look tired, and I'm starving. Shall I have the duke wait until after dinner to come up and see you?"

"Yes, please. Tell him I need a little nap so my mind will work again." Addison smiled and released her hand as she stood. "I'm glad you're home, Kate. We've missed you."

"I missed you, too, Papa. It was an interesting experience, but I got terribly homesick." She bent over and kissed his forehead, then left him to his nap.

Kate joined her mother and the duke in the parlor. Colton peered over his wineglass as she entered the room, searching her face for any sign of distress.

"How is he?" he asked gently, standing politely until she was seated.

"No' as bad as I was afraid he would be." Kate smiled at him, heartened by his concern. Reservation and wariness still hovered in his eyes, but at least they did not chill her soul. "He would like to take a wee nap before you go up to see him. He thought you might like to eat dinner first."

"Of course I'll let him rest. I'm anxious to get to the bottom of this whole affair, but I can't do much tonight anyway."

"Catriona, dinna Rory and John deliver my letter?" Myrna held out the decanter of wine to Kate, but she declined with a shake of her head.

"No, they hadna arrived before we left." Her face reflected

her concern as she looked over at Colton. "I hope they dinna have any trouble."

"I suspect if anything bad had happened, we would have heard about it on the way. Seems like the proprietor of every inn had horror stories to tell about those who had been stranded in the snow." Colton took another sip of his wine, pleased to see that the color was returning to Kate's face. Then he sternly reminded himself that he should not care whether she looked pale or not.

"MacAllister's men left as soon as the doctor had tended to Addison. I'm afraid I dinna have my wits together enough to send my men after Catriona until the next morning," said Myrna. She turned her attention to the duke. "Did you leave London soon after they arrived?"

"Yes, we did. It was only a few hours, in fact. I suspect your men reached Lord Blagden's the next day. I did not think we should delay, since we only knew Addison's condition was grave."

"Do you think your grandfather will come, Kate? I've pried what information I could out of His Grace. Lord Blagden dinna find out your identity in the best of ways, did he?"

"No, he dinna." She glanced at Colton, wondering how much he had told her mother. "He thought I was spying on him so we could blackmail him."

"So I understand. I know how your grandfather can be when he's angry. I've seen his wrath in action." Myrna gave her daughter a tiny, compassionate smile. "I know it wasna easy for you, lass."

"It wasna long after I started working for Grandfather that I realized the mistake of my charade. I couldna think of any way to tell him who I was without hurting him." She glanced at Colton. *Or you.*

The duke held his breath. The profound sorrow in her eyes gave him pause. *Is she speaking of me, too?* he wondered. *Does she really care whether she hurt me?*

Kate looked quickly back at her mother, realizing Myrna sensed the tension between her daughter and the duke. "I had already told Lady Millicent that I would be leaving as soon as the roads were passable. I had decided no' to reveal my identity to anyone. I suppose it was the cowardly way out, but it seemed my only choice." Unable to help herself, she looked apologetically at Colton. "I never meant to hurt anyone," she murmured.

The duke searched her eyes intently, wanting to believe there was more to her words than just a general apology. Mildly rattled, Kate broke away from his gaze.

"Once I overheard an argument between Grandfather and Richard about Father. I wasna intentionally listening, but everyone in the house could hear it." She shuddered. "There was so much hatred in Grandfather's voice. It made me afraid he would never forgive Papa. Then, the longer I stayed there, and the longer the deception went on, I dinna think he would ever forgive me either."

Again her gaze went to Colton, but she forced herself not to look away. "Your Grace, why did Grandfather think Papa was a French spy?"

"A French spy?" Myrna was so astonished the words came out in a whisper.

"It has been a rumor going around the ton for the last month or so. I have done my best, discreetly, of course, to quell it. Thankfully, there are few people in town this time of year. Most have simply taken my word that he is innocent. I am not sure why the rumor was started, but I have my suspicions."

Colton had traced the story back to Blake Denley, although he could not prove it had originated with him. He had not confronted the man, knowing he would only deny it. He suspected Blake used the rumor to further damage Addison in the earl's eyes, but he was not sure what he hoped to gain. With three people ahead of him in line for the title, it did not seem to be a likely goal. Still, it was troubling, and not a thought Colton could easily put out of his mind.

"I convinced Lord Blagden that Addison was not working with the French, but to do so, I had to explain about his dealings with me. I don't believe it did any harm. The earl would never put his son or you in jeopardy, no matter how angry or bitter he is."

"Thank you, Your Grace." Myrna looked at Kate. "Were you able to convince him that Addison doesna care about the title or the inheritance?"

"I think so." Kate saw a brief look of surprise move across

Colton's face. "At first, he was so angry I couldna talk to him, but I went back down later to see if Lady Millicent would give him Father's letters. She refused to give them to him." Seeing her mother's look of distress, Kate added quickly, "She wasna angry with me. She thought I should take them into him myself.

"I dunna think I've ever been so nervous in all my life as when I stepped into that room. He dinna move a muscle the whole time I talked to him. I asked his forgiveness for deceiving him and told him how much Papa loves him. I begged him to come to Scotland to make peace with Papa. Then I left the letters on the desk and started to leave."

"Did he stop you?" Myrna leaned forward slightly, her expression anxious.

"Yes." Kate's eyes misted over and she blinked hard. "He bade me Godspeed and told me to tell Father that he would be praying for him. He also said he wished him well."

"Thank the Lord!" Myrna clapped her hands in joy. Turning to Colton, she asked excitedly, "Do you think they will come?"

Colton nodded slowly. He was pleased to hear Kate had made some headway with Lord Blagden, but he did not like the thought of his mother and Thomas trying to make the journey on the icy roads. "I suspect they might, especially if he read Addison's letters. Were there several?"

"Yes, over two hundred." Myrna and Kate laughed at his startled expression. "Addison has written him almost every month since we've been married. He mailed the first ones, but when they were returned unopened, he just kept the rest. He always held the hope that someday his father would want to read them. I think they were something like a journal."

"I'm impressed." Colton shifted slightly, crossing his legs at the ankles. "Few men would have cared enough to write so often even if they were on good terms with their fathers. Thomas is fortunate to have so thoughtful a son."

"Thank you. I think so, too." Myrna grinned impishly, giving Colton a clue as to where Kate got her fun-loving nature. "He tends to be a bit too serious and arrogant at times, but we manage to keep him from becoming too full of himself, dunna we, dear?"

Kate squirmed, very conscious of the serious, arrogant man sitting across from her. She started to murmur some trivial reply and move the conversation onto safer ground, but just then she caught the sardonic lift of the duke's brow. Her smile held a trace of challenge. "Aye. The frogs around here have an uncanny knack for finding their way into his desk."

"We've found various ways to trick him into going on a picnic or fishing when he becomes too grouchy."

Kate laughed. "And, if that doesna get him off his high horse, Mama just might push him in the pond!"

Myrna grinned, though her face turned red in embarrassment. "Now, Kate, we dunna need to tell all of our secrets." She caught the amused twinkle in Colton's eye. "Well, I've only done it once." She faked a thoughtful frown. "Or maybe it was twice."

Colton laughed, thinking how much Myrna reminded him of her daughter. For a second or two, he let down his shield and allowed his warm, affectionate gaze to sweep over Kate. Her sparkling eyes and laughing countenance filled him with sweet pleasure.

She caught her breath. How she had longed to see that look in his eye again! She was afraid she had imagined it, but quickly decided the thrill that swept from her head to her toes would not have come from imagination. She knew she had not been forgiven all her transgressions, for the tenderness was too fleeting, the expression replacing it too unreadable.

But it brought her hope. In that split second, Kate made up her mind never to give up on the Duke of Ryland. She would win his love and forgiveness no matter how long, or what it took.

Oswald tapped quietly on the doorjamb. "Cook has dinner ready, madam."

"Good. If you dunna mind, Your Grace, I'll go up and peek in on Addison. You and Kate go ahead and eat. I had my dinner earlier, but I'll join you in a few minutes." She hesitated at the duke's slight frown. "Oswald will serve you. It just occurred to me that you dinna bring a valet. I will send Addison's man to unpack your things and prepare a bath for later if you wish."

"Thank you. I would greatly appreciate it. I felt it more

important to bring an extra driver than to put Gregory out of sorts." He smiled, giving Myrna a hint of that devastating dimple. "He is not fond of traveling in the winter. We would have heard his complaints all the way here. He has a sharp tongue on occasion, but he's a good man."

He glanced at Kate, remembering his valet's sharpness with her when Gregory thought she was slow in making the bed. She had come to him that night, if only in her sleep. He had not forgotten the wondrous feeling of her body next to his, the softness of her lips. An intense wave of longing swept over him.

Kate remembered Gregory's sharp tongue, too. As she met Colton's gaze, she knew he was thinking of that night, which seemed a lifetime ago. A light flared in his eyes, sending her heart to racing. She took a few steps and stopped at his side. "The dining room is down the hall to our right." She made a vague motion with her hand. "Will you join me for dinner, Colton?"

He nodded briskly, conscious of Kate's guarded look. As he offered her his arm, Myrna smiled her approval and walked out ahead of them. When Kate placed her hand formally upon the top of his forearm, he felt her fingers tremble slightly.

"I should have stopped sooner and fed you, Kate. You're weak from hunger."

"Yes, that must be it." Uncomfortable with her strong reaction to feeling his taut muscles beneath her hand, she stared down the hallway ahead of them. "Colton, thank you for no' telling mother about . . . about us."

He looked down at her, his expression mocking. "What could I tell her, my dear? That you played the temptress and I fell for your siren's song? Or that I played the rake and preyed upon an innocent young woman? Which would be the truth?"

"Both and neither." She hurried on as they came to the dining room. "But I thank you for no' relating Grandfather's opinion of me. I hope by now he has realized that I dinna go to London to use him to snare a rich, titled husband." She was unconscious of her fingers tightening on his arm. "If I ever marry, it will be for love, no' for a title or wealth," she proclaimed forcefully.

Colton pulled out an Adam-style cane-backed chair and

seated her without further comment. They ate in uncomfortable silence as the excitement of their arrival wore off and the weariness from the journey set in. When Myrna joined them a few minutes later, it was obvious that Addison was not the only one in need of rest.

Chapter 10

Colton took a long drink of ale, set the tankard firmly down on the wooden table, and wiped his mouth on the ragged sleeve of his coat. He leaned back slightly in his chair and studied the man walking across the dirty pub at Pemberton's side. They stopped next to the table.

"I think I've found ye man, Will. MacDonald 'ere says 'e can do the job."

The duke shoved a chair out from the table with his foot and nodded for the men to sit down. He rubbed the two-day stubble on his jaw and watched MacDonald in silence for a minute after the man sat down.

"Ye know 'ow to gut a man?" Colton picked up his drink and took another long, slow swig.

"Aye. There isna a man in Edinburgh who'd do better."

"I 'ear different." Colton let the front legs of his chair hit the floor with a soft thud. "I 'ear ye botched the last one."

MacDonald glanced to each side, then leaned toward Colton, resting his forearms on the table. "It wasna my fault the man's friends came along. If the two that was with me hadna run off, I coulda finished 'im off. That Denley gent was just lucky, that's all."

Colton pushed back from the table. "Let's walk and talk. I don't want nobody to 'ear wot we got in mind."

The other two men rose and followed him from the pub into

the cold, dark night. They stepped out the door and turned down the snow-covered street, three abreast. Half a block away, Lunan gently flicked the reins of his team, guiding the duke's carriage out into the street.

"Who ye want done?" MacDonald glanced around nervously.

Colton walked along, taking note of everyone on the street, but appearing completely at ease. "A jeweler over on the Royal Mile. I brought 'im some pretty baubles from London but 'e didn't pay me near wot they was worth. I risked my neck to get them diamonds and near got caught, then 'e turns 'round and cheats me."

As the three men passed a dark alley, the carriage pulled up beside them. Pemberton dropped back a step, reached behind him, and pulled a gun from the back waistband of his pants. He swung the gun up, bringing the handle down sharply on MacDonald's head.

Colton jerked the carriage door open as the man slumped forward. The duke and Pemberton shoved him inside the coach and climbed in themselves. Lunan drove carefully over the frozen roadway, turning down a street near the waterfront. He stopped the coach in front of a warehouse belonging to MacAllister.

Pemberton hoisted MacDonald over his shoulder and carried him inside the building. When the Scot regained consciousness a few minutes later, he found himself tied to a chair. His coat, hat, and boots had been removed. He was freezing.

"What's a'goin' on? What do ye want?" MacDonald squinted toward the eerie darkness of the room. A brace of candles sat on top of a crate nearby, illuminating him and several large boxes and barrels in a pool of light. All he could make out beyond the glare of the candles were the square shapes of more crates.

"Why did you try to kill Addison Denley?"

The prisoner strained against his ropes and squinted at the darkness. The voice sounded like the man he had talked to in the pub, the one named Will. But this man's speech was articulate and refined. "I'm freezin' to death," whined MacDonald.

"Yes, I suppose you are. I'm told it's not such a bad way to go. Once you turn numb from the cold, you'll simply fall asleep." Colton held up MacDonald's knife so the blade caught the light. With calculated slowness, he rose and walked across in front of the Scot. He was careful to remain in the shadows, taking equal care to assure that the light reflected off the blade every step of the way.

"What do ye want?" The thug's eyes were wide with fear; the catch in his voice exposed his growing panic.

"Why did you try to kill Denley?"

"It was a job. Pennyfeather hired me."

"Simon Pennyfeather? From London?" The duke's puzzled frown was hidden by the shadows. The man was one of London's more unsavory characters. He had never been convicted of a serious crime, but had a reputation as a man who could, and would, arrange anything for a price. He was also known to have connections with the French.

"Aye, that be him. He pointed Denley out and paid me fifty pounds to stick him. Me and the lads followed the gent. He sent his carriage home, so we waited for him to come out of the club." Sweat broke out on the Scot's brow. He swallowed hard, but his eyes did not leave the knife. "Put that knife away, will ye?"

Colton ran his finger down the blade, just a gloved hand extending from the darkness. "It is nice and sharp, isn't it, MacDonald?" His voice was filled with quiet menace. "I'd wager you put it to the stone just this morning." He twisted the blade again in the light, as if admiring its beauty. "Why did Pennyfeather want Denley killed?"

The Scot's voice shook, more from fear than from the cold. "He said some cove wanted him dead. I swear that's all I know. He dinna say anythin' about who hired him."

Colton stepped into the ring of light. Addison had remembered his assailant's words distinctly. The duke bent down, glaring into MacDonald's terror-stricken face, and paraphrased. "We got a present for ye, MacDonald."

The thug choked, fixing his gaze on the long-bladed knife. As Colton lifted it slightly, MacDonald closed his eyes, waiting for death.

Instead, the duke jerked the knife through the ropes which held the Scot in the chair. He slumped to the floor with a groan. As Pemberton hauled the half-frozen man to his feet, the magistrate stepped up beside Colton.

"He's all yours." The duke handed the official the knife. "As soon as I get back to London, I'll find Pennyfeather."

"Do you know him, Your Grace?"

"Not personally." Colton smiled slightly. "But I know who he is. We'll find out who is behind this. Thank you for your cooperation, milord. And for your indulgence of my theatrics."

"Got the job done." The magistrate chuckled. "Probably a lot quicker than my methods, too." The authorities let MacDonald put on his clothes, then hauled him off to the gaol.

A short while later, Colton eased himself down in the chair beside Addison's bed. It was late and the rest of the household was asleep.

"How did it go, Your Grace?" Addison's eyes sparkled with interest.

"Well. He sang like a canary." Quietly he told Addison about his escapade, going into detail like a true storyteller for his friend's enjoyment.

"You said Pennyfeather had French connections. Do you think they are involved?"

"They might be, but I doubt it." Colton rested his head against the back of the chair, clasping his hands casually on his middle. "No offense, my friend, but you're a little fish in a big pond. There's no reason for the French to suspect you in the first place, and even if they did, it is unlikely you would hear anything that would change the course of the war at this late date."

"True. Do you have any other ideas?"

"A few, but I'd like to keep them to myself for the moment. I don't want to cast aspersions on anyone until I have proof. However, be very careful. You may still be in danger."

"I'll admit it's a puzzle." Addison yawned. "Now, Your Grace, I think I'll go to sleep so you can go to bed." He met Colton's grin with one of his own. He held out his hand. "I'm grateful that you came. You accomplished more in two days than MacAllister and the authorities did in eighteen."

"The secret is in thinking like a criminal." Colton laughed and squeezed Addison's hand, then released it as he stood.

"Colton." There was an odd note in Addison's voice. "Thank you for bringing Kate home. Having her here has done more for my recovery than any of the doctor's medicine. I was foolish to let her talk me into going along with her charade, and I worried about her every minute she was gone."

She has a way of making fools of mortal men, thought the duke grumpily.

Addison hesitated. A few times during the past two days, Kate had been in the room when Colton came up to visit him. Both times, she had left rather quickly, but Addison had not missed the undercurrent of tension crackling between them.

"She's a good girl, Colton. Stubborn, I'll admit, but she has a heart of gold. She's young and bound to make her share of mistakes." He noticed Colton shift uneasily, but he was determined to say his piece. "She'll probably never be a truly biddable wife, but a strong man could keep her in line."

"I'm not looking for a wife," said the duke stiffly. He walked to the door, wearing the armor of his arrogance in front of his friend for the first time. As his hand touched the knob, Addison's words caused him to pause.

"She's her mother's daughter, Colton. When she gives her love, it will be with her whole heart and for life. There's nothing else like it in the world."

Without a backward glance, Colton silently left the room.

By the next afternoon, Kate's friends had learned she was home. So many people came to call that Myrna, with her husband's encouragement, threw an impromptu party in the evening. Colton had gone out to dinner with MacAllister at his club. When he returned close to ten, the festivities were in full swing. Nearly fifty people, most of them between the ages of seventeen and thirty, talked, laughed, and danced the night away. Myrna took the duke's arm, expertly guiding him around the room, making introductions. They stopped to chat with a woman he had known all his life, Lady Douglas.

"Colton, laddie, how's your mama?" Lady Douglas beamed a smile up at him and took his hand, drawing him down to sit beside her on a gold velvet settee.

"She is well, milady. Happily married, as I'm sure she has written you." Colton returned the lady's smile. He had always been fond of his mother's old friend. "I think she and Lord Blagden may be on their way to Edinburgh."

"Oh, lad, do you truly? Then you expect Thomas to resolve this infernal quarrel with Addison once and for all?"

"I am hopeful, milady. Kate talked to her grandfather after I did. His response seems to have been more favorable than at first."

"Ach, the lass told me how he learned who she was." Lady Douglas rolled her eyes and shook her head. "What a hiddie-giddie mess." She studied Colton thoughtfully as he unconsciously scanned the room for Kate. "Is your mama angry with me for taking part in Kate's deception?"

He forced his gaze back to his companion. "I doubt it. Mother saw through her disguise awhile before we left. I suspect she had an inkling of who Kate was. You know Mother, even if she were angry, she never stays that way for long. I'm sure she understands your reason for writing the letter. You did write it, didn't you?"

Kate's laughter reached out to him from across the room. Without thinking, he turned his head, searching for her. His action did not go unnoticed by Lady Douglas.

"Yes, I wrote it. The whole little adventure seemed harmless at the time." She touched his hand with her fingertips, bringing his attention back to her. "Was it, Colton? Or did it bring more pain than good? Did the harm fall where it was least expected?"

Her eyes held his. This old friend, this woman who had always seen what others could not, looked into his heart. He broke away from her penetrating gaze, scanning the room. All of these people were Kate's friends. Not just acquaintances, but friends. It showed in their relaxed manner and easy banter as she stepped into the center of the room.

Jamie Douglas joined her, carrying a bagpipe under his arm.

"Kate's going to dance!" Excitement filled the air as the guests hurried to form a wide circle around Kate and Jamie.

"Come, Colton, you willna want to miss this." The duke stood and helped Lady Douglas to her feet. They crossed the carpet, stopping on the outer fringe of the circle.

Colton tensed as two glistening broad swords were crossed on the floor at Kate's feet. For a heartbeat, her gaze met his, then she winked at him and grinned as a Highland war cry filled the room.

Kate lifted her tomato-red silk skirt to mid-calf as Jamie began to play the Jacobite Sword Dance on the pipe. Seconds later, she was moving around the crossed swords, her feet skipping back and forth between the blades in a variety of intricate steps. At times, her feet flew so quickly, they were almost a blur.

At first, all Colton could think about was how badly she would be cut if she made one wrong step. Her feet were only covered by red satin slippers, hardly sufficient to shield her from the blade. Slowly, he began to relax. Obviously, she had done this many times before, and she had not done any great harm to herself in the past.

He let himself admire her trim ankles and the curve of her legs until his eyes grew tired trying to focus on them. His gaze wandered slowly up her body. Her beauty filled him with pleasure and a strange feeling of pride. But when he finally looked at her face, his world came crashing down.

Her eyes sparkled, her cheeks were flushed from exertion, and her skin glowed from happiness. He did not think he had ever seen her so full of joy. *I could never give her this kind of happiness. Why do you care? You're a dunderhead, remember?* Reluctantly, Colton accepted what his heart had known all along. He would recover from his wounded pride, and he would still want her. In spite of how she made him look or even if she thought him a fool, he would still care for her.

He glanced around the crowd, watching the admiration on the faces of the others. His gaze came back to rest on her. *She thrives on this,* he thought. *The frivolity, the music and dancing, the admiration of her friends. Especially her friends. She needs a man who can give her this kind of life, not one who hates parties and has practically no friends to his name.*

Was this why she had said there could never be anything between them? He wondered if she had known all along that he could never make her happy. Perhaps being Thomas's granddaughter had not been the only reason she had not trusted him with her secret at Twin Rivers. A woman of her vibrancy needed the excitement and stimulation of others. To her, the type of life he preferred to lead would only be dull and boring.

Suddenly, he felt old, out of place, and heavy of heart. With chilling dignity, he nodded to Lady Douglas and excused himself. His friend watched him leave the room as the song wound to an end. She had caught the flicker of despair in his eyes and knew that harm had indeed fallen where least expected.

Lady Douglas glanced at Kate in time to see her crestfallen expression. She, too, watched as Colton's stiff back disappeared through the doorway. Lady Douglas rolled her eyes heavenward, wondering why the course of true love never ran smooth.

Kate felt sick at heart. Apparently, her dance had offended him, although she didn't quite know how. She plastered a false smile on her face as her friends praised her abilities and entertainment. Somehow, she got through the next few hours, laughing at the right moments, making witty conversation, hiding her pain from her friends.

When everyone left, she retired to her room, still keeping her pain inside until her maid, Bess, had helped her change for bed. The moment the girl completed her duties and closed the door behind her, Kate gave in to her heartache. Tears welled up in her eyes. *Did I embarrass him by my behavior? Did he find my dancing unseemly?* She muttered a mild oath in Gaelic. *Will you ever let me back in your good graces, Colton Lydell?*

Miserably, Kate crawled into bed, letting her tears fall until the pillow was soaked and her head throbbed. Finally, overcome by weariness, she dropped off into a troubled sleep.

"Miss Kate, wake up." Bess shook her mistress gently. "Miss, ye must wake up."

Kate struggled to open her swollen eyes. When she focused her gaze on the maid's urgent face, her mind cleared in a flash.

"What is it? Has something happened to Papa?"

"Nae, miss. But Edgar says the duke is leavin' this mornin' for London."

Kate blinked. Edgar, her father's valet, had been attending the duke during his visit. If anyone knew His Grace's plans, it would be the manservant. "When?" She pushed back the covers and sat up, swinging her legs over the side of the bed.

"He'll be goin' downstairs for breakfast any minute now. Then he be leavin' right afterward."

Kate jumped to her feet and grabbed a gold satin dressing gown from the foot of the bed. Slipping into it, she tied the sash quickly. "Where's Mother?"

"Eatin' breakfast with yer father. Oswald took the tray up a few minutes ago."

"Has he gone back downstairs?"

"Aye." Bess's eyes were wide as she watched Kate struggling to straighten her tangled hair with her fingers. "Miss, ye canna see him dressed like that!"

"I dunna have a choice, Bess." She grabbed the girl by her shoulders. "Please, dunna say anything to anyone. I canna let him leave without saying farewell. If I can get him to go in the sitting room, you watch the hall and tap on the door if anyone is coming."

"Aye, miss." The girl's eyes sparkled with excitement. "I'll keep a good lookout. But you canna take long." It was her way of warning her mistress not to do anything she should not do.

Kate grinned, understanding the maid's gentle admonishment. "I willna be with him *that* long." As she peeked out the doorway, she wondered vaguely just how long such a deed would take.

When Colton stepped out into the hall to go down to breakfast, Kate was waiting for him. He took in her sleep-tousled hair and the enticing way the satin dressing gown covered her curves. She looked a little pale and her eyes were suspiciously swollen and red.

"It's early. You should still be abed." *With me.* He spoke briskly; his expression was gruff.

"My maid said you were leaving this morning."

"As soon as I've eaten."

Kate pointed toward a small sitting room across the hall. "May I have a word with you?"

He raised a brow, raking his gaze over her. "It is unseemly for me to be alone with you, especially with you in *deshabille.*"

Kate's face flamed but she lifted her chin stubbornly and said softly, "It willna be the first time, and I would have a word with you."

"The temptress to the end," he muttered, then waved his hand toward the open door. "As you wish." He followed her into the room, admiring the gentle sway of her hips beneath the shimmering satin. She waited beside the door and closed it behind them.

"Kate, this isn't wise."

She ignored him. Instead, she studied his guarded expression for a long moment before turning away. She rubbed her upper arms with her hands, unconsciously trying to ward off the chill of the room. "Would you have left without saying farewell?"

"Yes." Colton stared at her tense back. The early light drifted through the open curtain, turning her hair into a glinting flame. He ached to bury his fingers in her curls, to pull her into his arms and kiss her senseless. He stood still.

She turned to look at him, her eyes filled with pain. She rubbed her hands over her upper arms again. "Do you hate me so much?" she whispered.

"No." Colton looked away, his jaw clenched against the emotion swelling within his chest. "I don't hate you, Kate. But it seemed best if I simply left. As you pointed out some time ago, there can never be anything between us."

Yes, there can be! She watched him struggle with his feelings, desperately wracking her mind for the right thing to say. She wanted to tell him how much she cared; that she would give anything to win his love and approval. Last night she had wept in frustration and disappointment. She had expected him to compliment her on her dancing. Instead, he had walked out in disgust. She longed to know why, but was afraid to ask. To her chagrin, she discovered that she, too, had no small amount of pride.

"I dinna ever thank you for bringing me to Edinburgh." Kate let her gaze wander over him, loving the way the maroon jacket fit his wide shoulders. And the way those buff britches fit his shapely thighs. She breathed a wistful little sigh.

Colton cocked his head slightly at the soft sound. "I knew you were grateful." A wicked part of his mind taunted him, silently mentioning a way she could show her gratitude.

"Yes, but I should have said the words. Thank you." She was stalling, trying to keep him there. They both knew it.

"I should leave, Kate."

"Not yet." Her soft plea revealed more than she intended.

She looked down at the floor, then walked across the space separating them. "Will I see you again?" She looked up into his eyes.

"If Thomas makes amends with Addison, we shall probably see each other on occasion," he said stiffly, trying to ignore the sadness in her beautiful eyes. He clenched his fists to keep from touching her. The scent of jasmine drifted up to him, tormenting him.

"I would like that." When he said nothing, she licked her lips nervously, then plunged ahead. "Colton?"

"What?" He swallowed hard and took a deep breath in an effort to slow his pounding heart. Instead, he filled his senses with her special scent.

"Remember me gently. Think of me once in a while."

I can't get you out of my mind! He sternly reminded himself that she had made him look the fool, but the argument had lost much of its force. Then a picture of her dancing the night before filled his mind, and he reminded himself that he was the wrong man for her. It made him feel noble to step aside, clearing a path for her happiness. Somehow, it served as recompense for his earlier mistakes.

"Once in a while," he said lightly. "And gently," he added, with a flick of his finger beneath her chin.

"Colton . . ."

"What?" His voice held a trace of exasperation.

Kate leaned toward him, just a fraction, and let her gaze drop to his lips. She wanted to kiss him in a way she never had before, to sear her name on his heart. She looked up into his eyes, then back down at his lips.

"One kiss," she whispered, leaning a little closer.

"Kate, no . . . I . . ." Colton's mouth went dry. He tried to swallow and couldn't.

Her palm came up to rest on his thundering heart. She met his gaze one last time, her eyes shadowed with desire. "Please, just one."

He tried to keep from leaning down to meet her upturned face but the battle was over in the blink of an eye. As his lips covered hers, she swayed against him, sending a shock wave through them both at the gentle impact of her satin-clothed body with his. His arms closed around her, drawing her even tighter against him.

The one kiss became another . . . and another, long and deep, filling needs and creating them. Colton slowly released her, moving his hands to her shoulders to ease her body away from him.

"You'd better go to your room, Kate." Even his voice trembled slightly.

Eyes still closed, she shook her head, brushing his fingertips with her hair. Dropping her head forward, she rested her forehead against his shoulder and took a deep, tremulous breath. "Colton, please forgive me for embarrassing you in front of Grandfather and your mother."

He hesitated. When she raised her head and looked up at him, he said, "You're forgiven. I was in the wrong also."

She searched his face and sighed. She sensed that he wanted to forgive and forget, but was not quite able to do so. Not yet.

"Please, Kate. Go to your room." Desperation lent a sharp edge to his voice. He was determined not to walk out on her as he had done at Twin Rivers. In fact, he wasn't even sure he could walk away from her. He released her, hoping for once she would do as he asked.

She stepped back and took another long look at his face, memorizing the rugged beauty there. She reached out a quivering hand and traced his lips with her fingers. "God-speed, Colton."

"Take care of yourself, Kitten," he whispered.

With a quick nod, she left the room, scurrying down the hall to her bedroom. Once inside, she leaned back against the door and closed her eyes, relishing the last few moments, cherishing them in her heart. An impish smile slowly lifted the corners of her lips.

"Now, Colton Lydell, perhaps you'll think of me more than once in a while."

Chapter 11

It was mid-afternoon, only a few hours after Colton's departure, but it seemed as if it had been a year. Dejected, Kate walked down the hall toward the back parlor. A loud knock sounded at the front door, and Kate turned to see who had arrived. When the footman opened the door, her grandfather and Lady Millicent stood there. Kate raced down the hall like a child and threw her arms around the earl when he stepped into the entry.

"Oh, Grandfather, I'm so glad you came!" She hugged him tightly, then stood on tiptoe to kiss his cheek. In her excitement, she bumped the brim of his hat and knocked it askew.

"Here, here, child," he said gruffly, "give a man time to get his coat off." His eyes were misty when she stepped back to allow him room to shrug out of his heavy coat. Once Oswald had taken his outerwear, the earl smiled at Kate. "Are you truly happy to see this old face, gel?"

"Oh, yes, Grandfather. Everyone will be."

He opened his arms and Kate stepped into them. They held each other for a few minutes, the earl's gray head resting against Kate's dark red curls. Then he released her so she could greet Lady Millicent.

"Thank you," Kate whispered to the countess as she kissed her cheek.

"I had nothing to do with it, my dear. You did it all. You and your father's letters."

Kate gave her a hug and stepped back, looking at her grandfather. "Father is doing well."

"Yes, I know." The earl smiled at her look of surprise. "We ran into Colton at an inn along the way."

Kate's face lit up. "Oh, did he come back with you?" She glanced at the door.

"No, he was determined to continue." The earl noted her look of disappointment and her quick effort to conceal it. "They required fresh horses at the same time we did. Thoughtful of Providence to intervene that way." He grinned. "I was sorry he had already started back to England, but I can understand. He's needed there." He paused, looking expectantly at Kate. "Now, tell me about Addison."

"It was a bad wound, but he is healing nicely. He is sitting up some, although he is still weak."

"He'll be that way as long as he has to stay in bed. Never did believe a man had to stay in bed forever to mend. Well, do you think he'll see me?"

"Of course, he will. Mama isna here right now, but she'll be back in about an hour. Do you want to wait or shall I see if Papa is awake?"

"I'd just as soon not put this off any longer, gel. I've waited far too long as it is."

Kate took his hand. "Then let's go up. Lady Millicent, will you come, too?"

"No, dear. Thomas needs to see his son alone this time. I'll go find a nice warm fire. Perhaps I can have your man bring me a hot cup of tea."

"Of course, milady." Kate smiled as the butler nodded. "Oswald will show you to the parlor, then bring you some refreshments. I'll join you in a few minutes."

Kate escorted the earl up the stairs and down the hall to Addison's bedroom door. Thomas hesitated as she reached for the knob.

"Why don't you go on in and tell him I'm here. I don't want to shock him too much." He ran a shaking finger across one bushy gray eyebrow.

"I'll just be a minute." Kate patted him on the arm, then

went into the bedroom, letting the door drift almost closed behind her.

"Papa, there's someone here to see you."

Addison took one look at her radiant face and sparkling eyes, and he knew. "Father?" he whispered.

Tears of happiness pooled in Kate's eyes, and she nodded. "He's just outside the door. He's very nervous."

Addison took a deep breath. "So am I." He looked around at the tousled bed. "Help me straighten up a little, lass."

Kate handed him a brush and a small mirror. Then she quickly smoothed the sheets and fluffed the pillows behind her father's back. She reached for the brush and mirror. "You look fine, Papa. May I send him in, now?"

He grabbed her hand. "After all this time, hoping for all these years—now, I'm not sure I know what to say to him."

"Dunna worry, Papa. The right words will come; or perhaps you willna need words at all." She leaned forward and kissed her father on the forehead. "I was so excited I almost knocked his hat off. He blustered a bit, but I dunna really think he minded."

Squeezing her hand, Addison took a deep, steadying breath. "You're right, Katie, my girl. Send him in."

Kate walked quietly from the room. "He's ready, Grandfather." He bent down slightly as she raised up to kiss him on the cheek. "Thank you," she whispered.

Thomas nodded, then straightened and squared his shoulders. He walked slowly into the room as she closed the door after him. The Earl of Blagden blinked back tears as he looked at his son. His heart ached for all the years he had missed. Addison was no longer the young man of his memory; still, time had been good to him. He had retained his handsome looks, although his brown hair was graying at the temples. Time and the trauma of his injury had etched his face, but as Thomas grew closer, he could see the most prominent lines had been caused by smiles, not worry.

"Good afternoon, son." The earl's voice was deep and husky.

"Father." Addison watched his father cautiously, still unable to believe that he had actually come to him.

Thomas cleared his throat. "How are you feeling?"

"Better every day. I sat up for an hour this morning and again this afternoon." He smiled, his eyes twinkling with a conspiratorial glint. "I'm about ready to do as I want and tell a white lie to the doctor. I'm disgusted with being in bed."

"That's exactly what you should do. As long as everything is mended inside, you'll get your strength back quicker if you get up and about."

"I'm glad you agree." He motioned for his father to sit down in the chair by the bed. "We always did see most things the same way, Papa," he said softly.

"Most things," the earl said gruffly. He sat still for a long moment, then looked up at his son. The pain of all the past years glistened in his eyes. "But on the most important thing, I let you down."

"Papa—"

"No, son. Let me say it. I've thought of little else ever since I heard you were hurt. No, that's not quite true. I was thinking about you before that, realizing how wrong I had been, but it was deuced hard to admit it to myself." Addison started to interrupt, but his father held up his hand to stop him. "There's something you need to know, and I've got to be man enough to tell you."

Thomas paused and took a deep breath. He'd known he would be uncomfortable confessing his discretions to his son, but he had not thought it would be so difficult. He released his breath slowly, swallowed hard, and cleared his throat.

"A few months before you brought Myrna home, I took a mistress." He grimaced at Addison's shocked look. "Aye, boy, you have a right to be surprised. After all the years your mother and I had been married, I met someone who turned my world upside down." A soft, warm look passed over his face as he thought of Leonore. "I can't say I loved her, son, because I didn't. In spite of my infidelity, it was your mother I loved."

Thomas paused, struggling for the right words. "For all her good points, your mother was a cold woman." He shrugged, as if apologizing for her. "It just wasn't in her nature to be warm and affectionate."

That's an understatement, thought Addison.

"My affair didn't last long, no more than a month or so, but it hurt your mother deeply. Leonore was a shopkeeper's laughter. She was young and pretty and knew how to please a man. I wasn't her first protector, don't suppose I was her last neither.

"Anyway, Elizabeth found out about it. She knew who the girl was, so when you brought Myrna home, her being a merchant's daughter and all, your mother was beyond all reason. She was disappointed because you could have had any woman among the ton you wanted." He smiled slightly, a sad, bittersweet smile. "She had such plans for you, boy."

"I know, Papa." Addison gripped the edge of the sheet with one hand, then slowly released it. "I didn't like hurting her or you. I couldn't help falling in love with Myrna. She was everything I had ever dreamed of and far more. She's been a good wife to me, Father."

"Yes, so you told me in your letters." The earl paused again. His eyes grew misty and he cleared his throat once again. "It was my fault. Everything. Without the affair with Leonore, I think we could have brought your mother around. As it was, my guilt would not let me stand with you." He looked at his only son with sorrow-filled eyes.

"I was trying to appease her for my own transgressions and was too blind to see how much I lost. I blamed you all these years for her death, because it was easier to accuse you than to live up to what I'd done. But I was wrong, oh, so wrong. If anyone was to blame, I was." Thomas sighed heavily. "Perhaps the doctor was right after all. Mayhap, the disease would have taken her anyway."

"Did she suffer?" Addison's face reflected his grief. He had never been sure of her love, but he had loved his mother just the same.

"Not greatly. She simply got weaker and weaker. The doctor said it was her heart. She had a couple of attacks right before the end. They were terribly painful, but the pain didn't last a long time." Thomas's voice grew thick and raspy. "Forgive me, son, for not letting you come home. Forgive me for all the terrible wrongs I've done."

"Oh, Papa." Tears slipped from Addison's eyes as he held his arms open to his father. The earl stood and leaned over his son, cradling his head against his chest. Addison wrapped his arms around his father and clung to him. "Of course, I forgive you," he said, his voice breaking. "I love you."

"I love you, too, son. Deep in my heart, I always have." Finally, the earl drew away, pulling his handkerchief out of his pocket before he sat down. Wiping his wet cheeks, he looked up to see Addison drying his eyes on the sheet.

"Papa, I want your forgiveness, too. You weren't totally to blame. I made mistakes, too. If I'd brought Myrna home before we were married and let you get to know her, perhaps it would have been different. I should have tried more to appease Mother, but I didn't. I stubbornly felt that she, and you, should welcome my wife, no matter who she was. I wounded you and Mother, even though it was mostly unintentional. Will you forgive me, too?"

The earl nodded. "Yes. Let's start anew, and promise each other we'll carefully talk out any disagreements we have in the future. I want to live my remaining years in total peace with my son and his family."

"Amen." Addison grinned. "Myrna will be so thrilled that you're here. She should be back any time now." He suddenly frowned. "You didn't come alone, did you? Did you bring your new wife?"

"Of course. I wouldn't go anywhere without my Millie. She's downstairs with Kate now. Ah, lad, you'll love her in no time."

"Is she much like Colton?"

"No, not really. He takes after his father, too aloof and serious. Millie tends to come off a little flighty, but she's as sharp as a tack, so don't be deceived. I think she was a little browbeaten by Colton's father, and mayhap, even Colton himself." At Addison's frown, he shook his head. "I don't think the lad meant to keep her under his thumb so much. It's probably the way the old duke treated her, so he just followed suit. Seemed like she didn't dare go against him, though I know he'd never raise a hand to her. Suppose just one of those icy looks of his were enough.

"She's coming around though. Developed a bit of a strong will of her own these past few months. Not a bit timid about saying her mind." He grinned and Addison laughed.

"I'd say you're rubbing off on her Father." Addison shifted, pushing himself up higher in the bed, and winced as he did so. "Tell me, what is there between my daughter and Colton? They wouldn't stay in the same room for more than five minutes at a time, but the tension between them was so thick you could cut it with a knife. Couldn't seem to keep their eyes off each other, either, although they tried hard enough."

The earl leaned back in his chair. "Kate didn't say anything to you?"

"No, nor to her mother. Myrna tried to talk to her about him, but Kate put her off, saying she was imagining things."

"I know they're strongly attracted to each other. Millie tells me that Colton first met Kate when Rowan—that's my Irish wolfhound—knocked the girl into him, then knocked them both to the floor. That's how wolfhounds stop people. They jump up, put their paws on the victim's shoulders, then push 'em to the ground. Then they stand over them."

Addison's eyes widened in amazement. "You're feeding me a Banbury tale."

"Upon my honor, my boy, I'm not."

"Just how tall is this dog?"

"When Rowan stands on his hind legs, he can drape his front paws over my shoulders, and the top of his head is about ten inches above mine."

"My stars! Does he bite? Is he safe to have around the women?" *Did you bring him with you?* Some of Addison's clearest memories from childhood were images of his father and his dogs. At least one of them accompanied him practically everywhere.

"No, he doesn't bite. He has a very gentle nature and is very safe to have around the women. He would never harm anyone, but his size alone is a great deterrent to would-be thieves."

"Why would he knock Kate and the duke down?"

"Playing. I suspect he spotted Colton and ran over to greet him. Rowan is very fond of him. Probably in his rush to see him, he bumped into Kate, and she bumped into Colton, throwing him off balance. Colton wouldn't have been knocked down if he'd had a chance to brace himself."

The earl's eyes twinkled. "I didn't bring him with me this trip. He was very disappointed, but I made him stay home. He'll be lonely, but the servants get along well with him. But

I got away from my story. It seems the dog licked the duke, and probably Kate, in the face, disheveling my immaculate stepson's appearance. Normally, I think he would have been provoked, but evidently that granddaughter of mine caught his eye right from the very beginning. When he finally reached Millie's sitting room—his original destination—he was in extremely high spirits. Millie was quite worried because he was smiling so much."

"He is rather somber, isn't he."

"Humph! If you ask me, the man is too high in the instep. Must inherit it from his father; Millie's not that way."

"I think he's lonely." Addison leaned back on the pillows. He looked thoughtfully out the window, absently enjoying the rare winter appearance of blue sky. "He's deeply involved with his work, and believe me, he's exceptionally good at what he does." He looked back at Thomas. "Since I've been confined to this blasted bed with little to occupy my mind, I believe my understanding of others has deepened. I'm not certain I can explain why, but I believe Colton has been hurt—or is afraid he will be. What else happened between them?"

Thomas grinned ruefully. "Well, Kate sleepwalked and wound up in Colton's room."

"Oh, no," Addison groaned. "Was she in her nightdress?"

"Yes, but I understand she was wearing two of them." At Addison's blank look, the earl shrugged. "Evidently, your mother gave an order years ago that the servants were not to have any heat in their rooms. I was unaware of it until Colton called me to task about it. At least, it served the purpose of keeping my granddaughter from displaying too many of her charms." The earl chuckled. "Colton said she also had on two mobcaps and two pair of stockings."

"How did he know she was wearing two pair of stockings?" Addison's worry deepened as his temper began to rise. Kate was a warm and affectionate young woman. She was obviously attracted to the duke. Addison's brow creased in a frown. He was not one to fret—except where his daughter was concerned.

"I didn't ask. But don't get upset, son. Colton is an honorable man. He would never take advantage of a woman, especially if she was asleep and didn't know what she was doing."

Instead of speaking with his normal frankness, the earl paused. He did not want to upset Addison any further, nor did he want to jeopardize his budding relationship with his granddaughter. And, he admitted to himself, I don't want to throw a hitch in the works between Colton and Kate. He decided not to give any hint as to the way he suspected Colton woke her.

"Colton said when he woke her up, she was appalled to find herself in his room and wanted nothing to do with him."

"What about before he woke her? Did he say what she did then?" Addison nervously toyed with the blanket, thinking of his wife's fiery nature. If his daughter took after her mother, they might indeed have a problem on their hands.

"She tried to make the bed." The earl smiled in reassurance. "Seems she thought it was morning and time to do the chores."

"That's all?"

"That's all he mentioned. I'll be honest with you, son." Thomas paused, thinking how good it felt to say the word 'son'. A soft, tender smile warmed his face as he stopped and simply looked at Addison. His son smiled in return, reading the love in his father's eyes.

"Knowing the attraction between those two, I'd be surprised if absolutely nothing happened after she was awake. But I'd wager that the most that went on was a kiss or two. Colton's not the type to rush a young, innocent girl into his bed. And even if he were, he knew I wouldn't stand for him dallying with one of my maids."

"Yes, I agree with you." Addison forced himself to relax. He had not realized how tense he was holding his body until his wound began to ache. "Is there anything more?"

"Well, somehow, she persuaded the duke to escort her to the Frost Faire being held on the Thames."

"I read it was frozen again. How did all that come about—the duke and Kate, I mean."

Thomas studied Addison surreptitiously for a moment, noting his weariness. He promptly decided his son didn't need to know all the details, just the few which were the most important. "I'm not quite sure. I know he went, and evidently had a very good time with Kate." He hesitated slightly, then plunged ahead. "I also have reason to believe he offered her *carte blanche*."

"He what?" Addison shouted, sitting further upright with a jerk. A sharp pain shot through his side, causing him to drop back down on the pillows with a moan.

"Addison! Did you hurt yourself?" Thomas jumped to his feet, hovering over him.

Addison took a shallow breath and waved feebly at his father. "It will pass," he said, his voice raspy. He motioned for the earl to sit back down. In a few moments, breathing became easier as the driving pain settled into a throbbing ache. "I shouldn't have moved so fast. I could use a glass of water, Papa."

The earl reached over to the walnut bedside cupboard and poured a glass of cool water from the pitcher, carefully handing it to his son. As Addison drank, Thomas shook his head. "My pardon, son. I shouldn't have been so blunt."

Addison gave his father a wan smile. "It was a shock. Of course, now that I've had a minute to think, I understand Colton was under the impression that Kate was a maid. He had no idea she was my daughter."

"Or my grandchild. I think he was hurt by her refusal, but even more so when he offered to help her find a more suitable position. Of course, she couldn't tell him who she was and couldn't accept his assistance or even tell him the reason why."

Addison frowned slightly, easing himself further down in the bed. "How did you find out about all of this?"

"Through Millie. She pried some of the information out of Kate and some of it out of Colton. A little of it is conjecture on our part."

"I'd wager Colton was highly embarrassed when all of you learned Kate's identity, especially if he knew Lady Millicent was aware of the situation."

"Yes, he was. Humiliated is probably a better word. Now, son, I'm going on downstairs. You need a nap. That wife of yours is liable to kick us out in the snow if I tire you out too much."

"Never." Addison grinned and reached for his father's hand as the older man stood. "She wouldn't dare. Besides, she's wanted us to mend our differences for twenty-two years. I need a few hours' rest, then you can bring my stepmama up to meet me. I also want to hear what you've been doing for the past twenty years." He clasped his father's hand and enjoyed the two short, quick squeezes in return. It was Thomas's gesture of love, just as it had been when Addison was a young man.

As they each released their grip, Addison looked up at Thomas with a speculative gleam in his eye. Strangely, he felt as if there had not been a twenty-year gap in his relationship with his father. The camaraderie they had shared when he was younger was just as strong at the present.

"Harboring ideas about playing matchmaker?"

"You mean Kate and Colton?" Thomas asked with an innocent look. At his son's nod, he grinned. "A few. We'll talk about it later." Thomas walked across the room. When he got to the door, he turned and stood watching his son for a moment.

"What?" Tiny lines of concern wrinkled Addison's forehead. He thought he saw a tear glisten on his father's eyelashes.

"I'm just thinking how happy I am, and how thankful I am that you're alive."

"Me, too." Addison grinned mischievously, making Thomas chuckle as he left the room.

Four weeks later Colton eased his tired body down in his comfortable green leather chair and stretched his legs out in front of him with a yawn. The clock struck midnight as he picked up a stack of mail from the small mahogany drum table beside him and thumbed through it.

"Would you like your dressing gown, Your Grace?" Gregory handed him a small glass of brandy.

"No, I'll be going up soon. There's no need for you to stay up." His eyes twinkled slightly at the tiny flash of annoyance that flickered over the valet's face. "I'll lay my clothes over the chair very carefully. No rumpled piles, I promise."

Gregory left the room, muttering to himself. Colton suspected the poor man did not quite know what to think on those rare occasions when he teased him.

He set the brandy glass on the table, loosened his cravat, and rotated the revolving top of the table to gain access to one of the shallow drawers. Taking a silver letter opener from the drawer, he slit the seal on a letter from his mother and held it toward the light with one hand. Absently, he lowered his other hand over the side of the chair to stroke Rowan's head. The moment he touched the animal's rough fur, a pair of lovely turquoise eyes, partially hidden by a crooked mobcap, danced across his memory. He jerked his hand away.

"I should never have brought you over here, no matter how lonesome you were," he grumbled. Sensing his displeasure, Rowan raised his head, staring at the duke with soft hound eyes.

"Oh, very well." Colton resumed petting his companion. "It's not your fault that I think of Kate at the strangest times." He scratched the dog behind one small, drooping ear. "Do you miss her, too?" Rowan released a heavy, doggy sigh and laid his head back down on the floor. Colton interpreted it to mean that he did indeed miss her. He turned back to the letter.

Dearest Colton,

It was so good to hear from you at last. I am so thankful the snow has finally melted and the Mail can move normally. Addison is doing very well. In fact, he has been going in to his office for half days this past week. I worry that he will tire himself and have some kind of relapse, but Thomas tells me not to fuss so. He assures me that Myrna's father and Mr. MacAllister are taking most of the load. Of course, Thomas has his fingers in the pie, too, from time to time.

I must admit, having another son and two delightful young women to fuss over has brought me much pleasure. I never realized what I missed in not having a daughter until now. Myrna and I get along wonderfully. She is such a jewel, very intelligent and wise, but can come up with the most amazing amusements at the drop of a hat. I only hope you will find a wife like her.

It is the oddest thing, Colton. To see Thomas and Addison together, one would think they had never quarreled. A nonacquaintance would never guess that they had been estranged for over twenty years. It is a miracle if I ever saw one.

Addison was upset, naturally, to learn that Pennyfeather character was killed while you were here with us. We are all disappointed, as I'm sure you were, not to be able to learn more about who wanted to kill Addison. However, I find it appropriate that Pennyfeather died in a brawl. If arranging murders and other distasteful things was his way of life, then it is only just that he should come to a violent end.

Colton chuckled as he paused. He moved his hand from the dog and picked up his glass, taking another sip of brandy. Rowan looked soulfully up at him but didn't even bother to raise his head. "Sorry, old boy, you've had enough attention for now. I need both hands." Colton shifted the sheets of paper, proceeding to the next page.

We keep up with the news here almost as well as in London. The newspapers here are excellent. I see where the fighting continues even though negotiations between the Allies and Napoleon have resumed. Personally, I think it was silly of the Allies to demand France to return to the frontiers of 1792. Even I know that Napoleon would never agree to such a thing. But I suppose with negotiations each side starts off with something outlandish and works their way down to what they truly want.

Colton nodded in agreement. He was pleased, but not surprised, by his mother's understanding of the situation.

We hear rumors that Napoleon and his army are worn out. I am disappointed we missed the "Great Rumor," although I appreciated you sharing it with us in your letter. I can just imagine the uproar when everyone thought Napoleon had been killed and the war was over. I do hope that when the war actually ends, our good British troops will be with the Prussians and Austrians when they enter Paris. After all, they cannot win the war without us. It is only right for us to share the glory.

Thomas says to thank you for taking care of Rowan.

The servants are good to the dog, but he is very fond of you. He is just so lost when Thomas is not around.

We should be coming home soon, in fact, not long after you get this letter. We expect to arrive on the twelfth or thirteenth of March.

Two days. Colton smiled, thinking of his mother and stepfather with affection. *I'll be glad when you're home,* he thought. He continued reading.

We're looking forward to the Season. I can't wait to present Kate to society.

Colton lurched straight up in the chair. His back rigid, he held the letter closer to the brace of candles. He did not notice that his fingers had a mild tremor.

It will be so amusing and exciting taking her around to visit the ladies in the afternoon, getting her vouchers to Almack's, and showing her off at the balls. It makes me feel like a girl again myself. She's such a beauty, I'd wager she'll be this Season's Incomparable.

At least she will be if she quits losing weight. Myrna says she hasn't been herself since she returned to Edinburgh. She's pleasant enough, but at times she has the most melancholy look in her eye. And she simply doesn't eat properly. Sometimes, she even forgets to eat at all unless one of us reminds her. She shrugs our concerns aside, saying she doesn't have much of an appetite now that she isn't doing household chores.

She was reluctant to come to London. In fact, just between you and me, I don't think she really gives a fig about being presented to the ton or whether she's a hit or not. But Thomas has his heart set on her coming. He's so proud of her and wants everyone to know what a beautiful grandchild he has.

Colton leaned back in the chair, allowing the letter to slip from his fingers to his lap. *Kate, here!* His heart pounded at the very thought of seeing her again. Memories of that last morning in Edinburgh came flooding back. She had been so beautiful, her hair mussed from sleep, her lovely body so delightfully covered by gold satin.

He closed his eyes, relishing the memory of her warmth and, yes, even her immodest behavior. A tiny smile lifted the corners of his mouth. He especially enjoyed her immodest behavior. He couldn't forget her kisses or the willing way she curled against him.

Doubt nudged aside the pleasant thoughts as he wondered for the thousandth time why she had kissed him that morning. Had she been teasing him? Did she know the memory of her touch would taunt him? Did she consider him some kind of conquest; one that she would laugh about in private or with her friends?

He shook his head as he stood and went up to his bedroom. "No," he murmured softly, "I don't think she would laugh at me." After he undressed for bed, it occurred to him that he had not finished the letter. He propped a pillow against the headboard, crawled beneath the covers, and reached over to the nightstand for the letter.

> Thomas wants Addison and Myrna to come, too, so Addison can take his rightful place in society. But, he says he is not quite fit enough to make the trip, nor is he willing to leave his business for any length of time again so soon. He does promise to come later in the year, however. I think he'd rather visit when we're at Heartlands and only spend a little while in town.
>
> Well, dear, I must go. We'll be leaving in a few days and will see you soon. Take care of yourself and get some rest. The Season will be upon us in no time. I do hope you'll try to attend more of the festivities this time.
>
> Love, Mother.

Colton tossed the letter back on the table and leaned over to blow out the candles. As he settled back against the pillow in a semireclining position, his thoughts returned to Kate. He found it hard to believe she was not overjoyed to be presented to the ton. From what little he knew of his female peers, society was the most important thing in their lives.

Even if it isn't important to her now, he thought, *it will be once she arrives and finds out what a success she is.* He grimaced, thinking of the scores of suitors who would be clamoring for one of her smiles. With her beauty and sparkling personality, she would have her pick of the ton.

She'll find the perfect husband, he thought. *One who has no problem being the center of attention. One who will enjoy the praise other men heap on her. One who loves to entertain. It's the right thing for her. She'll have plenty of eligible men at her beck and call.*

She'd never be happy with me, he reproved silently. *Maybe for a little while, but then the novelty would wear off and she'd grow restless and miserable. I'll just avoid her as much as possible. Someday, I'll forget about her. It's the right thing to do.* "The Duke of Ryland is always noble," he muttered sarcastically.

He slid down in the bed, pulling his pillow down with him. Turning over on his side, he bunched the pillow up under his head. A few minutes later, he pounded on it, and turned over to lie on his other side. A moment or two passed before he sat up in bed and pulled the pillow onto his lap, searching for lumps.

"I hate the thought of another man even looking at her!" Colton gritted his teeth so hard his jaw hurt. He gripped the pillow in both hands, raised it over his head, and flung it across the room. "And I hate being noble!"

Chapter 12

Kate carefully observed her reflection in the cheval glass as she turned first one way, then the other. The turquoise silk gown shimmered in the light, as did the fiery red of her hair. The gown was made simply. The neckline was cut wide, with tiny cap sleeves barely covering the curve of her shoulder. The décolletage was lower than most of her gowns, yet still very much within the realm of respectability. Gold ribbon trimmed the seam beneath her bosom where the skirt was attached to the bodice. The material fell in soft folds to the floor, gently following the curves of her body.

"Oh, Miss Kate, he canna ignore ye tonight. If there be a heart beatin' in the man's chest, it'll be captured forever."

"You're a romantic, Bess." Kate gave her abigail a wry smile. "But I hope you're right. I'm tired of the Duke of Ryland giving me an icy shoulder."

Kate had been in London for a little over four weeks. She had seen Colton several times, but on every occasion save one, he had simply acknowledged her presence and moved on to speak to someone else. When he had called upon the family a few days after their return from Edinburgh, his manner had been polite but extremely restrained. Other than smiling in greeting to his mother, no other look of pleasure had touched his face.

She turned once again, gazing at the cascade of hair down

her back. "I'll probably shock the ton by my unfashionable hairstyle, but this time, I'm wearing it the way I know Colton likes it."

Bess stepped up to her mistress and deftly arranged a few more soft curls around Kate's face. "Ach, miss, yer eyes look like jewels tonight."

"Thank you, Bess. I dunna know where Grandmama found this material, but it is the most beautiful I've ever seen." She clasped a simple strand of pearls at her throat and fastened tiny pearl earrings in her earlobes.

Lastly, she picked up a fountain ring and dipped it in a cup of her perfume. Pressing a little rubber ball at the back, she filled the tiny container with jasmine scent. She donned her gloves and slipped the ring onto her finger with a tiny smile, remembering the salesclerk's words.

"The fountain ring is the latest fashion, ma'am. If you find yourself in a mad crush, a slight pressure on the ring will release a bit of your favorite perfume to freshen the air." The older woman had leaned closer, dropping her voice slightly. "You're such a lovely thing, I'm sure you have a string of admirers. If you wish to show favor upon a particular gentleman, a lover perhaps, simply press the ring when he takes your hand to kiss it. He will be delighted with the honor of wearing your scent and will be unable to get you out of his mind, even though there might be hundreds of people about."

Kate checked her appearance one last time and gave the ring a tiny squeeze, releasing a jet of perfume into the air. She grinned at Bess, who had been with her when she purchased the ring.

The maid grinned back at her mistress. "Have a care if ye decide to 'favor one of yer admirers with yer scent', miss. The way that thing squirts, ye'll drown him."

Kate laughed. "Quite so. Some gentlemen wear strong cologne, but I think they would consider smelling of jasmine for the evening a dubious honor."

Bess settled a matching turquoise shawl around Kate's shoulders. An intricate floral pattern, woven in gold thread throughout the silk, sparkled in the light.

"Aye, the duke wouldna like it." The maid stepped back, admiring her handiwork before she met Kate's gaze with mischievous eyes. "Unless ye got 'im as he was leavin'. It would be one more thing to keep ye on his mind. I doubt if the poor man could catch a wink o' sleep."

Kate hugged her. "Bess, you're positively devious—and I love it!" Her face sobered. "Now, all I have to do is get him to speak to me before he leaves. The way he's been avoiding me, it will be no easy task."

"Ye'll think of something, miss. Is there a rule that says he must speak first?"

"No, I dunna think so. There are so many ridiculous rules in the ton that I dunna even try to remember them all."

"Kate, are you ready?" Lady Millicent stuck her head around the door, then walked on in to admire her new granddaughter. "Oh, child, you are a sight tonight." *If Colton's not there, I'll hang him by his thumbs*. "I knew that material would be perfect. You look absolutely enchanting."

"Thank you, Grandmama. Of all the gifts you've given me, I think this is my favorite." She kissed the older woman's cheek.

"You're welcome. It's my favorite, too. I almost wish I'd had you save it until our ball next week. But then, you have another lovely one to wear that night." Lady Millicent smiled gently at Kate.

"You brought so many pretty gowns with you. I hope you haven't minded letting me enjoy myself. I never had a pretty gel to rig out for a Season." Lady Millicent's light brown eyes sparkled. "I can't remember when I've had such fun." A tiny, impish smile tugged at her mouth. "I am glad I forewarned Lady Jersey and Countess Lieven."

"Forewarned?" Kate followed the countess out of the room and down the hall.

"Yes. I told them you were no schoolroom chit, but a woman of twenty who'd entered Edinburgh society long ago. I insisted there would be no milky, muslin gowns for you. Mercy, you'd have looked sickly."

"I did notice that all the younger women wore such pale colors, mainly white. I thought perhaps they belonged to some social club or something I dinna know about."

Lady Millicent laughed. "They do—the Coming Out Club! It's unofficial, of course, at least as unofficial as these things go. Somewhere along the way, some peabrain woman of enormous influence decided all the young ladies should wear pale, drab colors, and like the sheep that they are, the other ladies of society quickly agreed. I suppose they were afraid bright colorful clothes might overexcite our already lusty young bucks."

"Grandmama!" Kate chuckled. She had discovered that Lady Millicent was learning to speak as bluntly as the earl. "I do thank you for keeping me from a life of boredom."

Kate had made her official entry into London society a few weeks earlier, although Lady Millicent had invited Lady Jersey and Countess Lieven over for tea several days before attending the first ball. Kate learned that while her grandmother was not one of the all-powerful patronesses of Almack's, she carried a great deal of social weight. This prestige, along with Kate's mature manner and beauty, assured vouchers from Almack's and thus, initial acceptance from the ton. It also gained the ladies' concurrence that Lady Millicent's granddaughter could wear the type of clothes she preferred.

Kate was indeed a hit, although she artfully declined the title of Incomparable. She encouraged the men, both young and old, to bestow that honor upon another beauty, a lovely blue-eyed blonde who was a few years younger than her. Kate was not interested in the rivalry which threatened to erupt between them. She had no care to be the toast of society or the talk of the town. She did not care whether the members of society liked her or even accepted her.

True, she had come to London to please her grandfather, but she really only had one purpose in mind—to make Colton Lydell fall in love with her.

"Well, I suppose all the talk tonight will still be about Louis XVIII returning to France." The earl stepped into the carriage after his ladies, settling comfortably on the squabs as the footman shut the door. "I thought people would never quit discussing Napoleon's surrender. Great news, to be sure, but even good news grows tiresome after you've heard it a thousand times."

"But it was so exciting to see Louis XVIII go through London last week. You'd think he was our king the way the people cheered him," said Kate.

"Aye, we English love a celebrity," said the countess with a chuckle. Then her expression sobered. "Of course, there is more to it than that. As the Prime Minister commented a few months past, the English are insane on the subject of any peace with Bonaparte. They would not stand for him to remain on the throne of France."

"I don't think we need to worry about that," said the earl. "The French people are weary of war. Louis will find his role different from past kings. The French people have changed and so has the monarchy. He'll have to agree to a new constitutional charter or they'll not have him."

The earl smiled at his two lovely companions, noting that Kate looked particularly exquisite. His chest swelled with pride, pride for the granddaughter he might have never known. He asked casually, "Millie, do you think Colton will be there tonight? I wanted to talk to him for a minute last night, but never got the chance."

"He might be. He is attending far more functions this year than he has in the past." Lady Millicent gave her husband a speaking look, then glanced slyly toward Kate, who was watching the passing scenery out the window. "Of course, now that the war is over, he has much more time for such things. Perhaps he has decided to think more seriously about finding a wife. There are many suitable young ladies in this crop."

Kate winced, partly from being labeled part of a harvest, but mainly from the thought of Colton considering another woman to be his wife. *Am I doomed to loving a man who doesna care for me?* It had grown too painful to even entertain such a notion, though she had done so over and over during many sleepless nights. It canna be, she thought mournfully. He has to care. He just has to.

They arrived at the ball to find carriages lined up for a quarter mile down the street. "Good. Lady Tomlin has used some common sense. This shan't be such a crush as Lady Downey's event last week." Lady Millicent peeked out the window. "I daresay we'll be at the door in less than half an hour."

"And in the receiving line for another." Kate shifted in the seat. "Is the Tomlin house large? Will there be room for dancing this time?"

"Oh, yes, quite enough. I scolded Lady Downey for inviting so many, although I know it has become the thing to do. I simply find it ridiculous in the extreme to have so many people at a ball that the guests can barely move around, let alone dance."

Silently, Kate agreed. Lady Downey had invited over four hundred guests when two hundred would have been a crowd. They had waited in the carriage for two hours before reaching the door, then in the receiving line another two hours. They departed half an hour later.

Kate absently twisted the strings on her reticule. *Please be here tonight, Colton,* she thought. *Please dunna ignore me. I canna bear it if you ignore me again.* Butterflies fluttered in her stomach and her legs felt weak. She thought if she didn't see some sign of interest from him tonight, she would dry up and wither away.

A few moments later they disembarked the coach. Half an hour later, they were through the receiving line. As soon as Kate stepped into the ballroom, a throng of gentlemen clustered about her. In moments, her dance card was filled and she was being led out for the first dance.

During that number, and the next two dances, she secretively searched the room for Colton. By the beginning of the fourth set, she was making a conscious effort to keep a smile on her face. Throughout her time in London, she had been careful not to show favoritism to any man. She seldom even danced the acceptable two dances with the same gentleman, but if she did, she made certain she accorded the same honor upon at least one other man during the evening.

Each time, Kate allowed a different gentleman to escort her in to supper, and if she was seen in Hyde Park in the afternoons, it was either with a group or one of several admirers who took her for a drive.

She tried to be gracious to them all, only occasionally rebuffing some particularly odious fellow. Her partner in the fourth set was Viscount Heartly. He was a handsome young man, quite wealthy, with an endearing sense of humor. Kate was very fond of him as a friend, but at the moment, she was finding it difficult to keep up their light banter. All she wanted to do was find a quiet, deserted place and have a good cry.

Suddenly, she felt a tingling on the back of her neck and knew she was being watched by a certain pair of cinnamon eyes. *He's here!* She couldn't see him, but she knew he was present. She could feel his gaze boring into her. The sudden surge of happiness flooding her soul was like a powerful drug, lifting her spirits and putting the sparkle back into her eyes. A joyful laugh bubbled out.

"I say, my joke wasn't that good." Viscount Heartly studied her face briefly until the steps of the dance led them away from each other.

Kate spotted Colton standing alone in a tiny alcove along the opposite wall. She had but a few seconds to look at him before a side step turned her away, so she only noticed how fine he looked in his rose-brown jacket and soft white silk britches. The brown and white striped waistcoat picked up the shades exactly, quietly setting him apart from the other men by his understated elegance.

The next step turned her back toward him, and she focused on his face. He devoured her with his gaze. Even across the room, Kate felt the strength of his desire. It took her breath away and scrambled her thinking. As she stepped back to meet the viscount, she stumbled slightly.

He caught her arm to steady her. "Kate is something wrong?" His face was filled with concern as they automatically continued the dance.

"No, it is nothing. I was just momentarily distracted."

Lord Heartly glanced toward the wall. It was simple to determine who had distracted her. Although Colton was no longer gazing at her with undisguised desire, his eyes followed her every move.

"So that's the way the wind blows," the viscount murmured. He did not know Colton very well, no one did. But he liked him, just the same. He looked down at Kate as a soft blush stole over her cheeks. Yes, he thought, it would take someone like her to set a fire under Ryland. Lord Heartly felt a twinge of regret, but only a mild one. He was very fond of Kate, but at five and twenty was not quite ready to get leg-shackled.

He leaned down, speaking softly. "He's your choice, then?"

Kate's wide-eyed gaze shot to meet his. "I . . . I . . .

yes. But I beg of you, Gerry, say nothing to anyone. I know what I feel for him, but I dunna know what he feels for me.

"My lips are sealed, I promise." He chuckled as the song came to an end. "By the way, my dear, I failed to tell you that you're absolutely enchanting tonight." He slipped his arm around her possessively and led her off the dance floor.

Kate looked up at him again in surprise. "What are you doing?"

He leaned down, whispering in her ear in an intimate manner. "You're already driving him to distraction. I just thought I'd make him a little jealous."

"Oh, Gerry, do you think he would be?" she asked wistfully.

His arm tightened, drawing her a little closer. "Give me one of those dazzling smiles of yours, and when I release you, glance over your shoulder."

Kate obliged, her excitement adding a spark of liveliness to an already beautiful smile. They stopped, and the viscount released her. Kate glanced over her shoulder, then turned quickly back to face her companion.

"He's throwing daggers at you!" Her face glowed and her eyes danced with elation.

"Figuratively, I hope." The viscount scanned the room, noting Colton's dark look, but not appearing to do so. "I don't think I shall flirt with you any more tonight, my dear. I truly don't want to wind up on his bad side."

"Nor would I want you to be. But I must confess, you've certainly brightened my evening. Thank you, Gerry."

"Most welcome, most welcome. Ah, here comes your next partner. By your leave, my dear." Viscount Heartly smiled and bowed slightly as Kate was once again led onto the dance floor.

Kate laughed and danced and had a wonderful time. It was her most enjoyable party since she had come to London. Several times during the evening, she caught Colton's scowling face. Under other circumstances, his black looks would have caused her worry or concern, but tonight they filled her with joy. He cared.

Colton watched her glide through the quick steps of a country dance, wondering if she realized how the silk gown clung to her every curve. He knew she was wearing a petticoat because he caught a glimpse of the lace-trimmed edge as she spun around. Still, the gown draped around her, outlining her legs and curved hips every time she took a step.

He gritted his teeth as she smiled up at her partner, obviously teasing him. Colton turned away abruptly, setting his empty glass on a tray as one of the footmen walked by. He eased his way through the crowd, determined to leave. *If I have to watch her smile and flirt with one other man, I'll throttle him*. The jealousy gnawing at him was not new. It had been his companion from Kate's first London party.

He had told himself over and over that she should have her Season, that she should be given the opportunity to find a husband more suited to her way of life and personality. He had assigned himself the task of looking after her, intending to steer her clear if she appeared to be falling for someone who was unsavory or who might hurt her in some way.

But his jealousy was clouding his good intentions. It grew every time he saw her in the company of another man. Every smile, every laugh, every gentle expression nourished it. He was being consumed. If he could not stifle it, he was going to do something rash.

Colton's progress out of the room was delayed a few times as various acquaintances drew him into conversation. At last, he stepped through the doorway into the long hall. He turned around, unable to resist one last look at Kate. She was nowhere to be found.

Mulling over her disappearance, he decided she must have gone to the ladies' withdrawing room to freshen up. The room was in the opposite direction. Disappointed to not see her again, he turned and walked down the hall. As he neared the great staircase, Kate stepped from a small antechamber. His quick glance through the doorway revealed that she was alone.

"Why, Colton. How nice to see you." She smiled up at him, her face filled with genuine warmth.

"I see you have taken a break from dancing." Colton's demeanor was icy at best. His gaze dipped to the neckline of her gown and a frown creased his brow. The décolletage was much lower than it had seemed across the dance floor. The generous swell of her bosom flirted dangerously with him above the turquoise material. He had the insane desire to plant a whisper kiss on that smooth skin. When he looked up again, meeting her gaze, a fire burned in his eyes.

"I am worn to a frazzle. I decided if I dinna get a few minutes away from the crowd and sit down, my next partner would have to drag me around the room." She licked her lips nervously and fought the urge to pull him into the empty room. "I dinna see you dancing tonight."

"I seldom do. I tend to be on the awkward side."

"I canna believe anyone who waltzes with as much grace as you, could be at all awkward on the dance floor," she said softly. She looked up at him, her eyes glowing from the memory of the first time he had held her in his arms.

"My partners would beg to differ with you." A corner of his lip lifted in a wry smile.

"Then you havena been dancing with the right woman." Kate turned toward the ballroom, surprising the duke by slipping her hand through the crook of his arm. He automatically bent his elbow to accommodate her. They walked slowly down the empty corridor. "Did you have a chance to talk with Grandpapa tonight? He mentioned earlier that he wanted to see you."

"Yes. I talked with him shortly after dinner."

They both fell silent. Colton looked down at the top of her gown again and was filled with a strange combination of desire and rage. *How dare she flaunt herself that way? She shouldn't have been let out of the house looking like that!* He grimaced, deciding he would have to talk with his mother on the proper way to dress a young unmarried woman.

"Oh dear, I forgot my reticule." The look she turned on Colton was one of pure innocence. "As I distinctly remember, you were going the other way when I met you. You're such a dear to escort me back to the ballroom, but now I find I must go back and fetch my bag." They made a wide sweeping turn, evoking a giggle from Kate. "I promise I willna ask you to walk me back again."

"Hmmmm. Promises, promises." Colton had not intended to enjoy her company. He had struggled to maintain his somber façade, but found it crumbling when assaulted by her laughter.

Some of the tension went out of his body, then sprang back again when his arm brushed the side of her breast.

"Do you go to Lady Edison's musicale tomorrow night?" Kate looked up at him, hoping he would not notice how her pulse quivered at her throat.

"It was not my intention." He glanced down the hall, then leaned over to speak softly. "The lady is not noted for her good ear. Her entertainment invariably falls into the same category."

"Oh, dear. I fear your mother and I are promised at any rate. Perhaps you will be noble, Your Grace, and brave bruised eardrums to keep us company. Lady Millicent complains of no' seeing you enough these days."

They halted a few steps from the antechamber. Colton looked down at her, searching her eyes as she withdrew her arm from his.

"I dunna see you enough either, Cole," she said quietly.

Cole. All his life, Colton had wanted someone to give him the nickname. No one in his family ever had. Even the few people he counted as friends had not seen fit to do so. It surprised him at how much it pleased him.

He had always felt only a true friend would call him by a nickname. *Friend*—companion, confidant, soul mate—things he had never had, things his weary heart longed for. Painfully, he realized that even if she married another, he would always be her friend.

"Perhaps I'll reconsider." He lifted her hand to his lips, brushing a brief kiss on her knuckles. As he lowered her hand, she squeezed his fingers—and the ring. A jet of perfume squirted out, not in the misty cloud as promised, but in an abundant, straight stream. It splattered across his cheek, then ran down his jaw to drip off his chin.

"What the devil!"

"Oh, my! Oh, Colton, I do apologize." Kate caught a drip with her fingertip as he pulled his handkerchief from his pocket. "I forgot I was wearing my fountain ring." She frowned as he swiped at his face with the handkerchief. "Obviously it isna working right." His stern look made her pause. "Well, I dinna mean to squirt you with it. I forgot that if I squeezed my fingers together it would send out a mist of perfume." *Forgive me, Lord. It's just a little lie.*

"Some mist. A cloudburst is more like it." The duke coughed, overwhelmed by jasmine. "There's an old adage about too much of a good thing," he choked.

"Uh, well, yes." She glanced nervously down the hall. "You'd better go. Someone's coming. You dunna want them thinking you're a man milliner."

He looked at her in astonishment. "They wouldn't dare."

"No, of course no'. Still, you'd better go—I must go." Kate ducked into the room, all but slamming the door behind her. Breathing a sigh of relief, she glanced down at the shamefully low neckline of her gown—and gasped. Her face flamed as she leaned back against the door and closed her eyes. The gown had slipped down even farther than she had intended. She had come perilously close to disgracing herself.

She carefully eased the gown up to its proper neckline, the décolletage she had presented to everyone else except Colton. Only the very top curves of her bosom were exposed. She checked the mirror to make certain the gown was hanging properly, then picked up her reticule. She slowly pulled open the door, releasing her pent-up breath as she checked the empty hallway. With a tiny smile of triumph, Kate headed back to the ballroom.

Colton hurried out, thankful for the fresh air. Once seated in his curricle and whipping down the street at a fast pace, the jasmine mellowed out. He supposed he wouldn't be free of it for hours. A rueful smile touched his face. He wouldn't be sleeping for hours either.

Her image sprang to mind, and Colton grimaced. *It should be against the law for her to wear that gown!*

Chapter 13

Early the next evening, the duke finished the last lines of his report to Lord Liverpool, frowning thoughtfully. He reread the dispatch he had received a few hours earlier. Napoleon had accepted the Treaty of Fontainebleau, thus officially abdicating and ending the war. Colton's duties were coming to an end.

He supposed there would still be a need for getting information as the allies bickered among themselves about dividing all the lands Bonaparte had conquered. The duke wanted no part of it, and there were others who could do the job much better. He tapped the edge of the papers against his desk, molding them into a neat stack. His letter of resignation to Lord Castlereagh, and another to Lord Liverpool, the Prime Minister, were on top.

He leaned back in his chair, wondering why he was not elated. In a few weeks time, he would be free of the responsibilities. After a moment of reflection, he realized it was only proper to have mixed feelings about ending his job. It would be a relief not to carry so many of the concerns of his country upon his shoulders. The worry that inaccurate or misinterpreted information, or the wrong decision regarding correct information, would result in the tragic loss of life or even victory for Napoleon had been a heavy burden.

Mixed with relief was a strange restlessness and emptiness. He had functioned at his limit for a very long time. It would be hard to wind down to a slower pace. *Whatever will I do with my time?* he mused.

The small porcelain clock on the corner of his desk chimed half-past-eight. He had toyed with the idea of attending Lady Edison's musicale, but the arrival of the dispatch and resulting paperwork had delayed him. He shook his head again, knowing he should be relieved not to have to sit through the torment. He wasn't.

Colton reached in his desk drawer and pulled out a wrinkled handkerchief, holding it to his nose briefly. The jasmine fragrance had mellowed but still served to remind him of Kate. He shifted in the chair, resting his head against the cushion, and closed his eyes. The image of Kate smiling up at Viscount Heartly sprang to mind. Colton frowned and forced the unwelcome picture from his thoughts.

I dunna see you enough either, Cole. Had he only fancied the tinge of disappointment in her voice? Had her expression truly been wistful, or was his imagination working overtime? He glanced at the clock and gently tucked the handkerchief in his pocket. If he hurried, he could still make it to the last part of the musicale. More important, he could see Kate and perhaps even talk with her a bit after the program.

The duke shoved his chair away from the desk and stood decisively. He hesitated for a second before leaning over to blow out the candles on his desk. He had the feeling he had just made a decision that went far beyond the realm of how to spend the evening.

An hour later, Colton arrived at Lady Edison's. From the immaculate appearance of his gray navy coat and powder blue waistcoat, no one would have guessed Gregory had practically thrown his evening clothes on him. The duke had taken enough time to gulp down a sandwich, mindful that Lady Edison's supper provisions sometimes ran thin. If Lord Edison's luck had been poor of late, then the supper would be meager. If the cards had been with him, then the table would be overflowing.

Colton hovered at the back of the room, hoping to catch a glimpse of Kate and Lady Millicent. They were sitting a short distance in front of him. To his surprise, there was an empty seat next to Kate.

Lady Edison spotted him and came to join him. The lady did

not take care to move quietly, but there was no need. The Italian soprano screeched at the top of her lungs, painfully dismantling a normally lovely aria, and torturing the guests in the process. Colton and his hostess stepped out into the hall.

"Your pardon for arriving so late, milady. I was unavoidably delayed at the War Office."

"I am too pleased that you came to scold you for being tardy, Your Grace." Lady Edison dimpled up at him. In spite of her faulty musical tastes, the young lady was a bubbly scatterbrain and was liked by most everyone. "I do hope that it was not some problem of national significance that detained you."

"No, not a problem. Good news, in fact. Boney has accepted the treaty. His abdication is official."

"Oh, how wonderful! You will be so kind as to share your news with everyone at the intermission, will you not?" Colton nodded politely. "Oh, this is simply too good. We shall all know the *on dit* before anyone else! I'm *so* glad you decided to attend my little party." She laughed softly, then blinked as he gave her a tiny smile in return.

"Miss Denley and Lady Millicent are sitting near the back."

"Yes, thank you. I saw them."

"Miss Denley is saving you a chair." At his startled expression, she hurried on, her eyes twinkling. The dear lady was a helpless romantic. "She was very insistent upon keeping the chair vacant. Turned away several worthy gentlemen who were quite anxious to sit beside her. She graciously said your mother wanted you to sit with them."

Colton took a deep breath in an effort to calm the spark of excitement racing through him. *Of course*, he thought. *That's all it is. Mother wanted my company, not Kate*. A quick look at Lady Edison's face suggested she didn't believe a word of it.

"Well, perhaps I should go on in. Thank you for coming to greet me." As they stepped quietly into the room, Kate glanced back at the door. Her troubled, disappointed expression was instantly replaced by sparkling joy and a wide smile as she spotted him. She patted the tapestry-covered seat of the chair beside her.

That look sent a wave of pure happiness spiraling through the duke. He suspected even his toes were glowing. He turned one of his rare, dimple-cheeked smiles on his hostess. "By your leave, milady."

Colton moved away, not seeing her mouth fall open. Nor did he notice the way she gripped the edge of the door and made a feeble effort to fan her flushed face.

Lady Edison stared after him until he sat down, then came out of her shock and glanced around to see if anyone was watching her. To her intense relief, no one had paid any attention to her. She wandered back to her seat, thinking that any lady on the receiving end of that devastating smile would quickly change her opinion of the Duke of Ryland.

"I'm so glad you came!" Colton leaned over slightly so Kate could murmur in his ear. He suppressed a shiver as her warm breath tickled his skin. "Grandpapa absolutely refused to make an appearance. He went to his club instead."

Colton winced as the soprano hit a particularly obnoxious note. "I think he was the only intelligent one in the family tonight."

Kate grinned up at him, then turned her face back to the front of the room. To all appearances, her attention was on the program. In reality, she barely heard the sounds which her grandfather had appropriately dubbed caterwauling.

Instead, her every sense was focused on the man sitting next to her. Their chairs were placed close together, so the slightest movement, either by him or her, caused her shoulder to rub against his arm. Her thin, apple-green muslin gown and his superfine jacket did little to cushion the hard play of muscles in that arm.

The scent of his Hungary Water tantalized her, and when she ventured a sideways peek at him, she noted that his cheek was freshly shaven and baby smooth. Kate bit her bottom lip, wishing she could brush a kiss across that fragrant, sleek skin.

Moments later, the singer took a break. Before her guests had a chance to move from their seats, Lady Edison clapped her hands to gain their attention. "Ladies and gentlemen, His Grace, the Duke of Ryland, has some exciting information to pass on to us." Everyone, including Kate and Lady Millicent, looked expectantly at the duke.

His expression was somber, due not to his news but to being the center of attention. It was not a position he often allowed, and one with which he was extremely uncomfortable. He glanced at Kate, reading encouragement in her eyes. Surprised by the depth of her understanding, some of his tension dissipated.

"I suspect some of you have already heard the good news. Bonaparte has accepted the Treaty of Fontainebleau." A cheer rang throughout the room, then almost as if on cue, everyone grew quiet again. "He has abdicated as ruler of France and all the conquered territories. In return, he has been given the sovereignty of the island of Elba, where he will be emperor."

"Where is Elba?" someone called.

"Off the coast of Italy," another replied.

"But that's not far enough away!"

"He should be thrown in prison instead of being called an emperor!"

The mood of the evening had changed from boredom and persecution to excitement. The guests strolled around the room, hashing and rehashing their opinions of this latest event.

Colton turned to greet his mother, but changed his salutation from cordial to concerned when he saw her white face. Lines of pain creased her brow. "Mama, you're unwell!"

"It is only the headache, but I fear 'tis a bad one." She looked apologetically at Kate. "I'm sorry, dearest. You have had such little time to chat with your friends, but I cannot bear to stay."

"It is of no consequence. Of course, we must go. I noticed a quiet little sitting room just at the top of the stairs. Let us get you situated more comfortably, Grandmama, then Colton can send for the carriage, and I will make our excuses to Lady Edison."

Colton took his mother's arm, slanting Kate a contemplative look. It occurred to him that there had been little opportunity for him to observe her in a role which called for efficiency and authority. Evidently, she was quite proficient at both. He doubted if she even questioned whether he would follow her suggestion or not. He would, of course, for it made perfect sense.

Still, there were few people in the world who could simply tell the Duke of Ryland when to jump. He grinned to himself, for he found he really did not mind. *But I'll be hanged if I let you tell me how high, sweetheart.* His grinned widened, amazing a few of the other guests as they walked by.

"Make my excuses to Lady Edison, too, please. I'll accompany you home." He tried not to read too much into Kate's answering smile, but the sparkle in her eyes made it difficult.

Half an hour later, they arrived at Lord Blagden's. Colton rode in the phaeton with his mother and Kate. Lunan followed in the duke's curricle, suspecting he would have time for a good game of cards while he waited for his employer.

"Shall I fetch a doctor, Mama?" Colton escorted the lady slowly up the stairs. He could tell by the way she leaned on his arm that every movement was painful.

"No, dear. I just need a dark room and Crockett. I've been on the go too much of late. I shall simply insist that Thomas escort Kate tomorrow night to Lady Jersey's rout. Then we shall have a few days to rest. With our own party next week, I kept our commitments blissfully sparse for the days leading up to it." She turned her neck stiffly to look up at him. "You will be here for Kate's party, won't you? I'll never forgive you if you don't come and stay the whole evening."

"Upon my honor, ma'am, I'll be the first to arrive and the last to leave."

"Humph! I'll believe it when I see it. Good night, dear. Thank you for seeing us home. Now, go on down and chat with Kate. Thomas should be home before too long."

Colton kissed his mother on the forehead and dutifully turned her over to Crockett, Lady Millicent's faithful abigail. He found Kate waiting in the back parlor, looking out the window at the moonlit night. He pushed the door closed with a backward thrust of his hand and walked toward her, smiling as she looked over her shoulder.

"Since we dinna have any supper, I asked Bence to bring us a tray." She grinned at Colton. "Actually, I was going to do it myself, but he wouldna hear of it. I miss rummaging around in the kitchen. Sometimes, the things the cook views as failures are most tasty." She licked her lips and wiggled her eyebrows, before turning her gaze back to the window.

Colton laughed softly as he stepped up behind her. Then he tensed, fighting the urge to wrap his arms around her and smother her neck with kisses. Caution warned him to stay way from temptation. She had burned him before; she could asily do it again. He had come to understand and accept why he had spurned him at Twin Rivers, but it bode wise to tread arefully. He had no intention of appearing the fool for the econd time, especially in her eyes.

The belief that he would make her miserable with his dull ife was fading. However, he was still not convinced he could ive her enough happiness to keep her by his side for a ifetime. He realized she was holding her breath, almost as if he were waiting for him to touch her. A little tingle of xcitement raced down his spine. He was so close that if he lew gently, his breath would flutter a wispy little curl beside er ear, tickling it ever so slightly. After a moment's consid- ration, he resisted temptation.

"I've never rummaged around in a kitchen for something to at. In fact, I'm not even sure I've ever been in a kitchen efore," he said.

Her breath came out in a silent rush as disappointment lickered across her face. She hid it quickly. Colton felt a tinge f regret at disappointing her, but at the same time, his elf-esteem received a needed boost.

"Oh, you poor dear. Your education has been sorely eglected. Dinna you ever sneak into the kitchen as a child to eg treats from the cook?"

"I seldom received sweets when I was young."

"How about now?" She craned her neck around so she could ook at him and found herself so close that she had to ease way in order to focus her eyes. Finally, she simply turned to ace him. She leaned back against the windowsill.

"What do you mean?" he asked.

"Do you ever stop by Gunter's in the afternoon just to spoil ourself a little?"

Colton frowned. "Well, no."

"Do you ever order any of the pastries and have them elivered to your home?"

"It seems rather silly to order them just for me."

Kate was warming to her topic. The man needed to pamper imself occasionally, or even better, he needed a woman to do for him. She straightened, tilting her face toward him a little ore. There was a decidedly stubborn slant to her chin.

"You should order them—just for you." She tapped the middle of his chest with her forefinger to emphasize her words. "You can afford it, you know. Besides, what you dunna eat you can give to your servants. They like the taste of confections as much as anyone."

Colton gazed down into her intense eyes. His look dropped to her lips. "I know one little confection I'm dying to taste," he murmured. He lowered his head slowly toward hers, giving her plenty of time to turn away. Just as his lips touched hers in a tiny heartbeat of a kiss, there was a sharp knock at the door. They jumped apart guiltily.

Harlan brought in a silver tray of sandwiches and one loaded with pastries from Gunter's. Another footman followed right behind him, carrying the silver tea service. Bence rolled the tea table from along the wall to sit between the blue velvet settee and an ivory brocade chair. He lifted the top of the table, unfolding it to double the surface. Taking the trays from the footmen, he placed them on the walnut table with precision. Once things were set to Kate's satisfaction, the servants bowed and left the room, closing the door behind them.

Both Kate and the duke glanced at the door. Although propriety dictated an unmarried woman should not be in a closed room alone with a man, they both knew they had gone beyond those sanctions long ago. Evidently, the butler did not believe it was his place to remind them of society's rules, or perhaps he considered them family, of sorts.

Kate sat down on the chair and Colton took the settee. She poured a cup of tea and handed it to him. While she poured one for herself, he reached for a sandwich.

Colton ate quickly, smiling as he watched Kate eat one just as fast. "Madam, you are an angel. I was beginning to think I would keel over from hunger."

"Me, too." Kate grinned and reached for another. "With all the dancing I've been doing of late, I find my appetite is as hearty as it was when I was working as a maid. Sometimes I think I eat even more."

Colton ran his gaze over her, his eyes gleaming with appreciation. "It doesn't show." He picked up another sandwich and took a bite, eating more slowly. He watched her thoughtfully. "When you first returned from Scotland, you were thinner."

Kate swallowed hastily and brushed some crumbs from the arm of her chair. "At first I was too upset by father's injuries to eat much. Then, no' eating seemed to become a habit. I suppose it was the change from being a maid to being a lady of leisure. I wasna as physically active as I had been. I just dinna seem hungry." She took a sip of tea, hoping he wouldn't question her anymore. It would not do to have him guess she had been dying from a broken heart.

"Well, you look lovely, now. London must agree with you."

Being near you agrees with me, she thought. "I have enjoyed the Season so far, more than I thought I would, in fact."

"Oh? I thought all well-bred young ladies lived for a London Season."

"English ladies, perhaps. You forget, my blood may be half-English, but my heart is Scottish. No, I suppose that isna really true anymore. There are many things about town I do like, but it is so big. I long for a breath of good, clean country air. And the ton's rules! There are enough to drive a person to Bedlam."

Colton wiped his mouth on his napkin and leaned back on the settee. "Doesn't Edinburgh society have rules?"

"Of course, but there are no' so many, and they are logical and practical." Her eyes held an impish twinkle as she pursed her lips. "Well, most of them. Here, one can give offense without even knowing it." She leaned back with a sigh of frustration. "I canna seem to keep track of them all, so I gave up trying."

"Don't do anything too outrageous. It can be quite unpleasant to be on the outs with the ton."

"Humph! I dunna give a fig what those top-lofty hypocrites think of me. I will never look highly upon them, no' after what they did to my parents. I will live my life as I choose, and they can all go to the devil!"

"Kate!"

"Forgive me if I have insulted you or your friends, Colton." Kate sighed wearily. "Sometimes my temper gets the best of me."

"You have not insulted me, Kitten, for I have few friends. I believe those I do have like you just as you are. However, for the sake of Thomas and Mother, you need to stay within the bounds. You do not wish to cause a scandal, do you?"

"No, of course no'. But it's so annoying to be on my guard all the time."

"Once you are more established, the scrutiny will diminish somewhat. Although you must remember, gossip is the life-blood of society." He grinned and settled back into the corner of the settee, resting his head against the softly padded back. "Without it, they'd have nothing to occupy their time."

"What will you do now that the war is over? Will you still work at the War Office?" Kate leaned over the table and studied the confection tray, deciding on a creme-filled lemon cake.

"No. In fact, I turned in my resignation tonight. It will be a week or two before all the loose ends are tied up." Colton stretched his legs out in front of him and watched as she took her first bite. He found it hard to move his gaze away from her mouth. He had to think twice to pick up his train of thought.

"I have several estates around the country that I have sorely neglected for the past few years. They are all run efficiently by the estate managers, of course, but I should take the time to visit each one. Sometimes things are not as they appear on paper." He smiled faintly as she plopped the last bite in her mouth. "I might even take some time to relax. That, too, has been neglected for the past several years."

"Good for you! You're like my father, you work much too hard." Kate picked up her napkin to wipe her fingers, then impulsively decided to lick the cream and sticky lemon icing off instead.

Colton's mouth went dry. Her movements were quick and innocent, but it was one of the most sensual scenes he had ever witnessed. He swallowed with difficulty and finally lifted his gaze to her eyes as she dried her fingers on the napkin. A tiny puzzled look settled over her face.

"Come sit by me, Kitten." His voice was rich and deep and held an intimate tone that sent goose pimples up her arms. He patted the cushion beside him, much as she had done earlier in the evening.

Kate took a quick breath and her eyes widened. "I—I dunna think I should." Memories of their time together at Twin Rivers flooded her mind, sending a shiver down her spine. She rose hesitantly.

"I'll be on my good behavior."

"No' best?" Her voice trembled a little, but she moved around the table and sat down next to him anyway.

His gaze held hers, searching for a yearning to match his. He found a spark of desire, yes, but also uncertainty and a little fear. He smiled gently. "Not best, but I think good will do." Folding his hands casually on his lap, he resisted the temptation to brush her lip with his thumb.

"Thank you for saving me a seat tonight at Lady Edison's. It was kind of you."

"You're welcome. Your mother wanted you to sit with us."

"And you? Did you fend off numerous gentlemen just to please my mother?"

"No. I wanted you to sit with us, too," she said softly. Raising her chin a notch, she added defensively, "Well, we've no' had a chance to talk in ages." She abruptly searched her mind for a different topic of conversation. She needed to know why he had ignored her all these weeks and why he had walked out when she danced the Sword Dance, but not tonight. She did not want anything to ruin these special moments.

"Do you think it will be safe to go to France now that the war is over?"

Colton paused at the quick change in the conversation. "No, but I don't think it will stop people. I've already heard of some who are booking passage. We English are a strange lot. There is often an undercurrent of animosity running through us with regard to France; history tells us it has been there since William the Conqueror's time and before. But no matter how much we defame the French, we are drawn to them and their country like bees to honey."

"I suppose many are interested in seeing all the treasures Napolean has collected."

"Yes, although I'm not certain how many of them will be available for viewing. Many of the conquered nations will want their valuables returned."

"Will France return them?" Kate relaxed a little, even

though sitting beside him on the small settee made her intensely aware of him. The knowledge that her grandfather might walk in at any minute kept her common sense in control for the moment.

"They'll try hard to keep them, I'm sure." A tiny frown marred his brow. "You aren't thinking of making a trip to the Continent, are you?"

"Oh, it crossed my mind, but I quickly decided now was no' a good time. I'm no' anxious to see a lot of destruction, and I canna imagine that the French people would be happy to see us. I suspect, too, that the war has taken its toll. I canna see how the inns could be up to the standards to which we are accustomed. We have had some shortages here, but it must be worse where the fighting actually took place."

"Very astute, my dear. You are a wise young woman."

"Why, thank you, Your Grace." Kate batted her eyelashes at him, evoking a chuckle from the duke. She sniffed the air mischievously. "I see there are no lingering effects of my misfiring ring."

"No, although my face was still red this morning from all the scrubbing Gregory insisted upon doing."

"Oh, no! Was he truly aghast?" Kate grinned at him.

"Beside himself. I thought he was going to take my hide off. Fortunately—or perhaps unfortunately, I haven't decided which yet—he could do nothing to dispel the fragrance entirely." He looked deeply into her eyes and murmured, "My dreams were very interesting."

Kate felt a delicate color sweep across her cheeks. The things his eyes were telling her were positively wicked! She took a deep breath and prayed he wouldn't notice her thundering heartbeat.

"Bess checked the ring for me when I got home. She found the tiniest bit of lint in the opening. Once it was removed, the ring worked perfectly."

Colton pretended a look of alarm. "You're not wearing it now, are you?"

"No." Kate laughed. "I decided I'd better practice using it before I wear it again."

"Good." He smiled, letting his gaze roam over her. It settled on the creamy skin of her neck and shoulders. Tonight, less of her lovely charms were on display, for this gown was designed with a more modest neckline. Disgruntled, Colton wished she had worn the turquoise gown tonight instead of last night. That way, he would have been the only gentleman to enjoy the view.

"Why did Mother allow you to wear such a disgraceful gown last night?" he blurted.

"What?" Kate stared at him. As his words sunk in, a bright flush spread from the base of her throat up her cheeks. "It is a lovely gown. My favorite, in fact," she said in a defensive tone.

"It is immodest in the extreme. It would have been an unseemly display for a married woman, much less an unmarried one. No wonder the men were so eager to dance with you."

How am I going to get out of this one? Instead of enticing him, she had earned his displeasure. Kate looked down at her hands, twisting her napkin into a tight swirl. Her blush deepened. There was no way she could tell him the whole truth, but perhaps she could avert disaster by admitting part of it. She might have to stretch it a little, too.

"Colton, I have a confession to make. I realized after I got to the party that my gown was a little wide through the shoulders. I hadna noticed it before, but I expect the movements of dancing caused it to slip down gradually. All it took to keep myself respectable was a sly tug on the back. It would pull the front up to where it was supposed to be." It wasn't exactly a lie. She had pulled it up a couple of times to thwart the leer of certain dance partners.

Her cheeks were burning, but she glanced up at him anyway. His unreadable expression caused her to drop her gaze again. "When I met you in the hall, I realized it had slipped down and I had forgotten to pull it up. I couldna think of anyway to do it with you standing there, so I left it." She chewed on her lower lip for a second, then added in a tiny voice, "And, well, the look in your eye made me daring."

"All it takes is a lecherous look to make you daring? Dash it, woman, you get those from half the men in London even when you're covered up to your chin!" Colton sat up straight, glaring at her.

"You're twisting my words! You dinna leer at me. Well, no'

exactly." She threw up her hands, frustrated because she could not explain better. She took a deep breath, huffing out a heavy sigh. Finally, she met his angry gaze. At least he isna cold and indifferent, she thought. He may even be jealous. The thought warmed her heart.

"Colton, I would have been embarrassed and probably a little frightened if that look had come from another man." Her voice was quiet and lilting, her eyes warm and dewy. "After I returned to the anteroom and discovered how far down the gown had slipped, I was mortified. When we were talking, I had no idea how I looked." She grinned ruefully. "My face was as red then as it is now. I assure you, the gown will fit properly the next time I wear it."

Colton studied her face as the grin became a soft smile. *What is she telling me?* he wondered. *Am I the only man she trusts? Is she saying I'm the only one she wants to entice? Or is it all a game?* He leaned back against the corner of the settee. Feeling reckless, he decided to play a little game of his own.

"I think I'll have my treat, now. One of those with strawberry jam on top." His smile was vague. "Would you get it for me?"

Kate turned to pick up the dessert, puzzled by his swift change of mood. Had he accepted her explanation and was she back in his favor? She couldn't tell what he was thinking from his expression. *Drat!*

As she picked up the pastry, some of the thick jam dripped down onto her fingers. She straightened before turning to hand it to him.

"You feed it to me." His voice vibrated with sensuality. His eyes sparkled with a warm, deceptively lazy light.

Kate felt a tingle of excitement race over her. "You might be taking relaxation a wee bit too far," she said dryly. With a grin, she held the delicacy in one hand and a napkin beneath it with the other. Pretending to take careful aim, she held it to his mouth so he could take a bite.

Colton closed his eyes and smiled as he chewed. He swallowed, then said, "You're right. I should pamper myself more often." He opened his eyes, then stretched his mouth wide for another bite.

Kate giggled and held the food to his mouth. This time, he ook a larger bite, intentionally brushing her fingers with his ips. Kate's quick intake of breath and startled eyes told him ow much it affected her.

"Are you going to Lady Jersey's rout tomorrow night?" Kate told herself to calm down. It was silly to react so to the imple brush of his lips on her fingers.

"Yes, I'm promised. I doubt that I'll have an unexpected neeting with Lord Liverpool to use as a convenient excuse."

"For shame, sir." She shook her head in mock disapproval.

"Do you go?" He knew his mother would see to it that Kate ttended. It was the reason he had accepted the invitation in the irst place.

"I'm no' certain now." Kate's delicate brows creased in a light frown. "I dunna think Grandmama will feel up to it. I uppose Grandpapa could take me, but I doubt if he would vant to go if she is unwell. Nor would I."

"Let us hope she will recover quickly."

"Will you talk to me this time? Keep me company on ccasion?"

"I'll consider it." Colton laughed and ducked as she layfully swatted the napkin at him.

"Will you dance with me?" *There, I've said it*. She held her reath, waiting for his rebuff.

His expression grew serious. "I'll consider it. I'm not nxious to make a cake out of myself."

"You willna do any such thing. Remember, doing well lepends a great deal on the partner." A soft, delicate pink inted her cheeks. "We would do well."

"Hmmm." He opened his mouth for the last bite, chuckling t the way she avoided his lips when she popped it in his nouth.

He grabbed her wrist before she could pull her hand more han a few inches away and held it there. When he was finished vith the pastry, he drew her hand to his lips. His gaze captured iers as he slowly licked the dark red jam from her fingertips, ne by one.

Kate held her breath. She didn't know what had triggered t—the lazy desire simmering in his eyes or the erotic touch of iis tongue and lips on her fingers—but she was on fire. He started with her little finger, swirling his tongue around it, then drawing it inside his lips to the warmth of his mouth dissolving the rest of the jam. By the time he reached her thumb, her breathing was rapid and shallow.

He dried her fingers gently on the napkin and sat up. For a moment, she thought he might kiss her. Instead, he reached over and picked up another strawberry-topped pastry, noticeably smaller than the last one. When he straightened, he shifted on the settee, dropping one arm along the back cushion.

"Now, it's your turn." His voice was thick and compelling. As he brought the delicacy to her lips, he slipped his other hand beneath her hair, gently stroking the nape of her neck with warm fingers.

Kate took a bite, but did not think she could swallow. She knew she must before he would touch her. And, he had to touch her! She was not quite sure what to expect, but she knew it would be wonderful. She quickly forced down both bites, her heart pounding with anticipation.

She sat still, barely breathing as he lifted his little finger to her mouth. She noticed his breathing was quick and shallow, his pupils dilated so that his beautiful cinnamon eyes were almost black. She drew his finger into her mouth, and he gasped softly, closing his eyes. He let her lick the sticky jam off of his ring finger, then dipped the other two into her mouth at the same time.

Kate was trembling, and her heart pounded so hard she thought it would burst. A deep ache filled her, a longing so powerful it brought tears to her eyes.

Colton looked at her when she slipped his thumb into her mouth. Kate saw the longing in his eyes, the matching ache in the almost painful expression on his face. There was little jam on his thumb, so a few seconds later she parted her lips and expected him to withdraw it.

Instead, he traced her inner lip. When she gasped, he moved his thumb farther out, rubbing first across her bottom lip and then the top with feather softness. A violent shudder shook her.

"Oh, Cole, what are you doing to me?" she whispered. She sagged toward him, resting her forehead against the tip of his chin, her bent arms against his chest.

"Tormenting you. And myself." His voice was ragged, but

his breathing gradually slowed. His heart throbbed against her hand. He waited a few minutes until he could catch his breath. "You'd better go upstairs, Kitten. If your grandfather or one of the servants comes in, you'll be thoroughly compromised." *And I wouldn't mind a bit.*

Would that be so horrible? She nodded, unknowingly tickling his nose with her hair.

He eased back from her, a grin lighting his face. Tickling his nose had been effective in bringing him down to earth. He rubbed the offended appendage with his finger, then ruffled her hair. "Dangerous weapon you've got there."

Kate smiled back, relieved the tension had been broken. "I'd better go."

"Yes, and you'd better go up the back way. Any man with eyes in his head will know we've been up to something."

Kate quickly smoothed her hair and pressed a few wrinkles from her skirt. The duke caught her hand, stilling her movements.

"It isn't that your hair or clothes are mussed." He brushed her cheek with his fingertip. "It's here, in the soft radiance of your skin and the gently swollen lips. I didn't kiss you, but I might as well have." Wide-eyed, she met his gaze.

"It's there, in those lovely, expressive eyes. Desire still glows within their depths, sweetheart. You look like a woman who has had a taste of passion and aches for more."

Kate jumped up, irritated because he could read her so well. *And if you dunna quit talking like that, the ache will never go away,* she thought in frustration. She stormed toward the door, but stopped and looked back at him. She had the sneaky feeling he had irritated her on purpose, to get her to leave quickly. A saucy grin slowly spread across her face.

"Well, Your Grace, you canna get away with acting cold to me now. I'll save you two dances tomorrow night." She spun around, walking to the door with a perky step. As her hand touched the doorknob, she heard a muffled response from behind her.

"Oh, very well, two dances. But make them slow and simple," the duke growled.

Kate sailed out of the room with a musical laugh.

A short time later, Colton departed, wearing a secret smile.

Chapter 14

Kate slept late the next morning, not arising until almost noon. Stretching her arms above her head, she yawned then smiled at Bess. "Is Lady Millicent feeling better?"

"Aye, miss. Crockett said her ladyship was quite on the mend. Still has a touch of the headache, but it isna so bad this morning. She plans to rest today. Told Bence to receive no callers."

"I'm glad she's better. I suppose it will be nice no' to have a house full of company today." Kate sat up in bed as Bess fluffed the pillows behind her back. When she was comfortably settled, the maid handed her a cup of hot chocolate. Kate's forehead wrinkled slightly. She felt restless and mildly out of sorts, not at all sure she wanted to spend the afternoon quietly.

"Lady Millicent suggested you join her in her sittin' room when you're dressed. She thought you might want to take your breakfast there."

"Of course," Kate answered absently. She had lain awake for hours thinking of Colton and his surprising lesson in sensuality. The thoughts were still with her, thrilling her, troubling her. *I will never find another who excites me as he does,* she thought. *Surely, he wouldna be so passionate if he dinna love me.* She shook her head at her own naïveté. Presumably, men were very passionate with their mistresses, yet she doubted if there was anything resembling love in those relationships.

For once, Kate regretted not having any close friends in London. She had made many acquaintances; indeed, she got along with most everyone. However, there was no particular young woman with whom she would feel at ease sharing confidences. In Scotland, she had three or four dear friends to whom she could bare her soul. She thought of writing her closest friend, Alice MacArthur, but decided against it. Surely circumstances would not remain the same long enough for her to get any answer that would be of help.

After Kate dressed, she wandered down the hall to visit her grandmother. Rowan came trotting up the staircase and joined her. She stopped and raised her hand to pet his great head. "Another lost soul, eh, you big beastie? Well, come along. You can tell me your troubles and I'll tell you mine." She stopped at Lady Millicent's doorway. "Do you mind if Rowan comes in, too?"

"Of course not, dear." Lady Millicent was reclining on a deep-cushioned chaise lounge. "Have you eaten?"

"Nothing but chocolate. I'll ring for a tray. Do you want anything?"

"No. I ate a bit of toast earlier. That will be sufficient for now."

"You look as if you're better. At least you have a little color," said Kate, sitting down on a chair near her grandmother. "How is your head?"

"Better, but it still hurts. I shan't be going to Lady Jersey's tonight, but Thomas has agreed to take you."

"I dunna wish to go with you unwell, and I'm certain he doesna want to leave you."

"Nonsense, my dear. There is nothing wrong with me that a few days away from the noise and crowds will not cure. Your grandfather is quite pleased to take you. If I am still only mildly under the weather, as I am now, he will not be troubled by leaving me. You will go, child. I will not hear of you staying home. Lady Jersey's rout is one of the most important of the Season."

"Very well, ma'am." Thinking of Colton's promise to dance with her, she added, "I do think I will enjoy it."

Lady Millicent caught the minute blush that shaded Kate's cheeks. "Tell me, gel, did that scamp of a son of mine stay and visit awhile last night?"

Kate's blush deepened. "Yes, he did. We had a nice conversation." *That's no' all that was nice!* "He has submitted his resignation from the War Office. He believes his duties will be completed in one or two weeks."

"Good. He has worked much too hard. I suppose he'll find some other project to fill his time. He's not one to let the moss grow. I do hope he takes more time to relax. He seems far too weary of late."

"I believe he plans to visit his estates soon, although he did indicate that he might try to relax more. I encouraged him to do so." Kate smiled, not aware of the soft, blissful expression stealing over her face. "He plans to attend Lady Jersey's rout tonight. I'm saving him two dances."

Lady Millicent's eyes widened in surprise. "Colton asked you to dance? He practically never dances. The poor dear tried it a few times when he was younger, but made a muddle of it. Turned wrong and ran smack into Sara Miles. Knocked her flat on her backside."

"Oh, no! He must have been mortified!"

"Indeed," said Lady Millicent dryly. "That's not the half of it. Sara was a homely thing, tall and skinny with a face like a horse. She acted more like a . . . um . . . donkey. Instead of taking Colton's hand and letting him help her to her feet as discreetly as possible, the chit started to wail. She sat there in the middle of the floor, shrieking like a banshee, blubbering out all kinds of indecent things. Finally, her mother made her way through the crowd and jerked the gel to her feet."

The countess chuckled and shook her head. "Sara made such an idiot of herself that her mother never brought her back to town. Married her off to some unsuspecting third son of a baron."

"Has Colton never danced since?"

"Oh, I wouldn't say never. He's danced with me a few times and perhaps a few others over the years. His father spent a fortune on dancing lessons for him. The instructors swore he was quite accomplished, but I've never seen him display a particular talent on the dance floor."

"He waltzes wonderfully," said Kate quietly. Before the countess could reply, Bence appeared at the door with Kate's breakfast tray.

Once the butler deposited the tray and left the room, Lady Millicent all but sprang on Kate. "How do you know he can waltz?"

Kate smiled softly. "The first day I met him, he stopped by the music room after his visit with you." A bit of color touched her cheeks again. "I had finished cleaning the room, and being a little silly, decided to waltz around the room with an invisible partner. Papa taught me the dance several years ago after he learned it on the Continent. Anyway, Colton fell into step with me, humming the same tune, and waltzed me around the room. I've never had a partner who was more graceful."

"I see." The countess tapped her lip lightly with the tip of her finger. "I suspect that Colton's problems on the dance floor have more to do with his shyness than his abilities. Perhaps a few successful dances with you will make him realize it." She shook her head. "I still cannot believe he asked you to dance."

"Well . . ." Kate's eyes twinkled with impish delight. "He dinna. I asked him. I'd be too old to toddle out onto the dance floor if I waited for him to ask."

"My, my, such forward behavior." Lady Millicent chuckled and winked at her. "Tell me, did he jump at the chance?"

"No, he had to think about it for a while." A vivid memory of the past evening flashed across her mind, and Kate struggled to keep the red from rising to her cheeks. She was only marginally successful, and noticed Lady Millicent's eyebrow lift expressively. "Finally, he decided that if I would save him two of the slow, simple dances, he would do it."

"Pity the waltz is not acceptable. Colton's father and I danced it years ago on the Continent. It was lovely." She grinned at Kate. "I always thought it would be a deliciously exciting, yet reasonably prudent way for a young woman to be held in a man's arms. It would serve as a guide, you see. If she could not bear his nearness on the dance floor, how would she tolerate it once they were wed? But if she found the experience delightful, then no doubt they would rub along nicely when married. Don't you agree?"

Kate almost choked. "Yes, Grandmama. It would make sense."

Lady Millicent looked at her shrewdly. "You do love him, don't you, child."

"Yes, milady, I do. I canna bear the thought of living without him for the rest of my life."

"I assume that he is no longer cold to you."

"No, he is no longer cold." *Oh, why do I have to turn red every time I think of him!*

"Do you care to tell me how this miraculous change came about?"

Kate gave her a quick, laundered version of her chat with Colton at the ball two nights previous. "I suppose I must admit, but only to you, Grandmama, that I had thought of spraying him with my perfume even before I went to the ball. I wanted to make sure he thought of me, you see, but I certainly had no intention of giving him a bath in jasmine. Still, it turned out far better than I had expected."

"You have obviously found the secret that no other woman has considered."

"What is that, milady?"

"His sense of humor. Though it seems contrary to his nature, at least to his manner, Colton has always had a keen sense of the ridiculous." She pursed her lips thoughtfully. "Although if it had happened in front of others, I suspect he would not have found it so amusing."

"I dunna think he thought it was amusing until later. I believe at the time, he was afraid he would suffocate." Kate smiled at her grandmother, pleased to see more color in her cheeks and a sparkle in her eye. "How's your headache?"

"Completely gone. I believe I might be up to gracing Lady Jersey's rout after all. I'm curious to see how Colton does tonight. If he is open in his attentions toward you, it will bode well for our own little party next week. There's nothing like the flowering of a confirmed bachelor to lure the reluctant."

"But I dunna want to cause him any embarrassment."

"You won't. I doubt if he will even notice that he is the center of attention."

Kate frowned. "I dunna think he would like that."

Lady Millicent shrugged. "No, probably not, but most of us

ake center stage at one time or another. The important thing, ow, is for you to let him know, subtly, of course, that you refer his company to all others."

"I intend to." Kate picked up a piece of bacon and nibbled n it. "Actually, I dunna think he can help but notice. I feel ike my face lights up every time I see him."

"Good. If only he'd dance with you more than twice."

"But I thought that wasna allowed."

"It is if you have my permission, and you certainly have my ermission to dance with him—and only him—as many times s you like. Well, I'm sure you can think of some way to do it. 'll handle the talk." Lady Millicent waved her hand, indicat-ng that gossip was well within her control.

"Well, I will see what I can do, although I'm no' sure that uch action would be subtle." She hesitated for a moment, but oon her eyes began to sparkle. What better way to let him now she preferred him to other men? It would almost be like public proclamation. It was a bit deceptive, she admitted, for would be almost like a proclamation on his part too.

But perhaps I can gauge his feelings by his reaction, she hought. *If he is quick to dance with me the third time, then I vill be more certain of his feelings. If he doesna want to, I will now he doesna love me, or at least that he isna ready to give int to his intentions. If he is very much against it, I willna ursue that course.*

Kate picked up a piece of toast and spread strawberry jam hickly across it. Suddenly, she was very nervous about Lady ersey's rout.

"Good morning, Mr. Robin." Colton set down his paper and ook a sip of coffee, watching the bird through the open indow of the breakfast room. "It's a beautiful day, isn't it?"

The bird chirped a cheerful reply, cocking his head to one ide and watching him carefully.

"I'll tell you a secret, Mr. Robin," said the duke softly. He lanced around to make certain none of the servants had lipped into the room unnoticed. "I'm in love. Now, don't you o telling everybody, Bird. I'll do my own telling, in my own ood time, thank you." He grinned as the bird took a few hops loser on the branch. "Ah, you think I'll toss you a worm or two, don't you? Sorry, old boy, but I didn't have them for breakfast this morning." He grimaced at the thought. "But I suspect if you look in any one of the flower beds, you'll find an abundance. Be my guest." The bird flew off and Colton laughed softly.

"I'm in love," he murmured. "Undeniably, irrevocably, head-over-heels in love." He had known it for months, but in the wee hours of the morning, he accepted the finality of it.

Although he was certain of his feelings, he still had his doubts. He was not sure she loved him in return, though after their moments together the evening before, that doubt was not as strong as it once had been. He knew she was passionate by nature, but her response to his touch still amazed and elated him.

I made her tremble, he thought with a swell of pride. His thoughts traveled back to the time they spent at Twin Rivers. He had made her tremble then, too, but he had convinced himself it had more to do with the situation and her awakening passion than it did with any feelings for him. But, somehow, now he knew he had been wrong. She cared for him, he was certain. He did not know the depth of her affection, but he had made up his mind to discover it.

If I never seek her love, then, of a certainty, I will never have it, he reasoned. He decided to openly pay his attentions to her, with discretion and dignity, of course. He could not flaunt his feelings before the ton, but it was time to quietly let Heartly and the other men who flocked around her know that he was in the race.

He would be vulnerable, and it was scary. He smiled ruefully to himself before taking another sip of coffee. He had been in situations in the past several years that might have spelled an end to his life. Yet, he could never remember being more frightened. He risked ridicule. He risked heartbreak. But the prize was worth any risk.

He would move cautiously but purposefully. He was certain Kate would note the change in his behavior. He believed she knew him well enough to understand how easily he could be hurt. He trusted her enough not to publicly thrash his heart.

Once his decisions were made, Colton felt almost euphoric For the first time in months, he had no business requiring his immediate attention, no particular reason to even go into his office. The duke drained his cup and set it down on the table as he rose from his chair.

"It is a beautiful day, and I'm going to enjoy it." He sent for Lunan to bring his curricle around, and soon they were on their way.

"Where to, Your Grace?" Lunan had been a little surprised when the duke indicated he wanted the groom to drive. He cast a slanted glance at his employer, trying to gauge his mood. The duke sat next to him, relaxed and apparently relishing the sunshine at the moment. His face was tilted upward, eyes closed. Lunan raised one eyebrow.

Colton brought his attention back to the groom and grinned at his amused expression. "Quite nice, this springtime sunshine. I'd almost forgotten how good it feels on the skin. Let's take a turn around Hyde Park. There shouldn't be too many people about yet."

"Very well, sir." Lunan flicked the reins and the pair of high steppers moved out prettily. "Going to the War Office today?" He glanced at the duke, wishing he knew what was afoot. His Grace was occupied with watching the street scenes around them and seemed to be enjoying himself immensely.

"No, not unless they send for me." He smiled at his friend. "I have no meetings scheduled, no reports to read, no reports to write, no strategies to work out. And it feels wonderful! I was afraid I would be plagued with boredom once the war ended, but now I'm beginning to think I'll enjoy a slower-paced life."

They drove through Hyde Park slowly, taking pleasure in the flowers and the singing of the birds. There were few others about so early in the morning, which suited Colton's mood just fine.

"Let's go down to the river and see if we can find John. I should let him know how things stand," said the duke.

Lunan swung the team around the corner with a show of agility, avoiding a vegetable cart that was stopped in the road.

"How is Copper Halfpenny doing? I haven't had much of a chance to stop by the mews and check on his work. Are you satisfied with him?"

"Aye, Your Grace. You read that one right as rain. The lad

is a hard worker. Seems like he was born with a knowledge of horseflesh." Lunan grinned and looked at the duke. "Reminds me of myself when I was his age. Lives and breathes them animals. He'd sleep with 'em if I'd let him." His face grew serious. "He's a good lad. I like him."

"I'm glad he's working out. Does he get along well with the other stableboys?"

"Aye, though he's pretty much the quiet type. He took some teasin' at first about his name, but he was good natured about it and soon the other boys came to respect him."

"It's time he had a little respect. Ah, I see Pemberton heading our way." Lunan stopped the curricle and held the horses steady as the duke stepped down. "Drive over Blackfriars and pick me up on the other side. If you don't keep me waiting, I'll buy you something to eat." He grinned and turned away, walking down the stone River Stairs. He stopped a few steps above the lapping water.

"Good mornin', Yer Grace." Pemberton smiled at the duke and moved his boat up next to the steps, holding it steady.

"Good morning, John. How's business?" Colton climbed into the shallow boat and sat down. He waved to Lunan as the waterman shoved the wherry away from shore.

"Doin' well, what with all the lords and ladies in town for the Season. Are ye retirin' from the War Office?"

"Yes. That's one reason I came by to see you. I won't be involved in any more operations right away. Probably never. Do you want to continue? There might be need of someone occasionally until the spoils are divided."

"No thanks." Pemberton plied the oars with obvious ease, propelling the boat smoothly across the river. "Without ye runnin' things, Yer Grace, I'd just as soon not be a part of it. I could trust ye. Always knew where I stood. That ain't always true with some o' the other coves."

He grinned and winked at the duke. "Besides, it's time I made my Annie an 'onest woman. I been tellin' 'er for a year that I couldn't be tied down. But we got a baby comin' soon and it needs a proper name."

"Congratulations, on becoming a husband and a proud father. You're wise to marry first. It could save you legal problems down the line with the child."

"Aye. We don't want nobody callin' our babe a bastard. We love each other, and we'll love 'im just as much. I felt 'im kick last night for the first time. I tell you, Guv, it brought a tear to my eye when I put my 'and on Annie's belly and felt 'im move." He grinned, blinking a little. "I told 'er the babe was punchin' with 'is fist, already practicin' to be a waterman."

Colton laughed. "What did she think of the idea?"

"She told me I'd gone a few rounds too many myself." Pemberton rowed in silence for several minutes, then casually asked, " 'ow's Miss Denley? I 'eard she was back in London."

"She fares well. She's a hit, as you probably expected." Colton didn't question how the waterman knew Kate was in London. That was one of the reasons he had worked with the man; he knew how to find out most anything about anyone.

"According to my mother, Addison welcomed his father to Scotland with open arms. You'd never think there had been a twenty-year rift between them. The earl insisted on bringing Kate to London and presenting her to society." He smiled. "She bends the rules now and then, but so far has caused no great calamity."

"Ye goin' to marry 'er?"

A day earlier, Colton would have been annoyed, perhaps even angry at Pemberton's question. Today, however, he looked at life in a new light. "If she will have me," he answered quietly.

"I was 'opin' ye'd come around, Yer Grace."

"Me? It's Kate I'm unsure about."

"I don't think ye've got a worry on that score. From everythin' I could see, she was quite fond of ye. Besides, what woman would turn down a chance to be a duchess?"

"Kate—if it was something she didn't want to do. She has a mind of her own."

Pemberton drew the boat up to a stone stairway on the opposite shore. "Then she's worth 'avin', Yer Grace. I wish ye the best."

"Thank you." Colton climbed from the wherry and dug in his pocket. He placed the contents, a fistful of gold guineas, in Pemberton's hand. "Buy your wife something pretty for her wedding day. And John, let me know if you ever have need of anything. Tell Annie, too." He offered him his hand. Pemberton took it, shaking it firmly.

"Thank ye, Yer Grace. It's good to know my Annie and the babe will be taken care of if anythin' ever 'appens to me." His smile held a hint of sadness as they released hands. He would miss working with the duke. "When Miss Denley accepts yer offer, tell 'er I always thought she was a smart lady."

"Thank you." Colton chuckled and walked slowly up the steps. "I'll bring her by some day soon. She'll be happy to see you again," he called over his shoulder. Pemberton nodded, then turned his attention to a small group of passengers who waited at the top of the River Stairs.

Lunan was waiting in the curricle, parked in the shade of a row of trees on the street above. "Well, looks like you have to buy my luncheon." His eyes twinkled at the duke as he climbed into the curricle.

"I did promise such a silly thing, didn't I. Well, stop by the bank, then we'll head for one of the coffeehouses on St. James. Afterward, I want to pick up some flowers and sweetmeats and then drop in on my mother."

"You're takin' her flowers and sweetmeats? Your poor mum will have a heart attack instead of the headache."

"There's no need to go fishing, my friend. The flowers are for Mother. The sweetmeats are for Kate. In fact, I think I'll even buy some for myself. If you're nice, I'll let you have one."

Lunan laughed out loud. His slanted glance at the duke spoke volumes, but he added for good measure, "Are we goin' courtin', Your Grace?"

"We're goin' courtin', Lunan." Colton's gaze focused on a pretty young nanny pushing a baby carriage down the walk, and he recalled Pemberton's emotion when he spoke of the babe. For a moment Colton felt the sting of moisture in his own eyes as he imagined Kate round with child. His child.

He took a deep breath and cleared his throat. "We are indeed," he said softly.

"Good afternoon, dear Mama." Colton bent gracefully to kiss his mother on the cheek. "Here I am bringing you posies to cheer you out of your sick bed, and I find you up and about and sparkling like a diamond in the first water." He gave her a broad smile when he straightened and held out a bouquet of violets.

"Oh, Colton, they're beautiful!" Lady Millicent's surprise and pleasure shown on her face. Her son seldom gave her flowers. His father never had, and as in many things, the son learned from the father. "Thank you so much, dear."

"It is my pleasure, I assure you." Colton felt a little twinge of guilt, realizing how much this simple gift had meant to his mother. He resolved to be more open with his affection in the future. He glanced around the room at the numerous floral arrangements, some quite elaborate, adorning the tables. "Although perhaps flowers were not the best choice."

"Of course they were." The countess held the fragrant blossoms to her nose and sniffed deeply. "Not a one of these tokens is for me. They are all from Kate's admirers. I'm delighted with your gift. If I weren't already feeling better, I'd be bouncing right out of bed, much healed by your thoughtfulness." She smiled up at him, her eyes glistening with unshed tears.

Colton bowed slightly and sought to lighten the mood. He turned to Kate. "And, for you, Miss Denley. I could not bring a gift to one lovely lady without also honoring the other."

Kate's eyes widened in amazement and her mouth practically dropped open. Then her gaze narrowed in suspicion as she caught the dancing imps in his eyes and the way his fingers cupped the lapel of his coat.

With his free hand, Colton reached beneath the coat to retrieve a square box trimmed with turquoise ribbon. He handed it to Kate with a flourish and a wicked grin. "Hopefully, the candy isn't too warm. I wouldn't want it to melt."

A soft pink filled her cheeks. For a second, she wasn't sure what he meant to do, but then the mischief faded from his face, replaced by a tenderness that warmed her heart. She took the box from his hand, intentionally brushing his fingers with hers, and murmured her thanks.

"I won't offer to help you eat it," Colton said, sitting down on a chair between the ladies. "I bought a box for myself, so I really shouldn't indulge in yours." He smiled and winked at Kate. "I even bought some for my servants."

"You are most kind, Your Grace." Kate returned his smile, then turned to open the fancy box with a flourish of her own.

"Edinburgh Rock! Oh, Cole, wherever did you find it?" Her face beamed in delight.

"Oh, I had to search high and low." He grinned. "Actually, I just happened upon it. I was on my way to Gunter's when I spotted a new confectioner's called MacAlpine's. I stopped out of curiosity. Their cakes are rather plain, but they have a large assortment of sweetmeats and candy." He smiled warmly. "And a good supply of Ferguson's sugar-candy."

"They'd better. Edinburgh Rock is my very favorite." She offered Lady Millicent first choice, then turned to Colton.

"No, you go next, my dear. Forbid that I should take the one you have your heart set upon."

She pondered over the decision for a moment, her fingers wavering back and forth between a pink raspberry and a green peppermint. Finally she chose the raspberry one. As Kate bit into the soft powdery candy, she held the box out to the duke.

"Well, since you insist," he drawled. With a grin, he made a show of choosing also, finally taking a fawn-colored ginger piece. "Perhaps I should change my thinking." He met her gaze, a spark flaring in his eyes. "We could eat your candy first, then share mine."

Kate drew a sharp breath, her heart thudding. A warm sweetness slowly invaded her body as the memory of his touch flooded her mind. His comment seemed innocent enough, but knowing what he was suggesting filled her with excitement and daring. "As you wish, Your Grace," she murmured, sedately closing the box of candy and placing it on a nearby table. "But you must remember, too many sweets will spoil your dinner."

"In this instance, I believe they would only serve to whet my appetite." The words were uttered in a mild tone, but the promise in his eyes brought a flutter to her heart.

Later that evening Colton wove his way through Lady Jersey's crowded ballroom. He reached Kate's side moments before the music began for their first dance.

"I thought you had deserted me, Your Grace." Kate smiled up at him, her eyes sparkling with pleasure. She put her hand lightly on his arm as he held it out for her. "You're tense."

"Quaking in my boots, ma'am." His expression was bland, but she thought she heard a true thread of nervousness in his voice.

"You'll dazzle the assembly." She smiled again and squeezed his arm gently.

"I just hope I don't trip, or tear your gown, or knock some poor unsuspecting soul to the floor."

"You dinna think you could skate either, but you did."

"Only by hanging onto you."

"Then, by all means, sir, hang onto me." She sent him such a flirty little look that he laughed out loud.

"You may regret that statement, minx." He smiled down at her tenderly, his dimple prominently on display.

"Never, Your Grace." She returned his warm smile, but her eyes held a glint of seriousness that was not lost on the duke. She turned and they lined up in position for the beginning of the dance.

"I wish this were a waltz," he murmured, leaning down to speak into her ear. "I shall regret every step we are apart." *Lud, what a line. You'd better be more original than that!* He held his breath, waiting for her to laugh or deliver some belittling remark. *What the deuce am I doing,* he thought. *I'm no good at flirting.*

"I shall regret it, too, Cole." Kate's expression was tender and sincere, and she realized with some alarm that she had rattled him. The corners of her lips lifted in a tiny smile. With a wink, she added, "Now, Your Grace, dunna forget, you turn to the left first."

"And take my next partner's left hand with my right."

"No, no! You take her right hand." Kate relaxed as she met his twinkling gaze. "You do know your left from your right, dunna you?" she asked dryly.

"Yes, mine, but not hers." A mock look of horror spread over his face. "What if she has three hands?"

Kate laughed, delighted that he was joking with her. "Then you're in a pickle, sir." The music began and the dancers, including the Duke of Ryland, moved gracefully through the pattern.

Lady Jersey tapped Countess Lieven on the arm with her fan. "Look quickly or you might miss it."

"Miss what?" Countess Lieven turned her attention from an attractive viscount to sweep her gaze across the floor. Her eyes immediately focused on the Duke of Ryland as he completed the circle and rejoined Kate. The young woman said something, and his serious expression brightened into a wide, beautiful smile.

"The Ice King is melting!" Countess Lieven and Lady Jersey, along with a goodly portion of the others in the room, gaped at the startling transformation.

Lady Jersey shook her head. "I never thought I'd see the day when that man smiled, much less see him looking at any woman the way he's looking at Miss Denley."

"I do believe we are seeing a match in the making."

"From the way they're looking at each other, it may already be made," murmured Lady Jersey.

Countess Lieven nodded and watched as the couple once again came together in the figure of the dance. She could almost see the sparks fly from across the room. The countess had been impressed with Catriona Denley. She was no simpering miss; instead, she was intelligent and direct without being brazen. The countess knew there were some who wanted to drag up the old scandal about Miss Denley's father, for no other reason than to gossip, but she had squelched all attempts.

As the Russian Ambassador's wife, Countess Lieven found few people in London society whom she truly liked, although she went out of her way to make certain others think she held them in high esteem. However, she retained a certain fondness for the Earl of Blagden. To most everyone else, and especially to the Russian countess, membership in the ton was a power game. Lord Blagden, however, went about his life without pretense. He was a little blustery, but was honest and direct. The countess found it extremely refreshing, and felt his granddaughter was much like him.

She was not a close acquaintance of the Duke of Ryland, but she admired and respected him. He was a wealthy and influential man, although no one seemed to actually know what he did in the government. She suspected he was one of the most powerful men in England, for though he quietly worked behind the scenes, she was privy to enough information to know that he held great sway over the leaders of the country.

"It would seem the duke has kept his charm hidden from the rest of us." The countess smiled knowingly as Colton escorted Kate back to Lady Millicent's side.

"Indeed," acknowledged their hostess with a similar smile. "This may prove to be an interesting evening after all."

Colton grinned down at Kate. A tremendous feeling of relief filled him, and he suspected that after a few more dances, he would have no more qualms about stepping out onto the dance floor. "Ah, success."

"You're a born dancer. I dinna see you make a single mistake." Kate's appreciative smile turned teasing. "And you had the ladies charmed out of their stockings."

"I did?" Colton glanced back over his shoulder toward the dance floor. "You jest, my dear. There's not a single stocking lying around."

"They grabbed them up before anyone else could see." Kate joined his laughter and linked her arm through his. She did not realize the possessive way she hugged his arm to her side, but the duke noticed. So did several others.

"Well, son, you acquitted yourself nicely out there." Lady Millicent beamed up at Colton. "I do believe you actually enjoyed it."

"Part of the time." *When I was with Kate*. "I'll be more at ease after I've completed a few more dances without a disaster. But right now, I'm parched. Would you ladies care for some punch?"

"I don't care for any, dear. Thomas brought me a cup a few minutes ago before he wandered off to watch a game of whist."

"Yes, please, but I'm promised for this dance." Kate glanced from her approaching partner back to Colton. Her regret was obvious.

"You're promised for every dance," the duke teased, astonishing her by playfully flicking her beneath the chin with his forefinger. "Now, put a smile on that lovely face or the poor gentleman will think you're repulsed by him. It will probably take me two dances to work my way to the refreshment table and back. I'll meet you here."

"Thank you." Kate sent him a brilliant smile, then carefully schooled her expression to one of polite interest before turning to meet her next partner.

Colton chuckled, pleased she had favored only him with the radiant smile. It took him over two dances to make his way through the crowd. He returned in time for Kate to drink her punch quickly before she was whisked off by her next partner.

The duke stood at his mother's side, making small talk and watching Kate for the next three dances. He noted that even though she was charming to each gentleman, she did not flirt with any of them. Not a one of them received the kind of warm, tender gaze that could set his heart to pounding. Not even her current partner, Viscount Heartly.

Colton was particularly observant of her attentions toward Heartly. There was a different tone to Kate's manner when she was around him. He could tell they were engaged in light, amusing banter, but by the time the dance ended, the duke felt on firmer ground. To all indications, the two were no more than simply good friends.

Viscount Heartly escorted Kate across the floor, delivering her to Colton's side. "I believe you have the honor next, Your Grace."

"Yes, thank you." Colton nodded politely. Instead of offering Kate his arm, he slipped it around her waist in a possessive move, resting his hand against the soft curve of her side. He gently propelled her through the crowd to join a set. Turning to get into position, the duke glanced back at Viscount Heartly. The man barely nodded his head in recognition of Colton's action, a tiny smile of satisfaction on his face.

The duke was surprised at Heartly's approval, but more surprised by the sudden lightness that filled his heart. *Perhaps there is indeed hope*, he thought. He joined in the dance with a bit more enthusiasm and felt much more confident when he completed it without a single misstep.

A little while later, Colton was conversing with Lord Blagden when Kate joined them. He picked up her agitation immediately.

"What is wrong, my dear?"

"Oh, it is no matter of great consequence. Freddie Packard's sister tore her gown and he had to take her home. He was next on my card. I had thought simply to sit this one out, but now I see his friend, Lord Bell, heading this way. My toes are still tender from the last time we danced." Earlier Kate had thought it great luck when Freddie stopped by to make his apologies. She had been trying to think of some way to trick Colton into dancing with her. Then Lord Bell appeared, presenting a ready-made excuse for the duke's help.

"Colton, would you be gallant and rescue this maiden in distress?" She looked up at him, batting her eyelashes with theatrical exaggeration. But the closer Lord Bell came, the more earnest her expression became. The man had two very large left feet.

"It will mean three dances for us, Kate. There will be talk." His countenance was serious.

"I know." She cast a worried glance toward Lord Bell. He pushed through the crowd with the determination and the grace of a bear after a cache of honey. "But I dunna care if you dunna."

Colton looked at Lord Blagden. "Do I have your permission to dance with this lovely lady for a third time, sir?"

One glance at his granddaughter's pleading expression convinced the earl there was more here than met the eye. "Of course, son."

Colton quickly spirited her away, once again slipping his arm around her. He drew her even closer to his side when he noted Lord Bell stalk after them. Thankfully, the man stopped after a few steps in their direction. The scene had not gone unnoticed. Mixed murmurings met their ears, some only of interest, others of disapproval.

"Well, my dear, we're earning a bit of censure and the dance has yet to begin."

Kate tossed her head disdainfully. "You know I am no' overly concerned with what these people think of me."

"Yes, I believe you've mentioned that on occasion," the duke said with a wry smile. It occurred to him that he was not overly concerned with what they thought of him either, but he knew how cruel they could be, especially to a young woman.

He noticed his mother talking to Countess Lieven. The woman smiled in his direction as his mother moved over to talk to their hostess. Lady Jersey was frowning at him, but Lady Millicent said something to her which caused her to laugh. The paragon shook her head slightly, then shot Colton a mischievous look. He had the feeling she considered him an amusing, naughty little boy, caught with his hand in the cookie jar.

He looked down at Kate as the orchestra began to play. In spite of her brave words, there was a glint of worry in her eyes. Instinctively, he knew her concern was for him and not herself.

"Give me that beautiful smile, Kitten," he murmured, bestowing one of his own upon her. As his arm slid around her for a turn, he drew her much closer than was normal for the dance.

Kate looked up at him in surprise, keenly aware of the pressure of his body against hers. Excitement rushed through her as she realized he was telling all who watched that he was attracted to her. Her pulse quickened as she briefly stepped away to join another partner. Seconds later, the dance brought her back to Colton.

He pulled her close, swinging her around with the grace she had seen in the waltz. Before the dance separated them again, he dipped his head to whisper, "Let them talk."

His warm breath tickled her sensitive ear, but it was the quick, artful brush of his lips against her temple that almost made her trip.

Chapter 15

Only two floral offerings arrived the morning after Lady Jersey's party. One, a dozen carnations of varying colors, came from Viscount Heartly with a card that simply said, "Bravo!"

The other gift came from the Duke of Ryland. The small bottle holding a single yellow orchid and a delicate spray of jasmine was cleverly hidden in a silver filigree basket. Also resting in the basket, unfurled behind the flowers in all its glory, was the most beautiful mother-of-pearl fan Kate had ever seen. The card read simply, "Kitten—On Thursday, four or more. Cole."

Kate clutched the card to her breast. "I'd gladly save all my dances for you, my love," she whispered. She was also thrilled to see he had used the nickname she had given him. Tucking the card beneath the wristband of her long sleeve morning dress, she carried the bouquet into the breakfast room to show the earl and countess.

"Oh, my dear, how lovely!" Lady Millicent's delight slowly faded from her face. "Although, by rights, I suppose you shouldn't keep the fan. It's much too expensive a gift. Who sent it?"

Kate's sparkling eyes suddenly misted with happiness. "Colton."

"Will wonders never cease." Lady Millicent shared a joyful grin with the earl.

"You may keep the fan, child." The earl relaxed against the back of his chair. "I don't suppose it was accompanied by words of undying love."

"No." Kate grinned at him, all the mistiness in her eyes gone. "But he did ask for four or more dances at our ball."

"Then, by all means, child, save them for him. Won't do to discourage the lad."

Kate raised an expressive eyebrow. "Lad?"

The earl shrugged. "At my age, dear girl, anyone under forty is a youngster." He smiled at Kate, his expression soft and loving. "I'm beginning to think the *lad* might come up to scratch after all."

"I hope so, Grandpapa. And soon." Kate picked up the bouquet and took it up to her room. This was one token of admiration she did not wish to share with curious visitors.

The four days between Lady Jersey's rout and Lady Millicent's ball were filled with a flurry of preparations. As the countess had mentioned to Colton, they remained at home in the evenings so as not to become overtired. However, Lady Millicent and Kate continued to receive company in the afternoons.

There was a definite change in their type of visitors. Viscount Heartly dropped by, as did a few gentlemen who were not quite up to snuff and did not realize the Duke of Ryland had quietly staked his claim on the beautiful Scot. But the hordes of suitors vying for Kate's attention dwindled noticeably. Most of those who paid a call were ladies of the ton, young and old, striving for some hint as to what was afoot between Kate and the duke. They all left sadly disappointed, without any additional *on dit* to share with their cronies.

On Thursday evening, as Bess put the finishing touches to Kate's hair, Harlan knocked on her bedroom door. When the maid opened it, he held out another silver basket, wider and flatter than the first one. "The duke brought this personally. He's waiting with his lordship in the drawing room."

Bess took the basket and shut the door. "Oh, Miss Kate, 'tis perfect." She handed the treasure to her mistress.

Resting on a cushion of black velvet inside the basket was a delicate peach-colored orchid surrounded by wispy clusters of jasmine. Trailing from the bouquet were two peach-colored ribbons trimmed with tiny seed pearls.

"How?" Kate's gaze moved from the beautiful flowers to her gown. The peach of the orchid matched her silk gown to a shade, and the pearl ribbon adorning the bouquet was identical to the ribbon running beneath her bosom and around the flounce on her skirt. She looked up at Bess. "How did he ever match it so perfectly?"

Bess grinned. "Day before yesterday, Lunan asked me what ye were wearin' tonight."

"Lunan?" Kate noted a soft pink flow across the young woman's cheeks.

"Aye, miss. We've walked out a few times." Her blush deepened. "The day His Grace brought ye the candy, Lunan brought me a little box of it, too. It wasna large, nor nearly as fancy as yers, but 'twas the nicest present any man has ever given me. Some might think he's a bit old for me, but I dunna.

"But to answer yer first question, the duke told Lunan to find out exactly what ye were wearin' tonight, so I told him."

"Did you give him a scrap of material or the ribbon?"

"I gave him the teeniest piece of material, but there wasna any extra ribbon."

"He must have gone to the dressmaker's to find it. Oh, that dear, sweet man. Here, help me tie it on my wrist." Kate picked up the flowers, lifting them briefly to her nose to smell their fragrance.

"Oh, Miss, look!" Bess pointed at the basket.

When Kate set the flowers aside and looked down at the basket, she found an exquisite mother-of-pearl, fan-shaped omb for her hair. She picked up the fan Colton had sent her arlier and opened it with a flick of her wrist. The comb was smaller version of the fan, down to the tiniest ornate detail.

She laid the fan aside and picked up the comb with trembling fingers. Handing it to Bess, she said, "Put it where he will see the first time he looks at me."

The maid deftly swept a long strand of hair up to curl above Kate's ear and fastened it with the pearl ornament. The silky curl hung fetchingly along the back of her ear and down her slender neck to brush the tip of one creamy shoulder.

Bess tied the flowers at her wrist, then tied the white silk cord of her dance card beside it. Lastly, she handed her the fan.

"Ach, Miss, the peach is as pretty on ye as the turquoise. He's bound to declare himself tonight."

"We'll see. I want him to be certain of his feelings, but I'll admit, I hope it's soon. If it isna, I'm going to do something rash."

Bess took a string of pearls from the jewelry box and held them to Kate's throat. Addison and Myrna had given them to her two years earlier when they held her first ball in Edinburgh. It had seemed appropriate to wear them tonight, but since the arrival of Colton's lastest offerings, she changed her mind.

"No, Bess, put them away. My only adornment tonight will be the gifts from the man I love."

"Aye, Miss," the maid said softly, blinking back a sentimental tear.

When Kate stepped into the drawing room, both the earl and Colton stood up. She watched Colton as she walked slowly across the room toward them. He took in her appearance in one burning, sweeping glance, then his gaze darted from the flowers to the fan to the comb in her hair. His eyes traveled slowly over her face then down her neck to appraise her décolletage.

A tiny smile lifted the corner of his lip as he noted the wide but modest neckline of her gown. Her shoulders were completely bare, but not even a hint of the curve of her bosom was exposed. His smile grew deep and tender when he realized she wore no other ornament than his gifts. He moved across the room, meeting her halfway.

"You are enchanting tonight, sweetheart," he murmured bringing her gloved hand to his lips in a perfectly proper kiss except he kept her hand gently clasped in his.

The endearment sent a thrill racing through her and for a moment she thought she might not be able to answer him adequately.

"Thank you, Your Grace. Thank you, too, for the flowers both lovely bouquets, and the other gifts. They are beautiful." She ran her gaze over his much-loved face and quickly down his body and back up again. She thought she had never seen him dressed so fine as in his dark blue coat and embroidered sky blue waistcoat. "And so are you," she added softly.

He inclined his head slightly, acknowledging her compliment with twinkling eyes. She was still the only woman who had ever called him beautiful. "Is the waistcoat a bit much? Gregory thought it grand, but I'm not sure."

"It is more colorful than anything I've seen you wear, but it's in good taste and is quite flattering to you. You should wear bright colors more often."

"Perhaps I shall," he murmured, with a tender smile. "Fits my mood of late." He glanced at the comb, pleased to see how nicely it looked in her hair, yet thinking that the glossy locks far outshown his gifts. "I'm gratified that you are happy with my humble offerings. I wanted to give you diamonds or something else equally extravagant, but knew it would be unacceptable." *Soon, I'll shower you with any kind of gift I like*, he thought.

The earl cleared his throat. "Make that scamp release your hand, gel, and come over here so I can get a good look at you."

Colton turned, tucking her hand through the crook of his arm. "I think I shall hang on to this hand for the rest of the evening, sir." Colton grinned. "What do you think? Can I get away with it?"

"Not likely. You look lovely, Granddaughter. You do an old man proud." His quick glance took in the flowers, the fan, and matching comb. He tilted his head toward the duke. "Clever, son, clever. I'm beginning to think I might learn a thing or two from you."

Lady Millicent breezed through the door in a fluttery state of agitation. "What are you going to learn from him?"

"Oh, the way to pick appropriate baubles for the ladies. Dash it, Millie, calm down. Everything's in order, ain't it?"

"Well, yes, at least I hope so." She clasped her hands, then released them immediately. "I'm so afraid we've forgotten something. It's been years since I've hosted a party of this size, you know."

"You couldn't have forgotten anything, love. You've enough food to feed everyone twice over, the orchestra's here and tuned up, the flowers are lovely, the house is spit-polished, and the dog is banished to the mews for the night. Why even your son arrived early. Aren't you even going to greet him?"

"Oh, of course. Colton, you *are* the first to arrive!" Lady Millicent looked at him with wide-eyed astonishment.

"As promised, ma'am. And I'll be the last to leave, unless you kick me out early."

"Well, I do declare. You're simply full of surprises lately."

"He came bearing more gifts, Grandmama." Kate held up her wrist to show off her flowers and pointed to the comb with her fan.

Lady Millicent grinned at her son, giving him a surprise of her own when she winked. "If any other young man paid such lavish attention on Kate, I'd have sent his tokens back." Suddenly a frown wrinkled her brow and her eyes focused behind Colton. "Now, who put that fern in front of the terrace doors? Harlan. Harlan!"

The footman dashed into the room from the hallway.

"Move that plant over to the left about three feet. Yes, yes, that's better. Now, open up the doors so we can have some fresh air in here. The guests will be here any time."

Bence popped his head around the door in an unusually undignified position. "The first coach has arrived, milady." He promptly disappeared again.

"Oh, quick, take your places, Kate, Thomas. Colton, you can stand next to Kate."

"Oh, no, you don't, Madam Mother. You'll not corner me into shaking one hundred hands and kissing another hundred fingers." He grinned at his mother as he sidled toward a nearby door. "Or would that be five hundred fingers?" He winked and ducked through the doorway.

A second later, he stuck his head back through and called softly to Kate. "Am I on your dance card?"

She nodded and held up four fingers. "I dinna think I'd better save more. It would be rude to my other guests."

The duke nodded as Bence stepped to the ballroom door and gravely intoned, "Lord and Lady Webley, Miss Silvia Silverman, the Honorable James Silverman."

Colton held up his index finger and mouthed, "First dance?"

Kate nodded, glanced at the approaching guests, then looked back at him.

"Supper?" came the silent question.

She nodded again, and warmed by the softness of his smile,

turned to greet Lord Webley as he led a long line of guests through the receiving line.

An hour later, Colton appeared at her side. "The orchestra is about to begin." There were no others waiting to go through the receiving line. "Can you get away, now?"

"Yes, although my arm aches from my hand being lifted so many times." She giggled as they stepped away, her eyes sparkling with mischief. "My glove is actually damp from being kissed so many times." She raised up on tiptoe so she could whisper in his ear. "Some of these gentlemen are terribly sloppy with their kisses."

Colton chuckled and shook his head slightly. *Only Kate would say such a thing to me*. It was an intimate, heartwarming thought. "And am I sloppy with my kisses?" he murmured, leaning down a little so his lips were near her ear.

His words brought a flood of memories washing over her, and with it a longing so powerful it took her breath away. She found it impossible to speak, so she merely shook her head. By the time they took their places in the set, she had regained her composure.

The evening spun by like a whirlwind. Before she knew it, Colton had partnered her for the second time and then the supper dance. They sat with Viscount Heartly and Miss Amelia Hastings, a country miss in her second Season who up until that moment had been a confirmed wallflower. Although Miss Hastings's features were quite plain, she possessed a quick mind and dry wit which only seemed to feed Viscount Heartly's keen sense of humor. The two kept Kate and the duke laughing throughout the meal.

The viscount seemed captivated with the young woman, and although Kate sensed she was greatly pleased by his attentions, Miss Hastings was careful to keep a level head. When the supper was over, and the viscount asked her to dance a second time as well as go driving with him the next day, Kate suspected love might be in the air. She hoped so, for she was truly fond of Gerry Heartly and had been greatly impressed by the woman who sparked his interest.

Awhile later, Kate glanced at her card and estimated the ball would last another hour. She almost groaned. Her feet ached, as did her head. In spite of the open windows and doors, it was an exceedingly warm night and the room was stuffy and hot. The noise of the crowd had become a loud roar in her ears, and the orchestra blared a melody as they tried to be heard over the conversation.

Having stayed home for several nights, she had expected to be refreshed and enjoy the party immensely. She had, up to a point. But suddenly it was all too much. She was hot, tired, and wanted only one thing—to be someplace quiet with Colton.

"Kate?"

"Huh?" She came out of her muddle and gave Viscount Heartly a blank look.

"I said this is our dance. You look ready to drop. Would you like to sit this one out?"

"Oh, yes, please. I think my feet will fall off if I dunna give them a rest."

"Let's find you a chair." Gerry took her arm and propelled her through the crowd to some vacant chairs in a corner of the room not far from the garden doors. "Here you go. Now, what shall we talk about?"

Kate smiled wearily. "Would you mind dreadfully if we dinna talk at all?"

"You are done in, aren't you. Very well, I'll just sit here and watch the people while you try to shut everyone out for a bit. Do you want to take a turn in the garden?"

Kate shook her head. "No, this is fine." He was looking across the room at Miss Hastings. "If we went outside, you wouldna be able to watch 'the people.'"

Gerry glanced at her and grinned. "Obvious, eh?"

"Very. I like her, Gerry. From what I saw at supper, I think you two would suit."

"So do I, but don't you tell a soul I said that. A man likes to take these things slowly. Don't want to give up m'freedom without considerable thought and care." His smile had a dreamy quality to it. "Did you notice those pretty gold flecks in her eyes, and the way they sparkle when she laughs?"

To Kate, Miss Hastings's eyes had appeared simply brown, but she refrained from comment. Gerry wasn't really interested in an answer anyway. She tried to relax, rotating her neck around slowly to ease the tension, then let her thoughts roam where they would.

It was a mistake. Colton instantly filled her mind—his masculine beauty, the warmth of his voice, the tenderness and thrill of his touch. She toyed with her fan, thinking how simple it would be to let the language of the fan tell him how she felt, if she could remember all the signals. She had thought the whole idea silly when her governess gave her the instructions and had not paid too much attention.

If I let it rest on the right cheek, that means yes, she thought. *And resting on the left, means no. Drawing it across my cheek, means 'I love you'*. She contemplated doing such a thing the next time he looked at her, but decided she was being foolish. She dismissed the language of the fan from her mind and searched the room for her beloved's face.

When she spotted him across the room, deep in conversation with Lord Liverpool, it seemed as if the crowd and furnishings, and even the Prime Minister, blurred into the background. The noise, obnoxious to the point of a headache a moment before, mellowed to a low hum. A fierce ache swept over her. The yearning was so intense she actually felt a pain around her heart. How she wanted to be loved by this man! Physically. Emotionally. Intellectually. Spiritually. She wanted to share every part of her being with him and to share his in return. *Oh, Colton, love me! Please, love me!*

Colton nodded to Lord Liverpool. "Yes, I couldn't agree with you more." He felt Kate's gaze and turned his head to look across the room. His eyes focused on her immediately, although he had lost sight of her in the crowd a few minutes before. "We'll have to keep—" The look on her face stopped him cold.

The powerful emotions displayed in that unguarded moment sent a shiver clear down to his toes. Longing, loneliness, and—dare he hope—perhaps even love, filled that beloved countenance. Murmuring his apologies to the Prime Minister, Colton stepped away, drawn to her like a magnet.

He wanted to race across the room to her, shoving anyone aside who had the audacity to get in his way, but good breeding and a strong dose of common sense kept his pace leisurely. He reminded himself not only to walk slowly across the miles of carpet, but also to go slowly with her. After all, he might have misread her expression simply because he wanted so desperately to see those feelings there. It would not do to make a fool of himself again. It would be bad enough to do so in front of Kate, but sheer folly to do so in front of the ton.

When he reached her, she was obviously embarrassed and a bit flustered. *Kate, flustered?* A tiny smile tickled his mouth as hope sprang forth anew in his breast.

"Warm evening," he commented, stopping casually by her chair.

"Yes, it is." Kate didn't know whether she should be glad he had read her feelings or look for the nearest hole to crawl into. She suspected if she had been that obvious to him, then the exchange would not have gone unnoticed by others. Suddenly she thought she would scream if she could not get away from the crowd. "I could do with a breath of air. Would you walk with me in the garden, Colton?"

"Of course, my dear." He held out his hand, gently assisting her to her feet when she took hold of it. They passed by several ladies who were already irritated at Kate for attracting all the duke's attention. Some of them had harbored high hopes for their daughters, and a few of the younger but unhappily married ones had entertained certain fanciful daydreams of their own.

"Did you hear her? *She* asked *him* to walk in the garden," said one of the older women, her shocked countenance contorted like a bad actress overplaying her part.

"You can wager they won't be doing much walking," a younger lady muttered knowingly. Her heated gaze slowly moved over the duke, telling her companions that if she were in Kate's shoes, walking would be the last thing on her mind.

"Perhaps this is unwise," murmured the duke, even though he could have cared less what anyone thought.

"Perhaps, but I dunna care. Those old twigs are just jealous anyway." Kate tucked her arm more firmly through his and stepped out onto the steps with her head held high. She had to force herself to keep from grabbing his hand and drawing him off the lighted path into one of the darker recesses of the garden. His growing interest, apparent from his open attentions the past week, made her reckless and impatient.

A mild breeze sprang up, cooling her heated cheeks. Breathing deeply, she recovered from her earlier embarrassment.

"That's better."

"What?" She looked up at him as they strolled along the pathway. Even here, shadows and the light from the hanging lanterns played games with them. One minute his face would be visible, and therefore readable, but the next she could only see him in the moonlight.

"You're not so tense."

Kate chuckled. She was tied in knots, and he knew it. "I'm over embarrassing myself, but if you think I can be alone with you in a dark garden and no' be tense, then you're ready for Bedlam."

Colton laughed softly. "I'm not ready for Bedlam, yet, sweetheart." He drew her adroitly off the lighted path and down an unlighted one some distance from the house. After a few steps, he stopped and leaned over to nibble on her ear. "You'd better lead the way. You're more familiar with the garden than I am."

His touch and the warm, husky quality to his voice made her tremble with anticipation. She took his hand, leading him down the winding path. She guided him through a small opening in the trees and tall rhododendrons so that they were standing in a clearing. They were completely hidden from anyone who happened to pass by. A wispy cloud slid out from in front of the moon, bathing their hideaway in silver moonlight.

He settled his arms loosely about her and smiled down at her upturned face. "They were right, you know."

"Who?"

"Those ladies with their noses out of joint. We didn't do much walking."

"Probably more than most." She giggled softly. "I'd wager we're farther back in the shrubbery than anyone else."

"I have the feeling I'm acting like some young, randy buck."

"Well, no' quite." She raised her arms, slipping her hands around his neck. She could toy with the hair brushing his collar with only one hand, since she held the fan in the other. There was still a little space between them, which she hoped to soon remedy.

"How so?"

She tossed him a saucy smile. "If you were young and randy, you would have kissed me already."

"Minx! Such language for a lady." He grinned, remembering the time she chewed out the thugs in Gaelic. "But seems like I've mentioned that before."

"Well . . . if I canna say what's on my mind with you who can I speak plainly to?" She moved one hand, tapping her lips absently with the handle of her fan, wondering how much plain speaking it would take to get him to declare himself.

He watched the fan brush against her lips and subtly tightened his arms, pulling her a fraction closer. "Why don't you say what you want?"

She met his gaze, clearly puzzled. "What?"

"If I remember my fan signals correctly, you're asking me to kiss you."

"Oh . . . well, yes, I suppose 'tis true." Kate slid her hand back up around his neck. "But I must confess, it was unintentional. I had forgotten about that one." She tilted her head to one side, slightly exasperated. She had expected the kiss the moment he slid his arms around her. "Very well, I'll say what you know is on my mind. I'm tired of waiting. Come on and kiss me, Colton," she commanded softly.

He drew her fully against him, his hand caressing the contours of her back. One corner of his lip lifted in a silly grin. "You're misquoting Mr. Shakespeare. I believe the proper line is 'Come on and kiss me, Kate.' "

"Yes, my lord Petruchio," she whispered, her gaze dropping to his lips. To his surprise, she raised up slightly on tiptoe, pulling gently on the back of his head to bring his lips down to hers. She kissed him tenderly, not with the passion so carefully held in check, but with all the love that was in her heart.

It seemed to last forever. Finally, Colton broke away from her lips, lowering his to touch her just beneath the ear. She shuddered against him and his own legs felt wobbly. "Sweet, sweet Kate."

He slowly straightened to look down at her and slipped his fingers into her hair along her neck. His thumb brushed seductively along the smooth curve of her jaw. "Go driving with me tomorrow. I'd like to be able to talk to you without an audience."

"Can you get away for the day?" She ran her fingers along his collar and down the lapel of his coat, resting them against his chest.

"Yes." He waited with a half-drawn breath, hoping she would want to go to the country with him but doubting his good fortune.

"Will you take me out to Twin Rivers? I would like to see Mr. and Mrs. MacCrea again. I'm so sick of the city, and of crowds, and parties. I need some peace and quiet." She rested the side of her face against his chest. "I need to be with you," she added softly.

He released his bated breath, then filled his lungs to capacity, feeling her head lift with the swell of his chest. He wrapped his fingers in her hair, holding her against him. "Would noon be too early to pick you up? We're promised to Countess Lieven's party tomorrow night, remember. We'll only be able to stay at Twin Rivers until four or so."

"I can be ready by eleven."

"So can I." He eased her carefully away from him. "If I had a choice, I'd go right now, but I don't think either of us is ready for that kind of scandal." He grinned and stepped over to peer out of their hideaway. "I'll bring lunch. There's a nice meadow down between the rivers. It's a lovely spot for a picnic." He carefully drew her out onto the path, grinning like a mischievous lad. "I don't think I mussed you up too much."

"There will be talk anyway."

"True." *And if we keep finding dark corners in gardens, one of these nights I'll really give them something to talk about. You'd better make your move soon, Lydell,* he told himself, *or you may find it highly embarrassing to ask the earl for his granddaughter's hand.*

Chapter 16

Colton arrived promptly at eleven the next morning, driving his phaeton so there would be room for Kate's maid to accompany them. He was not surprised, however, when she met him in the front parlor without Bess. His gaze skimmed over her rich brown morning dress and the pert russet hat adorning her curls.

"No Bess?"

"No." Her chin went up a notch. "I dinna want a chaperon."

Colton smiled softly, his warm gaze caressing her face. "Nor did I. It's a good thing I didn't bring Lunan. He would have been quite put out with us if Bess had come along."

"If he were here, I wouldna even dream of leaving her behind. There's no telling what she would do in retaliation." Kate attempted a smile, but failed miserably. Her face filled with worry and she sank down on the settee.

"Sweetheart, what is it?" Colton was at her side in an instant, taking her hand in his.

"I received a letter from Mother this morning." She raised fearful eyes to the duke's face. "Someone took a shot at my father!"

"I was afraid they would try again. Was he hurt?"

"No, they missed him, but hit one of the guards instead. Thankfully, Frank was no' badly injured. My parents had gone to the country and were out riding, taking along several armed guards as you suggested. Their neighbors and some guests were out hunting, so Papa was no' overly concerned about the gunfire."

"Was more than one shot fired at your parents?"

"No, but they are convinced it was meant for Papa. If he hadna bent down to pull a burr from his horse's mane, he would have been the one wounded. Some of the guards searched the area, but the man had already fled. They did find where he had been standing. It was on a small hill which gave a good view in almost every direction. The guards questioned the neighbors, but they hadna seen anyone else. By the time the shot was fired, they had returned to their home."

Colton pushed to his feet and paced back and forth across the room a few times. "Is Addison staying in the country?"

"No. They returned to Edinburgh the next day. He has hired more guards and is being even more careful. I think he had grown careless since nothing else had happened."

"That's just what the killer is planning on." He pounded the ornate mantel with his fist, jarring a vase of flowers sitting there. "I wish I'd discovered who was behind this. I've had all my people keeping their ears on the twitch, but no one has turned up anything."

"Do you think you could help if you went to Edinburgh?"

Colton considered her question carefully. "No, not this time. Addison and MacAllister can handle it as well as I can, now that they realize there is still a problem. It becomes a waiting game. Your father will have to be extremely careful and not take any chances. If he makes it hard enough for the killer to get to him, the man will make a mistake and give himself away." He smiled a little ruefully. "I think MacAllister took a few lessons from me on how to be devious. He has a better understanding of what it takes to ferret out this kind of information now." He shook his head, pondering the situation. "It's obviously not the French behind this, although I never really thought it was."

"I canna understand why someone would want to kill Father. It just doesna make sense." She shook her head, throwing her hands up in the air in frustration.

"No, it doesn't, but I'll certainly increase my efforts to find out who is behind it." The only motivation that made even remote sense to him had to do with the title and the earl's wealth. But he knew Richard Denley well and found it inconceivable that he would ever plot to kill someone. Howard was not a consideration either, since he probably had only a short time to live.

That left Blake. A remote possibility, since there were four men between him and the title. Still, Colton believed Blake had started the rumor about Addison being a French spy. Colton's frown deepened. It was a farfetched idea, but the only one he had at the moment.

"If I send a note to Lunan and have him start on some further inquiries, do you still want to go to Twin Rivers?"

Kate nodded. "Yes, please. I need a change of scenery now more than ever." *I need to be with you more than ever.*

"Find me some paper and a pen."

Kate hurried up to her room, returning a few minutes later with the needed items. The duke dashed off a note to Lunan, telling him to contact Pemberton to see if he had gotten wind of this latest incident and to see what he could learn from the streets. He also instructed Lunan to contact two more of his associates, one to investigate Blake Denley, and the other to follow him at all times. Just as a precaution, although it galled him to do so, he told Lunan to have Richard Denley thoroughly investigated, too.

Feeling a little better after sharing her worry with Colton, Kate tried to bolster her flagging spirits. She desperately wanted to have a wonderful day with the duke, to share with him subtly, and perhaps not so subtly, all the love that was in her heart. She watched him as he quickly wrote out his directions to Lunan. *You're so decisive and confident in everything else*, she thought. *Why canna you be that way in love?*

An incident from the past evening came to mind, bringing with it a grimace of irritation. Colton had been true to his promise of being the last guest to leave—or so everyone thought. Kate had been the only one to see him off. Thomas and Lady Millicent, as well as the servants, conveniently chose to be elsewhere at the time. She had waved one last farewell before closing the door and turning to go upstairs to her comfortable, inviting bed.

Moments before she had reached the bottom of the stairs, Blake had stepped out of a shadowed alcove. He took advantage of her surprise, gripping her elbow in a powerful hold, and propelled her into the shadows with him.

"Well, little cousin, you're quite the talk of the ton."

"Release my arm this instant, Blake." Kate spoke softly, not wanting to stir up a fuss unless it proved absolutely necessary. "What do you want?" Her eyes adjusted to the dimness of the light in time to see his gaze roam very slowly over her. When he looked back up at her face, her blood ran cold, even though he released her arm, trailing his fingers down her skin slowly.

"You."

"Never!" She made a move to leave the alcove, but he anticipated the attempted escape. He reached for her quickly, halting her flight when he grabbed both her arms. His fingers dug into her flesh for an instant, then he eased the pressure to a point just short of pain.

"I'd be better than your poor, inexperienced duke. Do you know the man has never even had a mistress?" His chuckle was filled with malice. "Poor clumsy devil." He smiled, but there was no warmth in his eyes. Even in the dim light, Kate could see the cold menace lurking there.

"Tell me, lovely little cousin, what do you think the ton would do if they learned you had worked here as a maid? Wouldn't that be a delicious *on dit* to keep the gossip mongers busy for a week or two?"

"I hardly think it would signify. Now, do you release me, or shall I scream?"

He slowly lifted his fingers from her arms. "Ah, yes, you do like to threaten to scream, don't you. I remember that from the last time we were alone. Let's see, as I recall, you were very intent on playing your role. You had no qualms about doing whatever it took to keep your secret—even to surrendering your innocence to me on that big, convenient bed in the guest room."

"Liar! You know I would have brought the house down around your ears if you hadna let me go."

"Yes, I suppose you would have, but no one else knows that. A little word here . . . a little word there. A man can tell from looking at you that you were made for a tumble. It would not be hard to convince our peers of your wantonness. Any young woman low enough to work as a maid would certainly be low enough to give herself away."

"That's gammon and everyone would know it. Grandfather and Lady Millicent would see to it that no one believed it."

"Not likely, dear, but since I'm such a kind soul and really would not like to see your reputation ruined, I'll take a small sum of money for my silence instead of your body. Say one thousand pounds?"

"Dunna be a dunderhead! I couldna come up with that kind of money, and I wouldna give it to you even if I could." She was proud of the firm, commanding tone of her voice and took advantage of his momentary surprise by stepping from the alcove. To her relief, the footman was coming down the hall from the kitchen. "Harlan, please show Mr. Denley out. He seems to have forgotten his way."

With a haughty toss of her head, Kate had made her way up the stairs. She had felt her cousin's hatred every step of the way.

"Kate?" Colton spoke her name for the second time and nudged her chin with his knuckle.

"Um? Oh, forgive me. I was woolgathering."

"Don't worry about Addison. If he takes the proper precautions, he should remain safe." He held out his hand. When she clasped it, he gently pulled her up to stand. "Now, no more fretting. You will have a nice day. This day is for you." His smile held a shade of reminiscence as he thought of her words the last time they went to Twin Rivers. "Give me a smile. Ah, much better." He put his hand to the small of her back, guiding her out of the room and down the hall.

As they walked toward the door, they heard the thump, thump, thump of Rowan's tail on the tile. Stopping, they looked over to where the dog was sprawled beneath a window. "What's wrong, ol' boy? Have you succumbed to ennui?" Colton snapped his fingers and the dog jumped to his feet and trotted over to them. "Would you like to spend the day in the country?" The duke ruffled the crisp fur on the top of the dog's head.

"Oh, Colton, he'd love it. I'm sure Grandpapa wouldn't

nind. Why dunna we take him?" Kate giggled. "He could be ur chaperon."

"Hmmm, just the kind I like. Very well, you can come, Rowan, but you must behave yourself. Bence, would you lease tell his lordship that we've taken the dog with us? Also, ee that Lunan gets this message immediately."

"Yes, Your Grace." The butler opened the door and bowed lightly. "Have a pleasant day." If the man thought it odd for he young mistress to be going out so early in the day with the uke, he did not let it show.

A few minutes later they were whipping along the road, the uke skillfully guiding his team around any other vehicle that hanced to get in their way. Rowan had managed to cram his onsiderable length onto the back seat, causing more than one asserby to gape in astonishment. Colton teased and joked, oing out of his way to keep Kate in a jolly mood. They were njoying each other's company so much, they did not notice Blake Denley as they passed by him.

Blake held his team at a firm halt, waiting until the traffic leared to pull his curricle out from the side street onto the nain thoroughfare. Nell Kingsly, former maid to the Earl of Blagden and Blake's current mistress, perched prettily beside im. The fine quality of Nell's blue muslin dress and fashionble chip hat gave evidence to the high manner in which her rotector provided for her.

"Well, look who's heading out of the city." Blake watched he passing carriage with undisguised contempt. "It would eem my little cousin is getting reckless."

"Oh, she's always been reckless where the duke was oncerned," said Nell with a little laugh. "Did I ever tell you bout the night the duke came up to her room?"

"Tell me more, my pet." Blake guided his team out into the treet, barely missing another carriage in his distraction.

"The duke and his nitpicky valet spent a few nights at the arl's house during that awful cold spell. His Grace had a logged chimney or something. Anyway, the first night he was here, I heard voices in the hall. It was the middle of the night, o I was curious."

"Naturally." Blake grinned at his pretty Cyprian, glad on his occasion that she was curious as well as exciting in bed.

"When I peeped out the door, I saw Kate, with a blanke over her night dress. She had on stockings, but no slippers an her mobcap was all cockeyed. Oh, her hair was loose, too although she always wore it in a long braid at night. All th duke was wearing was a silk dressing gown, and it was to short." Nell smiled a secret little smile, remembering how sh had wanted to touch the rippling muscles beneath that sof material.

Blake shot her a sharp look, but Nell only grinned back an tickled him beneath the chin with her closed fan. "Now, lovey I was still a maid then, and not your light-o'-love. Besides, h was always a cold kettle of fish." She ran her hand down hi thigh and back up again, saying softly, "Not at all like you.

"Anyway, he went into her room and closed the door. H wasn't in there long enough to do anything, but the way h looked at her and touched her face when he came out told m they had been up to something earlier. I never really hear much about it, although the gossip was that she had sleep walked to his room. She did that sometimes."

"Sleepwalked?"

"Yes. But I'd go bail she faked it that time just to get to hi room. Then, a week or so later, she up and disappeared for couple of days. The servants said she had gone out to th country with him and got caught in a storm. They were *force* to spend the night at his country place."

"Does the earl know about this?"

"I don't think so. We were all warned not to breathe a wor of it around him. Lady Millicent threatened to dismiss anyon who let it slip. The old man would have kicked Kate out in th snow if he'd found out. 'Course that was before he learned sh was his granddaughter. I'd wager he'd go clear through th roof if he heard about it now."

"Yes, I suspect he would." Blake unconsciously slowed th team as he mulled over the information Nell had so sweetl provided. He wondered just how much the old earl knew Kate's escapades. Of course, even if the earl was aware them, Blake thought he might still be able to use them to h advantage.

With a rare sparkle in his eye, Blake unexpectedly stopp

the curricle in front of Nell's favorite modiste. "Why don't you run in and order yourself a couple of new gowns, pet?"

"Why, lovey, thank you! Will you join me?"

"No, I've got an errand to run. I'll stop back for you in an hour or so." He leaned over and kissed her pouting lips. "Then, we'll go over to the jewelers and buy you a bauble to go with your new dress." Blake nodded to his tiger, who jumped down from his perch behind the seat. When the boy had a firm grip on the reins, Blake climbed down and lifted Nell from the curricle.

"You'll let me thank you properly this afternoon, won't you, Blake?" Nell leaned against him provocatively. She got a thrill out of Blake's taste for public affection. He pulled her into his arms and kissed her roughly, sending a rush of excitement through her as he openly fondled her.

Finally, he raised his head, trailing his hand down across her belly. "Several times. Now, run along and enjoy yourself. Buy something to wear to the theatre next week. Something that will make all the other men envy me."

Nell smiled wickedly and brushed her hand across the front of his pantaloons. A matron, stepping from the modiste's shop, gasped at their vulgar display and hustled her spinsterish daughter down the sidewalk away from them. Blake laughed and pinched Nell on the bottom, evoking a little squeal and giggle as she scampered into the shop.

Blake drove the short distance to White's and joined a few of his friends for a game of cards. By the time the game was inished, so was his story of Kate's scandalous behavior. Nothing spread through the ton more quickly than a tale of disgrace, and he knew that by evening, well before the start of Countess Lieven's party, almost everyone would know about Kate's love affair with the Duke of Ryland.

Blake returned to pick up Nell, sure of himself and confident of his plan. The scandal would make the earl so angry that he would disinherit Addison again. And if Blake were truly fortunate, the uproar would prove fatal to the old man before he could change his mind. That would leave only his brothers between him and his goal.

At Twin Rivers, Kate leaned back against the trunk of a tree, wiping the last bit of apricot truffle from her fingertips onto

the napkin. She felt Colton's gaze and raised her head to lool
into his twinkling eyes. Knowing he was thinking of the las
time they shared sweets from Gunter's, a quick blush sprea
across her cheeks. When he made no comment, she breathed
sigh of relief and relaxed against the tree.

She took in the scenery slowly, letting her gaze roam fron
the meadow on their left, across the pond where a family o
ducks drifted lazily, and on to the woods to the right and i
back of them. "It is so lovely here. I can see why you never tir
of this place. And the MacCreas are such nice people. Yo
must have visited since we were here."

"Yes, Lunan and I have driven out a few times. He tol
them who you were. I think Mrs. MacCrea was relieved to hea
it. She was having a hard time getting you pegged." H
grinned as her gaze came back to him. "I do enjoy it here
much more than being in town. Before the war, I often staye
here during the Season or when business brought me to th
area. I would only stay in London when I had an evenin
engagement." He smiled wryly. "Which was as seldom a
possible."

"You truly dunna enjoy parties and such?" Since she wa
sitting in the shade of the tree, she reached up and removed he
hat, enjoying the gentle breeze in her hair. She carefully tosse
the hat over by the picnic basket, then smoothed a wrinkl
from the blanket spread out beneath her.

Colton stretched out on the blanket beside her, leaning bac
on his elbows, and watching the ducks with great interes
After a long pause, he said, "I must admit, I've enjoyed th
parties more of late." He turned his head to look at her an
grinned. "Probably because a certain young lady helped me t
overcome my terror of the dance floor."

Kate laughed. "I find it difficult to believe, Your Grace, th
you would be afraid of anything."

I'm afraid of losing you. His expression sobered. *I'm afrai*
I can't be everything you want me to be. "We all have ou
secret fears."

"Yes, I suppose." *And mine is having to live my life witho*
you.

"I do think I'll draw the line at Lady Edison's music
evenings from now on. I never thought I'd be happy for m

nother to get the headache, but we all would have had one if ve hadn't left."

"So true. 'Tis a pity she's so tone deaf." Kate took a deep reath, savoring the peaceful countryside and the nearness of he man she loved. Rowan came bounding across the meadow rom a woods on the other side. He made a wide swing, assing by them in an arc on his way to the pond. Gone was the ind and sensitive expression in his great hound eyes, replaced y the blazing fire of chasing some invisible stag or wolf.

"I'm so glad you brought Rowan. He's having such a good omp. Grandpapa makes sure he goes to the park every day, ut it is much nicer here. He can run anywhere he wants and nvestigate anything that catches his fancy."

Colton sat up and swung around to face her, grinning nischievously. "I know something I'd fancy right now."

"A walk?"

"Not exactly what I have in mind."

"A swim, perhaps? Do you think the pond is deep enough?" Kate lifted her fingers to her cheek and assumed an expression f exaggerated concern.

"Only if I were ten years old, which in case you haven't oticed, I'm not." He leaned forward until his face was about foot away from her.

"Oh, kind sir, dunna keep me in suspense." Kate opened her yes wide in mock innocence, though her lip quivered from ontaining her amusement. "Pray tell what is it you fancy?"

"You, naked in my arms, and not so much as the breeze etween us."

Kate gasped, her eyes widening even more in astonishment. Her face flamed, even as a fire of another sort coursed through er veins.

Colton groaned and closed his eyes, shaking his head. He eaned back, giving her more space. "I can't believe I said hat." A singular blush spread over his cheeks as he opened his eyes, meeting Kate's gaze sheepishly. He shrugged. "I meant o say a kiss, but instead I think a walk might be better after ll."

Kate nodded, doubting if she could say a word if her life lepended on it. He rose in one swift movement and reached lown for her hand. When he pulled her to her feet, she dropped his hand and stepped a little away from him. Rowan cam trotting up, wedging himself between them, effectively wid ening the gap.

Colton scowled down at the animal. "Sometimes I think thi dog understands every word we say. You might tell him that chaperon doesn't have to walk in the middle." His grump tone brought a reluctant smile to his lips. When he looked u at Kate, he found her smiling, too.

"At the moment, I think he's a very wise animal. Tell me of all your holdings, which is your favorite?"

"Almost all of them have some appeal. I have a farm in th Cotswolds that I thoroughly enjoy and a house on the coas near Brighton. But I think my favorite place is in Yorkshire.

She glanced at him, surprised at his choice. "Why?"

"The countryside is wild and rugged, the storms are won derful, and it has a drafty old castle with the coziest library i the world. The wind howls around the parapets, making on happy to be inside and curled up in front of the fire with a goo book." *Or with you.* He stepped around the dog and gentl pulled her into his arms.

"I've always thought it would be a fine place to spend th winter with a beautiful woman. On nice days, we could rid across the moors to the sea, and on stormy ones, we could cu up in front of the fire and, um, read poetry."

"This kind of poetry?" Kate tilted her face toward his, he eyes inviting his kiss.

"Precisely." He lowered his face until their lips touched an tried valiantly to keep the kiss light and gentle. Her fier response shattered his sterling intentions.

Kate slid her hands up around his neck, molding her body t his. When she traced the outline of his lip with the tip of he tongue, he groaned her name, giving her the freedom sh requested. Excitement and love made her bold as she darte her tongue into the warmth of his mouth. He teased her back following the invitation of her retreat. He deepened the kis drinking in the sweetness only she could give him.

Gradually he drew way from her, nibbling on her lip, the feathering her cheeks with tiny kisses, finally raising his hea to gaze down at her with burning eyes. "I need to sit down. He smiled tenderly, brushing away a lock of hair that ble across her face. "You have this strange ability to take the strength right out of my legs."

She hugged him fiercely, loving him all the more for his honesty. "You do it to me, too."

They turned back toward the shade tree and the blanket, each a little uncertain about the next few minutes. Rowan stopped and watched them briefly, then took off for another run. A few yards away from the picnic spot, Kate halted and shook her foot.

"Picked up a rock?"

"Aye." She took another step. "Ouch! Oh, botheration!"

"Allow me, madam." Colton swept her up in his arms.

"Oh, kind sir, you're too gallant." She giggled and silently hoped his legs weren't still weak. She slid her arms around his neck, reluctantly releasing them a few minutes later when he knelt on one knee and set her on the blanket. He dropped down beside her.

Kate discreetly lifted her skirt to mid-calf and began unlacing her half boot. It was awkward since it laced up the outside, and she had to bend her leg to the side in order to reach the boot.

"May I be of assistance, my dear?" Colton purposefully kept his expression and tone casual. He could sense Kate's discomfort as she attempted to unfasten the boot and keep her legs properly covered at the same time.

"Yes, please. I hadna realized how difficult these were to handle on my own."

The duke made quick work of loosening the laces and slipped the boot from her foot. Holding it upside down, he shook out the offending pebble. Placing the boot on the other side of her, he picked up her foot and examined it carefully.

"Colton, whatever are you doing?"

"Checking for damage."

"It was too tiny to have done any damage."

"True." He gently placed her foot back down on the blanket, but continued to scrutinize it.

"Now, what are you doing?" Kate watched him, puzzled by his serious expression. A smile flickered across his face, his dimple flashing for a second.

"Admiring your delicate foot and the pretty curve of your

ankle and calf. Those are very nice stockings, too. I like the stripes." He smoothed his fingertips over a few inches of her calf, hoping that he sent her heart to racing. His was doing double-time. "There's something very seductive about sleek silk over a woman's leg."

Kate drew an unsteady breath, willing her heart to calm down but doubting if it would ever return to normal. He picked up her foot and ran his fingers over the instep, then gently massaged her toes. *Oh, Lord, give me strength!*

"I was also wondering about something else," he said casually.

"Yes? Mmmm, that makes my toes feel good."

"I thought you just might be"—he wiggled his fingertips ever so lightly against the bottom of her foot and Kate yelped—"ticklish!" he cried in triumph.

Kate let out a whoop, kicking and squirming as he held her foot in an ironclad grip and tickled the bottom of it unmercifully.

"Stop! On, Colton, dunna do that!" She gasped and giggled, wailed and wiggled, pounding on his arm and shoulder until she collapsed back on the blanket in peals of laughter.

Colton promptly dropped her foot and pounced, applying his expertise to her ribs. Kate shrieked, laughing until tears rolled down her cheeks. Gradually, his fingers slowed and the movement of his hand became a firm caress, soothing yet tempting. He stopped, reaching up to wipe the tears from her cheeks.

"Ye are a rascal, my braw man." Kate shook her head and smiled up at him, her eyes shining with her happiness and love.

He moved his hand back to her side, his caress growing bolder. She caught her breath and her eyelids flickered closed. "Aye, that I am, my bonnie lass." *A rascal and your man*. He leaned closer, brushing his hand over her glorious curves. Devilment sparkled in his eyes and his smile would have melted butter on an icy day. "And I've got you exactly where I want you," he murmured, lowering his lips to hers.

It was a kiss full of passion, wild and free, and so much more—sunshine and rainbows, stardust and moonbeams, love and laughter when he was old and gray.

She loves me! Oh, God, I know it! I feel it! Thank you!

Thank you! He pulled away from her lips, sprinkling little kisses along her neck and up toward her ear.

I know you love me! It's in your touch, your kiss! Oh, Cole, please say it. Please, God, make him say it! He teased her earlobe with his teeth, but when his tongue traced the fragile curve of her ear, Kate lost all conscious thought.

At Kate's moan, Colton captured her mouth once again, telling her of his love over and over in his mind. Something pinched his backside, but he barely noticed. Suddenly it came again, sharper, harder. The duke jerked his head up with a muffled curse. When he looked over his shoulder, he found Rowan standing behind him, a distinct look of irritation in the dog's eye. The duke vaguely remembered the earl mentioning that the animal liked everything to be peaceful.

Colton sat up with a huff of exasperation. "Rowan," he bellowed, "you're going too far!"

Still in a daze, Kate pushed herself up to her elbows, looking from the dog to the duke. "What did he do?"

"He nipped me in the rump!"

Kate blinked, then shifted her gaze to the dog as she sat up. Rowan calmly stretched out beside them and dropped his head in the duke's lap. He looked up at his friend with serene, loving eyes.

Colton plopped back on the blanket, roaring with laughter. When he could catch his breath, he curled his fingers around her arm and smiled gently at her befuddled expression. "God moves in mysterious ways to protect the innocent, Kitten. We'd better pack up and go home."

The moment for expressing his feelings had passed. Colton decided it was for the best. He felt certain of her love and gladly accepted it. Tomorrow, he would go to the earl and formally ask for her hand in marriage. Then the earl would call her downstairs, and they would be left alone. He could declare his feelings without the temptation of consummating their love right there on the spot. She would return the sentiment and accept his offer. He would tell her that the earl had given them his blessing and they would start making wedding plans.

It would be all done precisely according to the rules of conduct. There would be no hint of scandal; nothing would be awry to cause the earl any more pain. Confident that he was doing the right thing, the duke folded the blankets and picked up the basket. Kate was unusually quiet, but he attributed it only to their interrupted passion. Surely, she knew how he felt. He had told her how much he loved her in practically every way except the spoken word.

"Come on chaperon." Colton whistled softly for Rowan to follow them. "We've got a party to attend."

Thoroughly confused, frustrated, and downright angry because the duke had not declared his love, Kate glared at the dog. She mumbled a Gaelic oath under her breath, and wished they had never brought the killjoy along.

Chapter 17

That evening the duke drew out his pocket watch, remorsefully taking note of the time. He should have been hearing Kate's sweet voice as they walked up the steps to Countess Lieven's ball with her grandparents. The intoxicating fragrance of jasmine should have been working its magic on his senses.

Instead, male voices droned in his ear and the acrid smell of stagnant smoke and port irritated his nostrils. At an impromptu meeting, the members of Foreign Secretary Castlereagh's cabinet, along with a few others, fretted over Napoleon's departure for Elba and the disposition of his empire.

Lord Liverpool had called the meeting of various secretaries and members of parliament to discuss the concerns put forth in Viscount Castlereagh's latest dispatch from Paris. Annoyed with being summoned, Colton found it difficult to concentrate on what was being said. He felt what he had to offer could easily have been sent over in written form.

Knowing these discussions usually went on for hours, he gave up all hope of spending the evening with Kate. He had planned to shower her with love and attention, even going so far as to broadly hint about his intended visit to her grandfather on the morrow. He was certain she knew how he felt about her, and thought it whimsically romantic and gentlemanly to refrain from declaring his love until he proposed marriage.

"I regret taking you away from the lovely Miss Denley, Your Grace."

Colton closed his watch with a click and slipped it back into his pocket as he turned to meet Lord Liverpool's twinkling gaze. "Your timing was dreadfully poor, my friend."

"Then I am indeed sorry," said the gentleman softly. "Unfortunately, I need your level head and wise counsel." He raised his voice slightly, breaking in on the other various discussions around the large walnut table. "Your Grace, what do you think of sending Napoleon to Elba?"

"I agree with Castlereagh. It's much too close to France. I do not believe Boneparte will be content to live out his life in such a mediocre existence."

One of the gentlemen snorted. "He's still an emperor. He's sovereign over the whole island."

"Do you actually think he will be satisfied with a tiny island when he has been ruler of an empire thousands of times larger? It would have been better if he had been banished to darkest Africa." Colton shook his head at the stupidity of the Treaty.

"Can't do that. The man's a great leader even for all the trouble he's caused. Can't just send him off to be eaten by cannibals. Besides, the Frenchies are sick of war. They'll be happy to get the monarchy back."

"For a while," murmured the duke.

The Prime Minister frowned and leaned forward, placing his forearms on the table. "Do you actually believe the people would follow him again if he returned?"

"Not now. But give them a little time. Life will not be much easier, even with the war over. True, the men will not be dying in battle, but there are severe shortages in food and other goods. Prices are high. The government is low on money and the people have even less. The disposition of the empire will be the government's primary concern and will take a great deal of time.

"Mark my words, it will not take long for discontent to set in. You can be sure Napoleon will find a way to keep his fingers on the pulse of the country. When he judges the time is right, he'll make one last bid to rule."

Some of the men laughed. "You actually believe the people will follow him again, do you?" They shook their heads, privately thinking the usually sensible duke had gone off the deep end.

Colton leaned forward, copying the Prime Minister's pose, and looked slowly around the room. His expression was impassive, but several men fidgeted visibly under the cold, knowing look in his eye.

"They will forget the past and see only the man they once loved, the man that led them to greatness, however brief. You dismiss his charm and amazing power to draw followers. I suspect that he will return in less than a year."

"You can't be serious." A few of the men laughed nervously; others carefully pondered his words.

"Gentlemen, I know the minds and hearts of the French people probably better than any of you. Through my agents and at first hand, I've seen the way they think in battle and, more importantly, the way they think and act before going into battle. Given enough time, if Napoleon successfully sets foot on French soil, the people will rally around him. They will dream only of past glories and will remember him with a fondness we find hard to fathom. They will not consider the impossibility of their task but will be caught up in the thrill and excitement of the moment."

"Louis XVIII and the new government would not allow such a thing to happen. They would immediately send an army to stop him."

"Yes, they would send an army, but there would be no battle. I'd wager the entire army would join up with him." Colton sat back in his chair and relaxed. *There, let them stew about that,* he thought.

"Surely not the entire army," boomed one of the lords, once an army general. "The commander would not go over to his side."

"If the man had served under the Little Emperor before, he would fall into his arms." The calm conviction in the duke's voice brought an uneasy hush over the group. "Even when they knew their cause was lost and they had to betray him to save their country, many of his generals loved him still. Do not be caught unaware, gentlemen."

Indignant, Kate stared at the long receiving line ahead of them. *Drat you, Lord Liverpool. Why did you need Colton tonight of all nights?* She grudgingly admitted that undoubtedly the meeting was important, but she didn't know why it could not wait one more day. *I just know he was going to propose tonight.*

Her visions of a moonlight stroll in the garden, followed by a tender declaration of love and proposal of marriage were nothing but wistful illusions. The party would hold little enjoyment for her without the duke's presence. It would be a dreadfully long evening.

"My, the countess was brisk tonight," murmured Lady Millicent some twenty minutes later. They had passed through the receiving line in a relatively short time, considering Countess Lieven had invited over four hundred guests. She frowned thoughtfully. The woman had not been rude, but she had not been as friendly as usual.

She glanced at the faces around her as they made their way into the ballroom. People she had known for years avoided her gaze, occasionally murmuring a distant greeting before obviously turning their attention elsewhere.

"Something is very wrong, Thomas." With growing apprehension, she watched Kate walk a short distance away to join a group of friends. Ladies who just yesterday had considered the young woman refreshing were actually turning their backs on her. Men who had noted her beauty with polite admiration now openly leered at her.

"I see it and feel it, but I don't want to believe it." The earl met her gaze with a look of pain. "I've been through this before, Millie. Has Kate done something I don't know about?"

Not lately. She drew him aside into a small alcove and quickly told him about Kate going to Twin Rivers with the duke during the winter and how they had been stranded there overnight.

Thomas's face was grim. "Someone got wind of it, Millie. They probably saw the chit driving out there with him today and now we're in a thick broth. I don't have to take a second guess as to what 'our friends' are saying about my granddaughter."

"Nor do I, but I intend to find out exactly what's afoot, even though it means wading through a pit of vipers." She studied his face, knowing how painful a second scandal would be to him. He carefully schooled his expression to hide his hurt, although it was barely concealed.

Kate slowly drew to a halt, her heart pounding in her breast. A queasy feeling of panic swept over her. She could feel hundreds of eyes watching her and it made her skin crawl. She took another step toward the group of young ladies she had considered if not quite friends, then at least more than acquaintances. As if they were one, nine aristocratic noses lifted a smidgen in the air, and with a look of haughty disdain, those purportedly unsullied virgins turned their backs on her.

Kate could not contain her gasp at their affront. Someone snickered nearby and when she glanced in that direction, she found several men ogling her. Hot color rushed to her face, although she managed to control her shiver of disgust. One of the men, considerably older than anyone she had ever danced with, sauntered toward her. His mouth curved in a sneer as he ran his gaze slowly over her. His look made her feel naked.

She could not refrain from shivering this time, but anger quickly shut out all other emotions. She squared her shoulders and that defiant chin rose a notch. When the man's gaze finally lifted to her face, her sneer faded as he focused on the incensed glint in her eyes.

When Lord and Lady Blagden reached her side, Viscount Heartly pushed through the crowd, unceremoniously knocking the insolent lecher aside. "Where in the devil is Ryland?" he asked under his breath.

"With the Prime Minister. What has happened?"

"I just got here, so I only heard a little. It's said you're Ryland's mistress."

"What?" Kate's eyes widened as astonishment lit her face for a moment.

"Then you are beyond the pale, my dear," murmured Lady Millicent. "You have become an outcast, a social impure, no better than a common Cyprian."

Her anger of moments before was nothing compared to the wrath that engulfed her now. Never in her life had she felt such hatred. "How dare they?" she whispered, her voice shaking with fury. With a scathing glance about the now silent room, Kate located Countess Lieven.

When Viscount Heartly realized her intention, he held out

his arm. "Let me walk the gauntlet with you, Kate," he said softly.

Kate glanced at his arm, then looked up to meet his sorrow-filled eyes. She could not bring herself to smile, but her expression softened for him. "Thank you for standing my friend, Gerry. But I will do this alone."

The crowd parted before her as she marched across the room like a flame-haired goddess of war. Many of the men felt a twinge of envy for the Duke of Ryland. No other woman in the room could match her beauty or her regal carriage. Kate stopped in front of Countess Lieven, with Lord and Lady Blagden trailing a few steps behind her.

"I would beg a minute of your time, my lady. In private, please." Kate's face felt so stiff that it hurt to talk.

The countess studied her for a second. "Of course." Glancing around the room, she waved for the orchestra to resume. "Continue with your entertainment, dear people. Please do continue."

The countess turned abruptly and led Kate and her grandparents out of the room and down the hall to a small sitting room.

"Please be seated." As she motioned with her hand, the diamonds in her ring caught the candlelight, sending tiny sparkles across the ceiling.

The three sat down and Kate looked up at her hostess. Countess Lieven's expression was kind. "I would like to know what has been said about me," said Kate.

"The first part of the story was merely interesting, albeit a little intriguing. I understand you came incognito to your grandfather's house and worked as a maid for a few months."

"Yes, that is correct." Kate did not care to enlighten the countess further.

"Kate came to London to try and find a way to reunite my son and me, milady." The earl's grave face softened as he looked over at his granddaughter. "There was too much bitterness in this old heart for her to come to me openly. She achieved her goal remarkably well."

"Still, you must admit, it has made an interesting tidbit to talk about. Of course, there is much more to the story. It seems the duke was seen going into your bedroom in the middle of the ight. You appeared to be wearing nothing but a blanket raped around you, while His Grace wore only a dressing own." The countess paused, thinking how much she would ike to see the handsome duke clad in so little.

"It does not take a person of keen intellect to imagine what vent on behind those closed doors, my dear. The tenderness vith which he departed only supports the most outrageous ssumptions."

"First of all, I was certainly wearing more than a blanket, nilady. I walked in my sleep, thinking it was time to do my hores. The duke only escorted me back upstairs after I tried to lean his room, nothing more." Kate could feel her blood oiling. How like the ton to paint the worst possible picture. he knew where they got their information, too. Only Nell ould have seen what went on in the hall that night, and she vould have been only too willing to share a juicy bit of gossip vith Blake. Dear cousin Blake. In all innocence, she had not xpected him to make good on his threat to ruin her.

"Sleepwalking is a paltry excuse, Kate. Many young vomen use it as a ruse to capture unwilling gentlemen in a ompromising situation."

"Kate has been a sleepwalker from childhood," snapped ady Millicent. "Although I know no one would credit such a ning." The good lady released a long, exasperated sigh. "I'm ure there is more, Countess. Do go on."

"A few weeks after the late-night rendezvous with the uke—oh, I know you say it was nothing of the kind, but it's ie way everyone else perceives it—you went to the country vith His Grace. Not only were you without a chaperon, but ou stayed several days with him at his country estate." She eld up her hand when Kate started to protest. "Believe me, ny dear, I hope you can refute this ridiculous accusation, but ou will need proof of your innocence or no one will ever elieve it."

Kate's natural honesty would not let her lie, even if she had een sure the earl and Lady Millicent would stand behind her eceit. Her back was poker still and she held her head up roudly. "I canna deny that I went to the country with His irace. However, we stayed only one night and that was ecause we were caught in a snowstorm. The duke is a

gentleman, and even though at the time he thought I was onl
a maid, he showed me the greatest respect. Nothing happene
to cause either of us shame."

"It does not matter whether you truly are his lover or not. T
all appearances, you have been thoroughly compromised. Yo
are considered unchaste, therefore you must be avoided by a
the other young ladies. Not a one of them will brave censor t
be your friend.

"If you were a married woman and decided to have an affair
it would be another thing. As long as you were discreet, peopl
would say little. But, of course, since you are not, th
gentlemen consider you fast and an easy touch. None of the
would ever consider marrying you, now. Any compliment
they give you will be for a different reason entirely."

"I did nothing immoral," Kate said staunchly. "And I dunn
care a fiddle what you or anyone else thinks of me. I will liv
my life as I choose, not by the ton's rules."

"Perhaps you don't mind what everyone thinks, but wha
about the duke? Would you make his life miserable, also? O
the one hand, you have behaved in a most unseemly way, bu
nor has he acted the gentleman. There will be those who wi
call him a spoiler of virtue. His good name is being smeared a
much as yours.

"One has only to watch the two of you to know ho
captivated you are with each other. The whole *on dit* will di
away soon after you are married, but only if you are we
quickly and discreetly. After an extended honeymoon, yo
both could resume your place in society with barely a whisp
being said about your past transgressions."

Kate jumped to her feet and paced around the small room. "
dunna think Colton is overly concerned with the ton's opinio
of him. I willna have the ton dictate how I live my life. I willn
have Colton forced to marry me." She spun on her heel an
paced around the room in the opposite direction. "I've a goo
mind to go back in that ballroom and dance with any and ever
man who asks me. I'll show your arrogant, hypocritic
English peers exactly what I think of them."

She fed her anger, trying to cover up the hurt which wou
not quite be buried. She did not want to admit it, but it di
matter what others thought of her, at least a little. Mainly, sh

felt guilty because of the slanderous barbs being tossed Colton's way. She was thankful he was not present to suffer the accusations, yet at the same time she desperately needed his support.

Kate came to a halt and nodded her head decisively. "Aye, that's exactly what I'll do. I'll show them it takes more than lies to cut down a Scot." She shot a look of defiance toward Countess Lieven, who glanced meaningfully at the earl. Kate had avoided looking at him since the horrid episode began.

Reluctantly, she turned to face him and was instantly contrite. In only moments, the strain and pain of the scandal had etched new lines on his face. She dropped to her knees in front of him, looking up at him earnestly.

"Forgive me, Grandfather, for being so selfish. I would never intentionally hurt you. We shall leave immediately, and out the back way, if you think it is best."

The earl patted her shoulder. "If Colton were here, child, perhaps we could stand against this talk. But without him, there is little we can do to refute what has been said. It seems cowardly, but I suppose simply leaving would be the wisest move at this point." He grimaced. "I'll not have you sneak out the back like some criminal."

"Thank you, Grandpapa." Kate squeezed his knee, then put one hand on the chair arm, and pushed herself up to stand. It only irritated her further to discover that her legs were shaking. "Milady, you have been very kind and gracious. Thank you."

"You're welcome, Kate. I'll do what I can to discredit the talk, but I still believe the only course open to you is to bring the duke to heel quickly."

"He is no' a dog. If we marry, it will be for the right reasons, no' because he is forced into it."

Countess Lieven walked them to the hallway, bidding them a cordial farewell. To the number of guests straining for a look from the ballroom doorway, their hostess appeared to be on the best of terms with Kate Denley. The countess returned to the party and was immediately cornered by Lady Jersey.

"Well, what did she say?"

"We have our work cut out for us. According to Miss Denley, she was sleepwalking and doing her chores. The duke only guided her back to her room."

"That won't wash. No one would believe it. What about the trip to the country?"

"She didn't deny going with him, but said they spent only one night due to a storm." The countess tapped her fan against her fingers, frowning thoughtfully. "I'm not sure how much good we can do, but I like the Denley chit. Nor am I anxious to make an enemy of the Duke of Ryland. Lady Millicent said the gel had been sleepwalking since childhood, so we'll let on like it was a common occurrence. Put her in her working clothes and have the duke dressed in a nightshirt and heavy robe."

Lady Jersey tittered. "I much prefer the thought of him in only a silk dressing gown."

The countess grinned. "So do I, but for the purpose of our story, we'd better let the man be so cold-natured that he sleeps in the robe! As to the night in the country, let's simply say they went for a ride in that clever sleigh of his and got caught in a storm. They were forced to spend one night, but Kate spent her time with the servants in their quarters. After all, she was pretending to be a maid at the time."

"It's a little weak," Lady Jersey murmured, smiling at a gentleman as he made his way to her side for their dance.

"I know, but it's the best we can do at the moment. If only the duke had been able to attend tonight. He would have squelched the talk in a trice with that cold stare of his—if anyone had dared to say a word, that is. Well, I must mingle with my guests." The countess floated off to join a group of middle-aged ladies and gentlemen who were only too anxious to hear what the Denley chit had to say in her defense.

A strained silence fell over the trio as they made their way home in the carriage. They had gone only a few blocks when Kate spoke up. "I hope you can forgive me for the pain I've caused you. I dinna mean for any of this to happen. When I went with Colton to Twin Rivers, I expected to leave London and never return." Tears welled up in her eyes. "I loved him so much, even then, that I couldna bear to go away without spending a little time with him. We did nothing wrong, Grandpapa. Please believe me. I canna deny he kissed me, but it went no further, I promise."

"We believe you, child," said the earl kindly. "And we'll stand by you. I'll not turn against you like I did your father. Even if you had done wrong, I'd still stand with you. I won't lose the ones I love again."

Tears stung her eyes, but Kate blinked them back. "Thank you." She returned Lady Millicent's loving smile. "You are both so special to me. I'm so thankful I found you." She took a deep breath and tried to relax.

Once they were home and safely nestled in the back parlor, she tried to make light of the evening's events. "Well, at least we dinna have to hear about Napoleon this time. If we're lucky, by next week there will be some other scandal and the ton will lose interest in us." She kicked off her slippers and curled her feet up under her on the chair.

"Yes, if we're lucky." Lady Millicent tapped the arm of the chair with her fingertips, her brow wrinkled in a frown. "What I cannot understand is how the rumor got started. I suppose someone might have seen you on the way to Twin Rivers, but how would they know you stayed the night? And, no one outside our household could have known about you sleepwalking." She released a heavy sigh. "I suppose I'll have to question each one of the servants and see who has been talking about our private business. Some of my friends have been plagued by their servants' prattle, but I never thought we would be. I dread the thought of dismissing anyone."

"There's no need. It must have been Nell."

"Of course! She's the most likely candidate." Lady Millicent frowned again. "But why are you so certain?"

Kate shifted and glanced uneasily at her grandfather. "She's the only one who would have seen us in the hall outside my room, and she knew I spent the night at Twin Rivers."

"And she is now Blake's mistress," said the earl quietly. "Are you telling me my nephew is behind this? Why would he want to ruin you?"

"Because I rejected his advances." Kate bit her lip.

"His what? Did he harm you?" Lord Blagden boomed, clutching the arms of the chair and leaning toward her.

"No, he dinna hurt me. Once, when I was working as a maid, he caught me upstairs in one of the bedrooms. He tried to force me to . . ." Kate blushed and hung her head. "When

I threatened to scream, he let me go. I ran downstairs to the kitchen where it was safe. Then, last night, he stayed after everyone else had left. He practically dragged me into one of the alcoves where it was dark.

"He threatened to tell the ton about my working as a maid here. He said he would tell how I wanted to protect my role so badly that I gave him my innocence. Then he said if I paid him a thousand pounds, he would keep quiet." Kate smiled a little. "I got mad and told him I couldna come up with that kind of money, and even if I could, I wouldna give it to him. I think he was surprised because I dinna cower at his feet. Harlan came by and I was able to get away from Blake."

"What the deuce has gotten into him?" The earl shook his head, clearly perplexed. "I never thought much of him, but he's always been careful to stay on my good side."

"Is he short of funds?" asked Lady Millicent.

"Not that I'm aware of. His father was a wealthy man and left all the boys well provided for." His expression sobered. "No, it's not money he truly wanted. He fancies himself quite the ladies' man. When Kate rejected him the first time, it only made her more appealing." He shook his head, his face grim. "But for him to actually imagine you might give in to him now—what rubbish!

"He must be the one who spread the rumor. He would not like being spurned twice and is just wicked enough to want to make sure no man would marry you." The earl muttered an oath. "I'll make him pay for this. He'll regret his deeds of this day!" The earl gruffly excused himself and went to his study intending to make two young men pay sorely for their deeds.

After the earl left the room, Kate said, "What I told Countess Lieven was true. I dunna really care what the ton thinks of me. I regret having caused trouble for you and Grandfather and for Colton, but society's opinion of me isna worth a pence. I dunna think there are more than a handful of people who are worth having as friends anyway."

"You're probably right. I was proud of Viscount Heartly. I do believe you've made a true friend."

"So do I." Kate sought to change the subject away from the night's events. She did not want to admit it, but the whole incident had wounded her deeply. What other people privately thought of her was of little significance, but being made a public spectacle was debasing. "He is quite taken with Miss Hastings."

"I noticed he was paying her particular attention. I met the gel last year and found her much to my liking. She has a level head and a good mind. She'll be good for a man like the viscount. Keep him on an even keel." Lady Millicent was aware of Kate's tactic and went along with it, chatting about unimportant things.

Once in his study, the earl poured himself a glass of port and sat down before the fire, happy to have only his dog's company. He could think out loud with no interruptions.

"Kate may not want to bring Colton to heel, but by jove, I will. The duke'll probably want to marry her anyway, but if I have any say in the matter, he'll do it immediately. I'll not have my granddaughter disgraced before the whole ton just because that buck couldn't keep his hands off 'er." He took a sip of his drink and stared into the fire, swearing quietly. "I'll have Blake's hide."

He cursed some more, then shook his head. He had never considered himself a swearing man. "But, the devil take it! Tonight's been enough to make the bishop utter an oath."

The earl moved to his desk, where he took pen in hand and wrote a quick note to the duke. He told him of the scandal and expounded succinctly on Kate's humiliation at the ball. Thomas demanded Colton's presence as early as possible the next day.

Then he wrote to Blake, tersely demanding his attendance at four o'clock the following afternoon. Lord Blagden took another long drink and sighed in disgust. He had no idea how he could make Blake pay sufficiently for his sins.

He stayed awhile in the library, then returned to the parlor and rejoined his wife and Kate. A short time later, they retired to their respective bedrooms.

In the middle of the night, Rowan nudged his master's hand, persisting until he awakened him. The earl sat up in bed, yawned, and scratched his head. Half asleep, he frowned at the dog. "What's the matter? I let you out before bed, didn't I?"

As if in answer, the dog trod gracefully to the bedroom door and looked back at the earl with an expectant lift to his ears.

"Oh, very well. Must be the oysters I slipped you at dinner. Never again, eh? Just roast and pheasant for you, my boy." The earl stretched his arms over his head, then swung his legs off the bed. After he pulled on his robe and slid his feet into his slippers, he shuffled sleepily across the room and opened the door.

When they reached the second floor, Rowan went to the closed ballroom door and stopped. The earl scratched the stubble on his jaw and glowered at his pet. "You can't do your business in there, you ninny." The dog only looked at his master, then back at the door, standing patiently. Lord Blagden's senses sharpened and his mind cleared from the haze of sleep. "Is there someone in here, boy?" he asked quietly. The dog pricked up his ears again.

Slowly and carefully, the earl turned the doorknob. Just as cautiously, he eased the door open and peeped in. At first he didn't see anything, so he pushed the door open wider. Rowan strolled through the opening ahead of him, then surprised Lord Blagden by stopping just inside the room and laying down.

The earl heard the soft rustle of a woman's gown. Then he spotted her. Dressed in her nightgown and robe, Kate moved around the room, walking this way and that. She would go a short distance and come to a sudden stop with a soft gasp. Then she would turn, almost in a panic, and go another direction, only to repeat the scene over and over. At last, she stopped in a beam of moonlight and the earl could see her face, wet from a stream of tears.

"Dunna turn away from me," she cried softly, her voice breaking with anguish. "Please, milady, we dinna do anything wrong." She turned again and took a few more steps. "Look at me. Talk to me. Dunna condemn me." Suddenly, she crossed her arms over her bosom and took a step back. "Dunna you dare look at me that way! Keep your hands off me! I'm no slut!" She twisted away as if jerking out of someone's grasp and ran across the room.

Weeping, Kate sank to her knees, covering her face with her hands. "I dinna do anything wrong. I love him. Dunna shame me this way. Stop it!" She shook her head as a sob wracked her body. "Forgive me, Grandpapa, forgive me. I dinna mean to hurt you. I'm so sorry . . . so sorry."

The earl hurried across the room, kneeling down stiffly eside his granddaughter. He gathered her in his arms, cradling er against his wide shoulder, and rocked her back and forth. Don't cry, child," he crooned. "You've not shamed me. It on't signify what the others think. Don't let them hurt you."

He rocked her for a few minutes, then eased her away from is shoulder and gently shook her. "Kate, wake up," he said oftly. He gave her another easy shake and wiped her tears way with his hand. "Kate, my girl, wake up."

Kate frowned, then blinked several times. She looked round the room slowly, then up at her grandfather as omprehension took hold. "What was I doing?"

"Reliving your humiliation. They hurt you dreadfully, didn't ey, child?"

"More than I ever thought they could." She winced and hifted on the hardwood floor. "Let's get up. My knees are illing me." She put her hand down on the floor and pushed, orcing her stiff legs to straighten. The old gentleman did the ame, grunting a little with the effort. He draped his arm across er shoulders, squeezing slightly.

"It does not signify what the ton thinks of us, my dear. They re a fickle bunch, you know."

"I know." They walked slowly across the room toward the oor. Rowan got to his feet, his tail swishing through the air in happy greeting. "It was being cut in public, being mocked nd humiliated in front of everyone that hurt so badly. To have hem treat me like . . . like I was something that had crawled ut of the gutter. And to know how it hurt you, Grandpapa. hat was the hardest thing of all."

"I am a proud old man, and I'll admit what happened tonight urt. But it wasn't so much the disgrace. I hurt for you and hat they were doing to you. There was little I could do to help ou. That's hardest of all, feeling old and useless."

"But you're no'!" Kate turned to him and gave him a swift, ard hug. "You stood by me. That showed great strength and ourage. It was as if you dared them to say anything more." he hugged him fiercely. "I love you, Grandpapa," she said, a voice watery with emotion.

"I love you, too, child." He squeezed her shoulders before

releasing her. "Now, run along to bed. And try to stay ther this time," he added with a smile.

"Yes, Grandpapa. Thank you." Kate gave him a peck on th cheek and left the room.

The earl looked slowly around the silent, moonlit roon Ghosts from the past, as well as phantoms from Countes Lieven's ball, haunted every corner. "You can all go to th devil," he muttered. In his mind's eye, the Duke of Rylan strolled across the room, full of arrogance and radiating powe "You'll do right by my girl, Ryland."

Wearily, Lord Blagden followed the dog out of the roon His thoughts were on his stepson, and they were not at all kin

Chapter 18

Colton's face contorted with anguish. He crumpled the earl's note into a tight ball and flung it into the cold ashes of the fireplace. A few choice words rumbled around the softly lit room as he pounded the mantel with the side of his fist. "I should have been there! No one would have dared to cut her if I'd been there! The devil take them! Take them all!" He leaned his head against the cool wood of the mantel, spreading his arms and resting his palms on the dark mahogany. "Forgive me, Kate," he whispered. "Please forgive me for letting them hurt you."

His first impulse was to run to her, to gather her in his arms and tell her it didn't matter what the ton thought of them. But since it was a quarter-past two in the morning, he rejected the idea. Wearily, Colton went upstairs to bed.

He had to return to the War Office at nine the next morning. There was no avoiding it. Several dispatches had been delivered shortly before midnight from his agents scattered across the Continent. He had spent the last two hours reading them and preparing a report to give to Lord Liverpool and the Cabinet. He suspected he would be tied up most of the day, if not in meetings with the Cabinet, then in training sessions with the man who would replace him.

In spite of his pain and remorse over Kate's humiliation, sleep came quickly. The earl had mentioned that Kate did not seem greatly overset by the night's proceedings, and Colton took some solace in that. He drifted off to sleep thinking how brave she was and how much he loved her. He'd set everything to rights.

The duke arrived at the Earl of Blagden's at precisely one o'clock the next afternoon. He had to be back at the War Office by half-past two and had skipped his luncheon to see Kate. Even the butler's face betrayed his irritation with His Grace as he showed him into the earl's study.

As usual, Lord Blagden got right to the point. "You're going to do the right thing by my granddaughter. You'll marry her within a fortnight." His eyes snapped with anger and he stood abruptly, shaking his finger at the duke as if he were a naughty child. "I'll not stand by and see her dishonored. You brought shame on this house, Ryland, and humiliation to Kate."

Colton accepted the earl's anger with calm grace, feeling that the old man's wrath was deserved. "I came over with the intention of asking for her hand, Thomas. It will be my honor to marry her."

"You're deemed right it'll be your honor. You're luckier than most." The earl nodded his head decisively, accepting Colton's offer. He was relieved the duke had not balked at marrying Kate. Colton had proven to be the kind of man Thomas thought him, but he was still angry with him. He sat down behind his desk and motioned for the duke to do likewise. "You took advantage of her, blast you. Taking her off to the country like that."

"I merely took your suggestion," the duke said dryly, sitting down in a comfortable chair across from his stepfather.

"I didn't know she was my granddaughter!"

"Neither did I. Still, it is regrettable that we were seen. I tried to be discreet."

"It was Blake who spread the tale, I'd wager my house on it."

"Blake?" Colton's gaze narrowed. "Why would he want to shame Kate?"

"The swine wanted her for himself. He had the gall to proposition her right here after our party the other night. Threatened to tell the ton about her being a maid and all if she didn't cooperate. At the time, I suppose he hadn't heard about her going to Twin Rivers with you. A gel that used to be one of our maids is his mistress now. Suspect she told him, and he used it against Kate when she turned him down."

"I'll throttle him." Colton's hands curled into fists and his jaw clenched with the effort of holding in his rage. He jumped to his feet and glanced around the room, wishing there was something within reach that he could punch. "The snake! When I'm done with him, his mistress won't even recognize him." Pemberton had dropped by before Colton received the earl's message, saying he'd gotten word from the man watching Blake advising that he was going to the country.

"You'll have to go to Brighton to do it. I sent for him myself, but his butler said he had been called away to his estate near Brighton in the middle of the night. Some sort of emergency." The earl snorted. "The only emergency was that he decided he'd better get out of town. I vaguely remember seeing him at Countess Lieven's ball last night."

Colton moved to the window and glanced out at the sunny day before turning back to the earl. Anger still churned within him, but he would have to deal with Blake Denley when he had more time. From the earl's expression, the old man was still fuming about the whole affair.

"Would you ask Kate to come down?" Colton drew out his pocket watch and checked the time. "I have to leave soon, and I'd like to have things settled between us."

"She's not here."

"What? Surely, she knew I would come by."

"I couldn't very well tell her I demanded your presence, now could I? How do you think she'd feel then, boy?" The earl stood abruptly and stomped around the end of the desk. "She's too proud to send for you herself. I expect she planned to tell you what happened whenever you next came to call. Millie took her over to the Foundling Hospital to visit some of the children and take them some gifts. Thought it might do her some good, make her feel better." The earl slammed his palm down on the desk. "Blast you, Ryland, you should have been there last night! If I weren't an old man, I'd teach you a thing or two."

The duke did not let the older man's ire irritate him. He understood it and agreed with him. "I did not miss the ball on purpose, Thomas. I had every intention of attending until I was summoned by Lord Liverpool. But you're right. If I'd been there, I do not think anyone would have been brave enough to treat her as they did." He paused, almost afraid to ask the next question, but knowing he needed to. "Was she wounded deeply? In your note, you thought it mattered little to her."

The earl moved back around the desk and slumped in his chair. "They cut her to pieces, Colton. She wouldn't admit that she cared what they thought, not even after we got home. She tried to make light of it. She felt badly because your name was slurred and because I was embarrassed and hurt, but she said she didn't give a pence what everyone else thought of her.

"Then in the middle of the night, I found her in the ballroom. She was reliving the evening, but this time instead of being brave and regal, she could not hide her pain."

"She walked in her sleep again?" asked Colton gently.

"Aye. She saw all those vicious faces in her mind, crying out to them, begging them not to treat her like dirt. Telling them she had done nothing wrong, that she wasn't a slut. Finally, she just crumpled to the floor in a sobbing heap." The earl's eyes misted and he shook his head sadly. "It broke my heart, boy, to see my proud Kate that way."

It broke Colton's heart to even imagine it. He clutched the back of a chair, his fingers digging into the green brocade material until his knuckles were white. He closed his eyes and drew in a stinging breath. "When will she be home?" He kept his eyes shut a minute longer, knowing if he opened them, they would be shiny with moisture.

"Not until around four or five."

"Oh, lord." Colton opened his eyes and ran his fingers through his hair in agitation. "I have to be back at the office soon. It's not something I can avoid. We're putting together a dispatch for an envoy to take to Castlereagh. The man who is replacing me is not familiar with all the details, so I must be there. It'll take hours." He released a heavy sigh and rubbed the tension in the back of his neck.

"Tell Kate I'll come back this evening if I can possibly get away. Otherwise, I'll be here bright and early on the morrow. I don't want her worrying about us over long." He looked at the earl, his expression troubled. "Reassure her for me, will you? I don't want her to think I've abandoned her."

"I won't let her think that, boy." The earl smiled for the first time and rose to walk Colton to the door. He slapped him on the back with affection. "I'll let her know everything is going to be just fine. You hurry back. I'm certain she'll be anxious to see you."

As Colton drove back to the War Office, he felt uneasy. He wished he'd been able to see Kate or had at least taken time to write her a note. He decided he would write her as soon as he got back to the office. Unfortunately, the minute he stepped through the doorway, he was set upon by three or four undersecretaries and clerks who felt they had urgent and important information to include in the dispatch to Castlereagh. He was not to have a moment's peace until almost midnight.

When Kate and Lady Millicent arrived home, the earl summoned his granddaughter to the library. He was stretched out on a comfortable sofa, reading *Poor Richard's Almanack* by Ben Franklin.

"You wanted to see me, Grandpapa?" Kate stepped into the room as the footman closed the door behind her. She glanced at the book in the earl's hand and smiled. He had a copy of everything Franklin ever published and treasured the collection above all else in his library.

The earl smiled up at her and put the book aside, sitting up. "Come here and sit beside me, child. I've good news." He waited until Kate sat down, then said proudly, "I talked to Colton. He's going to do right by you, gel."

Kate's soft gasp and the quick tension that filled her body went unnoticed by the earl. He continued blithely on, unconsciously trying to show her how he had stood up for her.

"I sent him a note last night, telling him what happened at the party, and asked him to pay me a call today. When he arrived, I pointed out his disreputable behavior in taking you to Twin Rivers and told him how much you had been hurt last night. He dishonored you, Kate. I demanded he do his duty and marry you. He agreed that it was the right thing to do."

"How noble," murmured Kate. *Do his duty! I dunna want him to do the right thing—I want him to marry me because he loves me!* She felt like shouting the words at her grandfather, but bit her lip to keep her silence. He was proud of what he had done and she knew he did it out of love for her. But it's Colton's love I want, her heart cried bitterly. I dunna want him to be forced to marry me.

"I knew he was an honorable man, but I made sure he understood what was expected of him." His expression was smug and self-satisfied. "I'm not such a useless old man after all."

Kate struggled valiantly to keep from screaming, curling her fingers into fists, digging her nails into her flesh. She took three slow deep breaths in order to control her unruly tongue. Finally, when she spoke, her voice was low and barely hinted at the rage churning inside her.

"Will he be coming back today?"

"He wasn't sure, dear. He's very busy at the War Office. Said if he couldn't get away tonight, he'd be here bright and early in the morning. I suspect he wants to pop the question to you in a formal way."

"Yes, I suspect he does," muttered Kate through gritted teeth. "Thank you, Grandpapa, for your efforts on my behalf. Now, if you'll excuse me, I feel a headache coming on. I'd like to retire to my room."

"Why, of course, my dear." He frowned at her and felt her flushed cheek. "You are a bit warm. Why don't you go lie down awhile. I hope you don't have a fever coming on."

"I'm just overtired. The visit to the Foundling Hospital took my mind off of last night, but it was a draining experience. So many who have so little, you know."

"Yes, yes, that's true. Well, run along and get a nap. You'll want to look refreshed and pretty when Colton comes to ask for your hand."

"Yes, indeed." Kate managed a wan smile but the moment she was out of the earl's sight, her face twisted with anger. "Marry me out of duty, will he! I'll teach that arrogant poppinjay something about duty." If she had not been so emotionally tired, Kate would have seen the circumstances in a different light, realizing Colton would not declare his love through her grandfather. But the experience of the night before had affected her far more than she realized. Her nerves were on lge, and her feelings were far too sensitive for her to think ıtionally.

She stalked into her bedroom, slamming the door behind er. Bess jumped and dropped her feather duster. She spun ound from the vanity where she had been working and stared Kate.

"What happened now?"

"Colton came to call while I was out. Grandfather has rdered him to marry me."

"And does he plan to obey the order?" A smile tugged at the orner of the maid's lip. She knew His Grace would never omply with an order, or even a request, unless he wanted to.

"Aye." Kate plopped down on the bed and grabbed a pillow, ugging it to her chest. "He says he'll marry me out of duty nd honor. I dunna want duty and honor. I want his love."

"Surely, ye know he loves ye, miss. It shows on his face very time he looks at ye."

"I know nothing of the kind. He's never said anything to me bout love. Wanting, yes, but never love." Kate sat sullenly on ne bed for a moment, then jumped to her feet. "I willna marry man who feels forced to marry me, whether he cares for me r no'. Bess, sneak out the back way and hire a hackney."

"Be we goin' someplace, miss?" Bess had a keen idea of hat her mistress had in mind.

"Aye. We're going home. We should have stayed there in ne first place. Go downstairs and tell Lady Millicent that I've ecided to go to bed early and willna be joining them for nner. I hate to lie to them, but if they get wind of our plans, ey'll stop us. Then, sneak out the back way and find a ackney to take us to the Swan with Two Necks. I'll pack some othes and meet you outside the back gate in half an hour. If e hurry, we might catch the mail coach to Edinburgh. therwise, we'll just have to find another one."

"Miss Kate, are ye sure ye want to do this? Wouldna it be etter to wait and talk to the duke?"

"No! I dunna want to talk to him. I'm too angry and I'll say omething I'd probably regret." She started pulling dresses om the wardrobe. "Dunna you see, Bess? Even if he tells me e loves me now, I willna know whether 'tis true or no'. He might just say it to make me marry him, so we will do the honorable thing in the eyes of the almighty, all holy ton."

Bess chuckled and took two pieces of baggage from a large oak chest in the corner. "Holy?"

"Well, they think they are; though their definition of holiness certainly differs from what I was taught."

Casting her mistress a sympathetic look, the maid left to do her bidding.

Kate threw clothes into the bags for both of them, laying their pelisses aside to carry along with them. She slipped a small box containing her jewelry and another containing her money into her reticule, then sat down at the writing desk in the corner of the room to compose a note to her grandfather. She scribbled the message quickly, taking few pains with neatness nor pondering over what to say.

When the note was finished, she propped it up on the vanity and started to gather up the baggage. The door opened and Kate jumped a foot.

"I'm sorry, miss. I dinna mean to scare ye," said Bess softly, her breathing labored from running up the stairs. "I dinna think ye could carry everythin'. The hack is waitin' halfway down the block. I thought if he waited by the gate someone might see."

Kate nodded gratefully and handed the girl a bag. "Did you talk to Grandmother?"

"Aye. She thought ye goin' to bed early was a good idea. She said she'd wake ye if His Grace comes to call."

"Oh, dear. I hadna thought about that. Well, if our luck holds, he willna come until tomorrow. I suppose the worst that could happen is that he might come after us."

"I dunna think it would be so bad. It would keep us from goin' all the way to Edinburgh—just so he can come after ye."

Kate paused, having a tiny misgiving about the worthiness of her plan. "True." She nibbled on her bottom lip. "But if he came all the way to Edinburgh, I'd be more sure of his love. If he only has to go to Hounslow Heath to catch us, he might only be defending his honor."

Bess grinned. "I ken there's some logic in there somewhere, but if ye were to ask me, yer makin' more of a burble out of everthin'."

"Well, I dinna ask you. Now, are you going with me?"

"Aye, miss. I canna have ye runnin' off on yer own." Bess set the bag on the floor and pulled the covers back on the bed. Rolling up a blanket, she placed it on the bed, along with some extra pillows. She pulled the covers back over the padding so it would appear someone was sleeping in the bed if the room was dark.

"Clever, Bess, clever."

The maid only grinned and picked up her pelisse, throwing it over her arm. Carefully, she opened the door and peeped out into the hallway. "'Tis empty." Kate gathered up her things and followed her out the door.

With hearts pounding, the two young women silently made their way down the hall and backstairs and through the garden undetected. They paused only a moment outside the gate while Bess made certain it was locked behind them. Minutes later, they were in the hired hackney, driving toward Lad Lane. They both breathed a sigh of relief.

Soon, they were securely situated in two of the four inside seats on the Edinburgh mail coach. One of the occupants sitting across from them was a young man of approximately eighteen, who kept sneaking glances at Kate. The other man, a rakish-looking soldier of fortune dressed in the guise of a gentleman, did nothing to hide his interest in her. Kate and Bess exchanged cool pleasantries with the gentlemen, then did their best to ignore them.

The coachman drove his rig to the General Post Office in Lombard Street. Although anxious to make her getaway, Kate could not help but marvel at the sight. Twenty-seven mail coaches, painted maroon and black with scarlet wheels and the royal coat of arms emblazoned on their doors, were drawn up in double file to await the boxes of mail. Promptly at eight o'clock, the coaches set off for every part of the kingdom, piled high with passengers and baggage. The guard in his royal scarlet livery stood on the boot with his feet on top of the locked mailbox, blowing his long brass horn to clear the way ahead.

After a few pointed remarks from the rogue, Kate realized he, and most likely the younger one also, fully believed she was a high flyer currently without a protector.

"You will keep your insulting remarks to yourself, sir." Kate sent him a scathing look, lifting her chin with an arrogance normally unknown to her. "Circumstances have dictated that I travel to Edinburgh by the quickest means possible, but I dunna have to put up with your audacity. If you continue to cast aspersions upon my character, you shall be answerable to my grandfather, the Earl of Blagden."

The rogue's eyebrow lifted slightly. "I am not afraid of an old man."

"It is true my grandfather is advanced in years," said Kate coolly. "No doubt he would turn the matter over to his stepson, who would be quick and sure in the defense of my honor."

The man stifled a bored yawn. "And who is this gentleman that he should set me to quaking in my boots?"

"The Duke of Ryland." Kate's eyes gleamed in triumph as the man tried unsuccessfully to hide his gasp. The younger man's eyes grew round, for even he had heard of the powerful Duke of Ryland.

"I beg your pardon, miss. It seems I have made a grave mistake." The man crossed his arms in front of him, unconsciously hugging his chest.

Kate accepted his apology with a curt nod. She was a little surprised because her bluff had worked. She was in no position to call for Colton's help, yet it filled her with an inordinate amount of pride that the mere mention of his name had vanquished her enemy.

A deep, painful ache filled her heart. In a desperate effort to contain her need to cry, she concentrated on what little scenery remained visible in the fading twilight. *Oh, my love, come for me!*

Colton had finally concluded his business around midnight. His work was now complete; he had turned everything over to the man who replaced him. He would leave it up to Lord Castlereagh and the others to thwart the rising ambitions of Russia and Prussia, and deal with dividing up the lands Napoleon had lost.

He was now free to shower his attentions on his beloved. He awoke early, in a buoyant mood. He took his time bathing and dressing, then went down to breakfast. It was only eight o'clock, but he decided to eat quickly and go see Kate.

He grinned, thinking that he might sneak up to her room and catch her still asleep or shortly after she awakened. A clear memory of the morning he left Edinburgh filled his mind. She had been delightfully enticing in *deshabille*, and his pulse quickened. It might not be the most acceptable scenario, but he could think of nothing more romantic than to propose to her when she was still tousled and warm from sleep. A spark flared in his eyes as he thought of her, soft and cuddly on his lap.

He was startled from his daydream by a loud pounding on the front door. Moments later, the butler rushed in, carrying a note on a silver tray. "It's from Lord Blagden, Your Grace. The footman said you should open it immediately."

Colton grabbed the letter from the tray and tore it open. Seconds later he jumped to his feet, shouting, "I'll throttle her!"

"Your Grace, what has happened?" Gregory rushed into the room, having hurried downstairs when he heard the knock on the door.

"Kate has run off to Scotland!" The duke bowed his head and closed his eyes, taking a deep breath, trying to deal with the anger and hurt.

"But why would she run away?"

Gregory's question brought Colton's head up. He opened his eyes and looked at his servant. "I have a few ideas. Knowing Thomas, he told her I was going to do the honorable thing and marry her. That little minx, when I get my hands on her, I'll—I'll . . ." His voice trailed off as he caught the twitch of Gregory's lip.

"Kiss her?" the valet supplied helpfully.

A derisive smile flickered across the duke's face. "Probably. But first, I'm going to shake her until her teeth rattle. Send for my horse. I'll go talk to Thomas and Mother and see what has happened. You pack while I'm gone and have Lunan prepare the coach. We'll leave as soon as I get back. I'm not letting her simply walk out of my life."

"Good for you." Gregory grinned at the duke, quickly adding, "Your Grace."

Colton took a quick gulp of coffee on his way to the door,

handing the cup to the valet. After he left the room, Gregory looked down at the hot drink, shrugged, and finished it himself.

The duke sped down the fairly empty streets, awakening more than one of his peers with the pounding hooves of his steed. When he approached Lord Blagden's, Harlan came running out, reaching the street as the duke drew his animal to a halt.

"Walk him about, Harlan. I won't be long," barked His Grace as he dismounted. He strode swiftly to the back parlor, knowing he would find his mother and Thomas waiting. He stepped into the room and closed the door behind him, his expression fierce. "Well?"

Thomas silently handed Colton the note Kate had written. Lady Millicent reached out and took her husband's hand while her son read the letter. She watched his face closely, knowing a volcano was about to erupt.

Kate had thanked the earl and Lady Millicent for their hospitality and their love. She told them not to worry about her, even though she and Bess were taking the mail coach to Edinburgh. She declared her confidence in a safe trip, ignoring the well-known fact that the mail coaches often had mishaps due to the speed with which they traveled.

But the last paragraph was the most enlightening and irritating to the duke. "I know you had good intentions, Grandfather, but I canna help but believe Colton has been forced into asking for my hand. Even if you hadna pressured him to do his duty, I'm certain he would have offered for me as a matter of honor. However, I willna marry because honor and duty declare it. I willna marry a man who doesna love me."

Colton looked up, letting his hand, and the note, slowly drop to his side. His expression was perplexed. *How can she believe I don't love her?*

Thomas cleared his throat. "Uh, um, I seem to have made a muddle of reassuring her, lad."

"What did you tell her?" The duke's eyes narrowed dangerously.

Thomas pulled his hand from Lady Millicent's, motioning for Colton to sit down.

The duke complied reluctantly, his glance going briefly to his mother's worried face. She chewed on her bottom lip and fluttered her hands nervously. He knew he was not going to like what Thomas had to say.

"Well, I suppose I was trying to impress the chit. I didn't realize it at the time, but now I see I wanted her to think I had stood up for her, made things right and all. Didn't want her to think I was letting her down like I did her father. I told her that you had dishonored her, and that I demanded you do your duty and marry her. I said you had agreed it was the right thing to do. I told her you were an honorable man and, of course, would do the honorable thing." He cleared his throat again. "You hadn't mentioned loving her, so I couldn't very well say anything about it."

"Of course I love her!" shouted the duke, jumping to his feet. He stormed around the room, frustrated and infuriated with both himself and Thomas. "Anyone with eyes in their head can see that I love her."

"Well, of course, we thought so, dear," said his mother gently, "but you've never actually told us such a thing. Until now, that is," she added feebly. She took a deep, bracing breath, reminding herself that she no longer depended on her son's good favor for her sustenance. "I take it from Kate's note that you have not told her as much either."

Colton stopped rambling around the room and let out a deep sigh. "No, I haven't. I planned to declare myself when I proposed. Guess I made a muddle of it, too."

"Well, you've never been in love before, dear. You can't expect to be an expert at something you've never done."

Colton smiled faintly at his mother's logic before a new wave of anger washed over him. "Still, she didn't have to go running off to Scotland. Good lord! If she took the mail coach, she left last evening." He scowled at his mother. "Why did it take you so long to discover she was missing?"

"She complained of a headache and said she was going to bed early. The poor dear had been through so much the night before, I didn't find it unusual. I did peek in on her when I went to bed, but she appeared to be sleeping so I didn't disturb her." Lady Millicent shook her head, a look of irritation spreading across her face. "The chit had put pillows and a rolled-up blanket underneath the covers to make me think someone was in the bed. She has entirely too good of an imagination."

"She does have a flare for drama," murmured the duke, mildly disgusted that Kate would go to such an extreme. His worry and anger grew. "That little idiot! The way those coachmen drive the mail, she could be killed. She's only inviting some scoundrel to make advances." His voice rose. "She has no man along to protect her. She might even be abducted at some lonely inn. And on top of that," he shouted, "I'll have to listen to Lunan gripe all the way to Edinburgh because she took Bess with her."

The duke stomped across the room and flung open the door. His boots clicked loudly on the tile floor as he practically ran down the hall. "I'm going after her."

"But, son, she's hours ahead of you. You can't possibly catch up to her." The earl and his lady followed him out the front door.

"Oh, I'll catch up with her all right, even if I don't do it until I reach Edinburgh." Colton swung up on his horse, and the animal shied at the tension emanating from him. "And when I do, we'll get this mess straightened out. Not love her, indeed," he muttered.

As he spun his horse around, the earl called after him, "Don't have the wedding without us. We'll leave this afternoon."

Colton tossed him a wave, acknowledging his request, and dashed down the street, almost running down a rag man and two stray dogs who were reckless enough to get in his way.

Chapter 19

he duke did not catch up with Kate en route. He stopped at e various inns along the way where the mail coach passen-ers took their meals and checked on her progress. A woman f her beauty did not go unnoticed. When the innkeepers arned who he was and the information he sought, they were nly too happy to divulge the presence of the young lady on the ail coach. As expected, they were more than adequately ewarded for their discernment.

Colton did not rush to the Denley home the minute he rrived in town. Instead, he took lodging for the night at a hoice inn nearby. He was given the best room the innkeeper ad to offer and was able to procure a room for Lunan and the oachman, as well as a smaller, but separate room across the all for Gregory.

He had pushed himself and his men to their limits, yet they ad been unable to make up more than a few hours of Kate's ad. Grimy and exhausted, he did not wish to confront her ntil he was thinking clearly and smelled better. He did not ant her telling their grandchildren that he was dirty and mpled when he proposed.

He sent a message to Addison, asking him to confirm Kate's afe arrival but not to tell her he was in Edinburgh. He wanted catch her by surprise. Addison delivered his reply in person, rriving moments after the duke had ended a long soak in a

steaming tub. Gregory answered the knock on the door a
Colton tied the belt to his robe.

"Good. I didn't arrive too soon." Addison held out his han
as he entered the room. The duke clasped the offered hand an
shook it firmly, returning the other man's grin.

"A few minutes ago, you would have found me decadentl
turning into a prune." He held out his hands, smiling at th
wrinkles caused by spending so long in the tub. "I ca
remember only a few times when a hot bath felt better." Colto
looked over at his weary valet. "That will be all, Gregory. Se
to your own comfort. I shouldn't need you until the morrow.
He shot a questioning glance at Addison, who shook his head

"No, there's no need to dash over to the house tonight." H
grinned again. "Kate's in a temper in spite of having slept mos
of the day. If I could stand it, I'd suggest you wait a day or tw
to call on her, just to let her stew." He laughed and took th
chair offered by his host. "But I don't think any of us coul
stay in the house with her. The way she's hissing and spitting
I expect her to claw someone's eyes out any minute."

"My poor little Kitten," murmured the duke, sitting down i
the other plush red chair in front of the small fireplace. He ha
done little else but think of her during the whole trip. His ange
had slowly dissipated, leaving in its stead a surprisingly gentl
understanding of her feelings. His face was sober when h
looked up at his friend. "She has been through a great deal
Did she tell you what happened?"

"Not the whole of it. She briefly explained about the scand
and Father's ensuing demand for marriage." He paused, a loo
of hatred passing over his face. "When I get ahold of Blake
I'll throttle him." He took a deep breath to calm himself, the
continued. "But it is not the problem of the moment. I believ
her main concern is that she is unsure of your love and will no
be forced into a marriage with someone who does not lov
her."

"I do love her," Colton said softly. "I don't quite know how
I'll go on if she won't have me." A tiny, rueful smile playe
across his features. "I thought she understood how I felt abou
her, even though I had never said the words. I had planned t
tell her of my love when I proposed." He shrugged. "I though

o play by the rules—ask Thomas for her hand, then declare my undying love to her, and ask her to be my wife."

"You know Kate." Addison's eyes twinkled. "She plays by her own rules."

"Yes. I should have told her of my feelings sooner. Unfortunately, Blake—at least he's the prime suspect—spread the rumor that she was my mistress and the ton was at their vicious best." His eyes filled with sorrow. "I cannot tell you how deeply I regret not being with her at Countess Lieven's party. I should have shielded her, protected her from their wickedness."

"She understood why you were not there, Colton. She does not blame you." Addison hesitated, looking down at his hands for a moment, before lifting his troubled gaze back up to meet the duke's. "As her father, I have to know." He cleared his throat self-consciously, not quite knowing how to ask his friend the question burning in his heart. "Is there need for a hasty marriage?"

"Only because I do not think I can live without her for another day. I did not defile your daughter, although by society's definition, I have plainly compromised her." It was Colton's turn to hesitate, then he plunged ahead. He had heard confession was good for the soul. "Back during the winter, when she was still posing as a maid, I took her out to the country to my estate, Twin Rivers. I confess my intentions were not particularly honorable, although they weren't totally dishonorable either." He blushed slightly. "I knew what I wanted to do with her, but I wasn't certain when I took her there that I would actually go through with it.

"I loved her even then, although I did not quite believe what those deep feelings meant. We had a wonderful time together; the best I could ever remember. I made up my mind not to try and seduce her or ask her to become my mistress, which I had been considering. Unhappily, when I kissed her, my good intentions flew out the window. Thankfully, she had enough sense to stop me before things got out of hand."

"And when you went to Twin Rivers this last time?"

"Again, I compromised her by being alone with her and kissing her. Nothing more." His expression turned a little sheepish. "I've discovered it's deuced hard to obey the rules of society or even morality when one is in love."

"Aye, I have not forgotten the feeling. Thank you for the reassurance, just the same. We will not stand in your way if you do not choose to wait long for the wedding."

"Is it true we only have to promise to take each other as husband and wife? We don't even need a witness?" Colton asked with a grin.

"Yes, in an irregular marriage. It can be questioned if there's no witness, but anyone can be a buckle-the-beggar, as the saying goes. I'm certain you know of any number of English citizens who have dashed to Gretna Green and been married over the blacksmith's anvil or even by the tollkeeper himself. It is legal in every sense of the word."

"Yes, but sometimes questioned in England even if there are witnesses. I suspect Kate will want a church wedding at St. Giles." He smiled at Addison. "I suppose I'd better ask her before I make too many plans."

Addison stood. "And I'd better go so you can get your rest. I won't tell her you are in town. Shall I expect you early in the morning?"

"Fairly so. I doubt if you'd let me go up and wake her."

"It would be pushing the limits of my tolerance," replied Addison with a chuckle. "But I'm certain she'll be up and about by mid-morning."

"Then so shall I." Colton walked his friend to the door, resting his hand upon the other man's shoulder. "Has anyone taken any more potshots at you?"

"Not for a few weeks now. I've been very careful. There are two guards outside your door at the moment and two more downstairs. I'll be glad when whoever is behind this shows himself. It's very uncomfortable being on the watch every minute."

"Quite true. I wish we had some better ideas, but my men haven't really turned up anything of significance. I've even gone so far as to have Richard and Blake investigated."

Addison looked at him in surprise. "Richard? You can't be serious."

Colton shook his head. "I can't imagine him doing anything like this, but since he is next in line for the title after you, I decided I'd better be safe than sorry. Nothing showed up in the preliminary report, but then my men had only worked on it for a couple of days before I left."

"I could see Blake involved in something unscrupulous, but murder?" Addison shook his head, a bemused expression on his face. "He's so far down the line for the title, it doesn't seem logical."

"I agree, but then murderers have a warped sense of logic. He fled to his country estate after spreading the rumor about Kate. I can't quite picture him having enough courage to try and kill you himself, but then one never knows. I have a man observing him. If he makes a move, we'll know."

The duke bade Addison farewell and watched the guards take their places, one in front of him and one behind him, as they descended the staircase. Colton yawned as he shut the door, then removed his robe and retired for the evening. Several bright stars winked at him through the open window, and he wondered if Kate was watching them, too. "Tomorrow, my little Kitten." He yawned again and turned over. "You'll be purring tomorrow."

Colton knocked on Addison's door at precisely ten o'clock the following morning. He was dressed to perfection in his favorite shades of brown, and for once had agreed with Gregory when he said he looked quite dashing. The butler showed him into the front parlor to join Addison and Myrna.

"Good morning, Colton." Myrna held out her hand and smiled as the duke took it and kissed her fingers in a gentlemanly fashion. " 'Tis good to see you again."

"And you also, ma'am. I trust you have been well?"

"Very, especially since Addison has mended. Although, I must admit, my daughter has hagged me a bit since she's been home. In a devilish temper, that lass."

"I suppose she has reason to be." He glanced at Addison, his eyes twinkling. "Is she up?"

"Very." Addison grinned as Myrna giggled. "She decided to clean the attic this morning."

Colton raised a bemused eyebrow. "Do you think I can find her amid all the boxes and trunks?"

"You might have to search a little," said Myrna. "Actually,

things are quite orderly. I think she just wanted an excuse to shove something around and grumble."

Colton chuckled. "I can see this won't be the easiest job I've tackled. Do I simply follow the stairs?"

"Aye, to the tiptop of the house." Addison waved his hand and smiled. "Even you can find it."

"My thanks," the duke said dryly. "If you'll excuse me, I think I'll scale the mountain and see if I'm welcomed or pushed off."

"Stay away from the top of the stairs and the windows. Like I said, she's in a shovin' mood." Myrna's smile wished him well.

Colton hurried up three floors, but slowed his pace as the staircase narrowed. Walking softly, he climbed the last flight and peered through the doorway into the storage part of the attic. The room was huge, covering almost the entire floor. Boxes and trunks, along with out-of-favor furniture, were scattered in random stacks about the space.

He waited for his eyes to adjust to the dim light. Small, high windows let in the sunlight, and though not as bright as the other rooms in the house, once he grew accustomed to it, he could see clearly. Soft mutterings and a scraping sound reached his ears. He looked around the room slowly, trying to find Kate.

A wooden box screeched as it was scraped against the floor. The noise was followed by louder mutterings. He cautiously moved closer and determined that the words were a mixture of Gaelic and English. He craned his neck, looking around a stack of boxes marked "winter clothes" and another labeled "Kate's toys." She wasn't behind them.

A soft smile lit his face as he moved a little farther into the room, coming across a highly polished cherry wood cradle. Beside it was a larger baby bed, also highly polished, except for one rail which bore several patches of tiny teeth marks. He ran a finger over the little indentations and his eyes grew misty.

A ray of sunlight in the back corner of the room caught his eye. Instead of the normal dust motes floating lazily through it, the golden light was filled with a veritable cloud of dust. There came a sneeze. Then another. Colton grinned at the sound. Although pitched in a definite feminine tone, there was nothing delicate about it. He tiptoed down the makeshift aisle and peeped around a large, cumbersome dresser.

Kate sniffed, twitched her nose, and finally swiped it indelicately on the back of her hand, then absently brushed said hand across her apron. "Canna you even remember to bring a kerchief?" she muttered. "But no, you're an idiot. Runnin' off like some ninnyhammer; no' givin' the man a chance to explain himself."

Kate swept the corner furiously, raising another cloud of dust and bringing on another sneeze. She was miserable and the dust had little to do with it. She moved a little farther down the wall to ply her broom, then jumped back with a little scream when she leaned into a cobweb. Frantically brushing the spidery web off her face, she knocked her mobcap askew.

She hung her head in defeat. Tears—which she blamed on the dust and the frightening encounter with the cobweb—stung her eyes. After a few seconds, Kate raised her head and staunchly wiped her eyes with the corner of the apron, refusing to let the tears fall.

"You might as well accept it, Kate Dunderhead Denley," she admonished herself in a voice that held a mild tremor. "The man isna comin' after you. You let your temper get the best of you, and you gave him the easy way out. He doesna love you and dinna want to marry you. He was only doing it out of honor and duty." She spat out the words like they were some foul concoction.

The duke stepped into the open area where she had been working and said softly, "Honor and duty are very important, Kate."

She gasped and spun around to face him. "You took your own sweet time getting here," she complained, her brow wrinkled in a frown. She glanced from his neatly pressed, immaculate new clothes to her old, dirty, and rumpled gown. Embarrassment flickered across her face, followed immediately by an expression of extreme irritation. "Why dinna you announce your arrival? How dare you come up here to find me in such a mess!"

Colton let his gaze slowly, lovingly travel over her. A sweet smile softened his face as he noted her wrinkled, dusty clothes. The mobcap sat cockeyed on her head, allowing several thick, beautiful curls to droop down along her neck, and reminding him of the day he met her. She had a smudge along one cheek and a light powder of dust on the tip of her nose.

"You look absolutely lovely."

"Humph." In her agitated state, his words sounded patronizingly sweet, and only served to irritate her more. She crossed her arms over her chest. Up went her chin. "I willna marry you, Colton Lydell. I dunna care if you are the high, mighty, and esteemed Duke of Ryland. I dunna want a man who is forced to marry me just to save his honor."

Colton took a step closer, then another. Kate's heart pounded in her chest. *If he touches me, I'm lost,* she thought desperately, *and then I'll marry him no matter what the reason.* She took a step backward, but came up against the wall—and another cobweb. Shuddering, she jumped forward and bumped into a wall of a different sort, one made of warm flesh and hard, strong muscles. His hands firmly grasped her shoulders to steady her, and his tender cinnamon eyes held hers captive.

He brushed the dusty powder off her nose and pulled the crooked mobcap from her head, letting her hair fall in a river down her back. He buried his fingers in the shiny locks, and in a gesture she knew so well, lifted a handful of hair to his nostrils. He watched her face as he breathed deeply of her special fragrance, then let the curls sift through his fingers to lie across her shoulder and breast.

"Did I tell you I've grown to love the smell of jasmine?" He smiled into her eyes and brushed the thundering pulse in her throat with his thumb. "Honor and duty are important, Kate but there are other, more important reasons for marriage."

He wrapped his arms around her and drew her fully against him as he lowered his lips to hers. His touch was tender and reverent, and so filled with love that tears sprang to her eyes and slipped down her cheeks, leaving a faint trail through the dusty film. He raised his head a little to search her eyes, his brows furrowing as he noted the telltale path of her tears.

"Oh, Cole, I've been so wretched without you," she whispered. She closed her eyes and parted her lips slightly begging for his kiss. *Kiss me hard, my love, or I'll turn into a complete watering pot.*

His arms tightened, molding her body to his. When his lips ouched hers the second time, passion replaced reverence. He issed her again and again, leaving her breathless with the romise of things to come. At last, he straightened and drew er head gently to rest against his chest. He simply held her for few minutes to allow them both to calm their desire and catch ıeir breath.

"Can you forgive me for running away?" Kate asked softly, er words slightly muffled against the silken fall of his cravat.

"Of course, my love." He settled her a little more comfortbly against him. "At first, I was at sixes and sevens and ıreatened to throttle you the moment I got my hands on you. ut, alas, it's a long trip from London to Edinburgh, and I had lenty of time to think. I can't blame you for being angry with ıe, sweetheart. I intended to tell you how much I loved you ıat last afternoon at Twin Rivers, but Rowan interrupted my, ı, train of thought."

Kate pulled back so she could see his face. "And do you ve me, Colton Lydell?"

"With all my heart and soul, and with my body as soon as e're married." If she had needed reassurance, which she dn't, the warm, tender expression on his face and the spark longing in his eye would have been more than enough. He ıshed the hair away from her face, cupping her jaw in one ınd. "And you, Kate, do you love me?"

"With every beat of my heart and every breath I take." She bbed her face lovingly against his hand. "Mmmm, it feels ce to have you here."

Colton grinned, his eyes sparkling with mischief. "I told yself that you'd be purring before the day was out, Kitten."

Her eyes narrowed and she moved her head away from his nd, toying with the lace edge of his cravat. "Did I do that the ght I tried to smother you with the bedspread?"

"What? Purr?" His eyes glinted as if he would like to tease r to exasperation.

"Well, that, and who knows what else. Just exactly what did u do and what did it make me do?" she said with a frown.

The duke fondly thought that it didn't take her long to reach point of exasperation and took pity on her.

"No, you didn't purr. Your hands were cold, and I touched

your face to check it, too. It was like ice. When I cradled your jaw in my hand, you gave the sweetest little sigh and rubbed against it, just like a contented kitten wanting to be scratched behind her ears."

"And did you?" Kate relaxed, enjoying the banter.

"Scratch behind your ears?"

"Aye."

"No." He leaned down and stole a quick kiss. "I kissed you."

"That's how you lured me into your bed?" Kate stepped back, hands on her hips, and attempted a glare. Unfortunately it was quite ruined by the twinkle in her eye and the laughter that insisted upon bubbling up.

"No, it's how I woke you. You were so terribly chilled that for a moment my only concern was to get you warm." He wiggled his eyebrows expressively. "It was the promise of warmth that lured you into my bed, not my virile, naked body." He grinned wickedly and crossed his arms in front of him, leaning back against a stack of boxes.

"It soon became apparent that I could not bear to have you lying in my arms, at least not asleep. I sought to wake you in the gentlest, most persuasive way I could think of. Unhappily your response was not all I had hoped for." He smiled at her lifted brow and mildly disbelieving look. "Oh, at first, while you were asleep, I thought perhaps I was going to be the luckiest man alive. But, sadly, when you were awake, you did not want to stay."

Kate took a step, resuming her place in front of him. He uncrossed his arms and slipped them around behind her. She slid her hands slowly up the front of his coat and around to the back of his neck, leaning against him. "Are you saying, Your Grace, that I kissed you back?"

"Yes, you did. And very nicely, too. It was a great disappointment when you jumped up out of bed and tried to flee."

She wiggled against him, her lips forming a teasing pout. "Well, you must understand, Your Grace, I'm no' used to waking up in bed with a man, much less with one as bare as the day he was born."

"Hmmm. Sounds like something you need to work on." He

expression grew seductive, and his eyes flamed beneath half-lowered lids. "Especially since I never wear anything to bed."

"Have I a reason to be concerned about such things?" Her expression was one of mock innocence and only mild interest, but her heartbeat quickened and her body grew warm simply from thinking of that bare chest she had viewed eons ago.

"Yes—if you're going to marry me, that is." He kissed her tenderly.

When they broke apart, and Kate looked back up at him, her eyes were sparkling. "And am I going to marry you, Colton?"

"Devil if I know. Suppose I haven't asked you yet, have I?" With that, he dropped down on one knee in the dust, and took her hand, giving her a most beseeching look. "Will you be my wife, Catriona Denley? To love and laugh with and grow old together?"

"Yes, I'll be your wife, my love." She tugged on his hand so he would get up off the dirty, drafty floor. "To love, honor, and occasionally obey."

Colton laughed and pulled her into his arms, kissing her soundly. "I'm tempted to go downstairs and make our promises to each other in front of your parents. Then I could haul you back up the stairs and make love to you with a clean conscience." He kissed her again, a little more passionately. Although she answered him with like passion, he sensed the tiniest bit of hesitation. It was answer enough for him. Slowly, enjoying every delicious minute of it, he brought their kisses and caresses to a halt. Finally, he settled his hands on her shoulders and eased her away from him.

"But we won't." He smiled tenderly at her mildly dazed and questioning expression. "No, it would be best by all accounts to be married in the church by a minister. We should be able to avoid any legal hassles in England by doing so. And I promised your grandfather that we'd wait for them."

"They're coming?" Kate's face lit up.

"Probably only a few days or so behind me. I'm sure they left soon after me, but they have too many years behind them to travel straight through like we did." He tipped her face up and studied it. "Is there some way the minister can marry us without waiting forever? I don't want to wait three weeks for you to become my bride."

"Well, if we went to see Reverend Murray this afternoon, he could read the banns tomorrow in service and then again next Sunday. It only takes two Sundays here, instead of three as in England. We could be married after services next Sunday or on Monday."

Colton frowned sullenly, knowing he was behaving like a spoiled child but not really caring. "That's still too long."

"All we can do is talk to Reverend Murray. Perhaps he will have a better suggestion."

"Is this Reverend Murray at St. Giles Cathedral?"

"Aye. Do you know him?"

"Yes, we met years ago when my family visited Lady Douglas. In fact, we had property here for some time. My father sold it a few years before he died."

"I'm beginning to think there isna anyone you dunna know."

Colton grinned. "We spies need to know a lot of people." He leaned closer and said softly, "In fact, I have worked closely with your good minister several times."

"Reverend Murray, a spy?" Kate's face registered her disbelief.

"Of sorts. Kept his eyes open, like so many with a patriotic heart. He never betrayed any confidences of his people, although he dropped some strong hints a few times to keep them from getting involved in something they shouldn't have. I suspect we'll find a way to speed up this marriage of ours." He smiled and puffed out his chest a little. "After all, I am a duke. If I can't pull strings, who can?"

Kate laughed and squeezed him tight. She drew back with a startled expression. "Mercy of heav'n."

"What is it, love?"

"I'm going to be a duchess!"

"Indeed you are. Don't tell me you never thought of it."

She shook her head, laughing at herself. "I'm sure I did, but the reality of it dinna hit me until just now." She met his eyes and giggled. "I can look down my nose at all those snooty young *ladies* who cut me."

Colton's smile faded and pain drifted into his eyes. "I feel so badly because they hurt you. I would give anything if I could have been there with you, to shield you and stifle their malicious tongues."

She brushed his cheek with her fingertips and kissed the tip of his chin. "Dunna fret over it, dearest. It hurt at the time, but I have no lasting scars. They are nothing to me, after all. I doubt if we'll ever see many of them again."

"You'll see them if we go to town for a Season."

"I dunna need another Season. I've already caught my man."

"I see. Let me chase you till you caught me, eh?"

"Something like that."

Reluctantly, they turned to go downstairs, walking arm in arm. When they stepped out into the stairway, Kate glanced down at her gown and moaned.

Colton stopped, checking her over quickly to find the source of her pain. "What is it, Kate?"

"Will you just look at me? If I know you, Colton Lydell, you'll tell our grandchildren I was dirty and rumpled when you proposed."

"Never, my dear, never."

If it hadn't been for his roar of laughter as they walked down the stairs, she might have believed him.

Chapter 20

The beaming couple strolled into the front parlor, smiling at the expectant look on the faces of Kate's parents. Addison looked pointedly at the dirty spot on Colton's left pantaloon leg and grinned. Jumping up from his chair, he crossed the room, opening his arms to his daughter. "May I be the first to wish you happy, Kate."

"Thank you, Papa."

Myrna hurried across the room to join them, hugging Kate as Addison pumped the duke's hand.

"You've got a fine woman there, Colton. Of course, I'm a bit prejudiced, but I don't think you'd find any better." Addison broke off the handshake and slapped the duke on the back. "We're quite pleased with her choice, too. Welcome to the family."

"Thank you." Colton's grin held a hint of mischief. "Actually, I already was a part of the family. Can't you see me trying to explain it to some poor, hard-of-hearing dowager—this is my wife Kate, who also happens to be my niece—stepniece, that is. And, this is my father-in-law, who also happens to be my brother, uh, stepbrother." His expression grew comically perplexed. "A man could get confused."

They all laughed, moving across the room to the sofas. When Kate sat down, Colton dropped down beside her, letting his arm rest around her shoulders. She glanced at the hand caressing her upper arm and blushed slightly, but when she looked up and met her mother's pleased gaze, she relaxed against him.

"I half expected you to come down the stairs proclaiming yourselves married." Myrna smiled lovingly at her daughter and her fine gentleman. "Come to think of it, I dunna suppose we gave you a chance. Well, what is it to be, a simple declaration or should I be in a panic planning a church wedding? I know you willna wait long."

Kate glanced up at Colton and smiled a little timidly. "We thought it would be nice to be married in the church." A soft pink filled her cheeks. "But we dunna want to wait long, so we'll go see Reverend Murray this afternoon. Perhaps there's a quick way to do it."

Myrna raised an eyebrow and asked dryly, "How quick?"

"Well, I did promise Thomas we'd wait for them." Colton glanced down at Kate.

"Sure of yourself, were you no', Your Grace?" Kate laughed and poked him in the ribs.

"Determined. I wasn't going to take no for an answer. He and Mother were leaving the same afternoon, but they can't travel as quickly as we did. I expect they'll be here in a few days. I suppose we'd better wait three or four days just to be on the safe side. How does Wednesday morning sound, providing the minister can swing it?"

Myra laughed. "I'm sure we can pull something together. There's not time for formal invitations, but if we work on it this evening, we should be able to send notes to most of our friends. Most everyone is in town, I think. I'll talk to the cook while you go to St. Giles. You'll have to wear something you have on hand, Kate. There's no time to have a new gown made."

"That isna a problem. I brought a couple of new dresses from London. There is a cream-colored one with blue ribbon which would be nice."

"Does the blue match your beautiful eyes?" murmured the duke. At her nod, he smiled in satisfaction. "Perfect."

They spent the next few hours with Kate's parents, making plans for the wedding and the dinner following. They talked and laughed all through luncheon, playfully arguing first about the musical selections for the ceremony and then what to serve at the dinner. After eating their midday meal, Colton and Kate paid a call on Reverend Murray.

The minister was surprised by the visit, but overjoyed to see the duke again. "Your Grace, it has been far too long since I've seen you. I suppose with the war at an end, your duties have ended also?"

"Yes. My work at the War Office is complete. I can't say that I regret leaving the position either. It had become far too heavy a load." He glanced at Kate, his love evident in his radiant smile. "I have other more important things to occupy my mind, now."

"Ah, so that is the way the wind blows." The minister smiled at the glowing couple. "I collected as much when you came in. May I wish you both happy." He watched them carefully as they murmured their thanks. A twinkle sparkled in his eye as he schooled his countenance into a serious expression. "I suppose you are planning on a long engagement?"

"Well, no." Colton glanced at Kate and colored slightly. "We would like a church wedding, but would like it as soon as possible."

The minister raised a skeptical eyebrow and turned a stern gaze on Kate. "You know what some people will think, lass."

"Aye, they'll think the worst. But those who know me will probably figure I'm being impulsive as usual. And they are the only ones whose opinion matters anyway." Her cheeks turned a becoming shade of soft pink. "This handsome rogue hasn't had his way with me, Reverend." She smiled mischievously at her old friend.

The minister ignored the strange choking sound coming from the duke and smiled benignly. "I'm glad to hear it, lass. You were raised to be a woman of integrity. Now, I need to ask you both a few questions. First of all, Kate, you are not promised or otherwise betrothed to anyone else, are you?"

"No, sir. There's no man I'd have but this one."

"And, you, Your Grace. Is there any contract of marriage or promise which would impede this marriage? Any agreement your parents entered into when you were young?"

"No, sir. Until I met Kate, I had not met a woman with hom I wanted to spend my life. Thankfully, my parents had e good sense to let me decide my fate on my own. Mother ill be here in a few days if you need further affirmation."

The minister studied him thoughtfully. "No. Your word is ufficient for me. I know you well enough to be certain you ouldna lie, especially over something so important as this. I m satisfied that there is no impediment to this marriage. If ou'll fill out this application for proclamation, we can read the anns in tomorrow's service. You can obtain a certificate rty-eight hours later, and we can perform the ceremony at ny time after that. You will need two householders to sign e certificate, but I'm sure Addison and perhaps Lady ouglas would oblige." He smiled at the couple, correctly ading their excitement as they quickly calculated the time ey had to wait.

"In that case, Reverend, are you free on Wednesday orning?" Colton tried to appear somber, but gave up and rinned instead.

The minister carefully checked his calendar. "Well, I do ave a meeting Wednesday morning at eleven." He leaned ack in his chair. "But since it is with my wife to look at new rapery material, I think it can be postponed a day or two. he'd be in a temper if she knew she stood in the way of true ve."

"Then shall we have the wedding at eleven, sir?" asked Kate agerly. "We will have a dinner at the house afterward. You nd your wife will come, of course. Colton and I wanted to pend our honeymoon at Papa's country house, so if we have e wedding in the middle of the day, we can still reach it efore nightfall."

"Eleven will be fine." The minister stood and held out his and to Colton. "Why dunna you come by Monday afternoon nd we'll go over the ceremony. You will need to let the rganist know what songs you want played. I collect you want keep things simple."

"Yes. We dunna need anything elaborate. We just want to be arried, with God's blessing."

Reverend Murray put his hand on Kate's shoulder as he

walked them to the door. "I'm sure you would have that eve
if you chose an irregular marriage, lass, but I always feel th
church marriage is best. There's something about saying th
vows in front of others and in a house of worship that seems t
make them more meaningful."

As soon as Colton and Kate returned home, Myrna put then
to work writing out invitations, along with Addison an
herself. She allowed them to escape in the evening to pay a cal
on Lady Douglas and Kate's good friend, Alice MacArthur, t
share their news.

The reading of the banns caused quite a stir in church o
Sunday. After the services, they found themselves in a crow
of people, some anxious to meet a duke, others anxious to mee
Kate's future husband, regardless of his title.

The Earl of Blagden and Lady Millicent arrived early in th
afternoon on Tuesday. They were quite pleased to find th
lovebirds, as Thomas called them, happily made-up and tha
the wedding had been scheduled so they could attend. Thoma
did have a few words to say about the timing being a little to
close for comfort, but the duke responded that he had ha
every confidence they would make it in time.

Thomas also mentioned that he had brought Rowan along
just in case the duke wanted the dog to be his best man. "Afte
all, if it hadn't been for this furry Cupid, you two might neve
have met," said the earl.

"True. But he might cause a few swoons if we parade hi
down the aisle at St. Giles." The twinkle in Colton's eye gav
way to seriousness. "I'd prefer his master to be my best man
It would mean a great deal to me, sir, if you would stand u
with me."

"I'd be honored, son." Thomas blinked back a tear, notin
with some satisfaction the mistiness in Colton's eyes.

Before any of them could quite believe it, the day and tim
of the wedding arrived. Kate adjusted a turquoise bow at th
edge of her creamy silk sleeve and peeked around her father'
shoulder at the packed church. As her gaze scanned the crowd
she touched the pendant at her throat. A wedding present fro
Colton, the delicate golden snowflake was covered in dia
monds and pearls. Diamond earrings sparkled from her ea
lobes, and the mother-of-pearl comb crowned her head.

Practically everyone they had invited was in attendance, as well as a few more Kate did not recognize. Joy made her generous, however, and she could not blame anyone who wanted to brag afterward about attending the wedding of the Duke of Ryland.

Her heart swelled with pride as she and her father walked down the aisle to meet her beloved. He wore a charcoal-gray jacket, black silk britches, and a gray and white striped silk waistcoat. *How beautiful he looks!* As Addison placed her hand in Colton's, Kate thought she would burst with love and happiness. A radiant smile lit her face, and many commented that she was the most beautiful bride they had ever seen.

Colton smiled briefly when he took her hand, but as the minister began to lead them through the vows, his face grew somber. He was no less joyful than Kate, but the actual ceremony brought home the responsibilities he would face as a husband and father. Too, he was filled with profound thankfulness to his Creator for the woman He had given him.

His expression softened with love as he gazed into Kate's eyes and promised to love, honor, and cherish her, but she decided he needed to show his happiness a little more. Everyone will think he's no' at all pleased with this marriage, she speculated with mild irritation, totally ignoring her oft-proclaimed statement that she did not care what other people thought.

Kate repeated her vows clearly and distinctly, allowing all the love in her heart to shine forth as she promised to love and honor him. But on the word "obey," she lowered her voice and spoke the word on a questioning lilt. Adding a quick, wry lift of her eyebrow, she succeeded in bringing a full, dimpled smile to his face. A look of happiness stayed there for the remainder of the ceremony and the following festivities.

Around four o'clock, Kate and her new husband bade their guests and loved ones farewell and departed for Addison's country estate not far from Edinburgh. They were alone inside the coach since Lunan, Bess, and Gregory followed in another one along with all the baggage.

"Ah, this is the way to travel," murmured Colton, dipping his head to kiss his wife one more time. Kate's legs were curled up on the seat cushion, her torso resting comfortably in her husband's arms.

"Aye, 'tis very pleasant, to be sure, but I'll be in complete disarray by the time we arrive." Kate grinned and carefully untied the duke's cravat.

"Doesn't look like you'll be the only one to arrive in great disorder," he muttered, as her fingers unfastened the top three buttons on his shirt. When she dropped several tiny kisses on his throat and upper neck, Colton buried his face in her hair. He nuzzled her ear, then nipped the earlobe gently. "There's a slight difference between great disorder and complete disarray. If you keep up this mad seduction, my beautiful duchess, we might very well be embarrassed when we reach our destination."

"Oh, very well," Kate said petulantly, heaving an exaggerated sigh and buttoning his shirt once again. She fussed a minute with her hair, only to have him run his fingers through it again. Kate laughed and kissed him lingeringly before glancing out the window. "We are almost there, and I know you want to make a good impression."

"Well, I don't want all the servants thinking their little girl has married a rogue." He helped her sit up, enjoying the shapely calf that was exposed when she slid her legs around so her feet rested on the floorboard. Colton retied his cravat and chuckled.

"What?"

"You've wilted the starch right out of my neckcloth." He watched affectionately as she tried to smooth the creases from her gown and ran a brush through her tangled hair. "Now, all will know I am not the austere duke of my reputation. I'm ruined." He shook his head sadly, then joined in Kate's laughter.

Kate sat primly beside her husband as the carriage rolled up the lane toward the house. Just as they reached the circle in front of it, she glanced up at her husband. "Do we have to wait until nighttime to retire to our chamber?"

He smiled wickedly and leaned down, whispering in her ear as Jonesy drew their vehicle to a stop. "If you mean do we have to wait until dark before I make love to you, the answer is no. We'll do the pretty for a few minutes, then quietly retire.

If the servants talk, believing I can't wait to get my hands on you, then they'll be absolutely correct." He dropped a kiss on her temple as the footman pulled open the door.

Colton climbed down first, then helped Kate out of the carriage. She looked up at porch steps and gasped. All the servants, from the housekeeper and butler on down to the lowliest scullery maid and stableboy, lined the walkway and stairs leading into the manor. Everyone was dressed in their cleanest, best clothes, and every face beamed with happiness for their mistress.

The butler slowly came forward to meet them, trying to keep his countenance impassive. After a moment, he gave up and grinned. "Welcome to Rolling Meadows, Your Grace," he said to the duke. Then he turned to Kate, his eyes growing a little watery. "Welcome home, Your Grace," he said softly.

"Thank you, Angus." She smiled affectionately at the man who had long served her father, then turned her attention to the others. "Thank you all."

Angus regained his composure and turned toward the house. With the greatest dignity, he loudly proclaimed, "The Duke and Duchess of Ryland."

Kate placed her hand gently on her husband's arm when he held it out for her, and together they proceeded up the walkway and stairs. The servants murmured their good wishes, bowing or curtsying as the couple walked by. When they reached the top of the stairs, the newlyweds turned to smile once again at those below.

"Kate . . ."

She looked up at Colton to find an imp dancing in his eyes. Before she had time to think, he leaned down and kissed her lingeringly. A rousing cheer rose from the onlookers, accompanied by much hand clapping. The duke reluctantly raised his head to find his bride blushing profusely.

"I know you're a braw man, Colton Lydell. You dunna have to prove it right here in front of everybody." She shot him a half-embarrassed, half-pleased smile and ducked through the doorway.

They spent a few moments with the butler and Mrs. Buchanan, the housekeeper, as Kate introduced them to the duke and politely inquired about their health and the estate. To her relief, no one was ill and the estate business was running along fine. They assured her and His Grace that there would be nothing to bother them during their stay.

Later, Colton was feeding Kate a bite of smoked salmon when Angus tapped quietly on the sitting room door. "I beg your pardon for disturbing you, Your Grace, but your man, Lunan, asked to have a word with you."

"That's fine, Angus. Send him in."

The butler stepped back from the door to admit Lunan and Bess. As they walked across the floor, Bess nervously reached for the groom's hand. He caught it, tucking her arm possessively through his.

"What is it, Lunan?" Colton frowned slightly, sensing the uneasiness of his old friend. Kate looked from one nervous face to the other and had a strong suspicion as to what their servants were going to request.

Lunan glanced down at Bess, who nodded encouragingly. By the time the groom had cleared his throat twice and looked at the pretty young girl one more time, Colton, too, guessed what they intended. Not wanting to make his friend appear foolish to his sweetheart, the duke waited patiently until Lunan took a deep breath and spoke.

"Well, it's like this, Your Grace. Bess and I've grown to love each other. Oh, I know I'm too old for her, but I haven't been able to convince her of it." His face colored a little and he grinned. "She makes me feel like a young buck anyway, so maybe I'm not as old as I think I am. We'd like your permission to marry." He turned his gaze to Kate. "Yours, too, Your Grace, since Bess works for you."

"You have it, Lunan. And my blessing, also." Kate smiled kindly at the couple as Colton nodded his agreement.

"By all means, Lunan, marry the girl as fast as you can. She might discover your true nature." Colton grinned and stood, holding out his hand. "May I be the first to wish you happy." He shook the groom's hand, then bent to plant a gentle kiss on Bess's cheek. Not to be outdone, Kate jumped up and kissed Lunan on the cheek and hugged her maid.

"Uh, about being speedy . . ." Lunan looked at the duke and grinned. "We don't need a church weddin', but we'd be mighty pleased if you'd witness our promise to each other."

"Oh, Bess, we'd love to." Kate looked expectantly at 'olton.

"It would be an honor, old man. Why don't we step out into ıe garden? It would be a perfect backdrop for your lovely ıdy. Besides, there's a beautiful sunset."

Bess giggled, looked at Kate, and rolled her eyes. "Oooh, ıe man's gallant, too."

Laughing, they stepped through the double doors into the ıady garden, awash with a summer profusion of roses, eather, asters, and numerous patches of wildflowers. Lunan ıme to a halt near a bush covered with red roses. Taking both f Bess's hands in his, he gazed down at her lovingly. The sky ehind her was painted in brilliant reds and oranges, indeed ıaking a beautiful backdrop for his bride.

"Bess, before these kind friends and Almighty God, I take ɔu for my wife. I promise to love, honor, and cherish you for long as I live, through good times and bad. I'll be faithful you, lass, and be the best husband I can be."

"Oh, Lunan, I know ye will." She glanced at Kate and niled sweetly. "Looks like my man is gallant, too," she said ɔftly. Looking back up at the groom, tears misted her eyes. I've had a good life, Lunan, but I've ne'er known such appiness as when I'm with ye. I love ye with all my heart and n honored to take ye as my husband, before Almighty God ıd these kind friends. I promise to love, honor, and obey ye ɔr as long as I live, through good times and bad. I'll be ıithful to ye, my husband, and be the best wife I can be."

"I know you will, lass." Lunan gathered her in his arms and ıssed her so thoroughly that Colton and Kate slipped away. hey had reached the doorway when Lunan called them.

"May we still work for you, even though we're married?" e looked a little sheepish at having been so lost in his kiss, ıt it was a question he needed to ask. Many employers would ɔt keep servants who were married.

"Of course, you may. I'd be lost without you. Bess, do you ant to continue as Kate's maid?"

"For a while." She blushed deeply. "Though when we start ıvin' wee ones, I'd have to quit."

"Fair enough."

Bess looked at her mistress. "Send for me when ye are ready

to retire for the night." The last thing the young woman wante to do was leave her new husband, even for a few minutes, bu she did not believe it would be right to ask for time off on suc short notice.

"I most certainly will no'. My husband can assist m tonight, and I'll have Mrs. Buchanan assign one of the oth maids to help me for a while. You may stay in the carriag house or if you prefer, you may take a bedroom in the ea wing of the house."

"The carriage house would be nice, Your Grace, if you' certain 'tis where you'd like us. A tenant house would do, said Lunan.

"No, I dunna believe there are any empty at the momen Besides, you wouldna have the furniture and things you nee No, the carriage house is best. You're less likely to b disturbed there and it should have everything you need. Com back in with us, and I'll have Angus give you the key."

"Yes, Your Grace. Thank you."

They all went inside where Kate first rang for the butle then for the housekeeper. They both showed up at the san time. "Angus, Bess and Lunan have married today, to Would you please get the key to the carriage house so they ma use it while we are here? Also, you might break out a bottle two of spirits this evening, so the staff can celebrate bo weddings." The butler nodded, smiled at Lunan and Bess, a bowed slightly to his mistress before leaving the room.

"Mrs. Buchanan, are there still linens and things in th carriage house?"

"Aye, Your Grace. It is fully equipped, including th kitchen, except for foodstuffs."

"Send over a few things, but since we'll only be here for few days, I would like meals taken over to them."

"Oh, mila—I mean, Your Grace, ye dunna need to do tha I dunna want to put anyone to any trouble."

Kate looked at the housekeeper, who read her mind a smiled. "It willna be any trouble at all to feed another pair newlyweds."

Kate grinned. "I thought no'. Now, run along, you tw We'll give you plenty of warning before we leave. Dun worry, we'll give you enough time to pack."

Lunan and Bess expressed their thanks once again, picked the key, and departed for the carriage house, stopping every tle bit along the way for another kiss.

"Now." Kate turned to Mrs. Buchanan. "We will no' quire dinner tonight. We had quite a feast after the dding." Kate blushed, knowing what the housekeeper was nking.

"I have a tray prepared in case you want a bit of supper later. l send it up right away. Will there be anything else, Your ace?"

"No . . . uh, yes. I'll need another maid to fill in for Bess rting tomorrow. Just for the time we are here."

"I'll see to it. Ring if you need anything. Otherwise, you llna be disturbed." With a slight curtsy, Mrs. Buchanan rried from the room, closing the door behind her.

Colton came up behind Kate and slid his arms around her. wering his head, he nibbled on her ear. "I'm ready to not be turbed."

Kate's heart fluttered. So was she, even though she was a le nervous now that the moment had arrived. She hid it well, ncing up at him impishly. "Are you ready to play lady's id?"

"I think I could be persuaded. I may be a bit clumsy." He aightened and moved his hands to her shoulders, gently ning her around to face him. For the briefest of moments, he oked uncertain.

"What is it, love?" Kate touched his jaw with her fingertips.

Suddenly, Colton felt ill-prepared for the night ahead. He d lain with few women in his life and none of them had been nocent. Feelings of inadequacy swept over him, and he und himself unable to meet her gaze. He pulled her into his ns, cradling her head against his shoulder.

"Kate, I may be clumsy with more than your gown." He ok a deep breath, and Kate felt a tremor run through him. 'm as nervous as a green youngster." Her arms slid around n, holding him, reassuring him through her touch.

"I heard you've never had a mistress."

"That's true." He hesitated, wondering why he had started s conversation in the first place. Finally, he plunged ahead.

"I can't say that I've never been with a woman, but m experience has been limited."

Kate leaned back against his arms and looked up at him, h expression gentle, but serious. "I've never even been kisse no' really kissed, by any other man, Colton."

He eased away from her, raking his fingers through his hai "But that's as it should be. I'm glad no one else has tasted yo sweet lips or touched you."

"And you think I'd be happier if you'd coupled with half t women in London?" Kate stared at him, her eyes wide, and h hands resting on her hips.

He looked away from her, clearly disconcerted. "I suppo not." He took a deep breath, and though he did not look at he his words came out in a rush. "But a man should experienced. He should be proficient enough to make woman's first time wonderful." He raked his hand through h hair again, leaving it tousled. "He should know all the ways arouse a woman and bring her pleasure." He sighed heavil and when he turned to face her, his expression was troubled. don't know all those things, Kate. I'm afraid I'll disappoi you, or worse, hurt you dreadfully."

Kate reached him in two quick strides, putting her arm around his waist and resting her head against his chest. "Y big, wonderful ninnyhammer."

"Thanks heaps." Reluctantly, he put his arms around he holding her close. "I pour out my soul, and the woman ca me a ninnyhammer."

Kate smiled up at him, her eyes bright with tears. H confession, and that he was so concerned about her welfare a her pleasure, had touched her deeply. She stepped back a took his hand. "Come, my husband. This is a conversati best continued in our bedchamber."

When they reached their chambers, and the door was firm closed and locked behind them, Kate turned to her dearest lo and began to methodically undress him.

"Colton, I canna tell you how much it pleases me becau you havena been with many women. I'm even jealous of t ones you have been with." She helped him shrug out of h coat and tossed it over the back of a chair. "It irritates the li out of me to think about them touching you and kissing you, ven worse"— she jerked off his cravat, evoking a mild umph" from her handsome, soon-to-be lover—"to think of ou touching or kissing them and then spending the night with ne of those strumpets curled up in your arms." She threw the avat off into the shadowy space of an unlighted corner of the om.

He quickly reached down and momentarily stilled her hands she fumbled angrily with the buttons on his waistcoat. Kate, I never stayed the night." She looked up to meet his nder gaze and took a deep breath. She knew she was being lly, but after all, she was nervous, too, and fussing and ming a bit helped. Her brow wrinkled as a deep red slowly ushed his cheeks.

"What's wrong?"

"I think I'd better not elaborate any further. Everything I ink of to say only seems to blacken me more."

"Wise man," murmured Kate, turning her attention back to e buttons of his waistcoat. She worked gently this time, her e pacified. She felt his fingers working at the fastenings on e back of her gown. "Gettin' wiser, I see."

Colton chuckled and planted a kiss on a tiny patch of bare in on her shoulder. Then he lifted his head and concentrated n the hooks until she interrupted him to slip off his waistcoat.

She placed it carefully on top of his coat, then started to ndo the buttons on his shirt. She felt the night air whisper gainst her back as the last of the hooks came undone. Seconds ter, his warm fingers heated her cooled skin. Kate took a ep breath and closed her eyes, savoring his touch.

"Colton, you dunna have to be an expert lover to excite e." Her words were spoken in a breathy whisper. "Dunna ou remember how your touch sets me on fire?"

"I remember," he whispered, his voice deep and full of notion. He moved one hand from the smooth skin of her back cup her face tenderly, tilting it gently. His lips touched hers d she parted them eagerly for his kiss. The whole world ploded.

Kate tugged at his shirt, jerking it from the top of his itches. As she slipped her hands beneath it and flattened em over his chest, a shudder rippled through her. She moved

her hands over his taut muscles and an answering shudde
shook him.

He kissed her over and over, each time more urgently tha
the last, each feeding their growing desire. Drawing away fror
her lips, Colton reached down and pulled the shirt over hi
head and slipped his arms from the sleeves. He let it drop to th
floor as he kissed her with tiny nibbling kisses.

Curling his fingers around the top of her gown, he eased i
from her shoulders and down her arms. Reluctantly breakin
off their kiss, he leaned down and pushed the gown past he
waist and hips. It drifted down to the floor in a soft, cream
heap.

Colton's gaze took in her beauty. The luscious curves barel
hidden by her shift and petticoat beckoned him. He leane
over, kissing the curve of her breast, and laughed softly.

Kate closed her eyes, her breathing quick and shallow. Hi
touch was sweet, and his breath warm on her skin. H
smoothed his fingers along the skin of her shoulder an
collarbone. Being with him was so beautiful, so precious, sh
wondered how she had ever lived without him.

"You're so beautiful, Kate. I want to kiss and touch yo
everywhere at once!"

Kate's chuckle was unknowingly sensual. "I dunna intend t
stop you." She ran her palms across his chest, evoking a moa
of pleasure from him.

Colton reached down to untie the ribbon at the waist of he
petticoat—and promptly pulled it into a knot. "Blast!"

Kate glanced at the offending bit of white satin befor
brushing a kiss across her husband's lips. "Break it," sh
commanded softly.

She did not have to repeat the order twice. Gripping bot
sides firmly, Colton gave it a quick jerk. The ribbon snappe
in two, and he quickly slid the petticoat past her hips and let i
fall to the floor. His fingers moved back to the straps of he
shift as he searched her eyes and caught the hint of fear there

Taking her hand, he led her over to the bed. "Sit down
Kitten, and I'll take off your shoes and stockings." Ka
complied, loving the gentle way he eased the shoes from he
feet. He untied the ribbon garters below her knee and carefull
rolled her stockings down her calf and off over the tips of he

›es. "You have beautiful legs, sweetheart." He ran his hand p her calf, stopping at the knee.

Colton stood and took her hand, drawing her up to stand eside him. "Are you afraid, my Kate?"

"No' afraid, just a little nervous." She smiled. "I have utterflies in my stomach."

Colton slowly moved his hand, flattening it tenderly against er stomach. "Here?"

Kate gasped at the pleasure sweeping through her. "Aye." nother tiny smile played on her lips. "There's more of them ow." His hand slid upward, caressing her ribs, then curving round the soft fullness of her breast. Kate moaned and slid her ands around his neck, seeking his lips.

Colton kissed her tenderly, letting his hands roam over her › she would become accustomed to his touch without the arrier of layers of clothing. As her kisses became more rvent, he clutched the fine linen shift and carefully drew it p. He straightened, guiding the shift over her head and plifted arms, then discarded it absently on a nearby chair.

As his warm gaze moved slowly over her, he was filled ew with a sense of gratitude that this beautiful woman was is. "You love me," he whispered in slight amazement.

"With all my heart."

Quickly he lifted her in his arms and placed her on the bed. little self-conscious, she pulled the sheet up modestly. He sat own on the edge of the bed and removed his shoes and ockings, setting them on the carpet beside Kate's. The sight ought a gentle smile to his lips. Standing, he moved his ngers to the buttons on his pantaloons, then stopped. Looking Kate over his shoulder, he asked, "Do you want me to blow it the candles, love?"

"No."

Colton stripped off his pantaloons and quickly crawled nder the sheet, stretching out next to her.

"You're so beautiful," they whispered together. They ughed, and Colton pulled her into his embrace, kissing her ith all the love and fire in his heart. Murmured words of love ingled with burning kisses and tender caresses. It did not take olton long to realize that when love was truly a part of

lovemaking, it did not require great experience to brin
pleasure and excitement to the marriage bed.

He wanted to be patient, to initiate his wife to the intimacie of their wedding night slowly, but it was not to be. Kate's so whimpers and trembling response to his touch, and her ow bold caresses and kisses made patience impossible.

His hands and lips moved over her in ways she had neve dreamed of, igniting a fierce, sweet passion she had scarcel imagined. The whole world seemed to stand still, existing onl for them, only for this moment and this loving pleasure.

"Make me yours, Cole. Be my other half, the other part c my soul," begged Kate urgently.

"You are my heart, my very life," he whispered, taking he mouth in a kiss that made her ache with its tenderness.

While she was lost in the wonder of his kiss, they becam one. The moment of pain was quickly forgotten as they share this greatest pleasure and fulfillment of their love.

Chapter 21

After three days of what could only be called wedded bliss, Kate and the duke returned to Edinburgh for a brief visit. Their time in the country had been one of discovery, delight, and the happiest moments either had ever known.

Kate snuggled next to her husband, wiggled a little on the carriage seat to get comfortable, and rested her head against his wide shoulder. After a moment, she released a soft, contented sigh. "Do you know what's the nicest part of being married?"

Colton grinned and looked down at the top of her head. "I can think of several things, but what's best in your opinion?"

"Being able to be with you whenever I want and as much as I want." She straightened and looked up at him, her expression serious and her eyes glowing with love. "I enjoy just spending time with you, no matter what we're doing."

"I feel the same, sweetheart. I knew it would be nice, but I had not realized how contented and totally, insanely happy I'd be. I'm glad you don't want to spend more than a few days with your parents. I'm anxious to get you to Yorkshire. I think you'll like the estate, and I can have you all to myself for a while. I heard rumors before I left London of great peace celebrations planned for the summer. Perhaps next month, we'll journey back to London. It seems most of the generals and other notables, like the Tsar of Russia, won't be here until June."

"I suppose I'll be ready to go by then, although right now, I think I'd be happy to stay in the country forever, with no one to intrude. But I know there will be many people you would like to see again."

"Only to show off my beautiful wife." Colton slipped his arm around her shoulder, giving her a quick squeeze. "Most of them never thought I'd find anyone who'd have me."

"And those idiots were leading our fighting men?" Kate shook her head in dismay. " 'Tis a wonder we dinna lose the war."

"Thankfully, they were better at war than at matchmaking." Colton chuckled and joined his wife in watching out the windows of the coach. Edinburgh teemed with visitors and residents, all going about their business in the afternoon sunshine. Suddenly, the duke stiffened and his gaze narrowed, focusing on one particular individual strolling along the street.

"What is it, love?" Kate peered out the window on his side, then looked at her husband in surprise. "Why, that's Blake!" She turned her attention back to the street, but her father's cousin was no where to be seen. "Where did he go?"

"Into the bank. I'm tempted to stop and go in and plant him a facer." Colton glared at the bank doorway as they drove past, wishing he were face to face with the man who had maligned his beloved.

"He's such a nasty little weasel, it would serve him right. But, alas, it would only cause another scandal, and I suppose we would be wise to avoid such things." Kate thumped her fingers thoughtfully on her reticule. "Of course, when he comes by to visit Papa, he might trip over a rake or something."

"Or walk into a door." Colton grinned at the thought of giving the scoundrel a black eye.

"Or two doors." Kate laughed. "He might even bloody his nose if he wasna careful."

"Aye. I have heard he's a terribly clumsy fellow." They were still laughing and plotting their retaliation against Blake when they arrived at Addison's town house. Colton's amusement quickly turned to caution and suspicion upon learning Blake had not paid his cousin a call.

"Don't seem likely that he would call on Addison after all

the trouble he caused Kate," said the earl. "You actually believe he might be the one who tried to have my son killed?" Thomas glanced at Addison, then settled his worried gaze on the duke.

"He is definitely a possibility. It's not only because he hasn't been by to see you. I've had a man following him since we learned of the last attack on Addison. Winston is very thorough and should have advised me of Blake's presence in Edinburgh."

"There's been no one here looking for you." Addison glanced at Myrna, who shook her head. "We certainly would have taken a message or given him your direction once we learned he was your man."

"Do you think something might have happened to him?" Kate looked up at Colton, who was standing behind her chair. When she reached up, he took her hand in his, holding it gently.

"It's probable," the duke said grimly. "He would have contacted me by now, even if Blake had only arrived in town this morning. Just as a precaution, I want the guards doubled around the house, with the advice to be specifically watchful for Blake or any strangers. If he is the one behind the murder attempts, he might hire someone again." Colton frowned thoughtfully, squeezing Kate's hand slightly. "Since the first two attempts were bungled, he might try to do the job himself.

"No one should leave this house without adequate guard. Addison, I don't think you should go out at all until we find out what your cousin is up to. Do you have some men who could check the inns and find his lodging?"

"Yes. I'll send them out right away. I collect they should only find out where he is staying?"

"Yes. If there's a confrontation, I'll be the one doing it." He looked down at Kate, sensing her concern. "I'm the logical one to do it, Kitten."

"I know, but I'll still worry about you."

The men were dispatched to check the inns, and Colton set off to check at the bank himself. The rest of the family tried to keep the conversations light and pretend a semblance of gaiety, but were only successful for a few minutes. Worry and uneasiness took the sparkle out of the conversation and soon a sense of foreboding settled over them.

"I feel like we're under siege," muttered Kate later in the afternoon. "I canna even go out in the garden without being edgy, like someone is watching me."

"We'll all feel better when Blake is found. I know he is an unscrupulous character, but I still find myself hoping he is not behind this madness," said Lady Millicent. "Perhaps he is simply here on holiday and has not worked up the courage to make peace with the family."

"Let's hope that's all it is." Thomas patted his wife's hand comfortably, then pulled out his pocket watch and compared the time on it to the large clock in the corner. "I hear a coach, now. Kate, run to the window and see if it's Colton." Thomas looked up to see the hem of Kate's dress disappear through the doorway. She had been on her feet the minute the carriage pulled to a stop in front of the town house. Thomas chuckled. "Suppose I wasted my breath that time." He settled his hand on Rowan's head as the dog pricked up his ears and looked attentively toward the drawing room door.

Moments later, Colton walked in, his arm around his wife. "Evidently, Blake only changed some money. The bank manager was kind enough to check the ledgers, but Blake had not participated in a transaction which would have been recorded separately."

Addison walked in behind them from his study down the hall. "My men returned a few minutes ago. If Blake's still in Edinburgh, he didn't register at any inn under his own name. Or he is staying with friends."

"He doesna have any friends."

"No, Kate, dear, there you're wrong. Blake can be a very charming fellow when he wants to be, a regular sport. Still, I can't think of anyone he might know in Scotland," said the earl. "Of course, I haven't watched over him, so he could know any number of people here."

"It's entirely possible he has nothing to do with this scheme and was only passing through Edinburgh on his way to visit someplace else. Of course, we must remember that someone has tried to kill you twice, Addison. Even if we learn Blake was not involved, you will have to continue to be careful, until the culprit is apprehended."

The rest of the afternoon and night passed without incident, as did the following day. Colton began to wonder if he was wrong about Blake, and if he had been in espionage far too long. Still, he was uneasy. The same foreboding feeling that had saved his neck time after time told him something was going to happen soon.

By evening, everyone, with the exception of the duke, had begun to relax. He kept his feelings to himself, but his nerves were tight as a bowstring. Kate, Mryna, the earl, and Lady Millicent were deeply engrossed in a game of whist, while Colton shared some of his adventures during the war with Addison.

Rown lay stretched out beside the earl's chair, but no one noticed when his ears pricked up and he raised his head. The dog stared at the French doors leading out into the garden for a few seconds before hefting himself to his feet. Rowan nudged the earl's arm, but the play was hot and Thomas ignored him.

Silently, Rowan walked over to the garden doors and looked back at Thomas. When it became obvious that the earl was still ignoring him, the quiet giant moved back across the room and stopped beside his master's chair. This time, the dog bumped the gentleman's arm soundly, almost causing him to drop his cards.

"Umph! Oh, sorry, ol' boy." Thomas pushed back his chair as the dog hurried back toward the doorway. The earl looked at Myrna as he stood. "Wolfhounds seldom bark, so one must pay close attention if he wants a run in the garden." He grinned back over his shoulder as he crossed the room quickly. "Rowan is a patient fellow, but even he has his limits. I wouldn't want him to leave a puddle on your floor. It'd be more like a lake!"

Thomas closed the door after the dog and walked back across the room, smiling as the duke's gaze followed his every movement. The earl spotted the alertness in his stepson's eyes. It gave the older gentleman a feeling of well-being to have the duke present. If any man could thwart their mysterious villain, the Duke of Ryland could.

As Thomas eased down in his chair, a bloodcurdling scream and the report of a pistol came from the garden. They were instantly followed by a crash and another yell, this one slightly muffled. Colton grabbed a pistol he had hidden beside him on the chair and dashed out the door. Addison and the earl followed at his heels as guards came running into the garden from all directions.

There, at the base of a large oak tree several feet from the garden steps, stood Rowan, illuminated in a beam of light from the open doorway. A wooden bench had been toppled over nearby. The dog did not move a muscle as the men approached. Neither did the man pinned between his legs.

"G-Get him off me! Don't let him chew up my face!" Thomas and the duke exchanged a speaking look.

"Blake?" asked Addison quietly, watching his father.

"Aye." The earl spat out a few disrespectful words about his nephew, then called his dog. "Rowan, come." As the dog stepped over Blake, he dragged a lightly muddied paw across the man's chest, as if he wanted to leave the victim a reminder of his conqueror. In spite of his anger, a grim smile flickered across the earl's face as he patted his dog's head. "The hunter becomes the hunted, eh, boy?" The earl checked him over quickly but was soon satisfied the dog had not been hit by the bullet.

Colton reached down and grabbed a fistful of Blake's waistcoat and shirt, hauling the trembling man to his feet. The duke glanced up at a high, yet sturdy branch that grew over the foot-wide, stone garden wall. "A little late for dropping in, don't you think?" Blake only made a garbled sound in reply.

Colton had been aware of the tree and its possible use. He even had Addison's gardener remove a couple of lower branches. The guards had been told to be especially watchful. Unfortunately, it was a cloudy night, and Blake possessed an agility for tree climbing they had not expected.

The clouds parted briefly, allowing the duke a glimpse of a hooked pole hanging from the tree above the wall. The hook on the end was securely fastened over the tree branch. Pegs, the width of a man's foot, stuck out from the pole at precise intervals, allowing the man to use the pole as a ladder.

Addison bent down at the fringe of the light and picked up

a pistol from among the violets. The barrel was still hot from the recent discharge. "Somehow, I don't think you came to make a social call, Cousin." He took two steps backward into the darkness, then said softly, "Colton, come here."

Two guards stepped up, each taking a bruising grip on Blake's arms. Only then did Colton release him and walk over to his friend. Addison said nothing, but looked pointedly toward the house. That particular spot in the garden, only four steps away from the tree and freedom, afforded a clear view of Addison's favorite chair in the drawing room, the one he had occupied only moments before. It would not have taken much of a marksman to send him knocking on heaven's pearly gates.

Colton strode back to Blake and took hold of his arm, hustling him into the house. Shoving him down on a chair, he walked away from him. After the others had taken their seats, the duke nonchalantly sat down on the arm of Kate's chair. He pointedly ignored Blake for a moment, choosing instead to clean a smudge of dirt from his hand with his pristine handkerchief.

Blake glanced nervously from the cool, unconcerned duke to the earl, whose face was purple with rage. His gaze shifted quickly to Addison, only to be met by a cold, hard stare. Blake swallowed the huge lump in his throat and looked back warily at the duke. He could practically feel the hate emanating from those around him, so he did not bother to seek a friendly face.

Colton put his handkerchief away and looked up at the miserable soul sitting in the middle of the room. Under other circumstances, Blake's appearance would have been comical. His normally perfect hair stuck out in all directions. His cravat was limp and half untied, and if one were to look closely, two large muddy paw prints were visible on the shoulders of his black evening coat.

"Do you always dress so elegantly when you attempt a murder?" Colton asked casually.

"Uh, no . . . I mean I just wanted to surprise everyone. Uh, thought it would be a great joke to come in from the garden instead of being announced by the butler." Blake gulped, fully aware that no one else was swallowing his line.

Colton lifted one eyebrow in a dubious manner. "Come now, Denley, surely you can think of something better than that." The duke's expression grew hard as he slowly rose to his feet.

Blake gulped again. Now he knew how the Christians in the Coliseum must have felt seconds before the gates to the lion's cages were thrown open. Trembling, he craned his neck first this way, then that, as Colton made a slow circle around his chair, finally stopping a few steps in front of him. Blake read the barely restrained fury in the Duke of Ryland's eyes and bowed his head, waiting for judgment day.

"Is it the title you're after, or did you have another reason for killing Addison?"

"Title," mumbled Blake, staring at the floor and wishing it would open up and hide him.

"Good lord, man! There are four men between you and the title. Did you intend to kill them all?"

"No!" Blake looked up, turning his attention to his uncle. "It should be mine—nobody else wants it! Why should I be last in line when I'm the only one who really cares about it?"

"You hired someone to stab Addison last winter?"

Blake's shoulders sagged in despair. "Yes. It all seemed so simple then. I wasn't in a hurry, not anxious for you to drop off or anything, Uncle. With Addison disinherited, Richard was next in line for the title. Howard probably won't make it through next winter, and since Richard is several years older than me, I figured there was a good chance I'd inherit the title someday.

"Then when Richard started pushing you to reconcile with Addison, I was afraid I might not ever become the earl. I wanted it so badly, you see. The prestige, respect, money, and property. If I were earl, I'd be important, not just the third son of a second son. I decided my chances would be better if Addison were dead. You said he was dead to you anyway, Uncle, so I didn't think it mattered overmuch." At Myrna's gasp, Blake looked at her almost apologetically. "I know it would have mattered to you, ma'am, but since I'd never even seen you, it wasn't much of a concern. But the lout Pennyfeather hired botched the job. So did the other lackey I hired, the one that took the shot at you."

"So you decided to come to Scotland and do the deed yourself," boomed the earl, jumping to his feet, and shaking a ist in his nephew's face. "By Jupiter, I ought to put a bullet in your miserable black heart."

Colton put a steadying hand on the earl's shoulder. The force of his gaze compelled Blake to look at him. "And after Addison—what of your brothers? Or your uncle? How long would it have been before you decided to hasten your cause?"

"I wouldn't kill my own brothers! Nor you either, Uncle Thomas."

"Why not, boy? There's been no love lost between the two of us. I've thought you were a no-good scoundrel since you were in short coats. What end did you have in mind for me?" The earl glowered at him and clenched his fist. He was itching o thrash the young man cowering in front of him. Only the resence of the ladies prevented it.

"I never thought about killing you, Uncle, I swear. I didn't hink you'd live much longer anyway," he added sullenly. With your temper, you're going to have a stroke one of these lays."

The earl raised his hand threateningly, but Colton once again ut out a hand to calm him. Thomas turned abruptly and talked across the room to drop down on the settee beside Lady Aillicent.

"But you did think about how you would kill Richard, didn't you?" the duke said softly.

Blake's struggle for an answer was obvious to all in the oom. Finally, he looked up at the duke in abject defeat. "Aye, thought of it. I figured I'd wait until he had been earl for ten ears or so. With all his daughters, there was no one to follow Richard."

"What method would you use? Pistols again?" the duke ressed quietly.

"Poison milk," muttered the villain.

"I didn't quite catch that. Did you say something about nilk?"

"Richard drinks a glass of warm milk every night before ed. I'd poison his milk. People die all the time from bad milk. No one would think anything about it."

"And since it would happen so many years after Addison's leath, no one would think to connect the two. Of course, Ioward would have died along the way of natural causes."

Colton shook his head and walked back to Kate's side. "You'r
a devious one, Blake."

There was total silence in the room. Everyone understoo
that Colton had turned the situation over to the earl. As head o
his family, it was his duty to decide what fate awaited Blake
No one expected Addison to press charges of attempted murde
against his cousin. It simply was not done among the aristoc
racy. Discretion was the deciding force in their lives.

The earl looked at the son he had lost for over twenty year
and came near to losing for an eternity. "You know I'd like t
see him in Newgate."

"It would not be worth the family's suffering, Father. I think
some good hard labor, in a hot, humid climate might do my
cousin some good," he answered grimly.

"Nephew, you are a disgrace to this family. I'd like to drai
every drop of blood from that worthless body of yours, bu
you'd still be a Denley. I won't shame your good brothers b
hauling you before the magistrate, but you will leave thi
country and never set foot in it again as long as I live. And
contrary to what you might think, I plan on living a long time

"I'm sending you to Barbados to work on my suga
plantation. You'll work hard and be under constant guard. I
you try to leave, you'll regret it. If you try to hire someone t
kill Addison or your brothers, I won't think twice about havin
your miserable life put to an end. If you somehow manage t
elude your guards and show up in England while I yet live,
won't give you a second chance. At that time, you'll b
brought up on charges of attempted murder."

Blake said nothing, only hung his head and thanked hi
lucky stars that he was getting off so easily. His devious min
was already at work. The old man wouldn't live forever an
perhaps his cousin would be more forgiving. He would simpl
be grateful for the opportunity to live out his days on Englis
soil.

Addison ordered four of his men to take his cousin to a sma
antechamber where he was to be detained until passage coul
be arranged to Barbados. Blake looked up at his cousin as h
was led out of the room. "You don't have anything to fear fro
me anymore, Addison. It's not worth the risk." And he mea
it.

As the guards and Blake reached the hallway, a stranger's oice bellowed, "Tie 'em up good, lads. See 'ow you like ein' trussed up like a pig on a spit, you . . ." The last words vere lost amid stamping feet and a loud howl from Blake.

"What in the world?" Kate looked up at her husband's miling face as they all jumped up and raced into the hall.

Blake was slumped forward, standing only because two of ie guards were hanging onto his arms. Blood dripped from his ose onto the polished tile of the hall floor.

"Good to see you, Winston. I was afraid something hapened to you." Colton held out his hand to his man.

Winston gripped it firmly and gave it a solid shake. "This oke caught me watchin' the house in Brighton. 'ad some of s men jump me. They knocked me out and tied me up. umped me in an old, abandoned barn at the back of the operty. Lucky for me, some lad lost 'is kitten and came oking for it, otherwise I'd a died there.

"I couldn't find out where the cove went until I was back in ondon. Got one of 'is servants soused one night and 'e abbered about the gent going to Edinburgh. I 'oped I'd get re in time to warn you, but looks like you found 'im out urselves."

"Actually, he was cornered by the earl's dog," said the ke, with a slight smile.

"Serves 'im right. Vermin like that ought to be brought to ound." Winston looked at Blake as the man raised his head. Vant me to black 'is eye, Your Grace? 'e ought to get a ashin' for all the trouble 'e put everybody through."

"No, that won't be necessary," murmured Colton, an unholy am lighting his eye. "I think I'll do it myself."

Before Blake or anyone else realized the duke was serious, lton drew back his left fist, and with a quick jab connected th Blake's eye.

The man groaned in agony as his head bounced backward. oggily, he eased it forward and asked in a weak voice, 'hat did you do that for?"

'For humiliating the woman I love." Colton swung around ckly to hide his own grimace of pain. It had been awhile ce he had done any boxing, and his hand hurt like the very

devil. He started up the stairs, reaching the first landing befo
Kate caught up with him.

She slipped her arm around his waist and kissed him on th
cheek. "Thank you for defending my honor."

"Your welcome." Colton kept walking. Once they were o
of view of those below, he groaned softly and bent his elbo
lifting his hand upward.

"Did you hurt yourself?"

"A little. It's nothing a good cold soaking won't cure."

Kate caught it gently, drawing him to a halt. "You did hu
yourself. It's turning red!"

"Where?" Colton peered down at his hand and smiled. H
loving wife was holding it as if it might break.

"There." Kate pointed to a small red mark on his knuck
and giggled. "You're going to need lots of love and attenti
to heal from this terrible wound."

"I'm sure the doctor would recommend plenty of rest, wi
a lovely red-haired nurse in attendance at all times."

"Of a certainty." Kate nodded sagely. "But no laudanum

Colton grinned and opened their bedroom door. "Definite
no laudanum."

Kate and the duke said their farewells and climbed into t
carriage with promises from her parents and grandparents
pay them a visit in Yorkshire at the end of the summer. Be
and Lunan were happily settled in the second carriage w
Gregory and all the luggage. Blake had been put on a boat th
morning bound for Barbados, accompanied by two of Ad
ison's strongest and most loyal men.

As the footman started to close the coach door, the e
stepped up, leading an Irish wolfhound puppy. "I have a lit
gift for you." His eyes twinkled as he urged the dog up into t
coach.

"Little? He's already a horse!" Colton grinned and help
the dog up on the seat across from him. "Rowan's offspring

"No, but a relative. Wolfhounds are rare enough that m
are related. He'll be a good guard dog and a loyal friend."

"Thank you, Grandpapa. He's beautiful." Kate reach
across and stroked the dog's rough fur. "What is his name

"Curran."

"Champion or hero," said Kate, cradling the dog's face in her hand, meeting his mellow gaze. "Let's hope you dunna have to live up to your name." She scratched Curran beneath the chin, cooing and fussing over him as if he were a baby. She was rewarded by a gentle, tip-of-the-tongue lick on her own chin. Giggling and wiping her face, Kate leaned back against the seat.

"Now, child, I only have one piece of advice regarding this new pet of yours." The earl's sparkling gaze shifted from Kate to the duke and back to Kate. "Don't let him knock you down."

With a chuckle, he closed the door and stepped back as the coachman cracked his whip in the air. The earl called over the clatter of the wheels, "You never know where it might lead!"

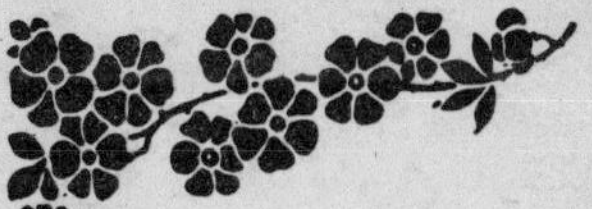

If you enjoyed this book, take advantage of this special offer. Subscribe now and . .

GET A ***FREE***

NO OBLIGATION (a $3.95 value)

If you enjoy reading the very best historical romances, you'll want to subscribe to the True Value Historical Romance Home Subscription Service. Now that you have read one of the best historical romances around today, we're sure you'll want more of the same fiery passion, intimate romance and historical settings that set these books apart from all others.

Each month the editors of True Value will select the four very best historical romance novels from America's leading publishers of romantic fiction. Arrangements have been made for you to preview them in your home Free for 10 days. And with the first four books you receive, we'll send you a FREE book as our introductory gift. No obligation.

free home delivery

We will send you the four best and newest historical romances as soon as they are published to preview Free for 10 days. If for any reason you decide not to keep them, just return them and owe nothing. But if you like them as much as we think you will, you'll pay *just* $3.50 each and save at least $.45 each off the cover price.(Your savings are a minimum of $1.80 a month.)There is *no* postage and handling – or other hidden charges. There are no minimum number of books to buy and you may cancel at any time.